Critical acclaim for the marvelous romances of

JUDE DEVERAUX

THE MULBERRY TREE

"Mystery, romance and good cooking converge in the latest by perennial bestseller Deveraux."

—*People*

"Her protagonist combines innocent appeal with wry experience in a way that readers will surely find irresistible."

—*Publishers Weekly*

"A twisted, unpredictable story (not wholly women's fiction, nor wholly mystery) that's indicative of Deveraux's penchant for telling fresh, new stories each time out."

—*Romantic Times*

THE SUMMERHOUSE

"Marvelously compelling reading. . . . Deeply satisfying. . . ."

—*Houston Chronicle*

"Deveraux explores that oft-asked question in a well-written book that varies from the normal romance style, but still blends three love stories into an emotionally stirring novel."

—*The State* (Columbia, SC)

"Entertaining summer reading."

—*The Port St. Lucie News* (FL)

"Jude Deveraux's writing is enchanting and exquisite in *The Summerhouse*."

—*BookPage*

"Deveraux is at the top of her game. . . . [She] uses the time-travel motif that was so popular in *A Knight in Shining Armor,* successfully updating it with a female buddy twist that will make fans smile."

—*Booklist*

"[A] wonderful, heartwarming tale of friendship and love."

—America Online Romance Fiction Forum

"A wonderfully wistful contemporary tale. . . . With *New York Times* bestselling author Jude Deveraux, one thing that's guaranteed is a happy ending."

—Barnesandnoble.com

"Thought-provoking, entertaining, and downright delightful."

—Amazon.com

"Jude Deveraux takes a fascinating theory and runs with it . . . a very compelling and intriguing story."

—*Romantic Times*

"Once again, Deveraux gives us a book we can't put down."

—*Rendezvous*

TEMPTATION

"Deveraux['s] lively pace and happy endings . . . will keep readers turning pages."

—*Publishers Weekly*

"Filled with excitement, action, and insight. . . . A nonstop thriller."

—Harriet Klausner, Barnesandnoble.com

"[A] satisfying story."

—*Booklist*

HIGH TIDE

A *Romantic Times* Top Pick

"*High Tide* is packed full of warmth, humor, sensual tension, and exciting adventure. What more could you ask of a book?"

—*Romantic Times*

"Fast-paced, suspenseful. . . . [A] sassy love story."

—*Publishers Weekly*

"Exciting. . . . Fans of romantic suspense will gain much pleasure."

—*Midwest Book Review*

"[A] fast-paced escapade . . . mysterious and sultry."

—*BookPage*

"Jude Deveraux not only keeps you guessing but mixes crime and human morality with humor in the most unexpected moments. . . . [A] fantastic read."

—*Rendezvous*

THE BLESSING

"Plenty of romance, fun, and adventure . . . fans won't be disappointed."

—*San Antonio Express-News*

"[A] fun and entertaining love story. . . . Wonderful. . . . A must for Deveraux fans."

—*The Advocate* (Baton Rouge, LA)

"A heartwarming story."

—*Kerrville Daily Times* (TX)

AN ANGEL FOR EMILY

"All sorts of clever turns and surprises. Definitely a keeper. . . . Wow!"

—*The Philadelphia Inquirer*

Books by Jude Deveraux

The Velvet Promise

Highland Velvet

Velvet Song

Velvet Angel

Sweetbriar

Counterfeit Lady

Lost Lady

River Lady

Twin of Fire

Twin of Ice

The Temptress

The Raider

The Princess

The Awakening

The Maiden

The Taming

The Conquest

A Knight in Shining Armor

Wishes

Mountain Laurel

The Duchess

Eternity

Sweet Liar

The Invitation

Remembrance

The Heiress

Legend

An Angel for Emily

The Blessing

High Tide

Temptation

The Summerhouse

The Mulberry Tree

Forever…

Wild Orchids

Forever and Always

Jude Deveraux

The Mulberry Tree

POCKET BOOKS
New York   London   Toronto   Sydney

This book is a work of fiction. Names, characters, places and incidents are products of the author's imagination or are used fictitiously. Any resemblance to actual events or locales or persons, living or dead, is entirely coincidental.

 POCKET BOOKS, a division of Simon & Schuster, Inc.
1230 Avenue of the Americas, New York, NY 10020

Originally published in hardcover in 2002 by Atria Books

ISBN: 0-7434-9985-9

This Pocket Books trade paperback edition June 2004

10   9   8   7   6   5   4

Manufactured in the United States of America

For information regarding special discounts for bulk purchases,
please contact Simon & Schuster Special Sales at 1-800-456-6798
or business@simonandschuster.com.

The
Mulberry Tree

One

❦

He needed me.

Whenever anyone—usually a reporter—asked me how I coped with a man like Jimmie, I smiled and said nothing. I'd learned that whatever I said would be misquoted, so I simply kept quiet. Once, I made the mistake of telling the truth to a female reporter. She'd looked so young and so in need herself that for a moment I let my guard down. I said, "He needs me." That's all. Just those three words.

Who would have thought that a second of unguarded honesty could cause so much turmoil? The girl—she had certainly not attained the maturity of womanhood—parlayed my small sentence into international turmoil.

I was right in thinking she herself was needy. Oh, yes, very needy. She needed a story, so she fabricated one.

Never mind that she had nothing on which to base her fable.

I must say that she was good at research. She couldn't have slept during the two weeks between my remark and the publication of her story. She consulted psychiatrists, self-help gurus, and clergy. She interviewed hordes of rampant feminists. Every famous woman who had ever hinted that she hated men was interviewed and quoted.

In the end Jimmie and I were portrayed as one sick couple. He was the domineering tyrant in public, but a whimpering child at home. And I was shown to be a cross between steel and an ever-flowing breast.

When the article came out and caused a sensation, I wanted to hide from the world. I wanted to retreat to the most remote of Jimmie's twelve houses and never leave. But Jimmie was afraid of nothing—which was the true secret of his success—and he met the questions, the derisive laughter, and worse, the pseudo-therapists who felt it was our "duty" to expose every private thought and feeling to the world, head-on.

Jimmie just put his arm around me, smiled into the cameras, and laughed in answer to all of their questions. Whatever they asked, he had a joke for a reply.

"Is it true, Mr. Manville, that your wife is the power behind the throne?" The reporter asking this was smiling at me in a nasty way. Jimmie was six foot two and built like the bull some people said he was, and I am five foot two and round. I've never looked like the power behind anyone.

"She makes all the decisions. I'm just her front man," Jimmie said, his smile showing his famous teeth. But those of us who knew him saw the coldness in his eyes.

Jimmie didn't like any disparagement of what he considered his. "I couldn't have done it without her," he said in that teasing way of his. Few people knew him well enough to know whether or not he was joking.

Three weeks later, by chance, I saw the cameraman who'd been with the reporter that day. He was a favorite of mine because he didn't delight in sending his editor the pictures of me that showed off my double chin at its most unflattering angle. "What happened to your friend who was so interested in my marriage?" I asked, trying to sound friendly. "Fired," the photographer said. "I beg your pardon?" He was pushing new batteries into his camera and didn't look up. "Fired," he said again, then looked up, not at me, but at Jimmie.

Wisely, the photographer said no more. And just as wisely, I didn't ask any more questions.

Jimmie and I had an unwritten, unspoken law: I didn't interfere in whatever Jimmie was doing.

"Like a Mafia wife," my sister said to me about a year after Jimmie and I were married.

"Jimmie doesn't murder people," I replied in anger.

That night I told Jimmie of the exchange with my sister, and for a moment his eyes glittered in a way that, back then, I hadn't yet learned to be wary of.

A month later, my sister's husband received a fabulous job offer: double his salary; free housing; free cars. A full-time nanny for their daughter, three maids, and a country club membership were included. It was a job they couldn't refuse. It was in Morocco.

After Jimmie's plane crashed and left me a widow at thirty-two, all the media around the world wrote of only one thing: that Jimmie had willed me "nothing." None of his billions—two or twenty of them, I never could remember how many—none of it was left to me.

"Are we broke or rich today?" I'd often ask him, because his net worth fluctuated from day to day, depending on what Jimmie was trying at the moment.

"Today we're broke," he'd say, and he would laugh in the same way as when he'd tell me he'd made so many millions that day.

The money never mattered to Jimmie. No one understood that. To him, it was just a by-product of the game. "It's like all those peels you throw away after you've made jam," he'd say. "Only in this case the world values the peel and not the jam." "Poor world," I said, then Jimmie laughed hard and carried me upstairs, where he made sweet love to me.

It's my opinion that Jimmie knew he wasn't going to live to be an old man. "I've got to do what I can as fast as I can. You with me, Frecks?" he'd ask.

"Always," I'd answer, and I meant it. "Always."

But I didn't follow him to the grave. I was left behind, just as Jimmie said I would be.

"I'll take care of you, Frecks," he said more than once. When he talked of such things, he always called me by the name he'd given me the first time we met: Frecks for the freckles across my nose.

When he said, "I'll take care of you," I didn't give the words much thought. Jimmie had always "taken care" of me. Whatever I wanted, he gave me long before I knew I wanted it. Jimmie said, "I know you better than you know yourself."

And he did. But then, to be fair, I never had time to get to know much about myself. Following Jimmie all over the world didn't leave a person much time to sit and contemplate.

Jimmie knew me, and he did take care of me. Not in the way the world thought was right, but in the way he knew I *needed*. He didn't leave me a rich widow with half the world's bachelors clamoring to profess love for me. No, he left the money and all twelve of the expensive houses to the only two people in the world he truly hated: his older sister and brother.

To me, Jimmie left a run-down, overgrown farm in the backwoods of Virginia, a place I didn't even know he owned, and a note. It said:

> *Find out the truth about what happened, will you, Frecks? Do it for me. And remember that I love you. Wherever you are, whatever you do, remember that I love you.*
>
>   *J.*

When I saw the farmhouse, I burst into tears. What had enabled me to survive the past six weeks was the image of that farmhouse. I'd imagined something charming, made of logs, with a stone chimney at one end. I'd imagined a deep porch with hand-hewn rocking chairs on it, and a lawn in front, with pink roses spilling petals in the breeze.

I'd envisioned acres of gently rolling land covered with fruit trees and raspberry bushes—all of them pruned and healthy and dripping ripe fruit.

But what I saw was 1960s hideous. It was a two-story house covered in some sort of green siding—the kind that never changes over the years. Storms, sun, snow, time, none of it had any effect on that kind of siding. It had been a pale, sickly green when it was installed, and now, many years later, it was the same color.

There were vines growing up one side of the house, but not the kind of vines that make a place look quaint and cozy. These were vines that looked as though they were going to engulf the house, eat it raw, digest it, then regurgitate it in the same ghastly green.

"It can be fixed," Phillip said softly from beside me.

In the weeks since Jimmie's death, "hell" could not begin to describe what I had been through.

It was Phillip who woke me in the middle of the night when Jimmie's plane went down. I must say that I was shocked to see him. As Jimmie's wife, I was sacrosanct. The men he surrounded himself with knew what would happen if they made any advances toward me. I don't mean just sexually, but in any other way. No man or woman in Jimmie's employ ever asked me to intercede for him or her with my husband. If he had been fired, he knew that to approach me and ask that I try to "reason" with Jimmie would likely earn him something far worse than a mere dismissal.

So when I awoke to Jimmie's top lawyer's hand on my shoulder, telling me that I had to get up, I immediately knew what had happened. Only if Jimmie were dead would anyone dare enter my bedroom and think that he'd live to see the dawn.

"How?" I asked, immediately wide awake and trying to be mature. Inside, I was shaking. Of course it couldn't be true, I told myself. Jimmie was too big, too alive, to be . . . to be . . . I couldn't form the word in my mind.

"You have to get dressed now," Phillip was saying. "We have to keep this secret for as long as we can."

"Is Jimmie hurt?" I asked, my voice full of hope. Maybe he was in a hospital bed and calling for me. But even as I thought it, I knew it wasn't true. Jimmie knew how I worried about him. "I'd rather have my foot cut off than have to deal with your fretting," he'd said more than once. He hated my nagging about his smoking, about his drinking, about his days without sleep.

"No," Phillip said, his voice cold and hard. His eyes looked into mine. "James is not alive."

I wanted to collapse. I wanted to dive back under the warm bedcovers and go back to sleep. And when I awoke again, I wanted Jimmie to be there, slipping his big hand under my nightgown and making those little growling sounds that made me giggle.

"You don't have time for grief right now," Phillip said. "We have to go shopping."

That brought me out of my shock. "Are you mad?" I asked him. "It's four o'clock in the morning."

"I've arranged for a store to open. Now get dressed!" he ordered. "We have no time to lose."

His tone didn't scare me in the least. I sat down on the bed, my big nightgown billowing out around me, and I pulled my braid out from under me. Jimmie liked for me to wear old-fashioned clothes, and he liked for my hair to be long. After sixteen years of marriage, I could sit on my braid. "I'm not going anywhere until you tell me what's going on."

"I don't have time now—" Phillip began, but then he stopped, took a deep breath, and looked at me. "I could be disbarred for this, but I made out James's will, and I know what's coming to you. I can hold off the vultures for a few days but no more. Until the will is read, you're still James's wife."

"I will always be Jimmie's wife," I said proudly, holding all my chins aloft in the bravest stance I could muster. Jimmie! my heart was crying. Not Jimmie. Anyone on earth could die, but not Jimmie.

"Lillian," Phillip said softly, his eyes full of pity, "there was only one man like James Manville ever made on this earth. He played by his own rules and no one else's."

I waited for him to tell me something that I didn't already know. What was he leading up to?

Phillip ran his hand over his eyes and glanced at the clock by the bed. "By the law of ethics, I can't tell you—" he began, then he let out his breath and sat down heavily on the bed beside me. If I'd needed any further proof that Jimmie was no longer alive, that would have been it. If there was a chance that Jimmie would walk through the door and see another man sitting on the bed beside his wife, Phillip would never have dared such a familiarity.

"Who can understand what James did or why? I worked with him for over twenty years, but I never knew him. Lillian, he—" Phillip had to take a few breaths, then he picked up my hand and held it in his. "He left you nothing. He willed everything to his brother and sister."

I couldn't understand what he meant. "But he hates them," I said, pulling my hand from his grasp. Atlanta and Ray were Jimmie's only living relatives, and Jimmie despised them. He took care of them financially, always bailing one or the other of them out of some mess, but he detested them. No, worse, he had contempt for them. One time Jimmie was looking at me strangely, and I asked what was going on in his mind. "They'll eat you alive," he said. "That sounds interesting," I replied, smiling at him. But Jimmie didn't smile back. "When I die,

Atlanta and Ray will go after you with everything they have. And they'll find lawyers to work on a contingency basis."

I didn't like what had become Jimmie's frequent references to his demise. "Contingent upon what?" I asked, still smiling. "How much money they get when they sue you to hell and back," Jimmie said, frowning. I didn't want to hear any more, so I waved my hand in dismissal and said, "Phillip will take care of them." "Phillip is no match for greed on that scale." I had no reply for that, because I agreed with him. No matter how much Jimmie gave Atlanta and Ray, they wanted more. One time when Jimmie was called away unexpectedly, I found Atlanta in my closet, counting my shoes. She wasn't the least embarrassed when I found her there. She looked up at me and said, "You have three more pairs than I do." The look on her face frightened me so much that I turned and ran from my own bedroom.

"What do you mean that he's left it all to them? All what?" I asked Phillip. I wanted to think about anything other than what my life was going to be like without Jimmie.

"I mean that James willed all his stocks, his houses, real estate around the world, the airlines, all of it to your brother and sister-in-law."

Since I hated each and every one of the houses that Jimmie had purchased, I couldn't comprehend what was so bad about this. "Too much glass and steel for my taste," I said, giving Phillip a bit of a smile.

Phillip glared at me. "Lillian, this is *serious,* and James is no longer here to protect you—and I don't have the power to do *anything*. I don't know why he did it, Lord knows I tried to talk him out of it, but he said that he was giving you what you needed. That's all I could get out of him."

Phillip stood up, then took a moment to regain his calm. Jimmie said that what he liked about Phillip was that nothing on earth could upset him. But this had.

I tried to get the picture of my future out of my head, tried to stop thinking about a life without Jimmie's laughter and his big shoulders to protect me, and looked up at Phillip expectantly. "Are you saying that I'm destitute?" I tried not to smile. The jewelry that Jimmie had given me over the years was worth millions.

Phillip took a deep breath. "More or less. He's left you a farm in Virginia."

"There, then, that's something," I said, then I took the humor out of my voice and waited for him to continue.

"It was a breach of ethics, but after I wrote the will for him, I sent someone down to Virginia to look at the place. It's . . . not much. It's—" He turned away for a moment, and I thought I heard him mutter, "Bastard," but I didn't want to hear that, so I ignored him. When he turned back to me, his face was businesslike. He looked at his watch, a watch that I knew Jimmie had given him; it cost over twenty thousand dollars. I owned a smaller version of it.

"Did you do anything to him?" Phillip asked softly. "Another man maybe?"

I couldn't stop my little snort of derision, and my answer was just to look at Phillip. Women in harems weren't kept under tighter lock and key than James Manville's wife.

"All right," Phillip said, "I've had months to try to figure this out, and I haven't come close, so I'm going to give up. When James's will is read, all hell is going to break loose. Atlanta and Ray are going to get it all, and what you get is a farmhouse in Virginia and fifty grand—a pittance." He narrowed his eyes at me. "But the one thing I can do is see that you receive as much as you and I can buy between now and the moment that James's death is announced to the public."

It was hearing those words, "James's death," that almost did me in.

"No, you don't," Phillip said as he grabbed my arm and pulled me upright. "You don't have time for grief or self-pity right now. You have to get dressed. The store manager is waiting."

At five-thirty on that cold spring morning, I was pushed inside a huge department store and told that I was to buy what I needed for a farmhouse in Virginia. Phillip said the man he sent couldn't see inside the house, so I didn't even know how many bedrooms it had. The sleepy store manager who'd been roused from bed to open the store for James Manville's wife dutifully followed Phillip and me about and noted down what I pointed at.

It all seemed so unreal. I couldn't believe any of it was happening, and a part of me, the still-in-shock part, couldn't wait to tell Jimmie this story. How he'd laugh at it! I'd exaggerate every moment of it, and the more he'd laugh, the more flamboyant my story would become. "So there I was, half asleep, being asked which couch I wanted to buy," I'd say. " 'Couch?' the little man asked, yawning. 'What's a couch?' "

But there was not going to be any storytelling with Jimmie, for I was never going to see Jimmie alive again.

I did as I was told, though, and I chose furniture,

cookware, linens, and even appliances for a house that I
had never seen. But it all seemed so ridiculous. Jimmie
had houses full of furniture, most of it custom-made,
and there were great, enormous kitchens full of every
imaginable piece of cooking gear.

At seven, when Phillip was driving me back to the
house, he reached into the back of his car and picked up
a brochure. "I bought you a car," he said, handing me a
glossy photo of a four-wheel-drive Toyota.

I was beginning to wake up, and I was beginning to
feel pain. Everything seemed so odd; my world was turning upside down. Why was Phillip driving a car himself?
He usually used one of Jimmie's cars and a driver.

"You can't take the jewelry," Phillip was saying. "Each
piece has been itemized and insured. You may take your
clothing, but even at that I think that Atlanta may give
you some problems. She's your size."

"My size," I whispered. "Take my clothes."

"You can fight it all, of course," Phillip was saying.
"But something's wrong. About six months ago, Atlanta
hinted that she knew some big secret about you."

Phillip looked at me out of the corner of his eye. I
knew he was again asking me if there were other men in
my life. But when? I wondered. Jimmie didn't like to be
alone, not even for a second, and he made sure *I* was
never alone. " 'Fraid the bogeyman will get me," he said,
kissing my nose, when I asked him why he avoided soli-
tude so diligently. Jimmie rarely—no, Jimmie never
gave straight answers to personal questions. He lived in
the here and now; he lived in the world around him, not
inside his head. He wasn't one for pondering why people
were the way they were; he accepted them, and liked
them or didn't.

"I was a virgin when I met him," I said softly to Phillip, "and there's only been Jimmie." But I looked away when I said it, for I knew that there *was* a secret between Jimmie and me. Only I knew it, though. Atlanta couldn't know—could she?

But she did.

By eight, my comfortable, safe world as I knew it had collapsed. I don't know how Atlanta heard about Jimmie's plane going down so soon after it happened, but she had. And in the time between when Atlanta was told and the press heard of Jimmie's death, she had accomplished more than in all the other forty-eight years of her life combined.

When Phillip and I returned from our crazy shopping expedition, we were greeted at the front door of what I'd thought of as my house by men carrying guns, and I was told I wasn't allowed to enter. I was told that, as Jimmie's only surviving relatives, Atlanta and Ray now owned everything.

When Phillip and I got back into the car, he was shaking his head in wonder. "How did they find out about the will? How did she know James left it all to them? Look, Lillian," he said, and I noted that up until Jimmie's death, he'd always called me Mrs. Manville, "I don't know how she found out, but I'll find the culprit who told and . . . and . . ." Obviously, he couldn't think of anything horrible enough to do to someone on his staff who'd leaked the contents of Jimmie's will. "We'll fight this. You're his wife, and you have been for many years. You and I will—"

"I was seventeen when I married him," I said quietly. "And I didn't have my mother's permission."

"Oh, my God," Phillip said, then he opened his

mouth to begin what I assumed was going to be a lecture on my irresponsibility. But he closed it again, and rightfully so. What good would it do to lecture me now that Jimmie was gone?

The next weeks were horrible beyond anything I'd ever imagined. Atlanta was on TV just hours after Jimmie's death, telling the press that she was going to fight "that woman" who had so enslaved her beloved brother for all those years. "I'm going to see that she gets everything she deserves."

It didn't matter to Atlanta that Jimmie's will stated I was to get nothing. Not even the farmhouse was mentioned in the will. No, Atlanta was out to avenge all the things she imagined I'd done to her over the years. She didn't just want money; she wanted me humiliated.

Yes, of course she'd found out that my marriage to Jimmie hadn't been legal. It couldn't have been difficult. My sister knew. She and her husband had divorced because she couldn't bear to stay in Morocco, but her husband wouldn't give up all that cash and luxury. My sister blamed me for her divorce. Maybe she called Atlanta and volunteered the information that I wasn't legally married to Jimmie.

However she found out, Atlanta waved my birth certificate before the press, then showed them the photocopy of my marriage certificate. I was only seventeen when we'd married, but I'd lied and said that I was eighteen, and therefore legally in charge of my own fate.

No longer did I have Jimmie to protect me from the press. Now every reporter who'd been mistreated by him—i.e., all of them—dug through his archives and pulled out the most unflattering photos of me he could find, then slapped them across every communications media there was. I couldn't look at TV, a magazine, or a computer screen that didn't feature all my chins and the nose I'd inherited from my father. I'd told Jimmie about a thousand times that I wanted to have my over-large nose "fixed." "Removed!" is what I said, but Jimmie always told me that he loved me as I was, and, eventually, the right hook of my nose didn't seem to matter.

When I heard what was being said about me, my ugly nose was the least of my concerns. How can I describe what it felt like to see four respected journalists—three men and a woman—sitting around a table, discussing whether or not I had "trapped" James Manville into marrying me? As though a man like Jimmie could be trapped by anyone! And by a seventeen-year-old girl whose only claim to fame was a handful of blue ribbons won at the state fair? Not likely.

Lawyers talked about whether or not I was legally entitled to any of Jimmie's money.

But when the will was finally read and it was seen that Jimmie had given it all to his brother and sister, I was suddenly the Jezebel of America. Everyone seemed to believe that I had somehow ensnared dear little Jimmie (the youthful Salome was the comparison used most often) but that he had found out about it and had used his will to give me "what I deserved."

Phillip did his best to keep me away from the press, but it wasn't easy. I wanted to get on a plane and go away, to hide from everything—but that was no longer an option. My days of jumping on a plane and going anywhere in the world I wanted were over.

For six weeks after Jimmie's death, while the courts

dealt with his will and the press hashed and rehashed everything they heard, I stayed locked inside Phillip's sprawling house. The only time I left during those horrible weeks was when I went to Jimmie's funeral, and then I was so shrouded in black draperies that I may as well not have been there. And I most certainly wasn't going to give the press or Atlanta and Ray the satisfaction of seeing me weep.

When I got to the church, I was told that I couldn't enter, but Phillip had anticipated such an event, and seemingly out of nowhere, half a dozen men the size of sumo wrestlers appeared and surrounded me.

That's how I entered Jimmie's funeral: walking in the midst of six enormous men, my face and body covered with black cloth.

It was all right, though, because by that time I had realized that Jimmie was actually never coming back, and nothing anyone did mattered much. And, too, I kept imagining that farmhouse he'd left me. One time Jimmie had asked me to describe where I'd like to live, and I'd talked of a cozy little house with a deep porch, tall trees around it, and a lake nearby. "I'll see what I can do," he'd said, smiling at me with twinkling eyes. But the next house he'd bought was a castle on an island off the coast of Scotland, and the thing was so cold that even in August my teeth were chattering.

After the will was probated, I made no move to leave Phillip's house. With the press still hovering outside and with Jimmie gone, it didn't seem to matter where I was or what I did. I took long showers, and I sat at the table with Phillip and his family—his wife, Carol, and their two young daughters—but I don't remember eating anything.

It was Phillip who told me that it was time for me to leave.

"I can't go out there," I said in fear, glancing toward the curtains that I kept drawn night and day. "They're waiting for me."

Phillip took my hand in his and rubbed his palm against my skin. For all that I no longer had a husband, I still felt married. I snatched my hand away and frowned at him.

But Phillip smiled. "Carol and I have been talking, and we think you should . . . well, that you should disappear."

"Ah, yes," I said, "suttee. The wife climbs onto the funeral pyre and follows her husband into the afterlife."

From the look on Phillip's face, he didn't appreciate my black sense of humor. Jimmie had. Jimmie used to say that the more depressed I was, the funnier I was. If that was so, I should have gone onstage the day of his funeral.

"Lillian," Phillip said, but when he reached toward my hand again, I withdrew it. "Have you looked at yourself lately?"

"I—" I began, intending to make a sarcastic remark, but then I glanced into the mirror over the big dresser across from the bed in the guest room in Phillip's house. I had, of course, noticed that I'd lost some weight. Not eating for weeks on end will do that. But I hadn't noticed how much I'd lost. My chins were gone. I had cheekbones.

I looked back at Phillip. "Amazing, isn't it? All those diet programs that Jimmie paid for for me, and all he had to do was die and bingo! I'm finally slim."

Phillip frowned again. "Lillian, I've waited until now

to talk to you. I've tried to give you some time to come to terms with James's death and his will."

He started on another lecture about my stupidity in not telling either him or Jimmie that I'd been seventeen when we married. "He would have given you a huge wedding. He would have loved doing that for you," Phillip had said the day after he found out. "It would have been so much better than the elopement you had the first time."

But I'd heard that lecture before and didn't want to hear it again, so I cut him off. "You want me to disappear?"

"Actually, it was Carol's idea. She said that as things stand now, the rest of your life is going to be one long press interview. People are going to hound you forever to tell them about your life with Jimmie. Unless—"

"Unless what?" I asked.

Phillip's thin face lit up, and for a moment I saw the "little fox" that Jimmie had always said the man was. "Do you remember when I told you that I'd tried to talk James out of writing his will as he did?" He didn't wait for me to answer. "I did persuade him not to put the farmhouse in the will. I said that if he was so afraid of what his sister would do, then she'd probably try to take the farm too. At that time I hadn't seen the place, and I thought it was—"

"Was what?" I asked.

"Valuable," he said softly, looking down at the floor for a moment, then back up at me. "Look, Lillian, I know the farmhouse isn't much, but it must have meant something to James, or he wouldn't have kept it all these years."

"Why did he buy it in the first place?"

"That's just it, he didn't buy it. I think he's always owned it."

"People have to buy things," I said, confused. "People just don't give real estate away, at least not while they're alive." It was then that understanding began to hit me. "You mean you think that Jimmie might have *inherited* this farm?"

For the first time, I felt some interest spark inside me. All three of them, Atlanta, Ray, and Jimmie, were maddeningly secretive about their childhood. When questioned, Ray evaded and changed the subject. Atlanta and Jimmie out-and-out lied. They would say they were born in South Dakota one day, and in Louisiana the next. I knew for a fact that Jimmie had given me four different names for his mother. I'd even secretly read all six of the biographies that had been written about him, but the authors had had no better luck than I had in finding out anything about the first sixteen years of James Manville's life.

"I don't know for sure," Phillip said, "but I do know that James didn't buy the place since I've known him."

At that statement, all I could do was blink. Jimmie and Phillip had been together from the beginning.

"When I said that Atlanta and Ray might try to take the farm away from you, all I can tell you is that James turned white, as though he were afraid of something."

"Jimmie afraid?" I said, unable to grasp that concept.

"He said, 'You're right, Phil, so I'm going to give the place to you, then when the time comes, I want you to sign it over to Lil. And I want you to give her this from me.'"

That was when Phillip handed me the note written

by Jimmie. It was in a sealed envelope, so Phillip hadn't read it. He'd kept it and the deed to the farm in Virginia in his home safe, awaiting the day when he'd turn them both over to me.

After I read the note, I folded it and put it back into the envelope. I didn't cry; I'd cried so much over the last six weeks that I didn't seem to have any more liquid inside me. I reached for the deed to the farm, but Phillip pulled it back.

"If I make this out to Lillian Manville, then register the property transfer, within twenty-four hours, you'll have reporters—and lawyers—on your doorstep. But—" he said, drawing out what he wanted to say as though I were a child he was enticing to be good.

I didn't take the bait, but just stared at him.

"All right," he said at last. "What Carol and I thought was that maybe you should change your identity. You've lost so much weight that you don't look like James Manville's fat little wife anymore."

That remark made me narrow my eyes at him. I did *not* want to hear what he and the rest of Jimmie's staff had sniggered behind his back. I guess I'd not spent all those years near Jimmie for nothing, because I could see Phillip beginning to wither under my gaze.

"All right," he said again, then let out his pent-up breath. "It's up to you, but I've already done a lot of the work, such as get you new documents of identification. I needed to use James's connections while they still remembered him. Sorry to be so blunt, but people forget fast. Now, it's up to you to accept it."

He handed me a passport, and I opened it. There was no photo inside, but there was a name. "Bailey James," I read aloud, then looked up at Phillip.

"It was Carol's idea. She took your maiden name and James's first name and— You don't like it."

The problem was that I did like the idea. A new name; maybe a new life.

"Carol thought that with your weight loss, and if you got your hair cut and lightened, and if you . . . Well, if you . . ."

I looked at him. What was he having such a hard time saying? But then I saw that he had his eyes fixed on my nose. I'd gone down headfirst on a playground slide in the first grade and had managed to knock my nose permanently to the right. "No wonder," sixth-grade Johnnie Miller had said as I stood there gushing blood. "Her nose is so big that it hit the ground half an hour before she did." I still remember the teacher holding me and oozing sympathy even as she tried hard not to laugh, even as she made Johnnie apologize for his remark.

"You want me to get a nose job," I said flatly.

Phillip gave a curt nod.

Turning, I looked at myself in the mirror. If Jimmie had left me his billions, I could have made a prison with high fences and locked myself away from all the gigolos and hangers-on that orbit around money. I didn't have the billions, but I did have the notoriety. I knew that, eventually, in ten years or so, Jimmie would fade in people's memories and I'd be left alone, but during those ten years . . .

I looked back at Phillip. "It's my guess that you have a surgeon all set up."

"Tonight." He looked at his watch, the twenty-thousand-dollar one that Jimmie had given him; Atlanta was now wearing mine. "If you're ready, that is."

I took a deep breath. "As ready as I can be, I guess," I said, then stood up.

That was two weeks ago. My nose had healed enough that I knew it was time to step outside Phillip and Carol's big house. It wasn't Lillian Manville who was to greet the world, but someone I didn't even recognize in the mirror, someone named Bailey James.

During the time I was recovering from surgery, I'd come to know Carol somewhat better. In the past she'd attended the parties that Jimmie liked to give, but he had always warned me that it was better not to get too chummy with employees, so I was courteous, but there were no secrets shared between us. I didn't share secrets with anyone other than Jimmie.

The surgery had been done in the doctor's office, and a few hours later I was driven back to Carol and Phillip's house. The first night a nurse stayed with me, but the second night I was alone when Carol tapped on my door. When I answered, she tiptoed in and sat on the edge of the bed. "Are you angry?" she asked.

"No, the doctor did a fine job. Nothing to be angry about," I answered, pretending that I didn't know what she was talking about.

She didn't fall for it; she stared hard at me.

"You mean, am I angry that I spent sixteen years giving my entire life to a man, only to be cut out of his will?"

Carol smiled at my sarcasm. "Men are slime," she said, then we smiled together, and when I touched my sore nose in pain, we laughed. It was my first genuine feeling of humor since I'd last talked to Jimmie.

"So what are you going to wear?" Carol asked, folding her legs and sitting on the corner of the bed. She was about ten years older than me, and I'd be willing to bet that she was no stranger to the surgeon's knife. She was blonde and pretty, and extremely well cared for. I knew what that meant because I, too, used to spend a lot of my time looking after myself. I may have been plump, but I was a well-coiffed, well-tended plump.

"Wear where?" I asked, and felt my heart jump a bit. Please, I silently prayed, someone tell me that I wasn't going to have to go again to some courtroom and hear Atlanta and Ray accuse me of "controlling" Jimmie.

"On your new body," Carol said. "You can't keep on wearing my sweats, you know."

"Oh," I said. "Sorry. I guess I haven't thought much about clothes lately. I—" Damnation, but tears were coming to my eyes. I wanted to be the brave little soldier and believe that, whatever Jimmie had done had been done out of love. But when I was confronted with issues such as the fact that the only clothing I now owned was what I'd put on the night Jimmie died, and the black shroud that Phillip had given me, I didn't feel very brave.

Carol reached out to touch my hand, but then she pulled back and moved off the bed. "I'll be back in just a minute," she said as she left the room. In seconds she returned with a foot-high stack of what looked like catalogs. She'd taken so little time to get them, I knew she must have had them piled outside.

She spread them across the bottom of the bed, and I looked at them in wonder. "What are these?"

"Phillip owes me five bucks!" she said in triumph. "I bet him you'd never seen a catalog. In nor—uh, most households, catalogs come through the mail at the rate of about six a day."

I knew she'd been about to say "in normal house-holds," but she'd stopped herself. In Jimmie's houses, a servant brought me my few pieces of mail on a silver dish.

I picked up one of the catalogs. Norm Thompson. Inside were the kind of clothes that appeared in my closet now and then, especially in the two island houses. Jimmie had someone he called a "shopper" who made sure that we had whatever clothes we needed in every house.

Carol picked up a catalog and flipped through it. The cover read "Coldwater Creek." "You know, I used to feel sorry for you. You always looked so alone and lost. I told Phillip that—" Breaking off, she bent down toward the catalog.

"You told him what?"

"That you were like a lightbulb, and you were only on when James was around."

I didn't like what she'd said. Not one bit. It made me sound so . . . so nothing, as though I weren't a person at all. "So what did you have in mind with these?" I asked, making my voice sound as cool as possible.

She understood my tone. "It's my opinion that we owe you for the wedding gift that you gave Phillip and me, so I thought we might order you some new clothes and whatever else you might need in your new life. We'll charge it all to Phillip; he can afford it." She lowered her voice. "He's going to be one of the attorneys for Atlanta and Ray."

At that my mouth dropped open, then I winced because my new, smaller nose hurt at the movement. I wanted to scream, "The traitor!" but I didn't. "Remind me. What did Jimmie and I give you for your wedding?"

"This house," Carol said.

For a moment I couldn't speak, and I had to look away so she wouldn't see my eyes. He gave a house to his attorney, a man he thought was his friend, but now that so-called friend was going to work for the enemy. I picked up a catalog. "Do you have one of these things for jewelry? I need a new watch."

Carol smiled at me; I smiled back; a friendship was formed.

Two

Phillip watched Lillian get out of the car and walk slowly toward the house. For all that she'd had a quick burst of tears when she first saw the place, he thought she was holding up well. Considering what she'd been through, she was holding up extremely well. Shaking his head in disbelief, he remembered all he'd done to prevent this moment. He and three of his associates had spent two afternoons and one morning trying to persuade her to fight James Manville's will—a will Phillip had come to see as immoral and possibly illegal.

But he hadn't always felt that way. When James had told Phillip what he wanted to put in the will, Phillip had raised his eyebrows. He hadn't dared let James know what he was thinking—that, obviously, James had found out that his young wife didn't deserve his money; that she was probably having an affair. But instead of speaking his mind, Phillip had tried to talk James out of causing what would surely be years of court battles. It never crossed his mind that James's widow wouldn't contest the will. Phillip told James that if he wanted to leave his brother and sister money, then he should split the fortune three ways; there was enough for everyone.

But James didn't seem to hear Phillip. His only concern had been how to make sure that Lillian got some farmhouse in Virginia. "She'll love it there," James said in one of his rare self-revelatory moods. "I stole a lot from her, and this is the way I can give it back."

To Phillip, cheating a woman out of billions of dollars didn't seem to be repaying her; it seemed more like a punishment. But he kept his mouth shut.

It wasn't until after James's death, when Phillip saw the true nature of Atlanta and Ray, that he wanted Lillian to fight. He wanted to head a team of the most clever, most conniving lawyers in the United States, and he wanted to take every penny away from those two greedy worms. In the weeks since James's death, Phillip had never seen anything like what had been done to Lillian, both by the media and by people he'd thought of as James's friends.

But Lillian wouldn't budge. Nothing anyone said could make her file suit. Phillip and the other lawyers told her that she could give the money to charity after she won it, but that still didn't make her change her mind.

"Jimmie was very smart about business," she said, "and he did this for a reason. There's something he wants out of this, so I'm going to abide by the will."

"Manville is dead," one of the lawyers said, his face red with exasperation. His thoughts were written on his face: What kind of woman could turn down billions of dollars?

After the third meeting, Lillian had stood up from the table and said, "I've heard all your arguments, seen all your evidence that shows that I could win, and I still won't do it. I'm going to abide by my husband's will." She then turned around and walked away from them.

One of the lawyers, a man who hadn't known James and certainly didn't know his wife, snickered and said softly, "Obviously, she's too simple to know what money means."

Lillian heard him. Slowly, she turned around and looked at the man in a way that was so like James Manville, Phillip drew in his breath. "What you don't understand," she said quietly, "is that there is more to life than money. Tell me, if *you* were a billionaire and *you* died and left your wife nothing, would she fight for it? Or would she love the memory of you more than the money?" She didn't wait for an answer, but turned and walked out of the room.

The other lawyers hid their faces from the man Lillian had just told off, unable to contain their laughter. He had in fact just been through his third very nasty divorce, and his ex-wife had fought him down to who got the antique doorknobs.

In the end, Phillip had given up trying to persuade Lillian to fight. The night of the last meeting, he'd fallen into bed beside Carol and said, "I don't know what else to do."

"Help her," Carol said.

"What do you think this has all been about?" he'd snapped at his wife.

Carol was unfazed; she didn't even glance up from

the magazine she was looking at. "You've been trying to make her into what she isn't. You're a worse tyrant than James was."

"Yes, and I can see that you're terribly intimidated by me," he said sarcastically. "So what's in that pretty little brain of yours?" After twelve years of marriage, he could almost read her mind, and he knew when she wanted to tell him something. As always, she'd waited for him to fail; only then would she offer her help.

"You've got to help her do whatever it is that *she* wants to do," Carol said.

"Any ideas what that is?" he asked, looking at her with skepticism. "She stays alone in the guest room and doesn't talk to anyone. All those so-called friends that James used to fill the house with haven't so much as called her to say they're sorry about his death." His voice was filled with disgust.

"I don't know her very well, but it seems to me that when she was with James, she tried very hard to have a normal life."

Phillip snorted. "Normal? With James Manville? Carol, did you have on blinders? They lived in vast houses all over the world; they were surrounded by servants. I took her into a department store right after James died, and I swear she'd never seen one before. Or at least not since she ran away from home and married him."

"That's all true, but what did Lillian do when she was in those houses? Give parties?"

Phillip put his hands behind his head and looked up at the ceiling. "No," he said thoughtfully. "James gave the parties, and Lillian put in an appearance. I don't think I ever saw anyone more miserable than she was at those functions. She used to sit in a corner all by herself and eat. Poor kid."

"Did you ever see her happy?"

"No, not—" Phillip began, then stopped. "That's not true. One day I took some papers to James to sign, but after I left his house, I saw that he'd missed one, so I went back. When I got there, I could hear voices, so I went through the house toward the back, and I saw them. They were alone, just the two of them, no guests, no servants, and—"

He closed his eyes for a moment in memory. It had been one of James's multimillion-dollar houses, "all glass and steel," as Lillian had said, and the voices had come from a room Phillip had never seen before. It was off the kitchen, and since the door was open, he looked inside. As he was standing near some flowing draperies that some designer had put up, he knew they weren't likely to see him. He knew he was playing the voyeur, but he couldn't move as he looked in on the scene.

Lillian, wearing jeans and a sweatshirt, not the designer clothes that he'd always seen her in, was serving James dinner. They were in a small sitting room with a tiny round table at one end. From the look of the room, no designer had touched it. The sofa was covered in a rose chintz; near it was a plaid chair. The table was pine and scratched; the two chairs with it looked like something from a country auction.

None of the furnishings had that fake look that designers managed to achieve. There was nothing "arranged" in this room. Instead, it looked like half the living rooms in America, and the couple in the room looked like what other American couples hoped to be. As Lillian filled James's plate from the food set out on a buffet, James was talking nonstop. And Lillian was listening closely. When she turned and put the plate in front of him, she laughed at what he was saying, and in that moment, Phillip thought she was beautiful. She wasn't just the billionaire's plump wife who never had a word to say, but a real beauty. As she began to fill her own plate, she started talking, and Phillip was astonished to see James listening to her with an intensity he'd never seen in him before. James nodded as she talked, and Phillip could see that he'd asked her opinion about something and she was giving it. *Partnership* was the word that came to his mind.

Silently, his paper unsigned, Phillip tiptoed away. How many times over the years had he heard people say, "Why doesn't Manville ditch the dumpling and get a woman who isn't afraid of her own shadow?" But obviously, as in everything else, James Manville had known what he was doing.

On that day, as Phillip walked back to the car, he thought that in all the years he'd known James, he'd never been jealous of him. Thanks to James, Phillip had all the money he wanted, so he didn't envy James his billions. But Phillip realized that when he looked in on that scene, he'd felt a hot wave of jealousy. Carol hadn't looked at him like that or listened to him in that way since the first year they were married.

Phillip had looked at the unsigned paper and was glad he hadn't made his presence known. It would be better if James didn't know that his private moments with Lillian had been observed.

"Yes," Phillip said to Carol. "I've seen her happy."

"Oh?" Carol asked, her voice full of curiosity. "When was that?"

James might be dead, but Phillip still couldn't bring himself to betray his friend by telling what he'd seen. The memory of it, though, just made him more confused. If James loved his wife so much, why hadn't he at least left her enough money to protect herself from the press? "You have something you want to tell me," he said to his wife, "so why don't you spit it out?"

"On the way to James's funeral, Lillian asked me if I'd seen the farmhouse that James left her."

"So?" Phillip asked. "What does that mean? The place is a pigsty. It's horrible. The countryside around it is beautiful, but the house ought to be torn down, and only a bulldozer would help the landscaping."

"Hmmm," Carol said, closing her magazine. "Nobody made as much money as James did without being able to plan. What do you think his plan was for that farmhouse?"

"Insure it for millions, then burn it down?"

Carol ignored him. "How can she ever live there in peace? She'll have reporters setting up camp in her front yard. She'll . . ." Trailing off, she looked hard at her husband, as though she expected him to figure out the rest of her idea.

Phillip was too tired to play guessing games. "What?" he asked.

And that's when Carol revealed her idea to change Lillian's looks, and even her name.

Now, as Phillip got out of the car and watched Lillian—no, Bailey, he reminded himself—look at the ugly old place, he had to admit that she certainly looked like a different person. He remembered one day when James had slammed a book down on a desk and said, "I can't concentrate. Lil's on one of those damned diets again."

Then he'd yelled for his secretary to come into the office—no intercom system for James Manville. He'd ordered his secretary to send Lillian a pound of every kind of chocolate the nearest Godiva store had. "That should do it," he had said, smiling. "Now let's get back to work."

Without her husband's sabotage, Lillian had dropped a lot of weight in just a few weeks. When Phillip told his wife what James used to do to keep Lillian off her diets, she'd said, "So that's the secret to losing weight," then she'd put her hand on her hip. "I'll remember that the next time you get on a plane."

Between the weight loss and the removal of that big schnozz of hers, Phillip had to admit that Bailey was a looker. Pudginess had been replaced with slim curves, and without that nose, you could really see her beautiful eyes and small, full lips. One morning at breakfast, Carol, holding a metal spatula, had leaned close to his ear and said, "You keep on looking at her like that, and I'll ram this—"

But Phillip did admit that Bailey looked good. "Do you think anyone will recognize me?" was the first thing Lillian had asked when the bandages were removed.

"No one," the doctor, Carol, and Phillip had all assured her, each trying not to say how much better she looked, because that would have been saying how bad she used to look.

Now Phillip got out of the car and motioned to the man in the car behind him to remove the suitcases from the trunk and put them inside the house. He'd arranged for two cars to be waiting for them at the airport: the SUV he'd bought for Lillian, and a black sedan from a local car service to follow them and drive Phillip back to the airport.

On the plane ride to Dulles Airport in D.C., Lillian had put her head back against the seat and closed her eyes. When Phillip had spoken to her, she'd just nodded. He figured that she wasn't speaking to him because he'd taken the job with Atlanta and Ray. He wanted to explain to her why, but at the same time, the less she knew, the better. If she wasn't going to fight for herself, then he was going to do it for her. And the only way he knew how to do that was from the inside out.

It had been a three-hour drive from the airport to the tiny mountain town of Calburn, where the farmhouse was. On the drive Lillian had put aside her anger and had pumped him for everything he knew about the town and the house.

Unfortunately for Lillian, Phillip could honestly say that even though he'd been James Manville's friend for twenty years, he knew nothing about his childhood. Truthfully, he wasn't at all sure that this farmhouse was even connected to James's past.

"How can Jimmie be related to people like Atlanta and Ray?" she'd asked. "I can't understand that."

Phillip was tempted to say, "That's because you never saw James do business. If you had, you'd know that he was more like them than you realize." But he didn't say that. Let her have her dreamy-eyed visions about her dead husband, he thought.

Lillian—Bailey, he corrected himself again—had walked around the house to look at the back. The investigator Phillip hired had taken photos of the property, so he knew that the back was more tangled than the front, and he dreaded having her see it. Using the key that James had given him when he'd signed over the deed to the house, Phillip opened the front door.

The door fell off its rusty hinges and crashed onto the floor, taking the jamb with it. In astonishment, Phillip turned and looked at the man behind him, whose arms were loaded with suitcases. Turning back, Phillip stepped onto the fallen door and into the house.

The place was ghastly. Thick, dusty cobwebs hung down from the ceiling all the way to the floor. He could hear creatures—mice, rats, and whatever else they have in the country—scurrying about under the floor. The sunlight that came through the dirty windows showed years of dust floating through the air.

"Take the luggage back to the car," Phillip said over his shoulder to the man behind him. "She's not staying here." He waited until the man was gone, then he turned, stepped onto the door and out into the fresh air. He'd never thought of James Manville as evil until this moment. That he'd leave his wife this filthy place and expect her to live here was either insane or truly evil. Since he knew for a fact that James was not insane, that left—

Lips tight with anger, Phillip walked toward the back of the house to find Bailey.

The photos hadn't lied: the back really was worse than the front. Huge trees, vines that were covered with lethal-looking thorns, bushes as tall as trees, and weeds as big as something in a science fiction movie fought each other for space and light. The tangled mass of plants around him made Phillip shiver. To his right were stones set in the ground to make a narrow path through weeds as high as his head. The many bees buzzing around him made him quicken his step. "Lillian?" he called, then caught himself. Like the lawyer he was, he looked around to see if anyone had heard him make the error of calling her by her former name. But as he looked at the tangle of weeds, he knew that an army could be hiding ten feet away, and he'd not be able to see them. "Bailey?" he called louder as he quickened his pace. Still, there was no answer.

Immediately, his mind filled with all the horrors of the country: snakes, rabid skunks, deer that could kick a person to death. Were there wolves in these mountains? What about wildcats that hid high up in trees and jumped on people? What . . . about . . . *bears?*

If the jacket she was wearing hadn't been bright pink, he never would have seen her. She was entangled in the biggest, ugliest tree he'd ever seen, and all he could spy were her denim-clad legs and part of one pink sleeve. Oh, God, he thought, she's hanged herself. In despair over James and this hideous place, she'd somehow managed to commit suicide.

Heart pounding, he ran toward the tree, ducked under two low limbs, and then saw her. She was alive and looking upward raptly as though she were seeing some heavenly vision. It's worse than suicide; she's lost her mind, he thought.

"Bailey," he said softly, but when she didn't respond, he said, "Lillian?" She just kept looking upward. Slowly, carefully, he stepped toward her—but he also inspected the ground. Weren't people supposed to stand still if they saw rattlesnakes? Was a poisonous snake the reason she wasn't moving?

"Bailey?" he said softly when he got closer to her. "We can go now. You don't have to stay here. If you want a little house somewhere, I'll buy it for you. I'll—"

"Do you know what this is?" she whispered.

He looked up, but all he saw was an old tree that

badly needed pruning—or better yet, removal. "I know," he said, "it's a horrible old thing. But you don't have to look at it." He put his hand on her arm to pull her away.

"It's a mulberry tree," she said softly, her voice sounding almost reverent. "And it's very old. It's a black mulberry tree."

"Nice," Phillip said, then pulled harder on her arm.

Bailey smiled. "The Chinese duped James the First."

At first he thought she meant James Manville, but then he realized she meant the English king, Elizabeth the First's incompetent successor. What did an English king have to do with a derelict farm in Virginia?

She spoke again. "James decided to grow mulberry trees in England so he could raise silkworms and make silk an industry in England. The silkworms feed on mulberry leaves, you know. So James imported thousands and thousands of mulberry trees from China. But—" She broke off and smiled as she touched a leaf of the big tree. "The Chinese tricked him. They sent the English king trees that bear black mulberry fruit instead of white. Black mulberries are great for eating, but silkworms won't touch them."

Phillip looked at his watch. It was 2:00 P.M. Three hours back to the airport, and his flight was at six. Of course he'd have to find a seat for Bailey on the same flight. "Look, why don't you tell me more about mulberry trees and the kings of England on the way back to the airport? You can—"

"I'm not leaving," she said.

It was Phillip's turn to want to burst into tears. Why did all women have to be contrary? "Bailey," he said firmly, "you haven't seen the inside of that house! It's falling down. The door collapsed when I opened it. How can you possibly spend the night here? The place is filthy! It's—"

"What's that?" she asked.

At the sound of a large truck on the rarely used gravel road in front of the house, Phillip started chanting, "No, no, no, no," even as Bailey leaped over two tree limbs and started running down the overgrown path.

The furniture had arrived.

Three

For a moment, the two burly furniture movers stood behind Bailey, looking across the fallen door into the house. A breeze blew in through a broken windowpane, and the cobwebs danced in the dust.

"Not quite ready for us, are you?" one of the movers said into the silence.

"There's been a mistake," Phillip said from behind them. "We're sending all the furniture back."

"I can't take the stuff back," the mover nearest Bailey said. "Look, mister, this is my truck but their furniture. They paid me to haul it one way. If I drive it back up north, they're gonna tell me that the expense is on my head, not theirs."

"I'll pay you whatever—" Phillip began, but Bailey cut him off.

"It's not going to be sent back. The furniture goes into the house just as soon as I get it—"

"Repaired?" the mover asked, his brows raised.

"Maybe I should back the truck into the house," the second man behind him said. "Looks like it would only take a nudge to topple it."

The first man, taller, bigger, the one who owned the truck, frowned as he looked down at Bailey. He was about twice as big as she was, and he'd always felt protective toward small things. "Maybe there's someplace else we could unload the truck until you get this place fixed up. You got any friends with a big garage, maybe?"

Biting her bottom lip, Bailey shook her head no. No friends, she thought, and didn't dare meet Phillip's eyes. She knew he was standing there waiting for her to "come to her senses," that universal male phrase meaning that she was to agree that he was right and do whatever he wanted her to.

The second mover seemed to think better of making any more negative comments about the derelict old house. "Why don't you put the furniture in the barn?"

Bailey's head came up. "Barn? What barn?"

The man pointed toward a dense growth of trees. Barely visible was what looked liked the peak of a building that had once been painted red. "Either that's a barn, or it's a fire station ready and waitin'," the man said.

No one laughed at his attempt at humor, but Bailey instantly set off through the undergrowth, one arm across her face for protection, the other one pushing aside hanging vines and bushes that blocked her path.

"Remind me not to tip you," Phillip said to the man

who'd pointed out the barn, then he went after Bailey, the two movers following him.

It was indeed a barn, not a hundred yards from the house. There was no path cut through the underbrush, so getting to the building had been difficult. Bailey had three long, bloody scratches on her left arm.

It wasn't a huge barn, not something that kept dozens of horses and cows. It was more of a "gentleman's barn," a place to store farm implements and maybe one or two horses.

Bailey was struggling to slide the heavy door open when the others arrived and the two movers stepped forward to help her. The hardware on the door was heavy-duty, but it had rusted from disuse. As Phillip stood to one side, his mouth a tight line of disapproval, the movers and Bailey pushed until the big door slid to one side. A thick gush of dust and dried straw came rushing out of the barn and set the three of them coughing.

"When was this place last opened?" the second mover asked, leaning over and hacking to clear his lungs.

"I have no idea," Bailey answered, straightening up and taking some deep breaths. "I never saw this place before about an hour ago."

"You bought it without seeing it?" the man asked, his voice letting her know that he thought she was this year's number-one idiot.

"Inherited," Bailey said over her shoulder as she looked into the barn. Sunlight came in through a high window, but it took her eyes a few moments to adjust. Inside were a few bales of dried-out hay, some horse harnesses hanging from a board wall, and a few broken shovels hanging on another wall. Toward the back she could see some empty horse stalls. All in all, the place looked in better condition than the house. At least the roof had held, and there was no sign of water damage.

She turned to the others. "We'll put the furniture in here."

"And how do you propose to get it back here?" Phillip asked, nodding toward the way they'd come. There was no path, much less a drive that a truck could use.

For a moment, Bailey had no answer, then she smiled. "Isn't that car you bought me four-wheel-drive? We'll *make* a path." With that, she turned and went down the narrow space that their four bodies had made in the weeds.

The first mover walked behind Phillip. "When a woman is as determined as that one is, you might as well give up," he said softly, then chuckled when Phillip ignored him.

Hours later, the barn was full of crates and boxes and furniture wrapped in packing blankets, and Bailey had given the men a fifty as a tip.

"You can't afford to do that kind of thing now," Phillip had said as soon as the men drove away. "If you must give a tip, make it a small one."

Bailey walked ahead of him, back toward the house, and she kept her head high. When they reached the house, Phillip caught her arm. "Lil—I mean, Bailey, we have to talk. You can't stay here alone. This . . . this . . ." He couldn't seem to think of any words bad enough to express what he thought of the forsaken old house. All he could think of was the life that Bailey had lived for as

long as he'd known her: servants, palaces, silk sheets.
Like Carol, Bailey had spent most of her days having
various beauty treatments. "For you to stay here is like
Marie Antoinette playing at farming," he said in frustration. "You don't know anything about the kind of work
that a place like this requires."

"Actually, I don't know much about anything, do I?"
Bailey said softly, looking at him in the fading daylight.
"But what is my alternative?"

"I'll take care of you," Phillip said quickly. "I'll buy
you a house, I'll—"

Bailey narrowed her eyes at him. "Do you mean that
you'll use the money you received from James Manville
to buy me a house, and then you'll"—she was advancing on him—"you'll put me in it and keep me very
well? Is that what you had in mind? Like Peter, Peter
Pumpkin Eater?" When she was nearly nose to nose
with him, she lowered her voice. "Or do you intend to
try to take Jimmie's place? Is that what you think?
That one man kept me, so now another one will? Any
ol' man? *You* maybe? Are you thinking that since I lived
in seclusion with one man for sixteen years, it will suit
me perfectly well to live in seclusion with *you* as the
head of the harem?"

Blinking, Phillip stiffened his spine and stepped backward. "That's not what I meant at all. This house is not
livable."

"No, it's not," she said, her face full of anger. "But you
know what? It's *mine*. I figure I earned it, if for nothing
else than for all those hideous parties Jimmie made me
attend where everyone watched—and commented on—
every bite I took." When she saw him flinch, she took
another step forward. "Did none of you think that I

heard you? You whispered behind my back that I was fat and not pretty enough to be worthy of a dynamic man like Jimmie. You said—"

"Not me," Phillip said softly. "I never said anything like that, so don't try to make *me* out to be the enemy."

"Then why are you working for Atlanta and Ray?" she shot at him, then closed her mouth. She hadn't wanted to say that, hadn't wanted to let him see how she felt about what he was doing.

Phillip took his time in answering. His natural reticence, mixed with what he'd learned as a lawyer, made it difficult for him to reveal anything to anyone—it was a characteristic that James had truly loved about him. "Trust me," he said at last. "That's all I ask of you: trust me."

For a moment, the two of them stood there glaring at each other, neither of them giving in, but then Phillip gave a bit of a smile. "Now, about that idea of setting up a harem with you as my favored concubine . . ."

For a moment, all Bailey could do was stare at him in openmouthed astonishment. Was he saying this for real? It was a full minute before she realized that he was teasing her—and teasing her in a sexual way! In her entire life, only Jimmie had done that, and even he hadn't done it much. She wasn't sure what to say, but then she thought, Why not? "I get to be second wife, after Carol, or it's no deal. And if I bear you a son, then he's to be made sultan. Are we clear on that?"

Phillip laughed, then looked at her in silence for a moment. "I'm sorry that I didn't make an effort to get to know you."

"Me too," she said quietly, smiling at him.

"Sorry that you didn't get to know me or get to know yourself?"

"Both," she said, then leaned forward and kissed him on the cheek.

Phillip's eyes twinkled. "About that son . . . ," he said. "I have a low sperm count, so it will take lots and lots of trying before—"

"Get out of here!" she said, laughing.

Reluctantly, after giving Bailey a list of half a dozen telephone numbers where she could reach him, Phillip got in the car behind the waiting driver. "Anything," he called out the window. "You need me for anything at all, let me know," he said as the car backed over the weed-infested gravel of what had once been the drive-way.

"Dinner," she called out as he backed onto the dirt road that ran in front of her property, but he didn't hear her. "Or a grocery store," she said into the silence.

She stood where she was until she could no longer hear the sound of his car, then she let out her breath and let her shoulders relax. Around her were tall weeds, trees with great hanging branches, and vines with thorns that could tear a person's skin. What was lurking behind the trees? There was a sound like slithering. A snake? Or was it a person? Someone who had been watching and waiting?

She closed her eyes and swallowed, then offered up a prayer. "Dear God," she whispered, "please continue to take care of me in the way that You have in the past." She wanted to add more, but that seemed to cover it. So far in her life, she'd been quite fortunate, and now all she asked was for the good to continue.

Turning slowly, she looked toward the slithering

sound and saw that it was just two branches rubbing against each other. But finding the source of one noise didn't alleviate her fears. Around her were more noises and more places where people and animals could hide.

She did her best to put some steel into her backbone, then turned and ran toward the barn.

Four

❧

When Bailey awoke the next morning, she didn't at first know where she was. As she'd done for half of her life, she reached out for Jimmie. When she didn't touch some warm part of him, she didn't worry. He was often away on a business trip, away making all that money— and spending it, he liked to tell her.

It was the sound of a truck that brought her more fully awake. Turning over, she looked up and saw the window high above, and slowly her memory came back to her. Jimmie was gone, and she was alone. Absolutely and totally *alone.*

Outside, she could hear birds calling, the wind in the trees, and that truck in the distance, its wheels heavy on gravel. It had been a long time since she'd heard any of those sounds. The houses Jimmie bought tended to have acres of lawns surrounding them, or many hundreds of feet of stone terrace, or the ocean. Gravel roads weren't something that Jimmie tolerated.

The movers had set up a bed for her. Incongruously, looking like an ad for linens, her pretty new bed—white-painted wood, artificially aged to look as though it had been used for many years—rested smack in the middle of the big front room of the barn. She'd had to look inside six boxes before she found the linens; then Phillip had helped her dress the bed in white cotton sheets, a fluffy white duvet on top, and half a dozen pillows at the head. When it was finished, they'd all laughed; it did look like a setting for a commercial, with the white-on-white bed in the midst of the hay bales.

After the men and Phillip left, Bailey had gone back to the barn and climbed into the bed. What have I done? she asked herself, and at that moment, if she'd had a cell phone, she would have called Phillip and asked him to come and get her. And she would have said yes, she would fight Atlanta and Ray for a share of the money. She'd buy herself a *nice* house somewhere and—

Bailey stopped her thoughts. The truck seemed to be getting closer. In the next minute, she heard the unmistakable sound of air brakes. Had the movers returned? she wondered as she threw back the covers and slipped her feet into her shoes.

It took a few moments to get the big barn door to slide open, and she thought, Oil can, putting it on her mental list of things she'd need to buy. She ran down what was now a wide path between the house and the barn, then stood in front of the house to watch a big white truck pull into the driveway. Viking Industrial Cleaners was written on the side of the truck, beside a picture of a muscular man wearing a horned headdress and holding a mop.

The truck door opened, and a man wearing navy blue overalls and carrying a clipboard jumped down to the ground. "You Bailey James?" he asked.

It took her a moment to remember that that was now her name. "Yes," she said, rubbing at her eyes, "but I didn't order any cleaning." Two more men got out of the truck on the other side.

The first man looked at the house. The door was flat on its back inside; there were several broken panes of glass in the windows and through them could be seen rooms full of dirt-encrusted cobwebs. "Maybe you just wished so hard, your fairy godmother sent us," the man said.

She wasn't used to such flippancy from service people, so Bailey stared at him in disbelief. Then she saw a twinkle in his eye, something that she'd been seeing rather often in men's eyes lately. Like Phillip, this man was teasing her. "Does this mean that you believe you're Prince Charming?" she asked, deadpan.

Had she said this to a man a month ago, she knew that he would have frowned and walked away, but now the three men behind him guffawed in laughter, and this man seemed to think that whatever Bailey said was okay by him.

"Whatever you want, we Viking men deliver," he said, then held out his clipboard to her.

"Ordered by Phillip Waterman" was written at the top of the page. Dear Phillip, Bailey thought as she signed at the bottom. Maybe he hadn't bought her dinner, but he had ordered a cleaning crew. Part of her thought she ought to send them away and assert her independence, but another part of her didn't relish spending weeks on her hands and knees scrubbing.

She signed and handed the clipboard back to the man.

"Yo, Hank!" one of the men called from the front porch. "What do we do with this stuff?"

Bailey stepped out around what looked to be an unpruned butterfly bush to see what the men were referring to. To one side of the front door, on the ground, were some boxes and bags. There were also several pieces of paper stuck into the frame of the window to the right of the fallen door.

Turning, the truck driver looked at Bailey for the answer.

Quickly, she went to the pile and began to examine it. Inside one box was what looked to be a tuna noodle casserole in a Pyrex dish. "Welcome," the attached card said, and it was signed "Patsy Longacre." There were two roast chickens wrapped in foil, no card. A greasy paper bag held about half a pound of nails. "Thought these might come in handy," read another note torn off the bottom of a page of lined school paper. Another bag held four apples, each one carefully wrapped in newspaper. A quart jar with an old zinc lid held homemade bread-and-butter pickles. The name Iris Koffman was on the label. On the windowsill were three bunches of wildflowers, each one tied with string. An old, rusty hoe was leaning against the wall. The unsigned note on it read, "You need it, and heaven knows my husband never uses the thing."

In the window frame (which had a half-inch gap in it, so there was plenty of room) were business cards and brochures. There was a card for an insurance man whose office was on Main Street in Calburn. There was a well digger, and a real estate agent. "If you want to sell, call me," was written on the back. There was a card for a handyman. Bailey kissed this card, then stuck it into her jeans pocket.

"Hey! I got a card," one of the cleaning men standing in front of her teased.

She had no reply to his teasing, so she said, "I'll take care of these things. You can start cleaning in there."

One of the men was looking through a dirty window. "I'm real sorry we left the flamethrower at the last job."

Bailey gave them her best Get busy! glare, but they didn't react as men did when Jimmie gave them that look. Instead, laughing, they went back to their truck and started removing machines and supplies.

She pulled down a big envelope that was stuck in the window and opened it. Inside was a welcome package from the Calburn Chamber of Commerce, the president of which was Janice Nesbitt. There was a map of Calburn, showing Main Street and the three streets running off it. Yesterday Phillip had driven her to the house from the opposite direction, so she'd not seen the town, and now she wondered what stores were there, and what services. At the far corner of the town map was an arrow pointing to somewhere off the map. "Your house is this way," someone had written.

"The middle of nowhere," Bailey muttered to herself, then looked up to see one of the cleaning men holding out an empty box toward her. Smiling her thanks, she took the box and put all the items that had been left by the townspeople inside. Odd, she thought, but when she'd . . . well, when she'd looked different, men hadn't been so thoughtful as to offer her boxes to put her things into.

Smiling, Bailey carried the box back to the barn. She was hungry, and she wanted some privacy to eat, and she wanted time to ponder the idea of living in a town where people left gifts of welcome on her doorstep. But she wasn't to have any privacy as someone started blowing a horn, and she instinctively knew that she was being called. With a chicken leg in one hand and an apple in the other, she ran down the path, then stopped at what she saw. There were three trucks in her driveway, another two parked on the road, and four more behind them looking for space to park. There were eight men walking toward Bailey, clipboards held out for her signature.

"Would you guys mind?" said a man in a FedEx uniform. "I need to get out of here. Are you Bailey James?" he asked, then barely waited for her nod before handing her a letter pack and a clipboard.

She signed, then, not quite knowing what else to do, pulled the tab and opened the package. Inside were two envelopes, both of them with Phillip's return address on them. "A housewarming gift," the note inside the first one said. "And don't worry, they can afford it." Bailey smiled. Obviously, Phillip was somehow charging everything to Atlanta and Ray. The second envelope held a stack of crisp, new fifty-dollar bills clipped together. "I know how you like to tip," he'd written.

Smiling, Bailey looked up—and saw what looked to be now about a dozen men, their faces impatient as they waited for her to sign their papers.

"Who's first?" she asked, then held out her hands and started signing. When she signed without reading the papers thoroughly, she knew that Jimmie's spirit was somewhere frowning at her.

"You want to show me where the gas lines are?" a man asked.

"And where do you want the telephone jacks?" asked another.

"Where's your fuse box?" asked a third.

"I don't really know," Bailey said, looking at the house. "I haven't been inside yet."

That announcement silenced them. It was her house, but she'd not been inside it. The men looked at each other. "Crazy dame," seemed to silently pass between them.

"I've been here twenty minutes, and I still haven't seen the place," a man walking toward her said. "It's such a jungle that I'm afraid I'm gonna step in quicksand. I'm from Spenser's Landscaping Service. We were told to clean up and prune and mow—and we're to do it all in one day. I've just sent one of the men back to get the chain saws and his brother-in-law's threshing machine. You have any special instructions for us?"

Bailey could only stare at him; she couldn't think of any instructions to give him concerning a garden she'd barely seen. She shook her head no, but as he turned away, she called after him, "Don't hurt the mulberry tree."

Glancing back at her, but still walking, he said, "Does that mean I can't saw out the man the thing ate?" He didn't crack a smile.

"He's needed for fertilizer," she returned in the same serious tone. "Just add his wake to the bill."

"Will do," the man said, then gave her a mock salute and turned back around. Smiling at the exchange, the other men walked away too, and Bailey followed them inside for her first look at the house that Jimmie had left her.

As she walked across the fallen door, she closed her eyes a moment and offered up the word *charming* to any listening guardian angels. She really hoped that the inside was a great deal better than the outside.

But after only four steps, she figured her guardian angels and her fairy godmother were all on holiday. She was standing in a small, windowless, airless, lightless room that was covered on all four sides with very cheap and very ugly brown paneling, made out of material that wasn't wood, wasn't plastic, wasn't anything at all. Cut into the wall in front of her was a narrow doorway that led into a large room covered with more of the dark, scarred, and dented paneling. There wasn't a window to the outside in the room, but there were five doorways leading out of it.

Cautiously, she opened one door and saw a long, narrow room, again covered in dark paneling. There was an aluminum-framed window high up on one wall, but little light came through it. She went back into the big room, then stepped over the cords of the men's vacuum cleaners, whose roar was deafening, to open another door. It was another bedroom, again with windows that were too high for her to see out of.

The third door led into a bathroom that had been done in pink tile with ugly little flowers on it. In fact, every surface in the room had a pattern on it: the ceiling had great swirls of fake plaster; the walls had flowered foil wallpaper above the flowered tiles, and the floor had more tiles that had been—what? she thought. Bred to look like leather? They must have grown for, surely, no one had actually *designed* the things.

When Bailey closed the door behind her, she looked to see if there was a lock on it. She didn't want anyone else on earth to see inside that bathroom. A weaker heart than hers might not live through it.

The fifth door out of the big room led into a small, narrow kitchen. There was a little window over the sink, but it wasn't enough to alleviate the darkness that filled the room. The kitchen cabinets were old, cheap, dirty, and falling off the walls.

"I can't do anything about them," said a man from behind her. He was from the cleaning service, and he was nodding toward the kitchen cabinets. "I can try to clean them, but I ain't no carpenter."

"Do what you can," Bailey said, then walked toward the door at the end of the galley-shaped kitchen. When she opened the door, she gasped, for it was the only room she'd seen that was what she'd imagined a farmhouse to be. At the end was a tall window with old-fashioned wooden panes in it, and below it was a stone sink set into a thick wooden slab, the top scarred from use. Beneath the top were heavy turned legs, and stored below were stone jugs and pottery crocks, the kind that were used to make pickles and sauerkraut. Both sides of the room were lined with shelves that had been painted white.

The shelves were filled with dirty, cobweb-encrusted kitchen equipment. There were old canning jars and big enamel kettles, funnels and racks to hold dripping cheesecloth bags. There were several tongs and stacks of yellowed tea towels that had nests of spiders on them. But what made Bailey's heart nearly skip a beat was a battered old metal box, "Recipes" printed on it.

"You want me to throw all this stuff out?" the man asked, again coming up behind her. "This is the only room with things in it. The rest of the place is empty. We could take all this trash to the dump for you."

"No!" Bailey said, then calmed herself. "No, just leave it. Clean in here, but don't throw out anything. I want to keep everything, every jar, every lid—" She reached up to touch the bail of an old Ball jar. They didn't make jars like this one anymore. "Everything," she said, looking at the man. "Clean it, but leave it all here." Then, on impulse, she grabbed the metal recipe box.

"Aye, aye, captain," he said, smiling, then smiled more as Bailey squeezed past him in the narrow space.

Outside the kitchen was a closet that held an old avocado-green washer and dryer, then a door to the outside. She opened the door cautiously, fully expecting it to fall on her head. When it creaked, she released the knob, covered her head, and waited. But the door held on its hinges, and she looked outside. The yard behind the house now held what looked like a colony of men, muscular-looking women, and machines. A huge green tractorlike machine with a man sitting inside a glassed-in room was cutting down the vegetation from the house to—well, she thought, to wherever the property led. Hadn't she read on the deed that it was ten acres? A workman was removing dead branches from an old apple tree, and she could see another one high up in an ancient maple tree, wide leather belts between his legs, as he cut out dead wood from its upper branches.

Leave it to Phillip to find the best and the most, she thought as she closed the door on the noise outside, then went back to the men, noise, and machines in the big, central room. When she opened the last door out of the big room, she saw that it led into a little hallway with several doors leading off it. Before her was a staircase, and she could see light streaming down toward her. To her right she found a large bedroom with a bathroom off it. There was a separate shower, plus a tub, and there was even a walk-in closet. The bedroom had a little step-out on one wall and more of the tall wooden windows, such as she'd seen in the room off the kitchen. It was obviously the master bedroom and where Bailey would be sleeping.

Although the proportions of the room and the windows were beautiful, unfortunately, all the walls were covered in the awful dark paneling, and the tile and fixtures in the bathroom were too ugly for her to comprehend. There was a dark brown bathtub, a white toilet, and two sinks that were the color of dried blood.

With a shudder, she turned away and went back into the hall, where she found two more rooms and a third bathroom. There were also a number of closets.

Without exception, all the rooms were paneled in the dark fake wood, and the bathrooms seemed to be a study in how many patterns could be put into one room. The third bathroom had been tiled in a green faux marble; another type of faux marble had been put on the countertop, and yet another one was on the floor. There was wallpaper above the tile, a pea-green foil version of marble.

"I'm going to be sick," Bailey said as she closed the door behind her.

She took a deep breath as she looked up the stairs. More bedrooms? she wondered. So far, she'd counted five of them. Had the previous owner had many children? Or if this place had been where Jimmie grew up, knowing him, maybe they'd had a lot of guests.

Slowly, testing each step to make sure it was safe, she

went upstairs to the attic. As soon as she entered it, she smiled. Sure, there were two holes the size of her fist in the roof, and someone had placed buckets under them to catch the rain, but under the dirt, Bailey could see that the room was lovely—at least, one side of it was. The steep pitch of the roof cut into the room on two sides, but on the side where the stairs were, a row of windows had been set into the roof, and they let in sunlight. They were high windows, but not too high for her to see out. Setting down the recipe box, she turned the rusty crank to open one, and fresh air rushed into the room. Without the dirty glass blocking it, more sunlight came inside. Turning back, she looked around the big, open room.

In the middle was a waist-high railing, looking as though it had once been a divider in the room. Someone had sawed an opening in the center and removed a piece of the railing; she saw it leaning against the far wall.

The walls of the half of the room at the head of the stairs had been plastered and painted white, but the other half was paneled in the same dark brown used downstairs.

"Yet *another* bedroom?" she said aloud, looking at the big, empty room. She started to step through the opening in the railing, but drew back and looked down at the floor. For some reason, she didn't trust that floor. The half behind her had wide, thick-looking planks for flooring, but on the other side sheets of plywood were nailed down. It looked safe, but something made her not want to walk on it.

Bailey didn't have a chance to figure out if the floor was safe or not; suddenly, someone blew a truck horn in three short blasts, and she knew she was being summoned. "Six weeks ago it was, 'May I get you anything,

Mrs. Manville,' and now it's a truck horn," she muttered as she grabbed the recipe box off the floor and ran down the stairs. "I should be glad it's not, 'Sooey, sooey,' " she said out loud as she leaped over three heavy-duty electrical cords, an electrician's toolbox, and a telephone man, who was on his stomach, looking into an outlet. As she ran out the front door, she told the man from Viking Cleaners not to let anyone go into the attic, as she thought it was dangerous.

Two women were standing in front of one of the trucks. They were both about five foot three, both in their early thirties, both pretty but not overly so. Physically, they were so much alike that she was sure they were sisters, but they were dressed very differently. One woman had dark hair and wore a cotton shirt, jeans, and sneakers. The other was blonde—artificially so—and wore a knit suit, hose, pumps with heels, and enough gold bracelets that Bailey wondered how she could lift her arms.

"Hello," Bailey said, walking toward them and extending her hand in welcome. "I'm Bailey James." She was pleased with herself for saying the name without faltering.

"I'm Janice Nesbitt," said the woman in the suit as she shook Bailey's hand.

"Ah, yes, from the Chamber of Commerce," Bailey said as she turned to the other woman.

"Yes," Janice said, obviously pleased that Bailey had seen and remembered her brochure. "It's a shame that no one else has come in person to welcome you," she said loudly.

"Just the two of you." Bailey smiled at the second woman.

"I'm Patsy Longacre," the second woman said, shaking Bailey's hand. "I would have thought that at least one person from this town would have shown up, maybe even someone from the Chamber of Commerce."

Bailey looked at Janice. "I thought you were from the Chamber of Commerce," she said, puzzled.

"I am. I'm the president of it," Janice said brightly, then looked at the house. "I see you're having it cleaned. I didn't know that anyone had bought it. When did you?"

"I—" Bailey began, trying to think up a quick lie. She certainly couldn't tell the truth.

"When did you come to see the house to buy it?" Patsy asked.

At a loss to make up a lie quickly, Bailey looked from one woman to the other. For all that they were standing quite close together, they were looking in opposite directions.

"The house was given to me," Bailey said slowly. "An inheritance. Do you know who owned it?"

"Don't you?" Janice asked, looking at Bailey with narrowed eyes.

"Who'd you inherit it from?" Patsy asked.

Bailey took a deep breath. She should have thought of this beforehand and planned a lie. "My husband. I'm a widow. I didn't even know he owned the place until the will was read." There, that was true.

"My goodness," Janice said. "Imagine not knowing all there is to know about your husband's finances."

Instinctively, Bailey opened her mouth to defend herself, but closed it. Jimmie kept three large law firms busy overseeing his "finances." Instead, she smiled. "I'd offer you something to drink, but—" She waved her hand toward the house helplessly. "As you can see, it's pretty busy here today. Right now, all my furniture is stored in the barn."

"That'll be just fine," Janice said, then walked briskly past Bailey and headed toward the barn. Obviously, she knew where it was located. That she had on a suit and hose, and that the weeds hadn't yet been cut, didn't seem to bother her.

"I, uh—" Bailey began, then walked after her. But she halted and looked back because the other woman, Patsy, was still standing in front of the truck. "Please come with us," Bailey said. "We're going to the barn, I guess. Not that I have so much as seating there, but—"

"Us?" Patsy asked. "I thought you said you were a widow. Who else lives with you? Children?"

Bailey looked at the woman in consternation. Was her hearing off? "No," she said. "By 'we,' I meant Janice. I do have the name right, don't I? Janice Nesbitt."

"Don't know her," Patsy said as she walked past Bailey toward the path to the barn, then she turned back. "Aren't you coming?"

"Sure," Bailey said, feeling as though she'd come in on the third act of a play. What was going on with these two women?

When Bailey got to the barn, both women were already there, and Janice had opened a box marked "Kitchen."

"Excuse me," Bailey said firmly as she closed the box lid practically on Janice's nose. "As you can see, I'm not moved in yet. Perhaps it would be better if the two of you—"

"No one's lived here since 1968," Patsy said loudly, not allowing Bailey to finish her sentence.

Jimmie would have been nine then, Bailey thought, and nine was a long way from sixteen, when his biographers had first been able to track him. "Who lived here?"

Both women turned to stare at her, their silent question being, Don't *you* know?

This isn't going to be easy, Bailey thought. "My husband was . . . was a good deal older than I was, and he liked to keep his past private. I really know very little about his childhood. I'd like to know what either of you can tell me about this place."

"Either of who of us?" Patsy asked. "You're confusing me." She narrowed her eyes at Bailey. "If you're going to live in Calburn, then you must understand that *no one else is in this room except you and me.*"

Bailey blinked. "I see." She turned to Janice. "And are you and I alone?"

"Oh, yes," Janice said. "Except for the mice and whatever else lives in a barn. I can assure you that *I* wouldn't know. I am as far from being a farmer as anyone on this planet is."

At that Patsy snorted in derision, and Bailey saw the red of rage spread on Janice's neck and upward, as her hands beneath all the bracelets clenched into fists. It seemed that whether or not Janice knew anything about farming was a touchy subject.

"I don't know anything about farming either," Bailey said softly.

"Then why would you move to Calburn?" Patsy asked.

The way Patsy had hurt Janice's feelings didn't sit well with Bailey. "You mean, as opposed to selling this place for millions and moving to the south of France?"

It was Janice's turn to laugh.

Patsy looked at Bailey in speculation. "You have a tongue on you, don't you?"

"You're not bad yourself," she said. "But I can warn you that I don't like petty snipping."

"Got ya," Patsy said, then smiled at Bailey.

"So what do you plan to do with your life, if I might ask?" Janice asked politely. "Or did your husband leave you well off?"

Bailey was thinking that she couldn't believe she'd just met these two women. Did all of Virginia ask personal questions ten minutes after meeting someone? "To tell the truth, I don't know what I'm going to do. My husband left me this farm and a bit of money, but not enough to live on for the rest of my life. I guess I'll have to get a job. Do you know of any openings?"

Janice looked Bailey up and down. "You don't look like the Wal-Mart type. What were you before you married?"

"A teenager," Bailey said.

"I've got two of those," Patsy said, "but they're boys, and they work for their uncle. You don't know anything about carpentry, do you?"

"I wish I did," Bailey said wistfully. "The house is falling apart. There are holes in the roof, and I don't think the floor in the attic is safe. And I'd like to knock out some walls to make a few of the bedrooms into something else. The way it is now, I could run a boardinghouse."

Janice had been standing to one side and looking at Bailey, but suddenly her eyes lit up. "What you need to do is get married again," she said.

At that Bailey laughed. "I don't think so. I was mad about my husband, and I don't think I'll be able to—"

"Of course there aren't too many eligible bachelors in Calburn," Janice continued, more loudly, as though Bailey hadn't spoken.

"I do *not* want to get married again," Bailey said with emphasis. Truthfully, the idea of marriage hadn't crossed her mind, and right now she didn't like the way the conversation with these two odd women was going. "Maybe we should go back to the house. I'll show you the bathrooms." The sight of those rooms should get their minds off matchmaking!

Bailey walked toward the barn door, but when neither of the women moved, she looked back at them. Janice was looking at her hard, but Patsy was staring at the loft, as though she were trying to remember something.

"You need a younger man this time, someone who would be *useful* to you on this place," Janice said, emphasizing the word. "Could *help* you."

"I don't—" Bailey began.

"That's it!" Patsy said. "I just had a brilliant idea: you should get married again."

"That's what Janice just said!" Bailey said in frustration. "Didn't you hear her? She's standing three feet away from you."

Patsy didn't so much as blink. "You need to get married again, and more than that, you need to marry my brother-in-law, Matthew."

Bailey gave the women a tight little smile. Nosing into her personal life was one thing, but this matchmaking had to stop before it went any further. "That's kind of you to offer," she said firmly, "and I'm sure your brother-in-law is a wonderful man, but I don't think that—"

Patsy acted as though Bailey hadn't spoken. "He's a great guy, but he was married to a real bimbo. As soon as Matt got some money, she ran off with someone else. Why she'd leave a wonderful man like my husband's brother, I don't know, but it's her loss. So now he's been at my house taking up room for six long months. Why don't I give him a call and ask him to take you out to dinner tonight?" she said as she lifted up her shirttail and unsnapped a case that held a cell phone.

"No!" Bailey said so loudly that both women stared at her. "I mean," she said more quietly, "I was *recently* widowed, and I need some time. I don't want to get involved with anyone right now. Not that I've thought about it, but I can't imagine . . . well, being with another man. Surely you must know what I mean."

For a moment, both women blinked at her in silence.

"All right, then," Patsy said, "how about dinner next Thursday?"

Bailey took a breath, let it out slowly, and counted to ten. She was not going to be bullied by these two women, each of whom refused to acknowledge that the other existed. "When I said that I needed time, I meant—"

"What this place needs is a building contractor," Janice said loudly, yet again cutting Bailey off.

Good, Bailey thought. She'd made her point, and they were going to change the subject. She smiled. "I have a card from a handyman."

"Walter Quincey?" Janice said with a sneer. "He'll take your money, and you'll never see any work. He's the laziest man in two counties. No, you need a real builder, someone who knows what he's doing."

Patsy wasn't saying a word, just looking around the

barn. Bailey hoped she hadn't hurt the woman's feelings by turning down her brother-in-law so harshly, but Bailey wanted to make herself clear from the beginning.

Patsy looked at Bailey. "Did I tell you that my brother-in-law is a building contractor?"

Instantly, Bailey was at war with herself. She didn't want to encourage this woman or her bimbo-marrying brother-in-law, but the image of those kitchen cabinets that were barely hanging onto the walls danced before her eyes. "Your brother-in-law is a building contractor?" she heard herself ask.

"More or less. He's an architect, but he can build things too."

"Is he any good?" She had a vision of green tiles being thrown out the bathroom window, dark paneling torn from the walls.

"He used to build skyscrapers in Dallas."

"Is he expensive? I don't have much money."

"Well, honey, that's obvious," Patsy said in a way that made Bailey blink. "Everyone in town is talking about how some man named Phillip is paying for all of this for you."

When Patsy didn't say anything else, Bailey realized that both women were expecting her to tell them who "Phillip" was. She didn't want to; it wasn't any of their business. "My husband's attorney," she said at last, then gave a sigh.

"But if you're broke, you came to a good place," Patsy continued. "Nothing in Calburn can be expensive, because no one could afford it. Except some people, that is," she said, then she glanced in the general direction of Janice.

"Some people—" Janice began, not looking at Patsy but finally acknowledging her presence.

Now what? Bailey thought. A catfight? She rolled her eyes skyward. What have you dropped me into, James Manville? she asked silently.

"All right," Bailey said loudly. "I'll marry him if he'll repair this house. Or does he want only sex? Or both?"

The two women turned to look at her, their mouths hanging open so identically that Bailey was sure they were related.

Patsy was the first to recover herself. "Sex might cheer him up," she said without a trace of a smile, "but if you start having sex with a man here in Calburn, it might ruin it for the rest of us. My advice is that you offer to pay him half what he asks and hold off on the sex." She punched in some numbers on her cell phone. "And it's my experience that hints are better than the real thing. When you ask him to clean out the septic system, wear short shorts."

Bailey smiled at the two women. We might get along after all, she thought. When Patsy said into the phone, "Matt, I've got a job for you," Bailey's smile grew even more wide.

Five

❧

When Bailey awoke the next morning, her first feeling was of fear, old-fashioned terror, because this time she did remember where she was. Her bed had been moved from the barn to the bedroom, and she was surrounded by dark paneling that seemed to make the room close in on her. Light was coming in through the bare windows, but it only showed the ugliness of the room to better advantage.

Last night she'd been so tired that she'd fallen into bed, barely remembering to pull her nightgown over her head. But she hadn't slept well; her dreams had been haunted by memories of Jimmie. In all their sixteen years together, they had never been apart for this long. If Jimmie went somewhere interesting, he took her with him. "Hey, Frecks," he'd said once. "How'd you like to see those turtles on that island?" It took her a moment to understand where he meant. "Galapagos," she said, and Jimmie had smiled at her. She had just finished high school when she'd met him, but she'd read a lot since then, and her knowledge pleased him. "Sure," she said. "When do we leave?" "Half an hour." "That long?" she said, then they'd laughed together.

Now Bailey wiped at her eyes, which had begun to mist over. Jimmie wasn't here, and he was never going to return.

Slowly, she got out of bed and went into the bathroom, with its various-colored toilet fixtures. When she looked into the mirror at her "new" face, it startled her. She'd lived thirty-two years with her large, bent nose, and she'd been plump all her life. To see something different was disconcerting.

"Now what do I do?" she asked herself aloud as she stepped into the shower. Yesterday she'd asked those two women if they'd known of any job openings, but Bailey knew she was lying to herself as well as them. What skills did she have that would get her a job? She'd never learned to type, and she was probably the only person in the United States under the age of eighty who didn't know how to use a computer. "Why waste your time?" Jimmie had said. "I can hire people to work computers."

She had no experience at anything in the world, really, except at being a wife.

She turned off the shower, then slowly dried off on the stiff, new towels that hadn't yet been washed and pulled on a pair of chinos from the clothes that she and Carol had ordered. Maybe I could call Phillip, she thought, then pushed that thought from her mind. She had a fear that if she called Phillip, the next step would be going to Atlanta and Ray and begging for money.

Taking a deep breath, Bailey opened the bedroom door and walked down the few feet of hallway and into the living room. Late yesterday, Phillip had sent a truck-load of heavyset men to open all the boxes and crates in the barn and set the contents inside the house wherever Bailey wanted them. Now, she tried to look not at the dark, windowless walls but at the furniture. She'd cho-sen it under circumstances of great duress, and a week later she couldn't remember any of it, but now she was pleased with it.

There were two couches printed with big red peonies, golden vines, and green leaves, and two comfortable-looking chairs in the dark gold color of the print. A big coffee table stood in the middle. At the far end of the room was a large dining table set on a red Oriental car-pet, surrounded by eight Windsor chairs painted a dark blue. Against the wall was a box full of curtains of red-and-black plaid. The movers hadn't known how to hang the curtains, and, besides, there weren't enough win-dows for all of them.

But in spite of the nice furniture, the room was not inviting. How could any room as dark as this one make people want to stay in it?

Bailey walked through the doorway to the kitchen. Yesterday the men had been wonderful. They'd done as much as they could to make the kitchen livable, but it hadn't been enough. One of the electricians and a plumber had pulled the overhead cabinets off the wall, saying that to leave them up there was dangerous. When the movers had wheeled the giant cooking range, a forty-eight-inch-wide Thermador, into the room, there had been nowhere to put it. One of the gardeners had solved the problem by taking a chain saw to the lower cabinets and cutting out a section. The electrician had hooked up the gas line. It had taken more sawing to put in the big Sub-Zero double-door refrigerator three feet from the range. The men had put the porcelain sink with its tall, integrated backsplash on the other side of the room. "We threw out one of those when we redid my grandmother's kitchen," one of the men said as they dropped the sink into place. Beside it, the plumber set the Miele dishwasher she'd purchased.

So now, looking at the kitchen, Bailey sighed. It was a mess. What was left of the base cabinets ended in raw, splintered edges, and the walls above showed half a dozen colors of paint where the overhead cabinets had been. The cookware she'd bought with Phillip, and later what she and Carol had ordered, had been put in the adjoining pantry, but there wasn't room to store so much as a spoon in the kitchen.

Opening the refrigerator, Bailey saw that all that was left of the food the residents of Calburn had left for her yesterday was a wing stuck to the naked carcass of a chicken. One by one, the workmen had helped themselves to the food.

Bailey found a big ceramic mug in the pantry, filled it with water from the faucet, took the chicken wing, and went outside.

After Patsy Longacre had called her brother-in-law, the women had left, and Bailey had shaken her head in wonder when she saw them get into the same car, an older-model Mercedes, and drive away. "Wonder if they talk to each other when they're alone?" she asked aloud as she went into the house and tried to answer questions about where she wanted what. During the rest of the day, she'd been kept so busy that she hadn't so much as looked out a window to see what the people outside were doing.

So now, when she opened the back door and looked into the garden, what she saw was a revelation. The day before yesterday, all she'd seen was weeds. She'd been able to follow a path to the huge mulberry tree, but beyond that, she could see nothing.

Now, before her was a garden. A real garden. It wasn't just the American idea of a backyard, with a lawn encircled by a few shrubs and "foundation plantings." No, this was something that Jasper, Jimmie's old head gardener, the man who oversaw all of Jimmie's houses, would have been proud of.

And, more importantly, it was the garden that Bailey had always dreamed about. There were no "long vistas," no lawn that had to be big enough to land a helicopter. No, there was nothing grand about the place, just trees and flowers and—secrecy, Bailey thought; the way the trees were sited, she couldn't see what was ahead.

Putting down her empty cup and the chicken bone, she stepped onto the flagstone terrace, then followed the stone path into the trees. There was the mulberry tree, huge, magnificent, regal, now that all the weeds and debris had been cleared away from under it and it could be seen in its entirety. Smiling, saying, "Good morning," to the wonderful old tree, she kept following the path to see where it led.

To the right there was a fenced-off area, not very big, that the gardeners had used a Rototiller on, and she could see the rich black soil waiting to receive seeds. Years of lying fallow had renewed the earth in what had obviously been the vegetable garden.

Past the vegetable garden was an orchard of fruit

trees that, years ago, had been pruned in the vase, open-center method. This meant that, although they were full-size trees and bore a great deal of fruit, they would never grow very tall; the lowest branches were just a couple of feet above the ground. A child could pick most of the fruit.

Since the trees had been neglected for many years and only just properly pruned yesterday, Bailey doubted if they would produce much fruit this year. She could see several blank spaces in the even rows of trees, and see the new sawdust where the gardeners had cut down trees that had died.

Beyond the orchard, the path took a sharp left turn, and as she walked around a stand of evergreens, she drew in her breath. Before her was a small pond, and from the hill above it a stream tumbled down into a little waterfall over rocks that had been carefully placed to look as though nature had put them there. Slowly, Bailey ambled along the path, looking in wonder at the little pond, its sides lined with reeds; then she followed the path upward, walking beside the stream.

At the top of the little hill, stepping-stones led across the shallow stream, and on the other side, under a huge, shady walnut tree, a wide iron bench waited, weathered by the years. It was set on flagstones that had been interplanted with wooly thyme.

Bailey didn't walk across to the bench but kept slowly walking, wanting to see more. At the very top of the little hill was another pool, this one surrounded by stones. Yesterday the gardeners had cleaned out the inside of the pool, and as she peered into it, she could see that they had put a new recirculating pump under the surface of the water to create the waterfall below.

Beyond the pool, the path again turned left, and to her left, down the hill, she could see the side of the house between the trees; to her right was the barn. But here, hidden and private, was a lawn that looked to be the perfect size for a game of croquet. Or kids playing soccer, she thought, then put that thought from her mind. On the far edge of the lawn were bushes and a vine-covered wooden fence that would have fallen down except that steel posts had been embedded in concrete, from which the wooden slats hung. When she stepped across the lawn to examine the bushes and vines, she smiled. The bushes were gooseberry and currant, and the vines were blackberries.

Past the lawn was a large patch just in front of the barn that the gardeners had obviously worked hard on. Weeds had been removed to show the bare soil; poking up through it were sticks with the distinctive serrated leaves of raspberry plants: rows and rows of raspberries.

At the end of the raspberry bed, the stone path branched, and she could see that one side meandered through the trees, then back to the house, but she couldn't tell where the other branch led because it disappeared into a densely wooded area. She chose the path toward the woodland. As she stepped under the canopy of trees, she marveled at the silence and the dark coolness of the forest. It was as though she were in a place no one else had ever entered, not in all the time of Earth. But she smiled at her fantasy; a man-made path lay under her feet, and she could see a little stone bench almost hidden by the trunks of two big trees.

The path took a sharp right, and Bailey stopped at the sight of a clearing that contained a big fire pit. A hole, three feet in diameter, had been dug, and rocks cemented all around it. Inside were the remains of logs burned years ago. There were no seats around the pit, but English ivy had been planted to make a soft, low groundcover. Above her head trees encircled the area, but straight overhead, she could see sunlight, so if a fire was lit here at night, the smoke would escape. Turning about, she looked at the place, feeling the intimacy of it. It was as though she could hear people talking quietly, could smell the smoke, even feel the warmth of the fire.

Smiling, she walked back down the path, out of the woods, and into the sunlight, then turned in front of the barn and went back to the house. As soon as she saw the house, this time from the front, her good mood left her. How could something as beautiful as that garden surround a house as ugly as this one? she wondered. It occurred to her that one person had been in charge of the house, while another took over the garden. "I hope they weren't married," she said aloud as she opened the front door. Two such opposites would never get along, she thought.

Once she was inside the house, all she wanted to do was go back out. But she had to figure out what to do with her life. With that thought, she laughed out loud. "I'm thinking like a soap opera," she said, then went to the bedroom to get her handbag. First things first. She needed to buy food; then she'd have to figure out what to do next. As Jimmie had said many times, "I always know when Lil is upset about something, because she heads for the nearest kitchen."

She got behind the wheel of the car that Phillip had purchased for her and took a deep breath. She'd not done much driving in her life, and the fact that she even knew how to drive a car was a testament to her tenacity.

Jimmie didn't usually fight her about anything she wanted, but he'd fought her about taking driving lessons. At first she'd been understanding, thinking that maybe he was afraid she'd leave him if she knew how to drive. But as the weeks went by and he wouldn't relent, she got angry. She knew that no amount of anger in his work life affected him, but she also knew that he truly hated for there to be any turmoil between the two of them. She'd looked him straight in the eye and said, "I'm not going to speak to you until you allow someone to teach me how to drive a car. I am a grown woman, James Manville. You can't keep me a child forever." It was one of the few times she'd ever seen Jimmie get angry at her, and she'd almost backed down. But she didn't.

He'd lasted a mere three days of her cold shoulder before he hired some ugly little toad of a man to teach her how to drive. And on the day she'd received her driver's license, Jimmie had given her the keys to a cute little yellow BMW. That she drove it only about half a dozen times didn't seem to matter to either of them. She'd attained the knowledge that she wanted, and that was what had been important.

That had been years ago. Now, Bailey wondered if she'd remember how to drive. Slowly, cautiously, she backed the car out of the driveway and onto the dirt road in front of her house. There were trees on both sides of the road, no houses, and about a quarter of a mile down, she came to asphalt. She knew that to the left was the way that she'd entered with Phillip, so to the right was downtown Calburn.

After a moment's hesitation, she turned left. She wasn't yet ready to enter the town. If the people of Calburn were anything like Janice and Patsy, then Bailey would be in for hundreds of personal questions, and she wasn't prepared for them. First she needed to get some food inside her and think about what her next step was going to be.

Three hours later, Bailey drove back into the driveway of the old house. The car was filled with groceries. The back had full plastic bags all the way to the roof, the floor below the backseat had crates full of just-picked strawberries she'd bought at a roadside stand, the seat held boxes full of big bags of sugar and huge bottles of vinegar, while the front seat and floor had more plastic bags full of groceries.

Bailey was smiling, for she had an idea about what she could, maybe, possibly, do with her life.

Six

❦

Matthew Longacre parked his pickup under a tree and looked at the clock on his dashboard. Six-thirty. He'd put it off as long as he could. Last night Patsy had been on him nonstop that he had to go meet "the widow." "She's pretty, she's nice, she's young. What more could you want?" Patsy had said, standing over him as she dropped a thick slice of her "surprise" meat loaf onto Matt's plate. The surprise was that anyone could eat it.

"Did you *and* Janice go over there?" Rick asked his wife as he dug into the meat loaf, the made-from-a-package mashed potatoes, and the green beans that had been boiled so long they no longer had much color.

"I went by myself," Patsy said, her chin up, her mouth set in that line of defiance that her family knew too well.

"Oh, ho," said one of her big, strapping, six-foot-tall, eighteen-year-old twin sons. "A fight is about to happen."

"I got fifty on Mom," John said.

"Twenty-five on Dad," Joe said.

"You two want any dessert, you'll can it," Patsy said in warning, then looked back at her brother-in-law, pretending to ignore her sons as they made silent betting gestures.

"Patsy," Rick said, "what's that woman going to think of the people in Calburn if you and Janice go over there together, then don't speak to each other?"

"I have no idea what you're talking about," Patsy said, her eyes still on Matt as he mushed the meat loaf with his fork. "We aren't talking about me. Mrs. James needs a contractor, and you, Matt, are it. I told her that you'd take on the job."

Matt didn't look up. He knew that his life was in his sister-in-law's hands. He was living in her house, so he was at her mercy. And he knew that she hadn't set him up with "the widow" for any reason except to matchmake—with the intention of getting him out of her house.

"Matthew, I am talking to you," Patsy said in the same tone she used on the other three men in her life. "Are you going to do this one tiny thing for me or not?"

"What did you tell her about me?" he mumbled, pretending to have his mouth full.

"Not to give you any sex," she snapped, and that made all four males stop eating and look up at her. When she had their attention, she said, "Are you going or not?"

"With that condition already in the works—" Joe

began, but the look his mother gave him cut him off.

"I'll go, but not tonight. Tonight I have to . . ." He couldn't think of anything.

"Watch *Buffy?*" John suggested, both boys obviously loving their uncle's discomfort. This summer they were working construction with him and, based on the way he was at home, they'd thought they were going to have an easy time of it. But Uncle Matt at home and Matt the boss were two different people. They'd learned that the first day, when they'd sauntered back from a two-hour lunch.

"What's she going to do with the old Hanley place anyway?" Rick asked, attracting his wife's attention and thereby letting his big brother off the hook.

"As she said, what else can she do but live there?" Patsy said as she went back to the stove. "I don't think her husband left her very much money, certainly not enough to live on. But her husband's lawyer seems to have bought her a lot. Anybody want any more meat loaf?"

All but Matt asked for seconds.

"Why did her lawyer buy her *any*thing?" Joe asked. "Was she having an adulterous affair with him?"

"Richard Longacre!" Patsy said to her husband. "You have got to do something with these boys. The way they talk is a disgrace."

"Now, Pats," Rick said, reaching out and putting his arm around his wife's trim waist. "They aren't children anymore." He gave a sideward glance to his brother, silently telling him that he could leave the table and get away from Patsy's questions.

That had been last night, and all day today, Matt had dreaded tonight's meeting. He and his nephews had been working thirty miles away, converting a garage into a guest room, so he'd been spared from hearing about the woman who had set all of Calburn talking. After work today, he'd hurriedly kissed Patsy's cheek, mumbled something about having to meet a client, and then had gone to the diner in Calburn for a grease burger.

"I hear she's loaded," Ruth Ann, the waitress, had said as she poured him a cup of coffee. She was talking not to Matt but to a couple of the locals who had gathered to discuss the goings-on out at the old Hanley place.

"She'd have to be rich to pay for all those men. But why waste it in Calburn? Why not go somewhere else, some place closer to civilization?" asked Mark Underwood. Mark was leaving in the fall for college, and he couldn't wait to get out of Calburn and never come back.

The others in the diner ignored him.

"You know what I think?" said Opal of Opal's Beauty Salon down the street. "I think she's up to something. I think she's planning to open one of them, what do you call them? Where you stay overnight and eat breakfast?"

Matt was looking into his cup to see what the coffee was like tonight: colored water or motor oil. Once, in an attempt to make a joke, he'd suggested that if Ruth Ann mixed the two together, it might make decent coffee. She'd told him that if he didn't like the coffee in Calburn, he could go back to his hoity-toity ex-wife and ask *her* to make him some coffee. Matt had sighed. There were no secrets in a small town.

As he pondered the contents of his cup, he suddenly became aware of the silence around him. When he looked up, he saw that everyone in the diner was looking at him, obviously waiting for him to give an opinion. Thanks to Patsy, he was considered to be the "big-city expert." "Bed-and-breakfast," he said. "It's called a bed-and-breakfast."

"Sort of a diner with a motel attached, isn't it?" Ruth Ann said. "Does that mean she thinks there's room enough in this town for two diners?"

Matt got up, put a five-dollar bill on the table, and walked toward the door. "Ruth Ann," he said, "I don't think you should worry. Your business is unique. No one could replace you and this diner."

At that he gave a big smile to all of the customers, who were looking at him as though wondering if what he'd just said was good or bad, and went outside. Chuckling, feeling that he'd got some of his own back for that coffee, Matt went to his pickup, a dark blue, three-quarter-ton, wide-bed Chevy, and got inside. "Now to the widow's," he said, then started the engine, backed out of the parking place, and headed toward Owl Creek Road and the old Hanley place.

Now he was here, and he could put it off no longer. Slowly he got out of the truck and began walking toward the house. He knew it and the grounds well. As kids, he and Rick had ridden their bikes along the creek, then forced their way through the weeds to find the trees that still bore fruit. For three summers, they'd had a roadside fruit stand with produce they'd purloined from the abandoned farm. But they'd had no luck selling much; every other farm in Calburn also had a roadside stand.

As Matt walked up the path, he looked around. He had to admit that a lot of work had been done in a very short time. He couldn't stop himself from turning around full circle to see the changes, then gave a low whistle. Someone had paid a lot for this. In fact, someone had paid double and triple to persuade company owners to pull all their men off other jobs and send them here for one day.

Influence and money, he thought. Someone with both had done this.

He walked up the narrow steps to the front door of the house and raised his hand to knock, but the door opened at his touch. He knew the layout of the house well; years ago, he and Rick had forced a window open in the kitchen and often played inside. Also, he used to spend time alone in the house. But then one day he'd found the broken window repaired, and he couldn't find a way in. He'd told his mother that someone had done some repairs on the old Hanley place, but she hadn't had the time to be interested.

"Hello?" he called as he stepped inside. "Anyone home?" When he stepped into the big living room, his eyes opened wide in shock. He'd always seen the house in a state of filth and disrepair. To see it clean and filled with furniture startled him. What was more, he liked the furniture. Most people in Calburn went to the local furniture discount store and bought "sets," whole rooms full of furniture that matched.

"Nice," Matt said, as he ran his hand across the chintz-covered sofa.

It was at that moment that he smelled food cooking—and the aroma almost made his knees give way under him. In the last months, Matt had found that after being away from his hometown for so many years, he'd become a little particular. He no longer liked food that had "helper" in the name, such as Hamburger Helper and Tuna Helper. Patsy said he'd become uppity, and maybe, when it came to food, he had.

"Oh, hi," said a woman as she walked into the living room through the doorway that he knew led to the kitchen. She was pretty, he thought. She was small and curvy, wearing light-colored trousers, tennis shoes—real tennis shoes, not those great, hulking running shoes—a T-shirt that didn't seem to have any writing on it, and an apron. Her apron was white and covered with food stains.

"You must be the contractor," she said as she held a wooden spoon out toward him. "Would you mind tasting this? I've tried it so many times that I can't tell anymore."

There was a yellowish gel on the end of the spoon that Matt wasn't sure he wanted to taste, but the enticement of a pretty woman on the other end of it was more than he could pass up. He couldn't help giving her a look to let her know that he knew she and his sister-in-law had been discussing him and sex.

When Matt's tongue made contact with the substance on the spoon, he forgot everything else. "What is that?" he asked, taking the spoon from her and licking it like a child.

"Apple jam with ginger," she said over her shoulder as she went back to the kitchen.

Matt followed her like a puppy on a string. The sight of the kitchen made his eyes widen.

"I know," she said, looking up from a pot she was stirring. "It's awful, isn't it?"

He had to blink a couple of times as he looked in wonder about the place. The walls had holes in them where someone had ripped the overhead cabinets down. And the lower cabinets looked as though someone had taken a . . . "Chain saw?" he asked.

"The gardeners," she said as she stirred another pot. There were six burners on the big, professional range, and each one had a pot of something bubbling on top of it. Now that he was closer, he could smell cinnamon, cloves . . .

As though he were a cartoon character following his nose, he let it pull him toward the big pots. "What're you cooking?" he asked, trying to sound merely polite, rather than desperate.

"It's too much, isn't it?" she said with a sigh. "I always do that. When I have a problem, I cook."

"Was this a big problem or a small one?" There was something red in the pan nearest him.

"Big. This is only half of what I bought today. A funny thing happened to me today. I—" She stopped and looked up at him. "I'm sorry, I'm being rude. I'm Bailey James." She wiped her hands on her apron and held one out for him to shake.

"Matthew Longacre," he said, holding her hand, but looking over her head into the pot behind the one filled with something red.

"Are you hungry?" she asked. "I made myself dinner, but I haven't had time to eat anything. Maybe you'd like to share it."

Matt pulled his eyes and his nose away from the food and looked down at her. Was this a trick? he wondered. Had Patsy told her he was coming over so that she could cook something to lure him? "Depends on what you're having," he said, with as much I-don't-really-need-food in his voice as he could manage. He had, after all, had one of Ruth Ann's "special" hamburgers.

"Pigeons. I got them from a man down the road."

"Old man Shelby," Matt said, looking at her with wide eyes. The cantankerous old farmer raised the pigeons and sold them to a fancy restaurant in D.C. As far as Matt knew, no one in Calburn had ever cooked a pigeon.

"Yes, that was his name. Lovely man, and so helpful."

"Shelby," Matt whispered. The man frequently chased people off his property with a loaded shotgun.

"Do you like pigeon? You're not a vegetarian, are you?"

"That depends on what Patsy puts in her meat loaf," he said, but she just looked at him with a polite smile, not understanding his joke. "Yes," he said at last. "I like pigeon." I guess, he thought.

"Good," she said as she went to the huge stainless-steel-fronted refrigerator and pulled out a porcelain platter covered with plastic wrap. "I'll just finishing grilling the livers, and dinner will be ready."

"Okay," he said faintly. Livers. "What can I do to help?"

"Would you mind if we ate outside? This house is . . ." Trailing off, she waved her hand.

"Dark and gloomy," he said, smiling down at the top of her head. Grilled livers? Pigeons? Apples and ginger? And what was it that Patsy had said? That "the widow" had said she wouldn't have sex with him? If this wasn't sex, then— "I beg your pardon?" He hadn't heard what she'd said. His taste buds were on such overload that his ears were shutting down.

"In there, in the dining area, are utensils. Could you get them out, please?"

"Sure," he said, then nearly ran into the next room to the sideboard and opened drawers to remove knives, forks, and cloth napkins. He opened a door to get out a tablecloth, candlesticks, and candles. With his arms full, he walked through the kitchen, then halted as he looked at what she was doing. She was putting some small, juicy-looking red things on the plates with what looked like slices of chicken. "What are those?" he whispered.

"Pickled grapes. If you'd rather not—"

"No!" he said sharply, then when his voice squeaked, he cleared his throat. "I mean, no, I'm sure they're delicious. I'm sure I'll love them. I'm sure they're the best pickled grapes that—I mean, well, I guess I'll put these things outside."

Once he was outside, Matt had a talk with himself. "Okay, Longacre, calm down. You're making a fool of yourself," he said as he spread the cloth on the ground, then set the candlesticks on top of it. "Stay cool. Stay calm. Get hold of yourself. You're selling yourself out for some chopped liver." That analogy made him laugh a bit.

"You do that too," Bailey said as she set two full plates down on the cloth.

Matt could hardly take his eyes off the food. It looked as though she'd made a paste out of the grilled livers, smeared it on toast, then put the sliced pigeon meat on top, with the pickled grapes sprinkled about. There was salad on the side, and it wasn't that tasteless, colorless white lettuce that Patsy and all of Calburn served, but dark green and red, curly and straight lettuces. "I do what?" he managed to whisper. He was on his knees, in a posture usually reserved for worship.

"You talk to yourself."

"Oh, yeah, sure," he said. A hypnotist's subject had never stared so unblinkingly as he was staring at that food.

"Go ahead, dig in," she said as she sat down on the opposite side of the tablecloth and put her plate on her lap.

Slowly, with hands that he hoped weren't trembling, he picked up the plate, sat down on the cloth, and lifted his fork. Moving as though in slow motion, Matt put a piece of toast with liver and pigeon on his fork, then carefully, reverently, brought it to his mouth. When the flavors touched his tongue, he couldn't keep his eyes open. It was divine. It was heaven. Ethereal. Never in his life had he tasted anything better.

Her soft laughter brought him back to reality. "Like it?" she asked.

"Mmmm," was all he could say.

"So do you have any ideas about how to go about remodeling this place? Did Patsy talk to you about money and the fact that I don't have much?"

Matt couldn't have talked about money at that moment any more than he could have walked away from that plate.

After a moment, when she didn't say anything, he looked up at her and saw that she was smiling at him. She wasn't eating much. "There's more, if you want it," she said softly.

"I'm sorry," he began. "It's just that . . ." He didn't know how to explain the fact that he was eating as though he'd not eaten in a month.

"You're tired of fried fish and fried shrimp and pizza?" she asked softly.

All Matt could do was nod and continue to eat.

After a while Bailey put her half-finished plate down on the cloth, leaned back on her hands, and looked up at the big tree overhead. "That's a mulberry tree," she said. "An old one. Did you know that even when it's five hundred years old, a mulberry still bears fruit? She's a true woman. I mean, to be fertile at that age."

His plate was nearly empty, and he looked up at her. Was she trying to tell him something? "Before, you said that something funny happened to you today."

"Oh," she said, "it was nothing. Not important, really. I just . . ."

"Go on, tell me," he said. "I could use some conversation that has nothing to do with business."

"I—" she began, then looked at him as though trying to decide whether or not to tell him.

Matt understood her hesitation. She was a widow, a recent widow, according to Patsy, and it hadn't been long since Matt's divorce. His marriage hadn't been much, but he did know what it was like to have someone to tell about the trivial happenings of the day. "I had a flat tire today" doesn't seem like much, but when there's no one there to tell it to, it can feel very big.

He didn't say anything, and he hoped that his silence would make her talk.

"Do you know how your life can change in a minute?" she said after a while.

"Yeah," Matt said, and his voice was full of feeling. He sure did. If he hadn't thought he was having a heart attack . . . "I know," he said.

"This morning, I awoke feeling . . . well, really, feeling useless. My husband left me this house and his . . . estate, I guess you'd say, cleaned it and furnished it for me. But from now on, I'm on my own. I have to support myself, but what talents do I have?"

At that Matt choked. As he was coughing and recovering himself, he pointed with his fork at his nearly empty plate.

"I know," Bailey said, "I can cook. I've had some great teachers in that area, but what can I do with cooking?" She put up her hand when he started to speak. "I know, I could open a restaurant, but I can't think of anything in the world I'd less like to do. Cooking the same thing over and over, dealing with customers and employees. Not for me."

"So what then?" he asked as he used a bit of bread to clean his plate.

Bailey held out her half finished plate to him, silently asking if he'd like the rest of it. "Today I went to a grocery store, a big one up the road. I don't know where I was. Took a left on the pavement."

"Sure?" Matt asked, and when she nodded, he took her plate. "What happened at the grocery?"

"I guess, really, I had an idea. Of something that I can do, that is. I like to preserve things. Canning, you know?"

Matt nodded. Now that he was getting nearly full, he could listen to her.

"Jimmie—he was my husband—said that he thought I was trying to preserve time, make it stay where it was and not move."

She looked at him as though she expected him to say something to that, but he was silent. He didn't know enough about her to make a comment.

"Anyway, I was in the grocery, and I saw a display of so-called gourmet foods. There were tiny jars of jam selling for seven dollars each. I thought, I make more interesting jams than this. And that's when it hit me: I could sell my jams and pickles."

"Sounds like a good idea," Matt said as he finished what she hadn't eaten. "Know anything about operating a factory?"

"Nothing, but I was thinking along smaller lines. Mail-order, maybe. Posh stores. *You* wouldn't know anything about selling jam, would you?"

"Nothing whatever."

"Mmmm," was all she said, then leaned back to look up at the mulberry tree.

"So what was the funny thing that happened to you today?" he asked as he wiped his hands on a red-and-white checkered cloth napkin.

Bailey smiled. "I was filling my basket with bottles of vinegar for making pickles, when a woman came up to me and whispered that I shouldn't buy it there. She said that if I was going to buy in bulk, then I should go to the Cost Club. I told her that I was new to the area and had no idea where that was, so she tore off the bottom of her grocery list and drew me a map. 'And get your fruit at a local fruit stand,' she said. 'But bargain, don't pay what they ask. Those farmers—especially the ones over near Calburn—will take everything you've got.' I told her thank you very much and she said—" Bailey paused, eyes twinkling. "She patted my hand and said, 'That's all right, dear. I knew by your accent that you were a Yankee, and they're always so helpless, but you looked like a nice one, so I didn't see any harm in helping you.' "

They laughed together at the story.

"What's especially funny is that I grew up in Kentucky," she said.

"You don't sound like it." Matt was looking at her speculatively, but she didn't comment further, just kept looking up at the tree. "More good teachers?" he asked in curiosity.

"The wine!" she said, then jumped up. "How rude of me. I completely forget to get anything to drink, and I have a lovely bottle of chardonnay." Before Matt could ask another question, she'd run back inside the house.

"Interesting," Matt said into the silence as he stood up and stretched. She'd very neatly managed to evade answering his personal question.

Minutes later she returned with two glasses of chilled white wine and handed him one. "I have peach cobbler if you want some."

Matt's first thought was to yell, "Yes!" but he controlled himself. Taking the glass of wine, he looked past the mulberry tree. "This place has been abandoned for years, but when my brother and I were kids, we used to spend a lot of time here. It looks different now."

"Yes," Bailey said, standing near him, but not too near, he noticed, and sipping her wine. "The workmen did a marvelous job. I have no idea how I'm going to maintain all of this, but until the weeds start to grow, it's beautiful." When she glanced up at him and saw that he was looking at her expectantly, she smiled. "Would you like the tour?"

"Very much," he said.

"Since I'd never seen the place before two days ago, you probably know more about it than I do, but I'll show you what I've seen."

"Lead on," he said, moving to follow and letting his eyes wander up and down the back of her. Trim, he thought. She was built, that was for sure, but more than that, she had a body that he recognized from his ex-wife and her friends: cared-for. This woman had spent a lot of time in gyms. There wasn't much of her skin showing, but he was willing to bet that cream-laden massages were part of her life. Or had been, he thought.

He was quiet as he watched her and listened while she gave him a tour of her garden. She knew a lot about plants. She talked about trailing blackberries versus erect blackberries, then the two kinds of raspberries. "And they all have to be pruned differently," she said, smiling up at him.

If he'd just heard her and not seen her, he would have thought she was a farm wife. But what farm wife makes a meal worthy of a four-star restaurant? He knew good home cooks, but that usually meant chicken-fried steak, or catfish and hush puppies. He didn't know home cooks who mixed pigeon livers and pickled grapes.

She was showing him the pond and talking about koi fish that hibernated over the winter, and how she'd have to put nets around the pond to keep out the raccoons.

On the far side of the house, she talked about gooseberries and currants, neither of which Matt had ever eaten.

And the more she talked, the more he was puzzled by her. Sometimes she pronounced words oddly. She said "extra-ordinary" instead of "extraordinary" the way an American did. And she said "dale-yuhs" rather than using the American pronunciation of dahlias.

"You learned all this in Kentucky?" he asked softly as he followed her past the barn and into the wooded area beside the house. "Did you grow up on a farm?"

"No," she said. "I didn't. Just suburbia. Look at this. Isn't it lovely?"

She was looking at the old fire pit set in the clearing in the woods, and he was aware that yet again she'd not answered his question.

Turning, he looked at the pit and smiled. "My brother and I nearly set the woods on fire here one night."

"Tell me," she said.

"Nothing to tell. Just stupid kid stuff. Rick and I gathered some fallen wood, doused it with lighter fluid, then threw a couple of lit matches onto it. It exploded." He shook his head in memory. "It's a wonder we weren't killed. If it hadn't started raining, I don't know what would have happened."

"Your parents must have been angry."

"My mom never knew about it. She worked long hours, so we were on our own a lot." He paused, waiting for her to ask the question that everyone did, but when she asked nothing, he continued. "My father walked out when I was five and Rick was three."

"I'm sorry," Bailey said, looking up at him, but he had turned his face away so she couldn't see his expression.

"It was a long time ago. So what about your parents?"

She turned back toward the path. "My father died when I was fourteen, and my mother died last year, but I have a sister."

"In Kentucky?" he asked.

"Yes," she said, and her curt reply told him that he wasn't to ask any more questions.

Matt didn't let her tone bother him. "So if you didn't grow up on a farm, where did you learn so much about plants, especially food plants?"

Turning back to look at him, she opened her mouth

to speak, then gave a great sigh. "Does everyone in this town ask such personal questions?"

"Oh, yes," Matt said cheerfully. "Everyone knows everyone else's business. There isn't a child in this town who doesn't know everything there is to know about me."

Bailey laughed. "You mean about the bimbo you married?" she asked.

"That's Patsy's version. She met Cassandra once and was snubbed. Patsy's revenge has been to tell people that I married a brainless beauty."

"And was she?"

Matt gave her a one-sided smile. "She lost me, didn't she? She couldn't have been too smart."

Bailey cocked her head to one side. "And a personal question not answered," she said.

"Touché," he said, smiling. "Now, how about that peach cobbler? I've worked up an appetite."

"You'd better watch it, or you'll get fat," she said.

"And what would you know about being fat?" he asked, and there was a hint of suggestion in his voice.

"Nothing." Her blue eyes were dancing with laughter. "I wouldn't know anything at all about diets, or the endless frustration of hours of exercise with no food but still no weight loss. Nope. I don't know a thing about being fat."

Laughing, she went back to the house, and Matt followed her. Minutes later, he was seated at the table in the living room and having his first bite of the peach cobbler. "What—" he asked, unable to complete his sentence.

"Oh? You mean, why does it taste different from other peach cobblers you've had?"

Matt could only nod.

"Cherries and vanilla. Add a little of each, and it brings out the flavor of the peaches. And I put crushed almonds in the crust."

Matt told himself that he would not, could not, burst into tears. He pointed at his plate with his fork. "Where? How?" he managed to say.

Bailey looked down at her hands, clasped on the table. She was eating nothing, just finishing her glass of wine, and she looked as though she was considering how much and what to tell him. "My husband had a cook and a gardener, and I spent a lot of time with them," she said after a while. "I learned from them."

Matt sensed that she was telling about one percent of the truth, but that was better than no truth at all.

It was when he was halfway through the cobbler that the Idea came to him. An Idea with a capital letter. Bailey was sitting silently, looking toward her right at the big, blank brown wall on the far side of the living room, and he almost slipped up and told her that there was a stone fireplace hidden behind it.

"So what do you think of this house?" he asked.

He watched her give a sigh of relief that he hadn't asked another question about her past.

"Awful," she said. "When I was told that Jimmie had left me a farmhouse, I imagined something cute, something with a fireplace and a porch. A big, deep porch with rocking chairs on it. Instead, I get this thing with twenty bedrooms and those bathrooms. Have you ever seen anything like them in your life?"

His plate clean, Matt wiped his mouth, drained the last of his wine, then stood up. "I have to get some tools from my truck, then I want to show you something. All right?"

"Sure," she said, a puzzled look on her face.

As Matt left the house and walked to the road, he told himself to take this easy and cautiously. He knew that he'd have one chance, and if he messed it up, he'd blow it forever. As he opened the toolbox in the back of his truck and took out a crowbar, he closed his eyes for a moment and thought of Patsy's meat loaf and this woman's pigeon and peach cobbler. With cherries in it. And almonds in the crust. With an expression of absolute seriousness, as though he faced the most important moment of his life, he strapped on his tool belt, gripped his crowbar, and strode back to the house.

Inside, he saw that she'd removed his plate from the table. For a moment he stood in the kitchen doorway, watching as she put a big pot of jam in the refrigerator. "Ready?" he asked, and she followed him to the front door.

"When I was in school studying to become an architect, for a project, I took measurements of this old house, drew it as it was, then remodeled it on paper. The assignment was to keep the same footprint, but to change the interior." Kneeling on the floor, Matt ran his hand along the bottom of the paneling. The only light in the dark room was from the open doorway. "It was Christmas, and I wanted to give Rick and Patsy time alone, so I spent a lot of time over here. And as I measured and began to really look at this house, I began to want to see what it had originally looked like. I could see that this paneling"—he said the word with a sneer—"had been added long after the house was built, so I began to inspect it. I pulled boards off the walls, looked under them, then nailed them back in place. Ah, here it is," he said as he found a handhold under the dark wood, then inserted his crowbar in the opening. "Do you mind?" he asked before he pulled.

"You can do whatever you want to that stuff," she said with great sincerity, then jumped when one side of the paneling came away with a loud sound of nails being dragged through wood. Within seconds, the whole sheet was off, and Matt set it to one side.

He turned to her with a smile of triumph, but all Bailey could see was the backside of the paneling in the next bedroom.

"You don't see it," he said, sounding disappointed.

"Sorry," she replied.

"See that?" He pointed to what looked like some sort of post against the outside wall.

"Yes," she said slowly.

Matt lifted his foot, gave a kick to the back of the thin paneling in front of them, and sent it crashing to the floor of the empty bedroom. Then he turned to her as though to ask, Now do you see?

"Two rooms made into one," Bailey said. "Nice."

Matt put his hand on the big upright piece of wood he'd pointed out before. "Do you see what this is?"

"A post of some sort, I guess."

"Right." He was smiling at her. "Now, what kind of structures have posts?"

"Mailboxes?"

Matt laughed. "Think bigger. Something with rocking chairs."

"Oh," Bailey said, then louder, "Oh. A porch?"

"Yes."

"You mean—"

"That's right. This whole area is a porch. It goes around about a quarter of the house in an L shape.

Somebody—some do-it-yourselfer, obviously—closed in
the porch and made it into an entryway, two bedrooms,
and a bathroom."

"A very ugly bathroom," Bailey said.

"If you take out these walls, lose the bedrooms and
the bath, you have your porch back."

Matt was pleased to see that she looked too stunned
to make any comment. Turning away to hide his smile,
he walked back into the living room, and this time it
was her turn to follow him like a trained dog.

Part of the longest wall in the living room jutted out
about three feet. "Stand back and cover your eyes—this
may be messy," he said. He hooked his crowbar under
the sheet of paneling, but then he halted. "I better not
do this. Dust'll get all over your furniture."

"I have a vacuum," she said quickly as she stepped
back and closed her eyes, but opened them when she
heard crashing. Matt had caught the sheet of paneling
before it fell on her furniture, but with it came a cloud of
dust. When the dust settled, she saw stones.

"It's a fireplace?" she asked quietly as he leaned the
paneling against the wall.

"That's right. It's a fireplace. Made from native
stone." He stuck his head inside and looked up the
chimney. "I don't think it would take much to get it in
working order."

"And you could do that? You could pull all this off
and make the fireplace work? And the porch? You could
bring the porch back to life?"

She made him sound like a doctor who'd found a way
to resurrect the dead. "Sure," he said, trying to sound as
though it were the easiest thing in the world. He wasn't
about to talk to her about structural damage or rotten

overhead beams. Nor was he going to mention termites or dry rot. And right now he thought it was best not to tell her about the buzzing he was hearing inside the chimney.

Trying not to seem as though he were frantic, he picked up the piece of paneling and held it against the studs that had been put in front of the fireplace, then, as fast as he could, nailed the sheet of paneling back into place. Under his hands, he could feel angry bees, or wasps, protesting the disturbance of their nest.

"The kitchen," he said loudly, pointing and moving both of them away from the fireplace. "I always thought that this wall should be torn out to make the kitchen and the living room into one big room. You could put an island here. You like marble or granite countertops?"

"Marble?" she whispered. "Granite?"

Again, Matt had to turn away to hide his smile, then he led her through to the bedrooms and told her how he could get plumbing fixtures wholesale.

"You do plumbing too?" she asked in wonder.

"No, but a high school buddy of mine is a plumber, so I'll have him do it all." He liked the furniture she'd put in her bedroom. It had a homey feel that appealed to him. Patsy liked furniture that was shiny enough to use as a mirror, and his ex-wife had liked antiques, the kind that cost so much you were afraid to use them.

He managed to keep talking when he went through the other two bedrooms and the bath. She didn't seem to notice that he took a bit longer in those rooms, or that he kept looking at how the bathroom wall was shared with one of the bedrooms. Yes, he could put a door through the wall and make a private entrance into the bathroom. At Patsy's house, he shared a bathroom with her two sons—and they were slobs. Every morning Matt risked bodily injury as he stepped over wet towels and underwear that the boys left on the floor. Patsy said it wasn't her bathroom, that she never went into it, so she refused to clean it. For the last six months, Matt had spent every Saturday morning scrubbing it down.

"What?" he asked Bailey, still looking at the bathroom with longing. It was ugly, but it didn't contain two teenage boys.

"What about the attic?" she was saying.

"Ah, yes," he said, then led the way up the stairs. On the third tread, he shifted his weight. He didn't like that; the stair didn't feel sturdy. "Needs work," he said over his shoulder.

At the head of the stairs, he paused and had to take a deep breath before he could walk forward. He used to tell his little brother that the attic in the old house was haunted. The truth was that he wanted to keep the upstairs as his private place; the attic of the old Hanley house had been Matt's sanctuary when he was a boy. It had been a place where he could escape when his real life became too much for him.

"Are you okay?" Bailey asked, looking at him hard.

"Sure," he said briskly. "I was just trying to remember what I found out about this attic when I was here. I think that the floor on the other side of that railing has been put in recently. Beyond the railing, I think it used to be open to the room below, but somebody covered the opening, cut a hole in the railing and made a room. Probably—"

"No!" Bailey shouted, making Matt halt. "Don't walk on that floor."

When he looked at her, he could see that she was embarrassed.

"I'm sorry, you're going to think I'm crazy, but it's just a feeling I have about it. I wouldn't let any of the cleaning people near it. I know it's silly of me, but . . ." She trailed off with a shrug of her shoulders.

"Let's have a look at it," Matt said, then bent and began to pry up the plywood sheets. After he'd removed three of them, he stepped back. "Good instincts," he said, his voice full of admiration. "Whoever put this floor in didn't know diddly-squat about construction. They might as well have used Legos."

Stepping closer to him, Bailey peered down into the cavity that he'd exposed and saw floor joists that were barely touching each other, unable to hold any weight.

"If anyone had walked on that, he"—he looked down at her—"or she would have fallen through to the floor below." His voice lowered. "Do you always have premonitions like this one?"

"Not often," she said. "But sometimes I . . . You'll think I'm silly."

"Not likely."

"Sometimes I seem to know when things are right or not. It's not like I know the future, but I know when something is what I should do. Maybe it's what you said, 'an instinct.' "

"Whatever it is, it's a good one." It was growing dark outside, and there were no lights in the attic.

Bailey started down the stairs, Matt behind her, but at the top of the stairs, he paused and looked at the room. He could almost see his computer and desk set against the wall. And over there, under the windows, would be his drafting table. If he built a little platform, he could raise his table so he could see out the windows; then he'd be able to see into that garden where she was growing all that food that she put into jars and onto plates. He could—

"Did you see something else wrong?" Bailey called up to him from the bottom of the stairs.

"No," he answered, then turned and went down the stairs.

When they were once again in the living room, she didn't ask him to sit down, didn't offer him anything else to eat or drink, and didn't sit down herself. It was obvious that she was ready for him to leave. After all, it was a little past nine o'clock now, and she probably had things she needed to do.

But then, so did Matt. He didn't leave. Instead, he stood there and waited for her answer.

"All right," she said as she moved toward the front door. "I'm ready to hire you. Could you give me a bid? I need to see what I can afford to do. I think I'm going to have a lot of other expenses, and—" Glancing toward the kitchen, she gave a little shrug.

Now's your chance, Longacre, he said to himself. It's now or never. "I have a proposition for you."

Immediately she took a step back, and he regretted his choice of words.

"Business," he said quickly, but she didn't relax the set of her shoulders. "Look," he said, "could we sit down and talk about this?"

He moved toward the couch, but she stood where she was, looking at him cautiously. He sat down, took a deep breath, then looked back up at her. "I need a place to stay, and you have extra bedrooms, so I thought maybe I could rent a room from you. I'd do the remodeling of this house on weekends and charge you only for materials."

"I see," she said, but she avoided his eyes. Slowly she walked around the couch and sat on a chair, as far as she could get from him without leaving the room. "So why do you want to move in here with *me?* Surely there must be other people in Calburn who have empty bedrooms."

"Lots of them, but—" He gave her a crooked smile. "They can't cook, and they have a houseful of kids to drive me crazy, and . . . Please don't take offense at this, but there's something I like about you, something peaceful and calm. You don't look like the type of woman who gets hysterical easily."

"No," Bailey said slowly. "I can guarantee you that it takes a lot to make me hysterical." She looked down at her hands for a moment. "Sooooo, what, uh, space would you take if you moved in here?"

"I'd take the larger bedroom in the back, the one nearest that green bathroom," he said quickly, "and I'd need to use part of the attic room for an office. I do book work on weekends."

"You'd do book work in addition to freeing my porch?"

"Right. Porch and fireplace. And the kitchen. Kitchen, most definitely."

"So what about food?" she asked.

"I think you should cook."

"No, I mean, who pays for the food? You eat a lot. And what if you have guests? Who pays for the extra?"

"I have an account at the local grocery in Calburn, so if you buy there, I'll pay the bill. Is that fair?"

"What if the food comes from my garden or roadside stands? And there's the Cost Club."

Matt blinked at her. When he'd had this idea, his concern had been that she'd be afraid that he'd try to pounce on her in the middle of the night. "What do you have in mind that I should pay you for room and board?"

"I'd say . . . six hundred a month, plus the price of groceries."

"What?!" he said. "That's outrageous!" He started to get up, all the while looking at her out of the corner of his eye, but she didn't flinch, just sat there in utter calmness.

"If you got a motel room," she said, "you'd pay more than that, and that's without food, plus you'd have to cook for yourself. That means that if you moved in here, you'd be getting the services of a cook for free, and my cooking should balance out your carpentry, especially if you also do paperwork on the weekends. Actually, six hundred is too cheap," she said thoughtfully.

"I think you're confusing Calburn with some big city. Prices are much cheaper here."

Bailey leaned back in her chair and crossed her arms over her chest. "Take it or leave it."

"I'll take it, but I don't like it," Matt said, frowning.

"Well, then, I guess that's that. Should we sign something?"

"I think that shaking hands will be enough," he said, still standing and smiling down at her. "Unless you intend to charge me for that."

"I don't know. Should I?"

Matt laughed. "No," he said, holding out his hand. When Bailey got up and took his hand in hers, he held it and looked into her eyes for a moment.

Bailey was the first to pull away, then she walked to the front door.

Matt followed her lead, then stepped past her to go outside. "I'll move in tomorrow, if that's all right with you."

"Yes," she said, then hesitated. "You aren't going to . . . you know. I don't think I'm quite ready for—"

"Sex?" he asked.

"Oh, no," she said, smiling. "I could stand that. It's just involvement that I don't want. I need to find out how I can support myself before I get involved with another man—if I ever do, that is. And I need privacy. *Lots* of privacy. Understand?"

"I think so," he said hesitantly. "Sex is okay, but stay out of your life. Do I have it right?"

"Perhaps," she said, smiling at him as she started to close the door. "But let me make it clear: if there's sex between us, your rent triples," she said, then softly closed the door.

Laughing, Matt walked down the driveway and got back in his truck, then leaned his head against the seat for a moment. He really and truly couldn't believe his good fortune. He was going to get out of Patsy's house!

As he started the engine, he kept smiling. And more than just getting out, he was moving in with a woman who could cook, a woman who seemed to know all the domestic arts. He couldn't believe his luck.

As he turned off Owl Creek Road onto the asphalt, he hoped that Bailey didn't find out that Patsy was charging him seven-fifty a month, plus he had to buy one week's worth of groceries for the entire family of five adults.

Seven

❧

Bailey didn't awaken the next morning until nearly eight, late for her, but then, she hadn't gone to bed until three. After Matt left, the ugly little house had seemed too empty, too full of all the things in life that she no longer had. She'd gone to bed, but she'd tossed about for over an hour, so she got up, pulled on her chinos and a T-shirt, then padded into the kitchen to get herself something warm to drink.

For a while, she'd sat at the dining table in the living room and looked at the wall that concealed a fireplace. It was when she heard a noise outside and looked at the front door, fully expecting Jimmie to walk into the room, that she knew she had to *do* something, or she'd spend the night crying.

In the kitchen, she had a refrigerator full of pots of jam that needed to be reheated, then put into jars, and on the floor were crates of strawberries that she'd bought at a roadside stand. Also in the refrigerator were bags of plums, a large box of blackberries, a big bag full of cherries, and the crispers were full of vegetables.

"Cry or work," she said aloud; then she put on her tennis shoes and an apron. After she'd put the crate of strawberries on the table and found her capper in the box where she'd put her canning equipment, she set to work. Phillip had sent a man to hook her up to a cable service, so she turned on the TV and watched HGTV while she cooked.

So now, this morning, yawning, she got out of bed, dressed, and went through the kitchen into the pantry to look at the rows of jars: blackberry liqueur, cherry cordial, strawberry jam, green tomato chutney, pickled carrots, strawberry conserve, plum jam, and pickled plums. On the windowsill was the recipe box that she'd been so excited to find. Unfortunately, it had turned out to contain only a few basic recipes for meat loaf and chicken-fried steak. It had not been the great find that she'd hoped it would be.

Last night she'd run Ball jars through the hottest cycle of the dishwasher to sterilize them, while keeping the lids hot in boiling water. Since there was little work space in the kitchen, she'd set up the table in the living room, covering the surface with layers of clean white tea towels.

She first mixed the blackberries with sugar and set them in a bowl inside the small proofing oven of the big range. The fat berries needed to stay in low heat for hours, until the sugar drew the juice from them.

She capped strawberries, then divided them into two pots, one for jam and one for conserve, where the berries were kept whole. While the strawberries were simmering, she pricked the plums all over with a big darning needle, then left them in a bowl while she put cider vinegar, apple juice concentrate, cloves, allspice, ginger, and bay leaves into a pot and let it simmer.

She tested the jam to see if it had jelled by putting a spoonful on a cold plate in the freezer for a few minutes, and when it was ready, she began putting it into jars. She lugged a big canner full of boiling water to the table. For the jars to properly seal, everything had to be kept as hot as possible, and as clean as possible. There couldn't be the tiniest bit of jam on the rim of the jar, or the lid wouldn't seal—or worse, bacteria would get inside the jar.

The plums went first. She packed the pricked plums as tight as she could inside a dozen hot, sterile jars; then, using a wide-mouthed stainless steel funnel, she poured the strained vinegar solution on top of them. She wiped each rim with a clean cloth, put on the lids, twisted the rims into place, then put the jars on a tray and carried them back to the kitchen. Using the big lifting tongs to set the hot jars inside the canning kettle, she set the timer for the hot water bath, an extra precaution needed to insure safe preservation.

She followed with the strawberry jam and the conserve, plus the jams that she had cooked the night before.

While she'd been putting the strawberries into jars, she'd run a two-quart decorative glass jar through the hot cycle of the dishwasher, and when it was ready, she filled it with cherries that she'd pricked with her needle, their stems still attached. She put these into the jar, covered them with white sugar, then poured enough grappa—that dry Italian brandy—in to fill the jar.

The lid had a plastic seal on it, and she put it on tight.

She spent over an hour chopping green tomatoes, which she'd also purchased at the roadside stand, onions, and apples to make green tomato chutney. Once the vegetables were cut, she put them into a pot with wine vinegar, raisins, cayenne pepper, ginger, and garlic.

She mixed peeled baby carrots with wine vinegar, sugar, celery seeds, white peppercorns, dill seeds, mustard seeds, and bay leaves.

When the blackberries she'd put in the oven were a mass of juice, she poured the liquid into a cheesecloth bag, tied it closed with heavy string, then hung it from the legs of a chair she'd turned upside down on top of the coffee table, a big ceramic bowl set underneath to catch the drippings.

When the chutney and pickled carrots were in jars and sealed, she measured the blackberry juice, poured out an equal amount of gin, put the mixture into jars, and sealed them.

Only after she'd labeled all the jars and carried everything into the pantry did she allow herself to go to bed, and by then she was so tired that she fell asleep instantly.

So now it was morning, and she was facing the question, What now? Yesterday at the grocery it had seemed a brilliant idea to sell her jams, chutneys, and liqueurs. But during the night while she was working, she'd begun to think about marketing. How did she get her jars to the consumer? She was used to making six jars of one item. If she was going to sell them, she'd have to make hundreds, maybe thousands, of jars of one kind. And what about liquor laws? What did she have to do to be able to sell cherries preserved in grappa?

In the past, all she would have had to do was tell Jim-

mie that she wanted something and he would have seen
to everything else—or had someone else see to it. Early
this morning, when she'd at last climbed into bed, she'd
seen her address book on the bedside table. She knew
that inside it were all Phillip's telephone numbers, and
she knew, without a doubt, that if she called him and
asked, he'd take care of everything. But she wasn't ready
to admit defeat yet.

So now, looking at all the jars, she didn't know what
her next step was. "Damn you, James Manville!" she
said out loud. "Why did you do this to me? How am I
supposed to support myself when I know nothing about
anything?"

For a moment her body was filled with anger, but in
the next moment she felt herself near to tears, and she
leaned her forehead against a shelf. Oh! but she missed
him! she thought. She missed the sound of his voice, and
the way his presence filled the room. She missed talking
to him, listening to him. She missed the way they solved
each other's problems.

And she missed the sex. Yesterday with Matt Longacre, she'd been half kidding when she'd teased him
about sex. It was obvious he'd been worried that she'd
turn down his suggestion of being a paying boarder. He
seemed to fear that she'd act like a virginal maiden and
defend her virtue. But the idea of being relieved of the
sheer awfulness of living alone had been everything to
her. She was used to waking up in houses where dozens
of people were living. Yes, nearly all of them had been
staff, but Bailey had formed friendships with those people. When she went into the kitchen, there was a chef
and his assistants there to say "Good morning" to. In the
houses that had gardens, she'd had landscapers to greet.

Their houses in the islands and on the sea had had men in boats outside.

Perhaps her existence with Jimmie had been odd, but it had been her life, and as long as Jimmie was there, she'd enjoyed it.

But now she was alone. There was no one to talk to, no one to consult. And there was no more sex. Part of her felt that she should put on black and be like Queen Victoria, mourning her dead husband for the rest of her life. But another part of her wanted to laugh and have a good time—and even to tumble about in bed with a man. To go from an active sex life to nothing hurt. It physically hurt.

Slowly she made herself leave the pantry, and a few minutes later, she was sitting on the stairs out the back door eating a bowl of Cheerios.

"We're on our own, kid," she said as she looked up at the mulberry tree. Tiny fruit was beginning to form. She'd learned from their English gardener that the mulberry tree was the most cautious tree in the garden. It didn't put out leaves until all danger of frost was past. "Watch the mulberry tree," she was told. If it was early April and the mulberry tree sent out shoots, then it was all right to put out tender bedding plants. But even if it was a sunny day in May and the weatherman saw no danger of frost ahead, if the mulberry tree was still bare, then the bedding plants stayed in the greenhouses. And, sure enough, there would be a late frost.

So what was she to do today? she wondered. Put up more fruit? Make more chutney? Even though she had no idea how to market it?

On the other hand, maybe she should spend the day

trying to find out whatever it was that Jimmie had asked her to find out. In the weeks since she'd first read the note he'd left her, the more often she'd read it, the more it annoyed her. *Find out the truth about what happened, will you, Frecks? Do it for me.*

The truth about *what?* she wondered. Couldn't he have given her a clue as to where to start? Everyone in Calburn called the farm he'd left her the old Hanley place. What did that have to do with Jimmie's name of Manville? Of course, she thought, Jimmie probably lied about his name. He seemed to have lied about everything else to do with his childhood, so why not his name?

But as Bailey looked up at the old tree, her eyes widened. There was one thing that even Jimmie couldn't lie about. There was a scar on his face, a scar that he hid under his big mustache, a scar that only she knew about. But the one and only time she'd mentioned it, on their wedding night, had been the one and only time that Jimmie had been really and truly angry at her. As a result, she'd never mentioned it again.

It was that memory that gave Bailey some hope. Maybe there actually was a way for her to find out whatever it was that Jimmie wanted her to know.

She went inside the house, put her empty bowl in the dishwasher, then picked up her handbag and her car keys. It was time to see downtown Calburn.

But as she opened the car door, on impulse, she ran back into the house and filled a wooden strawberry crate with jars of preserves. It wouldn't hurt to start letting people taste her product.

If she'd had to use one word to describe Calburn, she would have said "deserted." Or maybe "abandoned" would have done as well.

Her farmhouse was about two miles from the cross-roads that was "downtown" Calburn, and on the drive there, she saw one empty house after another. There were big old farmhouses set back off the road, their deep porches shaded by trees the size of rocket launchers. Some of the houses had lawns that were mowed, while others had been left to weeds and bushes. Now and then she saw a house that looked occupied, but for the most part, they had an air of emptiness.

"What in the world happened here?" she wondered aloud. "Why did these people leave?"

When she reached the crossroads, she saw that most of the stores were empty. Some of them had boards over the windows; others had dirty glass with nothing behind them. A few windows had yellowed signs that said, "For Lease."

There were still a few businesses open in Calburn. There was a building that looked as though it had been converted from two; one side was a post office, the other a diner. There was an antiques store, but the things she could see behind the dirty glass were more old than antique. There was a feed store that said it carried hard-ware as well, and a grocery store. Outside it was a bin full of tired-looking vegetables. Bailey thought that she and Matt were going to have to have a talk about where she bought groceries.

There was a dry-goods store that rented videos and sold ice cream. And at the end of the street was Opal's Beauty Salon.

Bailey didn't hesitate as she pulled into the empty

parking place in front of the salon. She knew that if she was going to get information, this was where to begin.

When she opened the door, a bell tinkled, but the teenage girl sitting in the chair and eating a candy bar didn't look up from her movie magazine. She had three-inch-long white-blonde hair with black roots, all of it sectioned off into tiny tufts that were fastened with various-colored ties. Her eyes were heavily lined in black. Even though it was a warm day, she had on a sweater big enough to cover a baby hippo, and tight black toreador pants.

"Yeah?" she said, turning her head vaguely in the direction of the door, but not looking at Bailey. "You want somethin'?"

"I was wondering if—" Bailey hesitated. Maybe this wasn't such a good idea. Maybe she didn't want this young woman to touch her hair.

"Carla!" came a voice from the back. "See who that is."

"Yeah, Ma," came the tired-sounding voice of the girl sitting in the chair. "In a minute."

Bailey started to say that she'd changed her mind, but suddenly a woman stepped out from behind the curtained doorway, then stood in frozen silence as she gaped at Bailey.

"You're her," the woman said at last.

For one horrible moment, Bailey feared that the woman was going to say that she was Lillian Manville, wife of the billionaire.

"You're the widow that got the old Hanley place, aren't you? And Matt Longacre is going to move in with you today, isn't he?"

Smiling, Bailey nodded. She'd been right: if she

wanted to know what was going on in Calburn, she'd come to the right place.

"Get up!" the woman hissed at the girl in the chair, who was now staring at Bailey as though she had just stepped off a spaceship. The woman had to push the girl's shoulder hard before she vacated the chair. "Go to the store and get her somethin' to drink," she said to the girl. "A Dr Pepper." She looked back at Bailey. "You want color? A perm? Or maybe you want highlights? Or a cut? I'm Opal, by the way."

"No, really," Bailey said. "I just wanted to—" Ask some questions, she started to say, but the two of them were staring at her so hard that she couldn't bear to disappoint them. "I just need a wash and blow-dry," she heard herself say, and the next moment the woman took over. She took Bailey's arm and almost pulled her into the chair, while her daughter came alive enough to scurry out the front door in search of the nearest Dr Pepper.

As *Bailey left* the hairdresser, she kept her back straight, and when she got into her car, she waved at Opal and Carla, who were watching her through the window.

With a smile plastered on her face, Bailey drove out of Calburn, but the minute she was on the outskirts, she stopped under some trees and turned off her car. Digging in her handbag, she pulled out her big hairbrush, then got out to stand in the shade and brush her hair. The woman must have used half a can of mousse on her hair! Then she'd lacquered it down with spray that Opal said was guaranteed not to let her hair move even in a windstorm.

For a moment, Bailey leaned back against the trunk of a tree and closed her eyes. The hour-long ordeal had been exhausting! She'd been quizzed about her marriage, her husband, and her childhood. It had taken all Bailey's energy to lie without seeming to lie, to give answers while giving no answers.

Since Opal talked nonstop, she didn't seem to notice that Bailey wasn't really saying much at all. But her daughter Carla, sitting in the second chair, now and then gave Bailey a sideways look, as though to say that she knew she was being evasive.

It had taken all the cunning that Bailey possessed to get Opal to give information rather than try to extract it. Since Bailey couldn't tell Opal anything that she didn't want all of Calburn to know, she had to be subtle as well as pushy as a Sherman tank. "I'm just so interested in Calburn," Bailey said, trying to sound young and innocent. Carla had given her one of her disbelieving sideways looks.

"Not much to know," Opal had said as she wrapped Bailey's hair around a little brush roller.

Bailey tried not to think about Shirley Temple. "I'm sure the history of the town is fascinating."

Opal had stopped rolling and stared hard at Bailey in the mirror. "You're not here about the Golden Six, are you?" There was hostility in her voice, and anger on her face.

"I have no idea what you're talking about," Bailey said honestly, and she was glad that she wasn't asking about whatever it was that made Opal look like that. On the other hand, she couldn't resist asking, "What's the Golden Six?"

"Calburn's claim to fame, that's what," Opal said,

then told Carla to hush up when her daughter snorted in derision.

"Now tell me more about your husband that died," Opal said as she picked up an even smaller roller and pulled Bailey's hair so tightly around it that her eyes began to water.

It was while Bailey was under the hair dryer that Carla walked past her and dropped a folded piece of paper on top of her magazine. Without thinking, Bailey hid the note and later slipped it into her pants pocket.

So now, Bailey removed the paper and looked at it. "Violet Honeycutt knows all about Calburn" was written on the paper. "Yellow house at the end of Red River Road." Below that was a little map, showing that Red River Road was very near where she was now.

Bailey gave her hair another brush, then went back to her car, smiling. For all that Carla's manner and looks were off-putting, Bailey rather liked the girl.

Using the little map, it was easy to find Red River Road. At the end of it was a pretty little farmhouse that had long ago been painted yellow, with dark brown trim around the windows. Huge willow trees almost hid the house from the road. As Bailey pulled into the driveway and saw the porch with the old rocking chairs on it, she couldn't suppress the thought: Why didn't you leave me a place like this one, Jimmie?

She stepped up on the porch and knocked on the door, but no one answered. "Hello?" she called, but still there was no answer. When she left the porch and walked toward the back of the house, she saw a woman bending over a patch of vegetable garden. It looked as though she was setting out tomato seedlings. She was a large woman, wearing a huge, flower-printed sundress that had been washed many times. Her bare feet were in rubber thongs, and a big straw hat with half the brim torn away was perched on her head. Bailey could see only part of her face, but she looked to be in her fifties.

"Hello," Bailey said and the woman turned to look at her. She had a face lined by years of sun, and if Bailey didn't miss her guess, a few drugs and quite a bit of booze. The phrase *old hippie* came to her mind.

"Aren't you just perfect?" the woman said, straightening up as she looked Bailey up and down. "You look like something off the page of a catalog."

Maybe Bailey should have taken offense at the woman's words, but just a few months ago, no one would have ever said she looked like a catalog model. "That's me," she said as she held out her arms and slowly turned around. "I'm an Orvis-Norm Thompson-Land's End special."

The woman laughed, showing that she had a couple of teeth missing on the bottom. "So what can I do you for?" she asked.

But Bailey didn't answer her question; her eyes were on the plants that the woman had just set into the ground. They weren't tomatoes; they were marijuana. "Isn't that illegal?" she asked softly.

"Only if you're selfish. I share what I grow with the deputy sheriff who looks after Calburn, so he says I have a real nice garden." She squinted her eyes at Bailey. "You want to come inside and tell me what you came all the way out here for?"

Bailey had to smile at that. She was used to spending the weekend in places you had to fly to. But it seemed that Red River Road was considered "all the way out here."

She followed the woman onto the screened-in back porch of the house, where there was a washing machine that had to be from the 1940s, plus a couple of well-used washboards. In the corner was a stack of broken wooden lawn furniture that should have been used for firewood, except that Bailey was sure she'd seen some just like it in a shop in Paris. Retro was all the rage there.

They entered the kitchen, and Bailey could tell it hadn't been changed in thirty years. The linoleum on the floor was worn through in places, and the cabinets were aged with grease and old paint. Along one wall was an old enamel range with an oven big enough to roast half an ox. Under the window stood an enamel sink: one enormous bowl, wide drain boards on each side, and an enameled backsplash with two faucets in it. It was an original version of the sink she'd bought for her farmhouse.

"Awful old place, ain't it?" the woman said as she settled her bulk into a chair, her back to the sink. Bailey had seen the exact same chairs for sale in exclusive Americana shops.

"No," she said honestly. "It's the real version of what the rest of us try to copy."

The woman chuckled. "You look pretty slick, but I'm beginnin' to like you anyway. Come and sit down and ask me what you want to. Unless you'd rather can tomatoes." She said this last as though it were the greatest joke she'd ever heard in her life. That someone who looked as citified as Bailey did could put up tomatoes seemed like the ultimate joke.

It was Bailey's turn to give a smug little smile. When she looked into the sink, she saw that it was full of homegrown, still-warm-from-the-sun tomatoes. Some of them had holes in them because, obviously, the woman hadn't bothered with the slugs, but Bailey knew she could save the fruit. Without looking at the woman seated at the table, Bailey opened a door beside the screened back door, guessing that it was a big pantry such as nearly all old farmhouses had. It was, and inside were hundreds of old mason and Ball jars waiting to be filled with the summer's produce. On the floor were a couple of canning kettles and new boxes of sealing lids.

"You talk, I'll can," Bailey said as she carried the canners to the sink to fill them. "I want to know why this town has been abandoned, and I want to know why Opal at the hair, uh, beauty shop was ready to shoot me when she thought I was trying to find out something about the Golden Six. What is that, anyway? I haven't stepped into a union, have I? And I'm Bailey James, by the way. I inherited—"

"The old Hanley place. I know," the woman said, watching Bailey as she moved about the kitchen as though she'd always worked there. "Your husband died and left the farm to you, and Matt Longacre is moving in with you today. Patsy is thrilled to be getting rid of him. He never stops grousing about what slobs her two boys are. Of course Patsy spoils those boys to death, so Matt probably had reason to complain. I'm Violet Honeycutt."

"That's what I was told." Bailey was moving jars from the pantry to put them into two water-filled kettles to sterilize them. "What I want to know most is anything you can tell me about the farm I was given. Who lived there, that sort of thing. Did the Hanleys have any children?"

"Who are you tryin' to find?" Violet asked suspiciously.

At that, Bailey sat down on a chair at the table and faced Violet. She knew her meaning was clear: if Violet wanted her tomatoes put up, then she had to answer questions, not ask them.

Violet laughed. "Somebody somewhere taught you to do business, didn't he?"

Bailey did not move from her seat.

Smiling, Violet opened a little wooden box on the table and withdrew a hand-rolled cigarette. "Mind?"

Bailey just looked at her, waiting for the answers to her questions.

"Okay," Violet said, leaning back against her chair, lighting her joint, then inhaling deeply and closing her eyes for a moment. When she opened them, she said, "The Hanleys used to own the place, but just because they moved away a long time ago don't mean that their name was ever taken out of people's minds as the owners of that farm."

Bailey got up, went to the sink, and picked up an old paring knife that had been sharpened so many times that the blade was curved inward. The original bird's-beak knife, she thought, thinking of the expensive French knife she used.

"Are you interested in the Hanleys?"

Bailey hesitated in answering. It would be better to reveal as little as possible. "No," she said. "I'm more interested in the sixties and seventies in Calburn."

"Ah, then you *are* interested in the Golden Six."

"I have no idea who or what they are."

"Six boys, graduated from high school in 1953. They are Calburn's only claim to fame. But then some jealous little nobody decided to make up stories about them, and everything fell apart." There was bitterness in Violet's voice.

Bailey knew that Jimmie hadn't been born until

1959, so he couldn't have been one of the so-called Golden Six. "I'm interested in later than that." She put a black-bottomed aluminum pan full of water on to boil so she could dip the tomatoes in it to peel them.

"In 'sixty-eight, one of the six boys shot his wife, then himself. That about the right date for you?"

There was 1968 again, she thought. But Jimmie was too young then to have been involved in something like that. "I'm really more interested in the people connected to my farm."

"Truthfully, I don't know anything about your place, but I know a girl that used to live in Calburn. Hand me that phone, and I'll see if she's home. Except that it's a long-distance call." She looked at Bailey expectantly.

"I'll pay for it," Bailey said as she wiped her hands on a towel and went to get the telephone. It was a black rotary dial telephone that Bailey was tempted to say should be in a museum.

Violet dialed, listened, then said, "Hey, babe! It's Honeycutt. I got a new resident of wild and woolly Calburn here, and she wants to know the history of the old Hanley place. Didn't somethin' happen there? I seem to remember somebody sayin' somethin' one time. Give me a call. We'll be here awhile, as she's puttin' up my tomatoes for me."

She put down the receiver. "She'll call me back when she gets in, and if there's anything to know, she'll know it."

After that statement, Violet didn't say anything for so long that Bailey realized that she was planning to sit there and do nothing but smoke her joint while Bailey put up what looked to be about twenty quarts of tomatoes. And if the woman hadn't called back by the time she'd finished, Bailey was willing to bet that there were green beans and strawberries to be canned as well.

"All right," Bailey said with a sigh, "tell me about the Golden Six." She'd grown up in a small town, so she well knew that each and every town had some great tragedy attached to it, and the residents loved to tell the story over and over. Maybe she should be glad that Jimmie hadn't left her a farm in Fall River, Massachusetts. If he had, she'd never find anyone who could get past Lizzie Borden.

Violet took a long, deep drag on her joint and let it out as slowly as she could. Since she'd obviously had a lot of experience in this, Bailey had time to peel six tomatoes while she was waiting. "It's hard to believe this now, but years ago, Calburn was a thriving little town. It had a couple of industries, lots of shops, and it even had its own high school. But in 1952 the high school caught on fire, and the top floor burned out. The fire department said the bottom three floors were safe, but the top couldn't be used. Since the top floor was where the seniors had their classes, the whole class had to be bused off to somewhere else."

Behind her, Bailey looked at the woman. From the rote, practiced way she was telling this story, Bailey was sure she'd told it hundreds of times.

Violet paused to take another long, slow drag. "This was all way before my time, of course, but I've been told that there was a lot a hoopla over where the seniors would be sent. No school within fifty miles wanted all of them, so the kids were divided up and sent to four different schools in the area. But whoever did the dividing did a poor job of it, because of the twenty kids sent to Wells Creek High School, only six of them were boys and the rest girls."

"The Golden Six," Bailey said as she walked to the stove and began to remove hot, sterile jars.

"Yeah, the Golden Six."

Bailey didn't know if it was memory or the marijuana, but Violet's eyes had a dreamy, faraway look to them. "They were golden, all right. They were magnificent boys. Less than a month after they got to the high school, they saved the whole student body from being blown up by a bomb."

"In this area? In the fifties?"

"Honey, don't let the accents fool you. People here in Virginia love and hate just like the rest of the world—and they always have. Now we just hear about what goes on in the world more. That summer someone had blown up two warehouses near Calburn, so everyone was a bit nervous. Then, one Monday morning, black smoke started pouring through the high school, and the kids and teachers all panicked. It was chaos! Who knows what would have happened if the six boys from Calburn hadn't stepped in and quietly and calmly ushered everyone to safety? That the bomb turned out to be a dud doesn't have anything to do with it. Those boys didn't know that, and neither did anybody else!" There was anger in her voice, as well as defiance, as though she were having to defend what she was saying.

When Violet looked up and saw Bailey staring at her, she said defensively, "You can read any newspaper in Virginia from the next day, and you'll see the story of those boys. They were heroes. For a while there was talk of their bein' given a medal by the president, but nothin' came of it."

"So why was Opal at the beauty salon so angry?"

"Parlor," Violet said, smiling. "It's a beauty *parlor*.

You already look like a foreigner, but you don't have to sound like one."

Bailey started packing tomatoes into the sterile jars. Since modern tomatoes have a low acid content, they had to be handled carefully, so she'd have to leave them in the water bath a long time to remove all danger of botulism.

"Opal's just like the rest of us. She's mad about T. L. Spangler. Ever hear of her?"

"I don't think so. Should I have?"

"Unless you've been livin' out of the country for the last five years, yes, you should know her name."

Bailey didn't comment on that statement. As a matter of fact, she'd been living all over the world for the last sixteen years.

"Does Congresswoman Theresa Spangler ring any bells?"

"Actually, no."

"Where have you—" Violet cut herself off. "Okay, no questions about you. But I warn you that the people of Calburn will find out everything, so you might as well confess now." She left a bit of time for Bailey to speak, but when she was silent, Violet gave a sigh, then continued.

"Congresswoman Spangler is from Wells Creek, Virginia, the next town over, the town where the six boys were sent to school. She was a year behind the graduating class of the Golden Six. Nobody knows what happened—and one heck of a lot a people have asked her— but she got her nose so put out of joint that year that after she graduated from her highfalutin college, she decided to do a hatchet job on the boys. She came back here to Calburn and asked ever'body lots of questions.

Ever'body thought she was gonna write a book on how great the boys were, so they told her ever'thing they could remember. But she wasn't writin' somethin' nice; hell, she wasn't even writin' the truth. She cut those poor boys to ribbons. She said that ever'thing they ever did was a myth, that they were nobodies and nothing. She even said that she believed that one of the boys had set the bomb in the school so they could fake bein' heroes."

For a moment Bailey paused with the tongs in her hand and looked at Violet. This had all happened many years before, yet she seemed to be as angry as though it had happened last week.

"So what happened after the book was published?" Bailey asked.

"Horror, that's what. Not long after the book came out, one of the boys shot his wife, then himself. His *pregnant* wife. Another one got on a bus and never came back. And the others were never the same again. It was horrible, what that woman did to them. They'd already had their share of tragedy, I can tell you that."

Bailey went back to the sink to pick up a tomato while Violet closed her eyes and dragged on her joint. Now is the time, Bailey thought. Her hands were trembling so much that she had to hold on to the sink. Every family seemed to have one unbreakable taboo, and with her and Jimmie, what she wanted to say now, say out loud, was their biggest secret.

Bailey took a deep breath and let it out slowly. "Did you ever know a boy in Calburn, born in the late fifties, who had a cleft lip?" There, she thought. It was out.

Violet didn't so much as open her eyes. "A harelip? Not that I remember, but then I wasn't here then. I only moved here in 1970."

Bailey wanted to kick herself. She'd just revealed her biggest secret needlessly.

"Of course, his lip would have been fixed right after he was born, wouldn't it?" Violet said. Then, before Bailey could reply, the telephone rang.

Violet nodded that the call was from her friend, then stayed on the telephone for quite a while. There was a great deal of personal talk, with Violet asking how the woman's children were, and listening for several minutes. When she at last got around to asking about the old Hanley place, Bailey listened as hard as she could, trying to hear what was said, but mostly Violet said, "Yes," and, "I see." A couple of times she glanced up at Bailey, who turned back to the tomatoes and pretended she wasn't listening.

At last Violet came to the end of the conversation, and was about to hang up when she said, "Did you ever know a kid in Calburn who had a harelip? He'd be about your age."

Bailey held her breath while she listened, but all Violet said was, " 'Bye, and let me know how Katy's recital goes."

Slowly, Violet put down the phone, then leaned back on her chair. Bailey knew the woman was waiting for her to ask what her friend had said, but she would die before she did.

"You're not gonna like it," Violet said at last.

"Try me."

"My friend told me a story I'd never heard before, but as I said, I didn't grow up here. In fact, my friend didn't hear of it until she was an adult." Violet hesitated. "You don't know how to fry chicken, do you?"

Blackmail, Bailey thought. This woman was blackmailing her in return for information. With a grimace, Bailey went to the old refrigerator—how many years had it been since they stopped making round corners?—and opened it. Inside, the freezer compartment was a solid block of frost; the flimsy door had been forced off long ago. On the shelves below were half a dozen plastic containers filled with fuzzy, gray-green substances; the stench was overpowering. With her breath held, cautiously, Bailey reached inside, grabbed a wet plastic bag that contained something looking vaguely like a chicken, and quickly shut the refrigerator door. Inside the bag was a poorly plucked chicken, head and feet still attached. She was not only going to have to cook it, but also remove the pin feathers, then cut it up. "So, tell me, Violet," she said without any animosity in her voice, "are you the laziest person on earth, or are there other contenders?"

"Ain't met anybody who can go up against me yet," Violet said cheerfully as she reached for another joint.

Bailey rummaged in the pantry until she found some potatoes that weren't rotten and a canister of flour. There were some cans of food also in the pantry, and she carried them into the kitchen and plunked them down on the table in front of Violet. "I take it that calories aren't a concern of yours," she said, and Violet snorted in answer. "All right. One lunch for information. What did your friend tell you about my farm?"

"Her great-aunt told her the story, and the aunt said that nobody knew all of it. The farm was owned by a woman nobody in town liked. She had a couple of kids—" Violet halted when Bailey looked at her sharply. "No, none of the woman's kids had a harelip, nor anybody else that my friend remembered did either. Besides, I think all this at your farm happened a long time ago, too long ago for the dates you want, so those kids had nothin' to do with the man you're lookin' for." She paused for a moment, smiling smugly at having figured out so much from the little Bailey had told her.

"But anyway, the woman went off for a while and came back married to a man from outside. My friend said she thought he was named Guthrie or something like that. I like a little more pepper on my chicken than that," she said as Bailey put salt and pepper in the flour to coat the chicken.

"Go on," Bailey said as she shook more pepper on the chicken.

"My friend—her name is Gladys, by the way—well, Gladys said that the man was a big, hulking giant and kinda simpleminded. She said that when the woman— Gladys couldn't remember her name—bought the farm, it was a run-down old place, and since the woman had a job in town, it stayed that way for years. But after she got married, her husband brought it back to life. You'll like this: Gladys said that her aunt told her that the man used to make jams and pickles. She said the general store in Calburn used to sell them."

For a moment Violet drew on her joint and watched Bailey as she fried the chicken in hot Crisco, then put sliced potatoes in another big cast-iron skillet to fry.

"So what's the part that I'm not going to like?" Bailey asked.

"Gladys said that she didn't remember all the details, but her aunt told her that the wife started having an affair with some man where she worked. And when she told her husband she was divorcing him and he had to get off her farm, the poor guy went out into the barn and hanged himself."

Bailey paused with her tongs aloft. "*My* barn?"

"That's the one. Told you you wouldn't like it."

For a few minutes Bailey moved the chicken about in the hot oil and thought about that poor man. She'd sensed that someone who truly loved the farm had lived there before her. Through marriage, the man had found a beautiful place where he could grow the things he loved. He'd even been able to sell what he made. But then he'd heard that it was all going to be taken from him by his adulterous wife. And if he was simpleminded, he could never hope to earn enough to buy his own farm. It *was* an awful story, she thought.

When Bailey was silent, Violet said, "You shouldn't take it so hard. All these old places have stories to them. A couple of years before my husband bought this place, the old man that owned it dropped a chain saw on his foot. Cut it clean off."

"But suicide . . . ," Bailey said softly as she walked to the counter by the sink and checked the seals on the quart jars of tomatoes. All but two of the lids had popped down, showing that they'd sealed.

"It happens. And, as I said, it was a long time ago. Who knows? Maybe he was sick, or somethin' like that. We never know what's in a person's heart."

"So what happened after that?" Bailey asked as she walked back to the stove to check on the chicken.

Violet chuckled. "Gladys said that after the woman's husband killed himself, she packed up her kids and left town. Gladys said that her aunt hinted that the man she was plannin' to marry already had a wife, so maybe he told the woman he wasn't gonna marry her after all. Or maybe he was freaked out about the suicide. Who knows?"

"Did she sell the farm?"

"I asked Gladys that, but she didn't know," Violet said. "Gladys said that the house has been empty all her life, but then so has a lot of Calburn."

"This town is empty, isn't it?" Bailey said. She was pulling open drawers to find paper towels to drain the chicken on, but there was nothing. Half of the many drawers were filled with empty bread wrappers, some of them quite old. Could bread wrappers reach antique status? she wondered. In the pantry, she found some paper napkins printed, "Happy birthday, Chuckie," so she took them back to the kitchen. "Are you keeping these for sentimental reasons?" she asked.

"If gettin' somethin' free is sentimental, then yeah."

Bailey washed a chipped dinner plate, covered it with the napkins, then put the chicken and fried potatoes on it to drain.

"Why *is* half of Calburn empty?" Bailey asked as she put creamed corn and peas—found in cans in the pantry—fried potatoes, and fried chicken on a plate and handed it to Violet.

"You're welcome to join me," she said, motioning to the empty chair across the table from her.

Bailey looked down at the food and knew that if she started eating it, she'd never stop. What was it about the food you had as a child that was so viscerally appealing? But she also knew the calorie content of such a meal. "No thanks," she said as she sat down on the chair. "Tell me about Calburn."

"Simple," Violet said, her mouth full of chicken. "New highway. It was a toss-up whether the highway was gonna go through Wells Creek or here. I think somebody paid somebody off, and Calburn lost. A year

after the highway was finished, Calburn was nearly a
ghost town, while Wells Creek got rich. You should
drive over there and see the place. It has"—she wiggled
her eyebrows in disdain—"boutiques. Fancy places that
carry little soaps shaped like hearts. And shops that
carry clothes that cost more than I make in a year. They
even changed the name of the town, give it the la-di-da
name of Welborn. Isn't that cute?"

"Welborn?" Bailey asked thoughtfully.

"Sure. Like in Australia except without the *e*."

"I think I've heard of that place. Isn't there something there? Something that brings tourists?"

Violet stuffed her mouth full of peas and corn. "Mot
mings," she said.

"What?"

She swallowed. "They have some hot springs over
there, but—"

"Yes! Of course," Bailey said. "Welborn Hot Springs.
Lots of people go there. I heard that it was a divine
place. I wanted to go, but Jimmie . . ." She trailed off.

"He your dead husband?"

Bailey nodded. Jimmie had refused to go to the hot
springs in Virginia that some of the people they knew
had sworn by. Lady something or other had said the
springs had completely cured her arthritis. Bailey had
hoped that a few days of lying about in hot water would
help Jimmie relax, but he wouldn't hear of it. The fact
that he wouldn't go was so unusual that Bailey had asked
him why. His face had turned dark for a moment; then
he'd laughed and said that if she wanted hot springs, he'd
take her to Germany or somewhere exotic. "But not to
the backwoods of rural Virginia," he'd said as he picked
her up and twirled her about, then nuzzled her neck

and succeeded in making her stop asking questions.

"You in there?" Violet asked.

"Oh, sorry," Bailey said. "I was just remembering something. Look, I need to go. I have to—"

"Fix that big, good-lookin' Matt Longacre dinner. You two sleepin' together yet?"

"Every minute we can get," Bailey said as she stood up. "We're regular rabbits."

Violet cackled with laughter, then leaned back on her chair and looked at the many quarts of tomatoes that Bailey had put up, and at the chicken and vegetables she'd prepared. "You come back any time you want to know anything."

"And next time I'll bring a sous-chef," Bailey said, making Violet laugh some more.

"Wait a minute," Violet said as she heaved herself up from the table. "You've been such a good sport, I have somethin' to give you."

"No marijuana!" Bailey said instantly.

" 'Fraid it'll loosen you up so you *do* start rollin' around with that hunk that's movin' in with you?" Violet asked as she held out a battered paperback book.

"I'm more afraid of jail sentences," Bailey said as she took the book and looked at it. *The Golden Six,* by T. L. Spangler, it said on the cover. "Were they glorious young men or were they instigators of a great hoax?" the copy read. "You decide."

"Take it and read it," Violet said, her eyes twinkling. "Maybe it'll give you somethin' to do when you're in bed alone at night." She shook her head. "Your generation are fools. In my day we—"

"Didn't have AIDS or herpes, or morals, as far as I can tell," Bailey said pleasantly.

Violet didn't take offense. "That Matt Longacre could make a nun forget her vows."

"I'll consider that before I take mine," Bailey said as she pushed open the door. She was smiling at Violet's laughter, but then she saw that Violet had an odd look on her face. "Is something wrong?" she asked as she wiped her hand across her cheek. "Do I have flour on my face?"

"No," Violet said, "no flour. I just thought for a moment that I'd seen you before. Probably the grass. You go home and take care of that man."

Smiling, Bailey left the house. Outside, she looked up at the shade trees. Violet Honeycutt was lazy, manipulative, could be taken away to prison at any second, and was quite rude at times, but Bailey felt as though she'd made a friend.

In the car, she tossed the book onto the passenger seat and started the engine. It was three P.M., she hadn't had lunch, and she had yet to buy anything to make for dinner for Matt tonight. Maybe she should stop by that nice Mr. Shelby's farm and see what he had for sale besides pigeons and rabbits. It had been his sign, "Rabits 4 Sale," that had made her stop at his roadside stand instead of the many others along the highway. If she remembered correctly, she'd seen some collard greens growing in the back.

Eight

❧

Matt parked his truck under a shade tree next to Bailey's Toyota, and for a moment he leaned his head back against the seat and closed his eyes. It was after eight in the evening, and he was exhausted. He wasn't used to doing construction. He'd had too many years sitting at a desk looking at a computer screen or at a drawing board. His visits to the work sites had been quick and nonstrenuous.

But, to be fair to himself, today he'd really pushed it. He'd driven his two nephews until they were threatening mutiny. But Matt had wanted to finish the job to have the weekend free, so he'd done three days' work in one. The fact that his brother and nephews had helped him move into Bailey's house during their lunch break didn't lessen his fatigue.

Of course it hadn't helped that Patsy had called him

six times today on his cell phone. By the fifth call, he was ready to smash the thing. "This better be good, Patricia," he'd said as he stood up on the roof and took the call.

"She's spent the entire day with that horrible old Violet Honeycutt," Patsy announced.

"Bailey—if that's who you mean—couldn't have spent the *entire* day there, because you've already told me that she spent the *morning* with the gossipmonger of Calburn, Opal. So which is it?"

"You know exactly what I mean, Matthew Longacre, so don't get smart with me. And are you seeing that my boys wear their shirts and that they have on sunblock?"

Matt glanced down at the ground. His big nephews had on no shirts, and right now they were drinking water out of plastic cups and letting the water pour down their sun-bronzed, muscular chests. They'd seen "some dude" do this on TV, and the girls had gone crazy. So now there were half a dozen teenage girls in the neighbor's yard across the street, studiously pretending that they weren't looking at Joe and John pouring water all over themselves.

"Yeah," Matt said into the phone. "I coat your babies down with sunscreen every forty-five minutes. Patsy, I have work to do. I don't have time to listen to everything that my landlady does."

"Oh? Then I guess you don't want to know that after she left that Violet Honeycutt's house, she visited Adam Tillman's house."

"She did what?" Matt yelled so loud that his nephews stopped pouring water down the front of their chests. Actually, he was so loud that the girls across the street stopped not looking at the boys and turned to stare at Matt on the roof.

"No, she didn't," Patsy said sweetly. "But she could have. I tell you, Matt, you better not let this one get away. So, are you two coming over on Saturday?"

"Patsy," Matt said slowly and with exaggerated patience. "I hardly know the woman. For all I know, she has friends in this area. Maybe she's going to spend the weekend with other people."

"Then that means you better step on it and get her locked up. Oh! The oven timer went off. I gotta go."

Matt flipped the phone shut and counted to ten, then shouted down at his nephews to get back to work. Yelling helped to alleviate some of his anger, but not much. Damn Patsy and her meddling anyway! Hadn't he already pushed Bailey as much as he could and as fast as he could? He'd just met her yesterday, and this afternoon he'd moved into her house.

But even that hadn't been fast enough for his sister-in-law. "She won't last long," Patsy had said at lunch as she helped toss Matt's belongings into boxes. "She won't stay in Calburn long. She'll get bored and get out of here. You have to do everything you can *now*."

"If I'm out of your house, what does it matter to you who I get involved with?" Matt had snapped at her.

At that Patsy had thrown up her hands as though to say that she'd never met a dumber man in her life. "You tell him, Rick," Patsy said. "I can't talk to him."

Rick said, "Well, uh, Patsy thinks, I mean, we all feel that—" He broke off and turned to his wife. "You're so much better at explaining things than I am, honey." Behind her back, he looked at his brother and shrugged his shoulders. He had no idea why she was pushing Matt so hard.

Patsy took on a tone that said she couldn't believe Matt couldn't see the obvious. "Because, Matt, dearest brother-in-law of mine, whoever you are 'involved with,' as you call it, becomes part of our family. We have Christmases and Thanksgivings together. Weddings. Funerals." She narrowed her eyes at him. "Look what you did *last time*."

"Right," Matt said. "I see what you mean." His former wife had not participated in any family affairs. For the most part, he'd been isolated from his brother's family for all the years he was married. If he did see them, he saw them alone. One meeting between Patsy and Cassandra had been enough for both women.

"This one is *nice*," Patsy said, letting him know, yet again, what she thought of his ex-wife. "Opal likes her a lot. She even gave Opal and that daughter of hers some jam, and you should taste it!"

"She can cook," Matt said, and there was reverence in his voice. "She can cook."

Later, as Matt and Rick were on the stairs carrying boxes down to Matt's pickup, Rick whispered, "The widow didn't go bananas about Patsy and Janice."

Matt nodded. After the one and only time that Cassandra had met his sister-in-law, she'd said, "Do you expect me to pretend that there is only one person in the room when there are two of them? That's absurd. I won't be visiting your relatives again." And that had been that. Nothing Matt ever said budged her.

When Matt got out of his truck and went into Bailey's house, he was amazed at how disappointed he was that she didn't come out to greet him. "Hello? Anybody home?" he called, feeling a bit odd to be entering without knocking. This afternoon, when they'd moved Matt's few belongings into the house, he'd known that she wasn't there. Patsy and her chain of informants had told him of Bailey's whereabouts every minute of the day.

The house smelled great, warm with cooking, but when he went into the kitchen, she wasn't there. There was a note on the refrigerator, "Dinner's in the oven."

It was the first time he'd seen her handwriting, and he liked it: easy to read, on the small side, neat and tidy. Like she is, he thought, smiling.

"Bailey?" he called, then thought, Maybe she wants me to call her something else. He went down the hall, and when he saw that her bedroom door was ajar, he pushed it open farther. "Bailey?" he called softly. No answer, and the open bathroom door showed that that room was also empty.

Did she go out? he wondered. Did she make him dinner according to their agreement, then leave him to eat alone?

Matt decided that the next time he saw Patsy, he was going to wring her neck. She was making him believe there was something between him and "the widow" that there wasn't, and making him believe that if he thought there was ever going to be anything between them, then he had to act instantly.

Shaking his head to clear it, Matt went back to the kitchen and opened the oven door. Inside was a big plate and a bowl, both covered with foil. Slowly, he took the plate out of the oven, then peeled back the foil. There were four filets of fish, each lightly breaded and sautéed; a red sauce was under the fish, and when he tasted it, it was spicy-hot. Beside the fish was a big pile of what

looked to be old-fashioned greens, the kind that they
didn't sell in stores and that he hadn't eaten since he was
a child. Beside it was a square of something that looked
like onions. They were. Caramelized onions.

Lord! but the woman could cook!

He was halfway through the plate when he again
began to wonder where she was. On impulse, he opened
the door to the big pantry off the kitchen, then drew in
his breath. Yesterday the room had been empty, but
tonight there were many jars on the shelves, all filled
and labeled. Stepping inside, he ran his hand along
them. On the shelf under the window was a big glass
jar filled with cherries, looking as though they'd just
been picked and swimming in a clear liquid. "Cherry
Cordial," the label said in her neat lettering. On the
shelves against the wall were jars filled with a dark liquid and labeled "Blackberry Liqueur." There were jars of
carrots surrounded by whole spices and a rich-looking
liquid. "Jam," "Conserves," "Green Tomato Chutney,"
he read.

Matt backed out of the pantry, unable to comprehend
what he was seeing. It was Pioneer Woman meets Julia
Child.

In the kitchen again, he finished his plate of food,
then removed the bowl from the oven and took off the
foil. It was bread pudding, one of his favorite things in
the world. There were fat raisins in the bread, and a
warm, custardy sauce floated on top. He took one bite
and thought he might swoon, then laughed at himself
for thinking of the old-fashioned word. Would he have
to be revived with cherry cordial?

With his bowl full of pudding in his hand, he pushed
open the screen door and went outside. It was early in

the year yet, but soon it was going to get hot. He looked up at the mulberry tree. "Know where she is?" he asked, then smiled when a breeze blew the leaves and they seemed to point down the path. Looking through shrubs and low-hanging tree branches, Matt could see a bit of yellow near the fishpond. Bailey's shirt.

"Thank you," Matt said, smiling up at the old tree as he followed the twists and turns of the stone path down, and there was Bailey, bent over an empty raised bed. She was planting some little green things she pulled from a bunch.

For a moment he didn't say anything, just stood behind her and watched her work. She was a very desirable woman. Very. But not in the way that most people would think of as "desirable." There was something about her that made him feel good. She wasn't the kind of woman that would make a man go wild with lust. No, she was the kind of woman that made a man think of quiet evenings in front of a fireplace. She made him think of coming home from work and telling her everything that had happened. She made him think of . . . well, of kids and catching fireflies in jars, and of grabbing her and them and rolling down the hill on the grass.

Matt had never liked to tell anyone his innermost feelings, so he couldn't tell Patsy that he had to go slow with this woman, because this woman was too important to make a wrong move with.

"Dinner was delicious," he said softly, and was pleased to see that the unexpected sound of his voice didn't make her jump.

"Glad you liked it," she said. "You probably know that Mr. Shelby raises catfish in a big tank in back of his house."

Matt sat down on the grass not far from her and noted that somebody was going to need to mow the big lawn and the patches of grass here and there. He thought he'd better do some research on lawn mowers. "I can't say that anyone around here knows much about Shelby. The shotgun tends to keep people away." He noticed that she started to say something, but didn't, then turned back to her planting. "What are you planting?"

"Strawberries. I got the sets from Mr. Shelby. Everbearing over there and June-bearing in this bed."

"What's the difference?" he asked.

She didn't look up. "Take a guess."

Matt laughed. "Let's see, those bear strawberries all season, and those just produce berries in June. So how'd I do, Teach?"

"Perfect." She moved on to the next row. "And before you ask, canners want all the berries to be ripe at once, so we can make great vats of preserves."

"So where'd you learn to make all that—" He waved his hand in the general direction of the house.

"As a kid. My grandmother canned out of necessity, and I do it because I like to."

He waited for her to say more, but when she didn't, he sat there and watched her. He didn't know her very well, but she seemed to be thinking hard about something. "Did Violet tell you something that upset you?"

Bailey sat back on her heels and wiped mud off her hands. "I guess I'll have to get used to small-town ways again. So everyone knows that I went to see Violet Honeycutt?"

"I'm sure they do. But I take it you weren't there to buy grass, although her stuff is good. The best I've ever—I mean, I've heard—" He gave her a crooked smile and filled his mouth with the last bite of the pudding.

Smiling, Bailey moved to another place, bent forward, and began planting again. "Did you know that a man hanged himself in my barn?"

"Yes," Matt said softly. "It's not going to spook you, is it?" And make you move away, he wanted to add but didn't.

"No," she said, "but I keep thinking about that poor, unhappy man. I know how he feels. He loved the soil and what it produces. But then to have it taken away from him . . ." She paused. "Poor man."

"Yeah, there's been lots of tragedy in Calburn."

"Oh, yes, I got an earful of your Calburn Six."

"Golden Six," Matt corrected automatically.

"There!" Bailey said, turning quickly to look at him. "There it is again."

"What?" he asked. "There what is again?"

"That tone of voice. Have those boys been canonized? At the hairdresser's—no, it's the beauty parlor, I've been told—I thought Opal was going to accuse me of heresy for not knowing about the *Golden* Six. Were those boys *that* important?"

Matt almost said, To me they were, but he didn't. "People in Calburn have become suspicious. They're afraid of what outsiders will say about the town. That book, *The Golden Six,* hurt Calburn. It didn't sell well, but it got some attention from the critics when it came out, and for a while Calburn had some tourists here asking questions."

"It seems sad that anyone would write about such tragedy."

"Yes and no," he said. "I guess it depends on how you look at all of it. In Calburn, people tend to think that they were six magnificent young men, but their luck changed."

"And the other side of it is?"

"That it was all a hoax made up by some imaginative boys. Whatever the truth, for a while, everything they touched seemed to turn to gold, but after graduation, it seems that their luck ran out. Or maybe their luck was attached to Calburn."

"But I thought they all lived here."

"Some did; some went away. But they were all in Calburn in the summer of 1968 when Frank killed his wife and then himself."

"Do people know why he did such a thing?"

"More or less. He'd been in a car wreck four years before and lost the use of his right arm. For about three years afterward, he was out of work, but finally he got a job as a night security guard and seemed to be doing all right, but . . ."

"Violet said his wife was pregnant."

"Yes. The autopsy showed that she was. Everyone guessed from that that maybe it wasn't Frank's child. He was a proud man, so maybe he didn't want the humiliation."

"So he shot her, then himself."

He didn't answer her redundant question. Instead, he looked at her. "Why are you so interested?"

"I'm not. I mean, that sounds callous, but I wasn't interested in them at all. Actually, I was asking Violet about this farm, about who owned it, that sort of thing. Opal sent me to Violet, and I was told about the Golden Six."

"Opal hates Violet. She wouldn't have sent you to her," he said.

"Right. Sorry. Her daughter Carla told me. Or rather wrote me a note. Why does Opal hate Violet?"

Now that they were on a different subject, Matt relaxed again and leaned back on his arms. "Violet didn't always look like she does now."

"So?"

"Take a guess."

"Ah. The great equalizer: sex."

When she said the word, Matt was pleased to see that, for the first time, she looked at him—looked at him as a woman looks at a man. He guessed she liked what she saw, because her cheeks turned a bit pink. The light was fading, but he saw her blush, then look back at her strawberries.

"Why do you want to know about the farm?" he asked.

He listened while she told him the story Patsy had already told him, that her husband had died and left her the farm. But as he listened to the words, he listened harder to her tone of voice. When she said, "my husband," she didn't sound as though she were talking about a man who was dead. She was talking about a man she seemed to expect to walk down the path at any minute.

"May I confide in you?" she asked, turning to look at him in the deepening twilight. "You won't—" she began, but his expression stopped her from asking if he'd tell the whole town.

For a moment he hesitated, and it occurred to him that she was sitting on one very big secret and that she was considering how much she could tell him. He could have reassured her, but he didn't. He wanted her to make up her own mind.

"I want to know about my husband," she said at last. "I was married to him for years, and I thought I knew him, but he was always silent about his childhood. It was something missing between us. Yet after he died, I was told that he left me this." She gestured at the farm. "It doesn't make sense to me. Why did he refuse to tell me anything when he was alive, but then give me this place and leave me a note asking me to find out 'what really happened'? If he wanted me to know about him, why didn't he sit down with me and talk about it while he was alive?" For a moment she looked down at her hands, then back up at him. "It's so strange to have been so close to a man, then find out that we weren't close at all. In the weeks after his death, nothing showed up about this place, not a photo, a piece of paper, nothing."

He watched as she tried to get her emotions under control—and as he tried to control his own. He disliked himself for it, but he was jealous of this dead husband of hers.

"How much do you know about computers?" he asked, then saw that he'd startled her.

"About as much as you know about strawberries."

"Nothing about the Internet?"

"Well, actually," she said, smiling, "Jimmie's lawyer's wife showed me how to order things over the Internet."

Matt groaned. "Come on, help me up, and we'll go upstairs and set up my computer and see what we can find out about this place."

"Find out?" she asked, her eyes wide.

"Yeah. Let's see who owns the title to this farm."

"But—" she began, then stepped away from him.

"All right," he said, still sitting and looking up at her. "Let's get one thing straight between us. I may have been born and raised in a small town, but I don't tell everything to everyone." He raised his right hand. "I swear to you that what we find out will stay between us. I don't care if we find out that you're Lizzie Borden's granddaughter.

"What?" he said when she began to laugh.

"It's nothing. It's just a thought I had today."

"So tell me and share the laughter."

She took a moment as she seemed to decide, then she told him about being glad her husband hadn't left her a farm in Lizzie Borden's hometown. "Those high school boys are bad enough, but can you imagine Lizzie Borden?"

Matt was having difficulty with the Golden Six being reduced to "those high school boys," but when he recovered himself, he smiled. And then, for the first time in his life, he laughed about something that had to do with "those high school boys." "All right," he said, "are we in agreement?"

"Meaning, do I trust you not to tell Patsy or Janice anything you may find out about me?"

"About you or your former husband?" he asked, teasing.

"Both," she said. "We're the same."

Matt took a moment to digest that statement. "I swear it on all I hold sacred," he said at last.

"And what if Patsy asks you point-blank?"

"I will lie point-blank," he answered. "And it won't be the first time. Now, are you going to keep asking me questions, or are we going to start searching? Hey!" he said as she slapped his forehead.

"Mosquito," she said, but her eyes were laughing. "Come on, let's go."

He made an attempt to get up, but there was a pain in his leg. Groaning, he sat back down.

"Are you injured?" she asked, concerned.

"It's a wonder I'm not dead. One of my idiot nephews helped a girl get a cat out of a tree today."

"And?" Bailey asked.

Matt looked up at her. "He used a ladder to do it."

"And?" she asked impatiently.

"It was *my* ladder. I was on the roof of the garage— and the cat was in a tree three blocks away."

"You aren't telling me that one of your nephews knew you were on the roof, but he took your ladder and left you stranded, are you?"

"He *said* he thought I was in my truck, but I think he was getting me back about the water."

When Matt made a second failed attempt to get up, Bailey reached out her hand. He took it, then made a great show of standing up.

"You might have to help me walk," he said.

"Here, I have a hoe, you can lean on that," she said quickly.

"Spoilsport," he said, laughing and limping as he walked behind her toward the house.

Bailey had her hands full of gardening tools. Turning around, she began to walk backward. "What did you do with the water?"

"Took it away from them," he said as he put his hand on his lower back and hobbled.

"You're not going to tell me this story unless I beg, are you?"

"Begging . . . Hmm, not a bad idea."

"You know what I found that had been left in this house?" she asked. "A recipe box."

"Yeah?" Matt asked, interested but wishing she'd wanted to hear his story.

"Yes," Bailey said. "It was full of recipes I'd like to try, things like chicken-fried steak, fried chicken coated with cornflakes, spaghetti sauce made out of Campbell's tomato soup, and something called 'surprise meat loaf.' "

The last item made the hairs on the back of Matt's neck stand straight up. "You win!" he said quickly. "I took my nephews' drinking water away from them because they were spilling it all down the front of themselves." He could see that she didn't understand—and he hadn't meant for her to understand. They had reached the house, and she had her hand on the door.

"Spilled their drinks?" she asked, puzzled. "You mean, like a child?"

"Here, let me demonstrate," he said as he reached over her head to open the door. "Wait right here and try to remember how you felt when you were sixteen or seventeen." He went into the house, got the tallest water glass he could find, then filled it at the sink. He knew that what he was about to do was shameless, but, well, all's fair, etc. He unbuttoned his shirt, took it off, and dropped it on the corner of the kitchen counter. On one hand, he hated the backbreaking labor of construction, but on the other hand, what climbing ladders and lifting concrete blocks had done to his body was something he did like. He flipped the switch that turned on the light over the back door, then stepped outside.

He pretended he didn't see her eyes widen at the sight of his bare chest as he raised the glass to his lips. "The girls were across the street, and my nephews were bare-chested and drinking. Like this," he said, then he let the cool water dribble down his chest, all while running his free hand over his chest slowly. "See?" he said when the water was gone. *"That's* what I had to put up with all day today."

"I see," she said in a way that made him feel foolish. "You know," she said, "I was up late last night, so I think I'll pass on your offer of helping to set up the computer. In fact—" She gave a jaw-cracking yawn. "Oh, sorry. In fact, I think I'll turn in right now."

With that, she went inside the house, and Matt was left outside, shirtless, with the front of his pants wet and at least eight mosquitoes stabbing him between the shoulder blades. He wasn't quite sure what he'd done wrong, but it was something.

With a sigh, he went into the house, turned off the porch light, then made sure all the doors were locked. It was too early to go to bed, so he picked up his shirt and buttoned it as he went upstairs to the attic. With any luck, he could get a search service to find out who had bought the house from the widow of the man who'd hanged himself. Maybe if he found out that for her, it would get him back into her good graces.

Nine

Bailey didn't sleep very well that night. She kept having dreams of seeing Matthew Longacre standing in the yellow light of the outside lamp, water cascading down his bare chest. Why hadn't she acted like a modern woman and taken him up on what he was obviously offering? She was a widow; he was unmarried. They were two mature adults. What was *wrong* with her that she'd acted like a prim and proper old maid, feigned fatigue, and gone running into her bedroom? Alone.

She got out of bed slowly. The house had a feel about it that said Matt was either asleep or not inside. "Probably ran off to a honky-tonk and got himself a *real* woman," she muttered, then smiled at sounding so country-and-western.

She showered, dressed, and did the best she could with her hair. She was used to hairdressers who did it for her, but then coiffed hair didn't seem very important in Calburn.

She opened her bedroom door so it didn't creak, then tiptoed toward the kitchen, but as she reached the bottom of the stairs up to the attic, she went up to have a look. Matt's computer equipment was no longer in boxes, the components of his desk no longer in pieces. The desk had been reassembled in the corner of the room, and on top of it was a big white computer screen, with various other pieces of equipment to one side.

Feeling as though she was prying, she tiptoed to the desk and looked at it. On a purple pad was a mouse, but it had no cord to it. Guess he didn't hook it up after all, she thought as she lifted the mouse and idly rolled the ball on the bottom of it. Then, to her disbelief, the computer started making noise and sprang to life. "What have I done now?" she said under her breath.

"Nothing. It was just on sleep mode," Matt said from behind her.

Bailey put her hand to her chest in fright. "You startled me."

"I guess gardening relaxes you, but computers make you nervous."

"I didn't think it was hooked up, but it came on."

"It's a cordless mouse, and when you touched it, the computer came back into active mode," he said, but he just stood there, not moving toward her or the machine.

It took Bailey a moment to realize that he was waiting for her to step away from the computer. Obviously, he wasn't going to get too near her. And no wonder, with the way she'd rebuffed him last night!

"About last night," she began slowly, looking down at her hands. "I—"

"I owe you an apology," he said. "Sometimes my humor can get a little crude."

"No!" Bailey said quickly. "It's me who was at fault. It's just that—" She took a deep breath. "You can't go from sixteen years of faithfulness to what seems like adultery in just a few weeks. At least, I don't seem able to."

"You don't have to explain anything to me. I know what it's like to lose people. You name a method, and I've lost someone that way, and however you lose them, it's hard on the survivor." He smiled at her. "I have a proposition."

His words made Bailey feel better. Although she'd met other people in Calburn, Matt was the closest she had to a friend. "The last one of your propositions took over my house," she said, returning his smile.

Matt grinned at her, and the awkwardness between them vanished. "Okay, you're right, but this time my proposition is that we lighten up. You make jokes, I make jokes, and we stay friends. No pressure to be more. Deal?" He held out his hand for her to shake.

Instantly, she took his hand in hers, gave a firm shake, then released her grip. "It's a deal. Now, about the attic. I don't remember agreeing to your taking over the whole thing."

"You want me to show you how to log on to the Internet?"

"Matthew, you're not listening to me."

"No, I'm listening, but I'm ignoring you. There's a difference," he said, his eyes fastened onto the screen.

"I was planning to use the attic space for my business."

"And what business is that?"

"I'm going to . . . Well, I haven't really figured that out yet. Not all of it, anyway." She squared her shoulders and tried to take the hesitancy out of her voice. "But when I *do* decide, I'll need the attic."

"You'll need a computer, too, so you can use mine." He was moving the mouse around on the pad and clicking it.

"But what if you're using the computer when I need it?"

"I have a laptop, and besides, I thought you didn't know how to use a computer."

"I don't, but I can learn."

"Before or after you decide what you're going to do to earn a living?"

"Before. No, after. No, I mean . . ." She looked at him. "Do you have any idea what I could do to support myself—besides starting a canning factory, that is? I have no training of any kind, no education to speak of, and I'm sure I'd never be good at working for anyone. I've had too many years of independence. Any ideas?"

"I think that whatever you do should have something to do with food. Ever thought of writing cookbooks?"

"Now *there's* an idea," she said. "How long has it been since you've been inside a bookstore? There are thousands of cookbooks out there. I need something to do on a regular basis."

Matt stood up from the computer, put his hands on Bailey's shoulders, and looked into her eyes. "You have recently been widowed after a long-term marriage. Give yourself some time. You need to heal a bit first, then you can make big decisions about what to do with your life."

His words made sense to her, and for a moment she

had to work hard not to lean her head against his shoulder and let him hold her. "I guess you're right."

"You know what I thought we'd do today?"

Some part of her thought she should protest that "we," but she couldn't do it. She didn't want to spend the day alone. She didn't want to stay in the ugly house by herself and look up at every sound and think it was Jimmie coming home. "What?" she asked, and her mind filled with what he could possibly suggest. Something romantic? Sexy?

"Buy a lawn mower." Matt looked puzzled when Bailey laughed. "You don't think you need a lawn mower?"

"Of course I do. It's just that—" She waved her hand in dismissal. "Never mind. How about breakfast, then we go buy a lawn mower?"

"Sounds good to me," Matt said as he turned back to look at the computer screen.

At the head of the stairs, Bailey paused to look back at him. He was a nice man, she thought. He was a good man, kind and thoughtful. And he was easy to live with. Smiling, she went downstairs and pulled out a bag of buckwheat flour to start making pancakes.

❧❧

"May I help you?" the salesman asked. He was young and dressed in a white shirt and khaki trousers, looking as though he meant to make manager by the time he was twenty-five.

"I want a push mower," Bailey said at the same moment that Matt said, "We want a riding mower."

"There isn't enough lawn to justify a riding mower," Bailey said quickly, looking at Matt.

"It's the repetition that makes a riding mower needed," he said patiently. "And there's some heavy cutting that needs to be done in the back."

"Then get a weed whacker with a saw attachment," Bailey shot at him. She hadn't spent years around professional gardeners and learned nothing.

"You need a whacker too, but—"

"Too?! How much do you plan on cutting?"

"The farm is ten acres, and—"

"And half of it is trees!"

"Excuse me," the clerk said loudly, interrupting them. "Could I suggest a lighter riding mower?"

Both Bailey and Matt glared at him.

The young man put up his hands in front of his face as though to ward off blows. "I would never get between a husband and a wife. If you two need help, call me—or a divorce lawyer," he added as he walked off.

Looking at each other, Bailey and Matt began to laugh.

"Okay, sorry," Matt said. "It's your farm, so you decide."

He was so nice that he was making her feel guilty. "It's not that I don't want a riding mower, it's just that I can't afford one."

"How about if I buy it?"

Bailey stiffened. "I don't want you buying things for me. I was supported by a man before, and that's my problem now."

"How about this?" Matt asked. "Why don't you hire me to do the work, and I'll use my own equipment?"

"How much do you charge?" she said quickly.

"A lot."

She narrowed her eyes at him. "How much?"

"You have to get my sister-in-law off my back."

"What are you up to?"

Matt gave her a crooked grin. "Patsy's big on family. She has these family get-togethers, and she . . ." He trailed off.

"She what?"

"She's going to skin me alive if I don't take you with me when I go."

For a moment Bailey considered what he was saying. He was, of course, making it up about his "charge." What he was really doing was offering to pay for the lawn mower and do the work for free. "In other circumstances I wouldn't agree, but since Opal told me you were paying Patsy seven-fifty for rent and me only six hundred, I figure you owe me."

Matt laughed, unembarrassed at being caught. "Opal didn't hear that from me. Janice does my books, so she's probably the one who told Opal."

"Whatever. When I think of the way you acted as though I was overcharging you, I could—"

Bending, he kissed her cheek. "You're cute when you're angry," he said as the clerk approached them.

"I'll get you back for this," Bailey said under her breath.

With his back to the clerk, Matt winked at her.

"You two lovebirds decide yet?" the young man asked.

"Yeah, that one," Matt said as he pointed to a behemoth of a lawn mower. It looked like something used to cut the north forty.

"Good choice," the young man said. "That's the one *I* would want."

"You and *all* the boys," Bailey said in disgust as she looked away. Only Matt heard her.

"And we'll need some hand tools too," Matt said, turning to Bailey, unperturbed by her sarcasm. "Come on, honey, let's get some loppers."

An hour later they were in Matt's pickup truck. The back was loaded with the oversize tractor lawn mower and one of every shovel, rake, digging fork, and garden cutting tool the store carried. After the first two shovels, Bailey had quit protesting.

When they were out of the parking lot, Bailey said, "You said Janice does your books?"

"Such as they are. When I ran a business, I had an accountant, but now Janice does the work. Not that Janice isn't as good as an accountant. She did the books for all four of her husband's car dealerships, until Scott decided that he shouldn't work with his wife. Between you and me, I think he didn't want his wife knowing everything he had."

Bailey didn't know how to comment on this information. Besides, she was more interested in Matt than in Janice. "Is your move back to Calburn permanent? Or are you just licking your wounds after the divorce, and in a few months you'll go back to being a big-city architect?"

Matt was quiet for a moment, turning on his blinkers and checking his mirrors before making a left turn. "The truth is that I don't know. But I don't want to spend the rest of my life driving nails, I can tell you that."

"So what do you want to do?"

"Domestic architecture. Personal dwellings. It's what I've always liked."

"So why did you work on skyscrapers?"

"More money in it."

"Ah, right. Money. That ever-important commodity.

Jimmie used to say that if you work for money, then you'll never have any."

"Spoken like every poor man."

Bailey said nothing to that, but she turned her head away and smiled.

"So what's *that* about?"

"What is what about?" she asked, turning back to look at him.

"That smug little smile. Did I just make a fool of myself in your eyes?"

"It's just that Jimmie wasn't poor."

"Oh? Then why'd he leave you broke?"

"He—" Bailey shook her head. "I don't know. I can figure out some of the reasons why he did what he did, but why did he leave me *this* place in *this* town? I always had the idea that Jimmie hated his childhood, and that's why he refused to speak of it. But if he hated his childhood, why leave me his childhood home? If it is his home. I don't even know that it is." She looked out the side window and willed herself to calm down.

"Last night," Matt said softly, "I got my computer hooked up, plugged it into a phone line, and got the Net up and working. I paid thirty-five bucks for a property search on your house. I should get some info on Monday."

Bailey didn't know whether to laugh or cry. If it came onscreen as belonging to James Manville, no matter how Matt planned to keep the knowledge a secret, it would get out. And would he change toward her when he found out?

"Bailey?"

"Yes?"

"Patsy's planned a little get-together this afternoon, and . . ."

"I'm invited?"

"You're the guest of honor."

"You mean, they're going to ask me thousands of questions about every aspect of my life?"

"Probably. Plus they'll, well, try to marry you off to me. Matchmaking is the major occupation of my sister-in-law."

"For everyone or just you?"

"Me, mainly. I think she's afraid I'll move back into her house unless some woman takes pity on me and marries me."

"What in the world did you do to offend her that she's so anxious to get rid of you?"

"My sister-in-law lives to sew. She has a room upstairs set up with a sewing machine and a big table to cut out her patterns. Sewing is her claim to fame in this area. Whenever there's money to be raised, it's Patsy they ask to supervise the sewing committees."

"And?" Bailey asked.

"For the last six months my bed has been in her sewing room," he said softly.

"Oh, my."

"Yes. Exactly."

"So. Is Patsy paying the rent at my house, or are you?"

"Very funny," Matt said, but he was smiling as he pulled into Patsy's driveway.

Just as he said, Bailey was the guest of honor—and all his immediate family was there waiting for them. There was Janice and her husband, Scott, who Bailey hadn't met, and who Bailey discovered she didn't like very much. He was what Jimmie used to call a "deal man": he was always, constantly, trying to make a deal about something. As Bailey shook his hand, she was very glad that he didn't know she'd been married to a billionaire, because she was sure that Scott would be trying to sell her something. As it was, three minutes after they met, Scott was trying to get her to sell her Toyota and buy a Kia from him.

Matt put his arm around Bailey's shoulders and led her away. "Don't listen to a thing Scott says. If he gets too much for you, I'll deal with him."

Bailey adored Janice's two young daughters, Chantal, seven, and Desiree, four. But she felt sorry for them because they were dressed in pink cotton pinafores that had been ironed. Both girls ate their hot dogs as though they were terrified of getting their dresses dirty.

Patsy's family seemed to be as informal as Janice's was formal. Her big, handsome twin sons seemed to be terminally bored, and they tended to fall asleep every time they sat down.

"Matthew works them to death," Patsy said when she saw Bailey looking at the boys sprawled on a quilt in the shade of a tree, sound asleep. In sleep they looked so young and innocent—rather like six-foot-tall toddlers.

Rick snorted. "They were up all night playing video games, and on the phone to half the girls in the county," he said. "Their laziness has nothing to do with work."

"Richard Longacre!" Patsy began and, smiling, Bailey walked away.

Contrary to what Matt had said, they didn't ask Bailey a lot of questions. Instead, they seemed to want to tell her their stories, and they wanted to watch her with Matt. Twice that day everyone stopped talking and looked at her and Matt. The first time was when Matt stuck a crinkled potato chip in some cream-cheese-based dip, then held it out to Bailey. "Try this," he said.

The four adults sitting at the picnic table fell instantly silent and watched with undisguised interest. Even the boys under the trees opened an eye each. The two little girls stopped swinging and looked at what had made the adults go quiet.

Self-consciously, Bailey bit the potato chip and chewed. Then everyone went back to what they had been doing, but she felt that she'd pleased them all. And, truthfully, it felt good to have pleased them. She was beginning to feel as though she belonged with them, as though she were part of them.

In the late afternoon, Matt leaned over and whispered, "Why don't you ask Patsy for a tour of her sewing room? She'd love to show it off."

So Bailey asked Patsy, and she saw Patsy's face light up before she led the way into her house. Silently, Janice followed them.

All day, surreptitiously, Bailey had watched the dynamic between the two women, who looked so much alike, yet dressed so differently. Patsy wore baggy old cotton shorts and a huge T-shirt that probably belonged to her husband. Janice wore dark brown shorts that had a sharp crease down the center of each leg, an alligator belt with a silver buckle, and a crisp brown-and-green-plaid blouse. Her hair was as perfectly arranged as Patsy's was messy. But under the clothes, the similarity between the women was very strong.

"How are they related?" she'd whispered earlier to Matt as he flipped hamburger patties on the grill.

"Their mothers were identical twins," he said. "But one sister married rich and the other poor. Guess which one was which?"

"Janice grew up poor," Bailey said instantly. Her own mother had been like Janice, so afraid the poverty would show on her that she overcompensated. No one ever saw Freida Bailey less than made-up and dressed perfectly.

"Pretty smart, aren't you?" Matt said, smiling at her.

"Smart enough to know that if you don't take those burgers off there now, they'll be charred."

He kissed her on the nose—and that was the second time everyone halted in midair for a count of three before resuming their activity.

Bailey did what she could to pretend that she hadn't noticed their movements freeze, but she had to turn away to hide her blush. "Would you *stop* it?!" she hissed at Matt. "They're going to think you and I are more than just housemates."

"Couldn't have that, now could we?" Matt said, and she could tell that he liked the idea of people thinking they were . . . well, more.

When Matt had called out that the burgers were ready, Bailey had stood back, sipping the awful, made-from-a-mix lemonade that Patsy served, and watched all of them. She watched the way Patsy and Janice worked together but never actually spoke to each other or made eye contact. They sat next to each other at the picnic table, but never spoke. Part of Bailey wanted to ask what had caused the split between them, but she was afraid she'd hear that they'd had a fight over a Barbie doll when they were nine and vowed never again to speak to each other. And, too, it was more interesting not knowing the cause.

Since everyone seemed used to the situation, it was obviously a long-standing feud. Janice's youngest daughter, Desiree, was the funniest about it. Bailey heard her say, "Mommie, you look so lonely standing there all alone," when Janice was six inches away from Patsy. Then the child turned big blue eyes to her aunt Patsy and said, "You look so lonely, Aunt Patsy. Don't you wish someone was *with* you?" Bailey had to turn away to keep from laughing out loud at the impishness of the child.

By the time Matt suggested that Bailey ask Patsy to see her sewing room, Bailey wasn't surprised when Janice followed them.

When she and Matt had pulled up in front of the house, she'd been impressed. The house was large and fairly new—no more than five years old, at a guess. It was what she would call "contemporary country," with a deep, old-fashioned porch set across the length of the house, but the upper story had a tall, round-topped dormer flanked on each side by two square dormers. It was a very pleasant blend of old and new.

They entered the house through the back door, and once inside, Patsy halted and stood there in silence. Bailey wasn't sure what she was supposed to do.

Janice solved the problem. "You'll probably want to see Rick's house," she said. "Or maybe I should call it Matt's house."

It took a moment for Bailey to understand. "Matt designed this house?"

"Yes, he did," Patsy said proudly. "Would you like me to show you what he did?"

Bailey understood that Patsy didn't think it was polite to brag on her own house, but she could brag on Matt's design. It was a nice house, Bailey thought as she followed behind Patsy and Janice. As though they were a well-rehearsed duet, the two women split into different directions. Patsy showed her a room, then Janice would call, and Bailey would go to her.

On one side of the ground floor was a big, open area that was living room, dining room, and kitchen with a built-in table and upholstered bench. Although no walls separated the spaces, Matt had managed to divide them in other ways. Over both the dining room and the living room, half the ceiling opened up all the way to the ceiling of the floor above. Partitions set off the ends of the kitchen from the living areas.

All in all, the house had a cozy feeling, open but separate. She said the good things she thought, but kept the fact that she truly hated the kitchen to herself. It had the sink and refrigerator against the back wall, an island with an electric cooktop in it, then, on the other side of the island, another island with four stools. To go from the sink to where the food was served at the bar, a person would have to walk around the cooktop island. It was a kitchen that made the cook walk many extra steps. On the other hand, from the look of the shiny surfaces, the kitchen wasn't used much, so maybe inefficiency didn't matter.

The other half of the ground floor was a master suite with his-and-hers walk-in closets and a home office. When Patsy showed off the bathroom, she said, "Have you ever seen a bigger bathroom in your life?"

Bailey had politely said that the room was beautiful, ignoring the piercing look Janice gave her. The truth was that Jimmie had a fetish about bathrooms: to him they couldn't be big enough or ornate enough. One of his houses had a bathtub the size of a small swimming pool. The shower could have been used to bathe an elephant, and there were two rooms within the bathroom that held toilets and bidets.

What was remarkable to Bailey was that everywhere in Patsy's house were home-sewn items. Bailey had never been interested in sewing, but since her preserving had kept her around local and state fairs as a kid, she'd picked up some knowledge. In the living room, the couch, the two chairs, and the curtains were all made of the same blue-and-green-flowered chintz, and a blinding array of other items were covered in the same fabric. There was a big pine armoire that Bailey guessed probably held a TV and a stereo. The panels on the doors had been removed, and gathered fabric inserted. The bookshelves beside the TV had covers on each shelf, all of them chintz, but piped in different colors—blue on one shelf, green above it, then blue, then green. The wastebasket had a cover on it. The side tables were covered; the lamp shade had been covered in the same fabric. Wherever there was a surface, a doily, a mat, a slipcover—something—had been made for it.

Every room Bailey saw was filled with homemade covers and curtains. The bedroom was upholstered in combinations of blue and burgundy, but again, every surface had been covered. Upstairs was the same. Patsy briefly opened the door to the big bedroom her sons shared, and Bailey had a quick glimpse of curtains, bedspreads, and pillowcases that had to have taken bolts of the blue fabric printed with airplanes. If she didn't know differently, Bailey would have thought that Patsy's sons were nine years old.

Across the hall, past a bathroom enveloped in handmade covers, was Patsy's sewing room, its walls covered with pink paper printed with rows of rosebuds. A worktable occupied the middle of the room; a sewing machine stood against a wall, with shelves full of boxes labeled with fabric swatches. The room and the work materials were all perfectly organized.

"And here are my patterns, and I keep the extra buttons from every garment my family owns in here, each labeled by size, color, and materials."

Bailey hoped she was looking appropriately impressed. She didn't want to blurt out, "Why?!" On the wall to her right were photographs of people, and to distract herself, Bailey turned and looked at them. There were five framed photos, each one a group shot, and in each Patsy was standing at the edge, wearing a white three-quarter-length coat that had a badge pinned to the pocket. "What's this?" Bailey asked.

"Just the factory over in Ridgeway. Would you like to see my sewing machine needles?"

"Patsy," Bailey said firmly, "were you the boss of all these people?"

"Yeah. But that was a long time ago," Patsy said in dismissal. "I want to show you my thread cabinet."

Reluctantly, Bailey pulled herself away from the photos and turned to look at the hundreds of different colors of spools of thread lined up on dowel rods on the back of a cabinet door. After a moment, she glanced up and felt Janice staring at her. When their eyes met, Janice seemed to be saying something to her, but then her eyes flickered and she looked away.

After a while, Janice said quietly, "We better go join the men."

When they were downstairs, Rick said that Matt couldn't stop bragging about Bailey's cooking. "So when are we invited over?" Rick asked. For the third time that day, they all froze in motion and looked at Bailey.

"How about next Saturday?" Matt said as he put his arm around Bailey's shoulders. "That okay with you, hon?"

"Sure," Bailey said, then slipped out from under Matt's arm. "Next Saturday is fine." When Bailey looked up, she saw that both Janice and Patsy were staring at her with identical gazes of such intensity that she shivered. They looked away, though, when her eyes met theirs.

Ten

Bailey looked at the clock on her bedside table. It was two A.M., and she hadn't gone to sleep yet. She should have fallen into bed at ten and gone to sleep instantly. After all, it had been a long day. She and Matt had left Patsy's house at four, and when they got home, Matt suggested that they start tearing out the walls between the exterior and the living room and begin to restore what had once been the porch.

"You mean I get to tear out that pink bathroom?" Bailey had asked.

Matt took a short crowbar from his toolbox and handed it to her. "Be my guest."

When she walked into the pink bathroom and looked at the tiles, the wallpaper, and the fixtures, she didn't know where to start.

"Leave the plumbing alone," Matt called to her from

the other room. "Wait until I can turn off the water. Start with the tiles. Or pull the wallpaper off."

"Okay," Bailey said as she put her wrecking bar under a flowered pink tile and pulled back. She had to duck as the tile went sailing across the room.

"You okay?" Matt asked from the doorway.

"Great," she said. "I'm doing great."

They had spent three hours working. Bailey would have gone on, but Matt called a halt and suggested they order in pizza.

"You mean the kind with the soggy crusts?" Bailey asked. "Do you think we should order one with pineapple on it or one with four varieties of meat? Which?"

Matt laughed. "So what do you have in mind?"

"How about some pasta and salad? In Calabria they—" Turning away, she didn't finish her sentence.

"Have you traveled a lot?"

"Some," Bailey said, then turned back to look at him. "Maybe we *should* get pizza. Maybe we should . . . Why are you looking at me like that?"

"Whenever you're ready to talk, let me know. I can be a good listener."

Bailey had been tempted by his offer, and thought about confiding in him about some things. Her secrets were beginning to feel heavy to her. Instead, she'd turned away and said she wanted to take a shower before she started cooking, but when she'd finished and gone back to the kitchen, Matt was upstairs doing something on his computer, so the moment was lost.

As she'd often done in the past, instead of pouring her heart out, she went to the kitchen. She quickly boiled some broccoli, removed it from the pot, then cooked pasta shells in the same water so the pasta would absorb some of the vitamins lost in the cooking of the broccoli—and also to give the pasta added flavor. This was a trick she'd learned from a woman she'd met in Calabria. While the pasta cooked, she sautéed garlic, anchovies, pine nuts, and crushed red pepper. When everything was done, she piled it high onto a big platter, sprinkled pecorino cheese on top, added a salad, some grilled peppers in three colors, and carried all of it outside to serve picnic-style.

During dinner, they'd talked about what the house had once been like, and what changes could be made.

After dinner, Matt had sat there looking at her expectantly. Bailey put her fingertips to her temples. "I'm reading your thoughts," she said. "Yes, yes, they're coming through clearly. You're thinking . . . do I have this right? . . . dessert. *'Where is dessert?'* " She opened her eyes. "So how'd I do?"

"Perfect," he said, smiling, but the look of expectation had not left his face.

"Dessert is in the kitchen. It's in bags and boxes labeled 'cinnamon' and 'nutmeg' and 'brown sugar.' "

Matt gave her a very serious look. "May I lick the bowl?"

Bailey laughed as she stood up. "You get cleanup detail while I make you the best oatmeal cake you ever tasted."

"Oatmeal?" Matt said suspiciously. "This isn't good for me, is it?"

"Not when it's topped with homemade ice cream, it isn't," she said as she opened the back door.

"Homemade?" Matt whispered as he began gathering dirty dishes.

Forty minutes later, Matt had a big bowl full of

warm-from-the-oven, spicy oatmeal cake topped with smooth, heavy-with-cream, jasmine-scented ice cream. With the first three bites, he'd pretended that he was about to faint from ecstasy, and, laughing, Bailey had grabbed his arm to keep him from falling.

In the deepening twilight, they'd strolled along the stone paths and talked about what could be done to the garden.

In a way, the evening had been quite impersonal, but at the same time, it had been very personal. Their shared laughter and the intimacy of talking about what "we" plan to do and what "we" need was somehow more private than if they'd spent the evening talking about lovemaking. Or, Bailey thought, if they'd spent hours making those idiot double entendres that moviemakers and bad writers seemed to find so sexy.

When Bailey finally said she was going to bed, there was a moment of awkwardness, but Matt had yawned and said that he too was done in. He's making things easier for me, Bailey thought as, a few minutes later, she got into her nightgown and climbed into bed.

But sleep hadn't come to her. Instead, her mind had filled with the thoughts of the first time she and Jimmie had gone to southern Italy, the first time they'd seen the ancient, walled city of Badolato. And the more she thought of Jimmie, the more restless she became. After a couple of hours of tossing about, she got up, pulled on her clothes, tiptoed into the kitchen, removed a flashlight from a drawer, and went outside.

Later, when the sky was growing light from the approaching dawn, she wasn't surprised to look up and see Matt standing over her, wearing just a pair of jeans and a T-shirt, his feet bare. He was looking down at her with worry on his face. She was on her hands and knees, weeding the strawberry patch, only half of the "weeds" in her pile were young strawberry plants. When she looked up at Matt, she wasn't surprised to realize that her face was covered with tears.

He didn't say a word, just dropped to his knees and pulled her into his arms.

She clung to him as his arms tightened about her, and the tears increased. She hadn't cried since she'd come to Calburn. She'd thought of Jimmie constantly— everything reminded her of him—but she'd held her tears in.

"I miss him," she said, her face buried in Matt's strong shoulder. "I miss him every minute of every day. I miss the closeness, and the sex. I miss talking to him. Oh, God! We used to talk so much. He ran problems past me, about business, about whether he should buy something or not. And I . . . I lived for him. He was my whole life."

"I know," Matt said, holding her, rocking her. "I know."

"I married him when I was seventeen, and he was all I ever knew. He saved me. I was so unhappy, so unloved, but he took me away. If I hadn't met him, I don't know what would have happened to me."

Matt didn't make any comment but just held her tightly, stroking her hair and rocking her.

"Why did he die? I don't understand *why*. I needed him so much. Why did he have to go away and leave me so very *alone?*"

"Sssssh," Matt said, soothing her. "You're not alone. You're with me. I'm here."

Bailey couldn't seem to stop crying. "He was the

most wonderful man, so full of life. Jimmie could do *anything*. He could accomplish anything." Her hands seemed to make claws as she clutched at Matt. His shoulder was wet, but she kept crying.

Turning, he sat down on the ground and pulled her onto his lap, cradling her to him as she cried.

"I more than miss him," she whispered. "Without Jimmie I don't seem to know what to *do* with myself. Jimmie never had an indecisive moment in his life, but I . . . I . . ." She trailed off and for a moment Matt held her in silence.

"Ssssh, baby," he said. "Quiet now."

The sun was beginning to come up, and Bailey was starting to feel better. Yes, she thought, sniffing, it was as though something inside her had been released. It was as though something heavy had been taken from her.

And, suddenly, she was keenly aware that she was sitting on Matthew Longacre's lap, and they were alone. Not that it was an unpleasant feeling, but she didn't want what this could possibly lead to. Not yet. Right now, she felt as though Jimmie's spirit was too close, as though he were hovering over her. But at the same time, she couldn't come up with a reason for moving away from Matt's comfort and warmth.

"Maybe you should learn how to—" Matt began.

Bailey pushed herself out of his arms. "Don't you even *think* of telling me that I should learn how to live for myself," she said. "Show me a person who lives for himself, and I'll show you a narcissistic personality disorder."

Matt laughed. "I know, and you're right. My ex-wife lived for herself and no one else, and I can tell you that she was as narcissistic as they come."

Bailey looked at him expectantly, waiting for more of

the story. But in the next moment a cold drop of rain hit her on the nose, and she got off Matt's lap.

"Let's go inside," he said as he stood up, "and I'll tell you all the most intimate details of my past. It'll take your mind off your own troubles."

"I see. You're hungry, aren't you?"

"Famished."

"And you're willing to bare your soul to pay for your food?"

"Sure am."

Bailey took a step toward the house, then turned to look back at him. "How many other people have you told this story?"

"No one on earth. And I can tell you that Patsy has done everything to get me to tell her why I married Cassandra."

Nodding, smiling, Bailey turned back and walked toward the house, Matt behind her. Twenty minutes later, he was seated at the kitchen table. Before him was a strawberry and mascarpone cheese muffin, and Bailey was mixing the batter to make a Dutch baby—a big, baked pancake that would be filled with blackberries and sliced nectarines, then sprinkled with confectioner's sugar.

"It's time to pay the piper," she said. She knew she should feel embarrassed about what had just passed between them, but she didn't. Instead, she felt better than she had since the night Jimmie died. In fact, the colors in the room, ugly as it was, seemed brighter than they had before. Her big silver range seemed to gleam as bright as a star. "Story," she said. "Tell me your story."

Matt didn't attempt to hide his pleasure at her asking.

"Have you ever wanted something that you knew was no good for you but you couldn't keep from taking it?"

"Yes," Bailey answered instantly. "Chocolate."

Matt smiled. "No, I mean, something bigger, more—"

"How about a basket the size of the one Moses floated in filled with Godiva chocolate? Raspberry creams. Caramels. Truffles. And you've been on a flavorless thousand-calorie-a-day diet for four weeks and three days, and you're so weak your head spins every time you stand up, then, suddenly, there's that chocolate, all that heavenly, rich, creamy chocolate. You could bathe in it, coat yourself in it. You could bite into it and watch it run down your arm, then lick it off. Is that the kind of wanting you mean?"

When she finished, Matt's eyes were wide, his mouth open. "You know, I don't think I wanted Cassandra that much."

Smiling, Bailey lifted her spoon from the custard and held it out to him. "Taste this."

As Matt tasted the creamy substance, he closed his eyes. "How?" he whispered.

"I used a whole vanilla bean. Makes the taste stronger. Enough of that. Now tell me your story."

"Okay, where was I?" He gave the spoon another lick. "I'd just graduated from school with a design in architecture. Top of my class."

"I'm impressed."

"And said to impress you. But don't be," Matt said. "Maybe if I hadn't been given so many awards and offered so many great jobs, I wouldn't have been so full of myself. And if I hadn't had so many offers, I wouldn't have been so disdainful of them, so I might have taken one in St. Louis or Minneapolis. I would have worked in an office and learned something. But I didn't take one of those jobs, and I didn't learn anything—not anything about architecture, anyway. No, I wanted to set the world on fire with my designs for personal houses, domestic architecture. No office buildings for Matthew Longacre. In the end, I took a job with a very rich man, old money, generations of it, on Long Island. I was to build a jewel box of a house for his only child, his daughter Cassandra, who was marrying Carter Haverford Norcott the Third the following spring. I had the idea that if I made a truly beautiful house for him, and it was seen at a huge, rich wedding, I'd get more commissions, then more and more."

"But you ran off with the bride instead."

Matt took a while to answer. "The irony is that I didn't really want her. In fact, I never really saw her. It was that life I wanted. My . . ." He hesitated. "My mother came from a family like that one. When she ran off with my father, her family disinherited her. Years later, even after my father left her and my mother was waitressing and taking on any job she could get to support her two kids, she—" Matt looked away, and Bailey could see the anger on his face.

"She had class," Bailey said.

"Yes. My mother had class."

Bailey watched him as he picked up his spoon and turned it about in his hands. "And you wanted that class back."

"Yes, I did."

Bailey sat down across from him, a mug of tea in her hand, and picked up a slice of whole wheat toast from the stack on the table. The bread was plain, not buttered. "So when did you meet the daughter, Cassandra?"

"On the third day I was there. She hit me with a tennis ball, and I fell into a fishpond."

Bailey drank three cups of tea while she listened to Matt's story, and she filled his cup four times. She sliced strawberries and bananas, poured cream over them, and pushed the bowl toward Matt while he talked.

She listened to his words, but she also listened to the intensity of what he said. He's a man who feels things deeply, she thought. He was trying to make light of what had been years of his life, but his white knuckles on his coffee mug handle and the little white line at the left corner of his mouth betrayed him.

He was telling how a tall, slim, blonde, patrician beauty wearing a set of tennis whites had snubbed him. She'd been having words on the tennis court with her overbred fiancé, Carter Haverford Norcott the Third, when she'd slammed the tennis ball into the back of the head of the architect for their new house, knocking Matt off balance and into a fishpond.

"If she hadn't been arguing with Carter," Matt said, "I doubt if any of what happened would have taken place. But there I was, sitting in a fishpond, all of twenty-five years old, wearing a wet T-shirt, and I made skinny little Carter jealous."

Matt said that he saw something in Cassandra's eyes that day, something that appealed to "way down deep inside me," he said. "Years later I decided I'd imagined it all, but for a second, I thought I saw a spark in her eye that said—"

"Please rescue me," Bailey said.

"Yes! How did—"

"Been there, done that. So she was being married off to a man of her own class, a skinny little wimp, and she saw a big gorgeous hunk like you sitting in a fishpond in a wet T-shirt, and her eyes begged you to rescue her."

Smiling, Matt leaned back against his chair, puffing out his chest a bit at her having called him "a big gorgeous hunk." "That's what I thought she was saying. But in the next moment, she looked down her nose and said, 'He doesn't matter in the least. He'll probably steal the fish and eat them for lunch.' "

"What a nasty thing to say."

"After I got to know her, I found out that that was the kind of thing Cassandra said when she thought she was being amusing. I'm not sure how she came to believe that she was funny, since no one ever laughed at what she said, and heaven knows *she* never laughed at anything, but if you asked Cassandra, she'd tell you that she had a marvelous sense of humor."

"What did you do?" Bailey asked, picking up a strawberry and eating it.

Matt ran his hand over his face as though to clear his thoughts. "We're our own worst enemies, you know that? Nothing anybody else can do to us is as bad as what we do to ourselves. When I graduated from school, I pursued the job with Cassandra's father with everything I had. He wanted one of my professors to design his daughter's house, but I flooded him with my own designs and ideas and talked my way into the job. And that's what I did with Cassandra. I went after her."

Bailey ate more strawberries as Matt told his extraordinary story of how he had pursued Miss Cassandra Beaumont. Bailey paused a couple of times with a strawberry on the way to her mouth as Matt told of his escapades. Like something in a fairy tale, he'd climbed up a rose trellis and entered her bedroom. Then, like a bad TV comedy, he'd hidden under her bed when the maid entered.

"She must have been overwhelmed," Bailey said. "She—"

"She was fascinated with me. She looked at me like an anthropologist would look at an undiscovered tribe of natives, and she thought everything I did was strange. She'd sit there and coolly blink at me with her big blue eyes, fascinated, but not involved."

"So let me guess. The cooler she was, the harder you tried."

"You *have* heard this story before," Matt said, making Bailey smile.

"So how did you get her to agree to marry you?"

For a moment, Matt looked down at his hands, then back up at Bailey. "Truthfully, I think she did it to make herself more interesting in her own social set. To me, raised by a single mother, dirt-poor, Cassandra was an exotic creature, but to her own set, she was as ordinary and as bland as skimmed milk. I think she imagined that a six-week marriage to me would make her the center of attention when she returned to her daddy and the Hunt Club."

"And what about you? What happened after you were married?" Bailey asked softly.

"Nothing. We had nothing in common. I vainly thought that once I got her alone with me, she'd loosen up. You know, fire beneath the ice, that sort of thing." Matt gave Bailey a one-sided grin. "But by the end of two weeks, even the bed passion was gone. The truth is, I saw the depth of my mistake the morning after the elopement. I woke up, rolled over to her, and said, 'Good morning, Cassie,' and she said, 'Don't call me that. It's so common-sounding.' "

Matt took a couple of deep breaths before he spoke again. "She genuinely couldn't understand that I couldn't afford to send her to a riding stable or even buy her a membership in a country club. And her father knew what I'd done. He said, 'You wanted her so much, so now she's yours.' " Matt looked away for a moment, then smiled at Bailey. "This is hard to admit to a woman I . . . I like as much as I like you, but the truth is, I think I had some pretty mercenary reasons for going after Cassandra. When I look back on it, I think I was prepared to play the insulted hero and say that I loved his daughter and not his money. But I also envisioned myself eventually accepting, say, a house—of my design, of course—and a few manicured acres from her father as a wedding gift. And he'd tell his rich friends, 'Let my son-in-law design your house in Barbados. He's family, but he's also the best there is.' But—" Matt smiled. "But he was a wily old man, and all I got from him was a handshake. Not so much as a toaster."

Matt laughed, and now that he'd confessed to Bailey, he seemed to relax.

"Truthfully, I think Cassandra's parents were dying to get rid of her. They'd given her everything she'd ever dreamed of having, and as a result, they'd created a beautiful monster. She seemed to have love and money mixed up. I think that instead of time and attention, her parents had bought her things, so when I married her, she expected me to buy things for her too. It's what I was to do if I really loved her, that's what she used to say, and no amount of showing her my bank balance made her understand."

"So why didn't you divorce her right away?"

"Pride," Matt said. "I'd bragged to every man I knew

that I was going to get her. And I'll go to my grave seeing the smirk on her father's face when Cassandra told him we were married. That look made me push to achieve, to make more and more money, because money was the only way I could stand up to my illustrious father-in-law.

"I—" Matt paused for a moment. "I hadn't been consciously aware of it, but all the time I'd been pursuing Cassandra, I'd imagined myself with her at her father's dining table. You see—" Matt looked at Bailey and gave her a smile of irony. "Because of my mother's background, I knew certain things, like which fork is for oysters, and which knife is for fish, that sort of thing. I had this fantasy running through my head that her father would say—" Matt smiled. "I don't know how I could have been this naive, but I imagined her father saying something like, 'I thought my daughter had married beneath her, but now I see that you're one of us.' "

Bailey knew he meant for her to smile, but she couldn't. She'd too often been on the receiving end of being snubbed. Jimmie treated garbagemen and kings all the same—and because they were all after his money, they didn't dare snub him. But Bailey had often caught them looking down their noses at her. Why did a man like Jimmie Manville have a dumpy little wife like Lillian?

"But you know what happened?" Matt asked. "The night we went to their house to inform them we'd eloped, they were at dinner—no accident on my part—and I looked behind the old man, and there was Carter sitting at the dining table. He was in; I was out; nothing had changed."

"But weren't they even upset that their only child had eloped?"

Matt shrugged. "I couldn't tell that they were. When I look back on it, I think they thought we'd be divorced in a few weeks, then everyone could pretend it had never happened. I was as temporary as a shadow to them."

"But you wanted to prove them wrong," Bailey said.

"More or less. I think I wanted to prove to myself that I hadn't been a complete and total fool. And if I couldn't beat them at class, I'd try to beat them at work. I started calling companies I'd turned down for jobs, and I asked. And if that didn't work, I begged."

He went on to tell how he'd worked for years, nonstop, just to make money. He'd had no home life, nothing but work. But he'd been able to give Cassandra her country club, her big house, her life of ease, while he got the bills and the stress.

"So what made you finally come to your senses and divorce her?"

"I had a heart attack," Matt said, smiling. "At least that's what I thought it was. At the hospital they told me it was just indigestion and to go home and stop wasting their time. But it'd been enough of a scare to make me want a second chance at life. I went home in the early afternoon, something I *never* did, and—"

"And what?"

"Cassandra was in the hot tub, naked. With Carter. I stood there looking at the two of them together, and all I could think was, I paid for that tub, but I've never had time to get into it. And it was then that I started laughing. I was so relieved. Now I could get rid of her without guilt. I said, 'Isn't this where we began?' then Carter said, 'Listen, Longacre—'

" 'No, please, don't get up,' I told him. 'Continue what you were doing. Be my guest.' Then, as I turned around and walked out, behind me, I heard Cassandra say, 'Don't worry. He'll be back. He adores me.' And that's when I was really and truly *free*."

Matt told Bailey how he quit his high-powered architectural firm, sold everything he owned, paid off his considerable debts, gave his ex-wife half of what was left, then returned to Calburn.

"And now what?" she asked softly.

"Now I want to find out who I am. It's taken some soul-searching, but I realized that part of why I was drawn to Cassandra was the sense of family. I was raised without a father during a time when living in a single-parent household made my brother and me objects of pity."

"And now that you're here?" Bailey asked softly.

"I'm not sure, but I'm beginning to get some ideas," he said, his eyes locked with hers.

For the second time in one day, Bailey didn't know why she pulled back, but she did. "How about another slice of Dutch baby?" she said as she got up from the table. What is wrong with me? she wondered. Why don't I take what this beautiful man is offering? Or is it that Jimmie will always stand in my way?

"So what do you want to do today?" Matt asked. "It's Sunday, no work, so what's your pleasure?"

"Fly over to India and see the Taj again," Bailey said, trying to make a joke, but Matt didn't laugh. Instead, he just looked at her, and Bailey turned her face away. "I want to work on the porch more," she said. "And I want to get this kitchen into decent shape."

"Can do," Matt said, but he was still looking at her hard.

Eleven

SIX WEEKS LATER

Bailey moved the salad around in the big wooden bowl and frowned at it. Not that it wasn't good. It had mandarin orange segments from a can, and hard little slivered almonds, but the lettuce was fresh. Her drink was iced tea with a squirt of bottled raspberry juice added. All in all, it wasn't a bad lunch, but she wasn't interested in it.

Instead, she kept looking at the real estate brochure on the table beside her. "That place sold two days ago," the realtor told her when she'd inquired an hour ago.

She was sitting alone in a booth in a cute little restaurant in Welborn, having a late lunch by herself and trying to figure out what was wrong with her. Jimmie used to say, "You're restless again, aren't you, Frecks?" then he'd sweep her away to somewhere wonderful. But now Jimmie was gone, and there was no money to go sweeping away to anywhere.

She looked again at the brochure. Actually, it was just a single piece of paper, but it had a nice color photo of the shop that was three doors down from this restaurant. It wasn't a big shop or especially impressive, but she and Janice and Patsy had liked the place. In fact, they'd liked it very much. So what had happened? she wondered, picking up the paper and looking at it.

Five and a half weeks ago, Patsy had called Bailey and said she had to go to Welborn, would Bailey like to go with her? Since it was a weekday and Matt was out working, and since Bailey had already filled her entire pantry with bottles and jars of homemade preserves, pickles, and cordials, she had nothing whatsoever else to do. Even her search into Jimmie's past had been halted. Matt's search on the title to her property had come up empty. Any buying and selling of the house had been done earlier than the records that were put into the computer data banks.

When Patsy drove into Bailey's driveway, she hadn't been surprised to see Janice sitting in the backseat. It was on the tip of Bailey's tongue to ask how Patsy had asked Janice to go with her, but she didn't ask.

On the thirty-minute drive into Welborn, Bailey chatted with both Patsy and Janice, finding out more about their lives while trying her best not to give away anything about herself.

Welborn was what Bailey had expected it to be: a thriving tourist town with the usual shops that catered to the rich. As the three of them walked along the streets and looked in the windows, Bailey was glad that the highway had bypassed Calburn. For all that Calburn looked abandoned, there was something real about it that Welborn didn't have.

"People should work here and live in Calburn," Bailey

had said, looking into the window of a shop that sold New Age books and crystals.

"Then they could afford to rebuild the old houses," Patsy said.

"Calburn needs a business, a place where the women could work," Janice said, and there was such bitterness in her voice that Bailey had looked at her sharply.

Maybe it was these words that set them to thinking, and ten minutes later, when they saw a gift shop that had a small For Sale sign in the corner of the window, none of them commented. But when they went to lunch, at the same restaurant where Bailey was today, they could talk of nothing else. Janice and Patsy sat on one side of the booth so they weren't facing each other, and Bailey on the other.

It was Janice who started it. She was looking down at her big, plastic-coated menu when she said, "If we owned a shop, we could sell all those pickles and jams you make."

In the next instant, all three of them were talking on top of each other, and, although Janice and Patsy didn't make eye contact with each other, everyone was talking to everyone else.

"Crafts," Patsy said. "I can sew anything."

"Gift baskets!" Janice said. "We'd have a shop for gift baskets. They'd be full of your homemade jams and jellies and—"

"And Patsy's sewn things," Bailey said. "One time a rich woman I knew got a little dragon with her name on it from her husband, and I swear she liked it better than the diamonds he gave her."

"He probably gave her the diamonds out of guilt," Patsy said.

"As a matter of fact, he did," Bailey said, and the three of them laughed.

The idea of their buying the little shop in the tourist town seemed to grow with every minute. They were three women with too much time on their hands. Janice had two young daughters, but Bailey had found out that her husband's mother lived with them, and the girls would just as soon be with their grandmother as with their mother. When Janice said this, Bailey saw something in her eyes, something she'd seen when she'd toured Patsy's house, but Bailey wasn't sure what it was. Anger, maybe. Or perhaps it was a sense of having surrendered.

By the time they'd finished lunch, the women were talking money. They walked back to the shop, went inside, then began to rearrange it in their minds. At the moment the shop was one of many in Welborn that sold a little bit of several things but specialized in nothing. There were T-shirts that said "Welborn, Virginia," on them, a couple of shelves full of candles, some cheap toys for the kids. The owner came out from the back and showed them around. There was the pretty little glassed-front showroom, and in the back was a three-room area that could be used for storage and work. "It used to be a florist's shop," the woman said.

When she opened the back door and let them out into a big parking lot, for a moment the three women just stood there blinking in the sunlight, not quite sure what to do next. They knew that this was the turning point. Did they go home and forget about this, or did they pursue it?

It was Janice who made the decision. "First we need to find out about the competition. Are there any other gift basket shops in Welborn? I'm not sure this area is big enough to handle two of the same business. And somebody needs to talk to the realtor about money. And we need a researcher to find out just how we go about running a gift basket shop—and even if that's what we want to do."

Now, thinking about that afternoon, Bailey smiled. Janice was like a drill sergeant. Instantly, Bailey and Patsy had snapped to attention, and each woman had instinctively known what her job was. Patsy ran off to find out about other shops in the area, and Bailey went to the local library to see what she could find out, while Janice went to the real estate office to talk about money.

By the time the women met again, it was six P.M., and they had a thousand things to report to each other. Patsy drove them back to Calburn, stopping on the way to go to the grocery, the women pushing their three baskets down the aisles while talking nonstop.

And when they got home, they talked the same way to the men they lived with. Janice told Scott how she was going to keep the books for their new company, Patsy told Rick that she was going to be the creative director, and Bailey told Matt that she was going to look into renting a commercial kitchen so she could start producing her best-tasting products on a larger scale.

"We don't know what to call the business," all three women said to their men. "Do you have any ideas?"

Now, sitting in the same booth where she and Janice and Patsy had first talked about opening the business, Bailey looked at the brochure again. Yesterday the shop had been sold. But it hadn't been sold to the three of them.

So what had happened? Bailey wondered. When

they'd driven home that day, they'd been on top of the world. Bailey, laughing, truly laughing for the first time in a long time, had said, "We are three *very* bored women."

That night, they'd been on the phone to each other, with Bailey receiving twice as many calls as Janice or Patsy because they would not get on the phone to each other, so Bailey had to tell Janice what Patsy said, and vice versa.

And throughout those first days, all three of the men had been wonderful. Matt volunteered to renovate the shop. Scott said he'd donate two vans, each only two years old. Rick, who owned three service stations and who, according to Patsy, could fix anything in the world, was going to provide free gasoline for the vans, plus maintenance. Patsy said her sons—and the word *volunteered* was not used—were going to do the driving to deliver the baskets that were ordered.

For an entire week, Bailey's life had been very exciting, with constant phone calls and arrangements to be made, books to read, and Web sites to consult. With Matt's help, she figured out how to use the Internet in record time. She had no idea how to use anything else on a computer, but Matt said he'd never seen anyone master the Web faster.

But after the first week, things had begun to change. Janice had called Bailey on Monday morning to say that Scott was in trouble with the IRS, and he desperately needed her help in straightening out a few things. She was sorry, but Scott said that she was the only person on earth he really trusted, so she hoped Bailey would understand. Two days later, Rick had thrown Patsy a birthday party and given her a sewing machine that could be

hooked up to a computer and programmed to sew pictures. Patsy started spending so much time with the new
machine that she didn't have time to talk about the
shop.

It was on Saturday morning that Matt told her his big
news. He'd been asked by his old architectural firm to
draw some house plans that could be sold on their Web
site. In the past, plans sold through catalogs had had to be
fairly bland, but with the introduction of the Internet to
the world, people could have a wider selection.

"What do you think?" Matt had asked Bailey.

She was in the kitchen, and she was in a very bad
mood. Janice and Patsy had given out on her. She'd
wanted to spend today with them planning the new
business, but instead, Patsy was trying to copy a tiger
from a coloring book onto one of her son's shirts, and
Janice was deep into Scott's finances from eight years
ago.

Bailey barely glanced at the sketch that Matt held out
to her. "Hate the kitchen," she said, then gave a brutal
stir to the pot of *soupe au pistou* that was simmering on
the stove.

"Yeah? What's wrong with it? It's called a 'gourmet
kitchen.' I thought you'd like that."

"Why is it that when it comes to kitchens you men
think that 'big' equals 'gourmet'?"

"What have I done to deserve this 'you men'?"

Bailey knew she wasn't being fair, but it was the men
who'd taken Janice and Patsy away from the project that
the three women wanted to do.

When Bailey didn't answer him, Matt said, "You
think you could design a better kitchen?"

"With my eyes closed," she said, her lips tight, and

that's when Matt thrust a grid-lined pad of paper in front of her, and ten minutes later they were bent over the blueprint, and Bailey was redesigning the kitchen in Matt's house plan.

And that's where they were now. Matt was considering doing an entire book of house plans, and creating his own Web site. If he could get hooked up with a big company like Home Planners, he could earn a living and remain in Calburn. He'd already asked Bailey to go into business with him as the kitchen designer.

"Lillian?"

"Yes?" Bailey said absently, her eyes still on the brochure.

"It is you, isn't it? When I first walked in, I knew I'd seen you before, but it took me a while to figure out who you were. Are you like me and here for a spa treatment? Ask for Andre. He's marvelous."

In openmouthed horror, Bailey watched a woman from her past, Arleen Browne-Thompson, aka Baroness von Lindensale, slide into the bench on the other side of the booth.

"I'm sorry," Bailey said, "you must have the wrong person. I'm not—"

"Sure, sure," Arleen said, looking hard at Bailey. "You look great. Really, you do. How much did you lose? A hundred? More? And your nose! Removing that thing must have taken half a dozen procedures."

Bailey just glared at the woman, her head reeling with what the consequences of this meeting could be. Arleen could sell what she'd found out to a tabloid, and tomorrow Bailey's front yard would be full of reporters. Or she could—

"Would you stop looking at me like that?" Arleen

said. "I have no intention of giving away your little secret. If you want to go about the country dressed like . . . that"—she didn't seem to have words to describe Bailey's cotton trousers and T-shirt—"it's none of my business. Besides, you know a few secrets on me too."

At that Arleen gave a naughty little laugh, and Bailey was tempted to say, Not any secrets that anyone would pay to read about. Twice, Bailey had found Arleen in a compromising position with young men who worked for Jimmie. When Bailey told Jimmie, he'd howled with laughter. "The old bag must be a hundred and twelve at least. Good for her!"

Arleen tossed a Gucci bag onto the table and began rummaging inside it. Bailey knew she was searching for a cigarette; this was the longest that she'd seen the woman without one. It used to be a joke whether or not Arleen had ever eaten anything in her life, as she seemed to live on booze and cigarettes. Her skin was dried-out, her body emaciated.

"So tell me everything," Arleen said once she had her cigarette lit.

"This is a nonsmoking section."

"I just had sex with the owner, so he won't throw us out," she said, then laughed at Bailey's expression. "Darling, you always were so easy to shock. No, I haven't had sex with the owner. But it's three in the afternoon, and you know how these Americans are, they're finished with lunch by one, then they go back to the dreary little offices."

Bailey happened to know that Arleen had grown up in Texas, but she loved to pretend that she was a "citizen of the world," as she called herself.

"Everything," Arleen said again. "Tell it all."

"I have no intention of telling you anything," Bailey said, then had the satisfaction of seeing Arleen's thin eyebrows lift slightly.

"Then maybe you want me to tell you what's happened to all your friends."

"The ones who called me after Jimmie died and said how sorry they were for my loss? Are those the friends you mean?"

"My goodness," Arleen said, drawing deeply on her cigarette and looking at Bailey through a haze of smoke. "When did you gain a tongue? You used to sit in a corner and say nothing. You just hung your head and waited for James."

Bailey picked up her handbag. "I think I'd better go."

"Then I'll just have to tell my driver to follow you," Arleen said calmly. "He's former FBI, you know."

Bailey sat back down. "All right, what is it that you want?"

"Some of whatever you took to make you look so good and get so angry."

"I'm not angry!" Bailey said, but then she looked around at the mostly empty restaurant and lowered her voice. "I'm not angry," she said quietly, "and I don't know what's given you that idea."

"Let me see. You were married to a man who slept with everything in skirts, then he died and left you nothing. And now—"

Again, Bailey grabbed her bag, but Arleen clamped down on Bailey's wrist and held her. "Okay, I apologize. We don't have to talk about what was done to you."

"You're right. In fact, we don't have to talk about anything." Bailey was still half out of the seat, and

Arleen still had her wrist in a viselike grip. "What is it you want, Arleen?"

"Is it really true that Jimmie left you nothing?"

"I see," Bailey said. "You want money."

Arleen shrugged. "One has needs."

When Bailey didn't sit back down, Arleen's voice lowered. "Please," she said, "sit and talk with me. I miss James. And I promise, no more cracks."

Bailey knew she should leave, but something was holding her back. For one thing, Arleen was familiar to her. Not by any stretch of the imagination had they ever been friends, but Arleen had been one of the hangers-on around Jimmie. He used to think Arleen's bitchiness was amusing. "And she knows everybody," Jimmie said.

Slowly, Bailey took her seat again. "All right, what do you want to talk about?"

"You," Arleen said. "I really do want to know what's made you look so good. Before, when you were with James, you always looked dreadful."

"Thanks," Bailey said. "And the same back to you."

Arleen leaned back against the booth, drew on her cigarette, and looked at Bailey speculatively. "You really are angry. Were you always like this, or is it something new?"

"I'm not—" Bailey began, but then she too leaned back against the seat.

"Is it your new husband?" Arleen asked.

"What makes you think I already have another husband?"

That made Arleen give a dry laugh. She couldn't laugh too hard because her lungs were so full of carbon that if she started coughing, she'd never stop. "You? You, dear Lillian, were made to be a man's wife. And now you look like a pregnancy waiting to happen. We used to wonder if you even existed when James wasn't around. Bandy—you remember him?—used to say that you were a ghost and James had paid someone to conjure you. He said a voodoo priestess had performed some ancient ritual and from it had sprung this woman who was what all primitive men like James thought a wife should be."

Bailey was looking at the woman in horror. She'd heard whispers and had been given looks, but when Jimmie was around, no one had dared say anything like this to her. "Go on," she heard herself say. "What else did Bandy say about me?"

"Oh, darling, it really was most amusing. You know how bitchy Bandy can be. He said that only a ghost that'd had its spirit removed could be a billionaire's wife and still go around the world putting cherries into bottles the way you did. He said that you had everything, but all you really wanted was to disappear inside James Manville—of course, that's what James wanted you to do. That's why James sent all those chocolates every time you lost a pound or two."

"The chocolates were gifts from other people. Thank-you gifts, mostly. Jimmie said . . ." Bailey trailed off because Arleen was looking at her as though to say, How could you be so naive?

"Bandy was with him one time when he ordered the chocolates. Bandy said, 'I thought Lillian was dieting,' then James laughed. But you know how Bandy is, once he gets hold of something, he doesn't let it go. He coaxed and wheedled until he got James to tell why he wanted a fat wife. James said he wouldn't have a beautiful wife. I remember that night so clearly. We were on

Jimmie's yacht, that big one he had, what was the name of it?"

"The *Lillian*," Bailey said, her jaw clamped shut. She didn't want to hear anything this woman was going to say, but at the same time she couldn't possibly leave. "What did Jimmie say about me?"

Arleen lit another cigarette off the first one. "It was one of those nights after you'd gone to bed early, but then, you always went to bed early, didn't you, dear? One of the reasons so many people disliked you is because you made no effort to hide the fact that you despised them."

"You were all after Jimmie's money," Bailey said.

"Yes, dear, we wanted his money. But you wanted his soul. Now, tell me, which one is more expensive?"

Bailey wasn't going to reply to that. "Tell me what it is that you're dying to tell me," she snapped.

"Such hostility! My goodness. I never knew. If I had known, maybe you and I could have been friends." At that, Arleen gave another one of her cackles. "Anyway, that night, as usual, we'd all had much too much to drink, and Bandy asked James to tell us his secret for a happy marriage. I'm sure you know that, usually, you were off-limits to the rest of us. When James was around, your name wasn't mentioned. But that night, James talked. Maybe he was drunk, I don't know. And, too, he was in a good mood because he'd just met that starlet, the one with the red hair and the heart tattoo on her arm. She couldn't act, but she was divine looking. What was her name?"

"Chloe," Bailey said in a whisper.

"Ah, yes, Chloe." Arleen stubbed out her cigarette and lit another one. "So anyway, James was in a talking mood that night, and he said that the secret was in finding a girl who didn't have anything, a girl—he said girl, not woman, I remember clearly—who was loved by no one on Earth, and had no ambition to be anything. 'An empty bottle waiting for me to come along and fill her up,' is what James said. 'And if you fill her up with love, that's all that'll matter to her.' "

Arleen paused to draw deeply on her cigarette. "And you know James. Once he started talking, he didn't stop. Not that he ever told much about himself, but Bandy could get things out of him now and then. James said, 'Now take . . .' Oh, what was her name? That model before Chloe? That Italian girl?"

"Senta," Bailey whispered.

"Yes, Senta. James said, 'Now take Senta. She would make a dreadful wife. Too beautiful. Too ambitious. Too full of herself. There wouldn't be room for me in there. Women like that, you use them for what they were made for, then you get rid of them when they bore you.'

" 'But not Lillian,' Bandy said, and I can tell you that we all held our breath. You know what James's temper was like. He could put up with a person feeding off him for years, but then that person could rub James the wrong way just once, and James would never see him again, never speak to him, and—in my set, worse— never pay his bills again."

"What did Jimmie say about me?" Bailey asked, her voice so low she could hardly hear herself.

"He said that he made sure that you had no one but him to love. He said that if you started to get bored and wanted to actually *do* something, he'd whisk you off to someplace new. 'Lillian's problem,' James said, 'is that she's smart. She may not seem so with the way she doesn't say much, but what you people don't realize is that in the mornings while the whole worthless lot of you are sleeping off the night before, Lillian is in the kitchen with the chefs, picking their brains. Or she's out with the gardeners, or with the mechanics. She likes to learn things.' 'But never gets to use them,' Bandy said, then James laughed. He said, 'That's the key. If you marry a stupid woman, you have to live with her. If you marry a smart woman, in this day and age, she turns around and starts competing with you.' 'You mean a career,' Bandy said. 'But you couldn't really think that Lillian could compete with *you*.' 'Not with making money, but a business would take her mind off of *me*.' 'Is that why you sent the man from Heinz away?' Bandy asked."

Arleen stopped talking and looked at Bailey for a moment. "Do you remember the time that man from Heinz was doing some business with James? I think we were staying in the house in Antigua then."

"No," Bailey said softly. "The castle in Scotland."

"Oh, yes," Arleen said. "That's where you had the hundred-thousand-dollar kitchen put in and then lived in it. Jimmie said you were too cold in the rest of the house, but we all knew you couldn't abide *us*."

"What about the man from Heinz?" Bailey asked, unable to look into Arleen's eyes.

"He ate some of those jams of your yours, and he wanted to franchise you, but James wouldn't let him. James said that you had no interest in having a business, but Bandy said behind James's back that he was the only business you were allowed to have. Do you remember any of this?"

Bailey kept her eyes downward. She'd asked Jimmie

to ask the man from Heinz if maybe he could help her start a line of specialty items. All that day, Bailey had been a nervous wreck while waiting for the man's answer. But when Jimmie came home that night with a huge bouquet of roses in his arms, she knew what it was.

Jimmie had been wonderful that night, holding her, making her laugh after he said that the man had turned down her idea. Jimmie said, "I didn't tell him who made the jams he was eating, because I wanted an honest reaction, but I can tell you that I wanted to hit him when he said they were 'ordinary' and 'nothing special.' " When Bailey heard that, she'd had to work hard not to burst into tears. Over the years many people had told her that what she made was delicious and extraordinary, different from anything they'd ever eaten before. But it looked as though they'd been politely lying.

When Jimmie saw that she was close to tears, he'd become very angry and said that he'd buy her a factory for making jams if she wanted one. "We'll call them Lillian's Jams," he'd said. "Hey! I know what I'll do. How about if I buy Heinz for you?" His righteous indignation had been so sincere that he'd made her laugh.

But the rejection had so hurt Bailey that she hadn't canned anything for months after. Now Arleen was telling her that the man from Heinz had wanted Lillian's preserves so much that he'd had a contract drawn up giving Lillian complete control of that branch of the company.

"You should have seen him at breakfast that morning," Arleen was saying. "The man was nearly begging Jimmie. He said that the gourmet market was just opening up, and your products would be perfect for taking Heinz into it."

Bailey looked down at her hands and saw that her nails were cutting into her palms. That morning she'd wanted to go to breakfast and tell the Heinz man just what she thought of him. She'd wanted to show him all the blue ribbons she'd won over the years in contests and at fairs. But Jimmie had told her that he was going to "take care" of the man, and when he'd said it, his face had been full of rage. "Let me do it, Frecks," he'd said. "I'm better at revenge than you are."

So Bailey had stayed in their bedroom until she saw the man get into the car that would drive him back to the airport. Later, she'd wanted Jimmie to tell her the details of what rotten thing he'd done to the man, but all he'd said was, "You can be sure that he won't be coming around here again," and the way Jimmie had said it made Bailey believe that he was her champion.

"So how's your life now?" Arleen was asking.

"I—" Bailey said, but then couldn't seem to form any more words. What was she going to say? That she was already living with another man, and cooking for him while he paid for nearly everything? And that she was going to be working for him, doing about one percent of the planning in the man's new business venture? In other words, that in just a few weeks she had come close to re-creating her life with Jimmie.

"I bought this place," Bailey heard herself say as she thrust the brochure across the table at Arleen. "I'm going into business with two other women, and we're creating a line of specialty foods."

"Really?" Arleen asked, looking at Bailey through a haze of cigarette smoke. "*You* in business?"

"None of you ever really knew me," Bailey said, taking a deep breath. "And none of you ever knew how deeply involved I was in Jimmie's businesses. I did more than just follow him around, more than just—" She couldn't say any more, as what Arleen had told her was ringing in her head. "A girl who didn't have anything," Jimmie had said. "Who was loved by no one on Earth and had no ambition to be anything." "An empty bottle waiting for me to come along and fill her up." She knew they were Jimmie's words; she could hear him saying them.

"And what about a man?" Arleen asked. "Or did Jimmie sour you for all men?"

"There's a man," Bailey said, her jaw rigid. "Blue-blood type on his mother's side. You'd probably know the family name if I said it, but I really would like to keep my anonymity."

"I understand," Arleen said, then she smiled. "Blue blood is what James craved, isn't it? It's why he put up with people like Bandy and me. James could have all the money in the world, but he couldn't go back and change his breeding."

"No, he couldn't," Bailey said. She exchanged a conspiratorial smile with Arleen, and in that moment, they were close to being friends.

"You know something?" Arleen said. "I'm glad you aren't in that kind of a relationship again. And I'm glad that the new man in your life isn't a controller like James was, and that he isn't the kind to stop you from having your little shop. And I hope he doesn't stop you from finding out whatever it was that James wanted you to find out."

"What do you mean?" Bailey asked. Had Jimmie told people about the note he'd left his wife in his will? He seemed to have blabbed about a lot of other parts of their private lives.

"It was just something that James said once. I'm sure it wasn't important. But he said that after he died, he was going to ask you to find out something that he couldn't."

When Arleen said no more, Bailey looked at her hard. "Okay, what is it that you want?"

Arleen inhaled cigarette smoke so deep that it must have gone down to her toes. "There aren't many men like James left," she said softly, then waited for Bailey to figure out what she meant.

"Ah, right," Bailey said. Arleen meant that there weren't many vastly wealthy men out there who had some deep need to surround themselves with people whose only claim to fame was that they "knew people."

"The rich ones today," Arleen said, "are these boys from the computer world. What do they need introductions for? They want to stay up all night and play games on their computers." She stubbed out her cigarette in Bailey's salad bowl with such force that Bailey thought she might break a nail.

Bailey just looked at the woman, her eyes asking, What do you want?

"If you make a go of your little company, perhaps you'd like to have some good names on your masthead."

Bailey narrowed her eyes, unintentionally looking very much like her late husband. "Maybe I might like to have someone tell others about how wonderful my products are for say . . . one percent of the gross?"

"Ten percent of the net," Arleen shot back.

"*Two* percent of the *gross* will make sure you do some work," Bailey fired back.

Arleen smiled. "I wish I'd spent a little time with you when James was alive. All right. Three percent of the net."

"Two," Bailey said, unsmiling. "Gross."

"So what's the name of this company that I own . . . two percent of?"

"I have no idea," Bailey said, then she smiled. "I haven't started the company yet."

For a moment Arleen blinked at her, then when she realized that Bailey had lied, she threw her head back and really laughed. It was a good ol' Texas girl hee-haw, something that Baroness von Lindensale would never have given into.

Bailey couldn't help smiling back, and when Arleen went into a coughing fit, she handed her her glass of water.

"Now would you tell me what Jimmie said about what he wanted me to find out?"

"Oh, yes," Arleen said as she reached into her handbag and withdrew her compact to check her makeup. She wore a lot of it, with eyes heavily blackened, and cheeks painted scarlet. "James said that all his money couldn't right a wrong that had happened when he was a kid. Since he never talked about his childhood, you can imagine how all of us were on the edge of our seats. 'Murders called suicides', that's what he said. We said, 'Jimmie, you have enough money that you could set the record straight. Expose the murders.' Of course we were all volunteering to help because we wanted to find out the truth about his mysterious past. 'Do you think they would talk to *me?*' James said. 'I was there. I was involved. But those six shining boys were—' "

"What?" Bailey said, her eyes wide.

"He said he was involved so 'they' would recognize him. Whoever 'they' are. Even Bandy couldn't get James to tell more."

"No," Bailey said. "You said, 'six shining boys.' Did

he say that *exactly?* Or did he say 'six *golden* boys'?"

"Is there a significant difference between those two phrases?"

"There is if you live in Calburn. Okay, what did Jimmie say about the 'six shining boys'?"

Arleen took a maddeningly long time to light another cigarette, then she looked back at Bailey. "I think James's father was one of those boys."

"Do you mean that Jimmie's father was murdered? Or did he commit suicide? Or was he accused of murder? Or did he murder someone?"

"I have no idea. James spoke of 'murders called suicides,' then said he would be recognized if he went back to wherever it was that he was talking about, and he said that 'those six shining boys' "—she looked at Bailey—"or 'six golden boys,' I guess, were a religion and couldn't be touched. Then he got a nasty look on his face and said that someone had once tried to touch them; 'Look what happened to her,' he said. Is any of this making sense to you?"

"Some of it, yes. What about Jimmie's father?"

"James said, 'My father was one of them, but he—' Then he broke off. That's all he'd say. Bandy asked him to tell more, but James said, 'I talk too much,' and that was that. He never said another word about his past to anyone else as far as I know. I even asked one of the girls, that Swedish girl, uh . . ."

"Ingrid," Bailey said as she leaned back against the seat. "No, Jimmie wouldn't confide in any of them."

"Dear, your hand is bleeding," Arleen said softly.

Bailey looked down and saw that two of her nails had cut into her palm. Quickly, she put her hands out of sight under the table.

"Are you going to find out about James's father?" Arleen asked. "If you did, you could write a book about him and make a mint."

Bailey gave her a look of disgust. "No, I'm not going to write an exposé of my late husband."

"But, darling, you should. You could tell all about the fabulous parties, about the women, about—" Arleen stopped. "Yes, I could see why you wouldn't want to do that. So what do you plan to do with this information?"

"Nothing," Bailey said. "Sitting here with you has made me realize that I don't owe James Manville anything. I'm sure he had his reasons for leaving everything to people he hates and leaving me nothing but a—" When she saw Arleen's eager eyes, she stopped. She didn't want to give away too much about herself, including hints about where she was living. "What I plan to do is make up for lost time." She leaned across the table so her face was close to Arleen's. "I want some work out of you. There'll be no paper contract between us, just word of honor. Ever hear of that concept, Arleen?"

"A time or two," Arleen said, smiling slightly. "From way back when."

"You don't bring us customers, you don't get paid. Understand?"

"Clearly. I don't have to eat any of the product, do I?"

"I seem to remember that you rather liked my cherries in brandy."

"I threw all those awful little red things over the side of the ship," Arleen said. "Then I drank the brandy."

Bailey couldn't help smiling. "Give me your address and your cell number, and I'll let you know what's going on. And when we make any money, I'll send you a check."

Arleen took the brochure, scribbled some numbers on it and an address in London, then shoved it back across the table. "And who is this 'we'? The man in your life?"

"No," Bailey said firmly. "This will be a company run by and for women. No men allowed." She looked at her watch, and as she did, she could feel Arleen's derision. It wasn't an expensive watch. "I have to go," Bailey said as she stuck the brochure with the address into her handbag. "I'll let you know what happens."

"Thanks," Arleen said softly. "I'm depending on you."

As Bailey slid out of the booth, she avoided Arleen's eyes. There was something empty in them that she didn't want to see. Arleen made Tennessee Williams's immortal phrase, "I have always depended on the kindess of strangers," come to life.

With her head held high, Bailey left the restaurant and went to the lot where her car was parked.

Twelve

Her bravado lasted only until she was inside the privacy of her car. She put the key in the engine, but she didn't turn it. Instead, she put her head down on the wheel and closed her eyes.

While she was married to Jimmie, when he was there in the flesh, she could pretend that those other women didn't exist. She could tell herself that Jimmie's "friends" were odious creatures, and she didn't want to be around them—that way she heard little and saw less. She could hide in the kitchens of all the houses and pretend that she and Jimmie were just an ordinary couple, and that Jimmie was coming home from an office job to her home-cooked meal. In fact, over the years, she'd become brilliant at hiding from the truth.

And now she was doing with Matthew Longacre exactly what she'd done with Jimmie. She was again hiding and letting a man make all her decisions, letting a man decide her life.

She looked up through the windshield to see a woman holding the hand of a little boy and walking toward the stores. She'd very much wanted to have children, but Jimmie had had a vasectomy long before she met him. He never said so, but Bailey figured he'd rendered himself infertile because he was afraid that a child of his would inherit his cleft lip.

But now that she'd had some time away from the physical presence of Jimmie, she thought that maybe he hadn't wanted children because he knew he would have been jealous. He wanted Bailey all to himself.

"You were a very selfish man, James Manville," she said out loud as she started the car. "And what is worse, I allowed you to be."

On the drive home, she hardly looked at the road. Her mind was so full of what she'd heard this morning, and what she was being forced to remember, that she could see little.

Worse than what had been done to her in the past, she thought, was the fact that she was doing it all over again. She had no doubt that soon Matt would ask her to marry him, then they'd have a sweet little wedding in some adorable little church, and she'd probably be pregnant a week later. "A pregnancy waiting to happen," is what Arleen called her.

But what would Bailey tell her children when they asked for her opinion or guidance? "Go ask your father. He makes all the decisions. I just follow." Is that what she'd say?

And Bailey had firsthand knowledge of how suddenly things could change. What if she and Matt had three kids, then he fell off a scaffolding and was killed? How was she supposed to support her children? Work double shifts waitressing and never see them? She'd read articles about adults who were angry at their stressed-out, over-worked single mothers for never having spent much time with them when they were children.

What would she do if Matt had an affair? Would she do what she'd done with Jimmie—bury herself in thirty-five quarts of grapefruit marmalade and pretend that she didn't see what was going on? If Matt wanted to have a party with guests she didn't like, what would she do? Plead fatigue and go to bed? It was one thing to escape from a party in a twenty-thousand-square-foot mansion, but quite another to try to get away in two thousand square feet. No, this time, Bailey wasn't hiding; this time, she was frying cheese and onions for them.

And she was doing it in her own house!

When Bailey pulled into her driveway, she remembered when she had first seen the farmhouse with Phillip. It had been so ugly then! But in just six weeks, that had changed. Weekend after weekend Matt's friends and relatives—as if they were holding a barn raising in a western novel—had helped them restore the house to what it had once been.

At first, Bailey had enjoyed the remodeling. Cooking for people who lavished praise on everything that she put before them had been a dream come true. It was what she'd envisioned that life could be. Matt was always there, laughing, smiling at her, his arm often around her. He bragged on her cooking and on the designs that she did for the kitchens in his house plans. With each week he was receiving more commissions for design work, and if he could get a permanent job with a

New York company that sold house plans over the Internet, he would be able to remain in Calburn and earn a good living.

During the week, she and Matt had settled into a quiet, easy life. They knew each other's favorite TV shows; he learned not to bother her when she was reading one of her beloved murder mysteries. They both disliked going out during the week, so they stayed at home and rented videos, or they worked on the thousand-piece puzzle set up in the corner by the fireplace and listened to Enya. Sometimes one or both of Matt's nephews would spend the night; then Bailey would make popcorn, and she'd have to sit through some dreadful horror movie that would give her nightmares.

But there was no sex. When Matt and Bailey were alone, it was as though they were brother and sister. He was polite, but a bit distant. And since Bailey's experience with the only man in her life was that he didn't like aggressive women, she had no idea about how to approach Matt. And did she want to? She was afraid of messing up something great.

On the other hand, when people were around, Matt joked about sex often. He teased Bailey in a way that made the others look at them with approval; she knew that they all wanted her and Matt to stay together.

Matt's lack of aggression when they were alone made Bailey feel, well, somewhat undesirable, so she teased him back when they were in public. To outsiders, she was sure they sounded as though they were having a great sex life. But sometimes, when she and Matt were alone, Bailey wanted to scream, "I know I said I wasn't ready yet, but try me *now!*"

But Bailey didn't yell anything. Instead, she cooked

huge, wonderful meals. She made a big pot of chili and homemade bread when Matt and four of his friends from high school spent the day clearing the beehive out of the chimney. She made pizzas for the same men when they tore out the green bathroom.

And when Matt told her that he'd heard the boss of the company he was trying to get to hire him was considered a gourmet, he'd looked at Bailey with pleading eyes. Would she please make a killer dinner and help him get the job? he was silently asking her. Of course she'd volunteered, then spent twelve hours in the kitchen preparing a Moroccan feast. She made phyllo-pastry-wrapped olives and tomatoes, whole fish baked in spices, a seafood tagine fragrant with cardamon and cumin, and saffron chicken sprinkled with apricots, raisins, and almonds. And, of course, she made a b'stilla, that divine Moroccan dish of spiced, chopped chicken, eggs, and almonds wrapped in thin layers of pastry, baked until golden brown, then topped with sugar. For dessert, when the six men were groaning that they couldn't eat another bite, Bailey served them plum-raspberry sorbet with tiny sugar cookies in the shape of houses. The six men had laughed at the joke, and the boss told Matt that he would be a welcome addition to their firm. "If you can design half as well as she can cook, you'll double our sales," the man had said.

During those weeks, Bailey often saw Janice and Patsy, but when Janice said that she'd "found nothing wrong" in her husband's account books, even though she'd gone back through nine years, Bailey said nothing. And when Patsy said that her husband and sons had asked her to please not embroider another animal, plant, or fantasy creature on any of their clothing, Bailey had also said nothing. No, Bailey hadn't wanted to upset the lovely, peaceful life that she'd always craved. Her life with Matt was what she'd tried to make with Jimmie. But Jimmie's money and his . . . his need for "attention" got in the way of perfect happiness.

Now Bailey got out of the car and walked onto the front porch of the place. The house was beautiful now, the kind of place she'd always wanted. The deep porch wrapped around a third of the house, furnished with two wooden rockers with cane-bottom seats and three wicker chairs with flowered cushions. Matt had even hung a swing up at one end of it.

But Bailey didn't sit on the porch very often. For one thing, she'd rarely seemed able to get out of the kitchen since the porch had been finished. Patsy said that Matt was trying to make up for lost time. "Rick said that when they were kids, Matt was too proud to participate in anything social because their family was too poor to reciprocate. Rick doesn't have the ridiculous pride that Matt does, so my Rick went to any party anywhere; he and I had a great time in high school. But not Matt. Matt stayed alone. Then, of course, he married Cassandra." Patsy said the last as though no further explanation was necessary.

Because of Patsy's words, Bailey had felt an obligation to entertain half of Calburn and a great deal of the surrounding county over the last six weeks. She couldn't very well deny Matt something he'd missed out on as a kid, could she? Besides, true to his word, Matt paid for all the food. And he always asked her if she minded cooking for so many people and so often. "No, I love it," she'd said every time he asked.

Now she looked at the porch, but what she really saw

was the chairs, the swing, and the two little tile-topped tables that had come out of a rented storage unit. It was part of what Matt got in his divorce settlement. "Since Cassandra bought them, I'm sure they must have cost the earth," he'd said. "And they're just sitting there, so we might as well use them. If it's okay with you, that is?" he'd asked, looking at her. "Sure," Bailey'd said. "Of course we should use them. It would be silly not to." But she'd never liked the chairs. They were too slick, too "designer," and the pattern of the chintz was too bright, too modern. Bailey would rather have taken a trip to North Carolina and purchased something made by a craftsman there. But she didn't tell Matt that.

Inside the house, she looked around. The living room was a far cry from what it had been when she'd moved in. The kitchen was now open to the living room, with stools at the granite countertop. For the last three Saturdays she'd served the men something called "fried cheese" while they watched a baseball game on the big-screen TV that Matt had brought home one Friday evening. "They're not used to foreign food," Matt had said the night before the men, all of whom he'd known in high school, were to come over and help him replace the unstable floor in the attic. "Don't get me wrong, I love what you cook, but these guys grew up in Calburn, and, well . . ." He didn't have to finish; she understood what he meant. The second Saturday the men came (and there were more of them that day), one of them brought her a thank-you gift. It was a machine to cut onions into segments, which, when deep-fried, would make an "onion flower."

The men, under Matt's supervision, had made the room beautiful. The kitchen was small and efficient, with its huge walk-in pantry for storage. There were no overhead cabinets, just open shelves where she stored her most-used items. Matt had borrowed a friend's wood-working shop, and he'd made her lower cabinets out of knotty pine that he'd pulled off the walls of the garage he'd remodeled. They'd laughed together over the fact that the woman didn't like the beautiful old pine, but wanted Matt to put up plasterboard in its place. "And she covered it with wallpaper that was printed to look like knotty pine," he said, making them both howl with laughter.

Matt filled the nail holes, sanded the pine just enough to take off years of grease and soot, then finished the wood with a matte-finish sealer. The cabinets were so beautiful they made Bailey smile every time she saw them.

But if the kitchen was all hers, other parts of the house seemed to have no relation to her. What Patsy said about Matt making up for lost time rang in her ears. In a way, Matt seemed to be trying to rewrite history. Matt had been a recluse, Patsy said, when he was in high school, and later he'd left Calburn "before the ink was dry on his diploma." But now he was constantly calling men he'd gone to high school with and trying to renew friendships that, according to Patsy and Rick, had never existed.

"You hated him in high school," Rick said one day when Matt said that a certain "old buddy" was coming over on Saturday. "That jerk wanted everyone to think that he was the best football player Calburn had ever produced, even though he knew that you could out-throw and outrun him. But you had to work after school and on weekends, so you couldn't be on the team.

Remember the showdown you two had in the parking lot when you worked at the Dairy Queen? The manager fired you that night." "That was a long time ago," Matt had mumbled, then turned on the TV and refused to comment on the matter any more.

Now framed photos of Matt's family hung in Bailey's house, along with a couple of landscape paintings. They weren't bad, but Matt had bought them with his ex-wife. "Friend of her father's painted them," Matt said. "Not worth much now, but they may be someday." "So why didn't Cassandra take them?" Bailey had asked. Matt shrugged. "Carter didn't like them." Bailey had wanted to say, "Neither do I," but she hadn't.

The hall closet was packed full of Matt's sports equipment; she could barely squeeze a broom in the front. The third bedroom was filled with boxes that hadn't been opened since Matt's divorce. He said he was going to unpack someday, but he never seemed to find time to do it.

Upstairs, "her" loft was now packed with Matt's business equipment. He had bought something called a CAD system to make his designs. The floor on the far side of the attic had been repaired, the little railing taken down, and that area too was filled with Matt's possessions. He'd set up another drawing board with a drafting machine that slid up and down the surface. "I think better with a pencil in my hand than with a mouse," he'd said, smiling. In the corner was a fat easy chair with a light over it and a big ottoman. Matt had built shelves all along the walls and filled them with hundreds of his reference books.

Bailey walked out the back door, across the newly exposed porch, and into the garden. At least the mulberry tree was the same, she thought. Pausing, she looked up at the big, old branches, at the fruit that was nearly ripe. Until today, she'd thought that she loved the way her life was heading, but the double blows of hearing that the shop had been sold, then being taken back to the past by Arleen, seemed to have changed how she was seeing things.

As she looked up at the mulberry tree, she knew she had reached a turning point in her life. Jimmie's death had started it, and that event had led up to this moment. She had some important decisions to make. She could allow things to continue as they were—and with that thought, she remembered how she'd always let things "continue as they are." It was true that Jimmie was already rich and famous when he'd met her, but he'd been as famous for his daredevil stunts as for anything else. After their marriage he'd stopped his more flamboyant pursuits and entered what the media called "the world of the big boys." Only after he married the young, quiet, plump Lillian Bailey did he become a contender for the coveted title of richest man in the world.

She knew that what she'd given Jimmie was the knowledge that someone on earth knew him, the real him, and loved him anyway. To be truly loved, wasn't that the most powerful drug in the world? Jimmie used to pick her up, whirl her about, and say, "You give me the strength to do it, Frecks. I don't need much in this world, but I need *you.*"

And now, just as she'd done with Jimmie, she was beginning to disappear into Matt. She was putting the burden on him that she'd put on Jimmie of being everything and everyone to her. She was staying home, hiding in the kitchen, and expecting Matt to bring the world to her. Bailey was making no effort to create a life of her own. And inside, she was smoldering about furniture she didn't want and guests she didn't like.

Bailey put her hands over her face. She didn't want to remember it, but she'd been very unhappy the last two years with Jimmie.

During her twenties she'd been so enamored of him that anything he did, she saw as wonderful. But when she'd hit thirty, just two years ago, something inside her changed. She had no idea what caused it, but seemingly overnight she grew short-tempered and angry about everything. Jimmie would ask her what was wrong, she'd snap that nothing was; then she'd tell him she wanted to go somewhere, anywhere. "You'll just take yourself with you," Jimmie had said once, looking at her hard.

Bailey leaned back against the tree and took a couple of deep, calming breaths. What did she do now that she realized these things about herself? The truth was, she had no idea how to go about doing what the self-help books called "becoming your own person." Should she say to Matt at dinner tonight, "I've decided to become my own person?" Then what? Get up and fetch him a second helping?

No, Matt wasn't the problem. He was a nice man. She liked him. There wasn't much fire between them, but it was comfortable, something that she could live with.

The problem was that Bailey had spent a lifetime accommodating herself to others, and she wasn't sure how to change that. She'd grown up under the rule of her mother and her sister Dolores. Both of them were . . .

For a moment Bailey closed her eyes and remembered her father. Like her, Herbert Bailey had been willing to let others make the decisions and take on the responsibilities. "You and I need people like your mother and Dolores to help us along," he'd said to Lillian many times. "And, besides, it makes people like them angry when you go against them, so it's better to let them rule the show."

And he'd lived by that ethic. He'd gone to work each day, come home at exactly the same time each evening, and on Friday handed his paycheck to his wife. He let his wife do whatever she wanted with the money, with the house, and with their daughters, content to sit in his easy chair and read his daily newspaper.

He died one Sunday afternoon while sitting in that same chair. Lillian had been in the kitchen all day, getting ready for a 4-H competition, and she'd gone from the kitchen up the back stairs to bed. Since the lights had been turned off in the living room, she'd assumed that her parents and her sister had already gone to bed. They weren't the kind of family that informed each other where they were going or when.

Early the next morning Bailey had gone down the street to baby-sit for a neighbor, and hadn't returned until after lunch. When she walked into the living room and saw her father sitting in his chair in exactly the same position as the day before, she knew he was gone. When she pressed her lips to his forehead, his body was stiff and cold. The night before, her mother and sister had seen him asleep in his chair, but they hadn't tried to wake him. Instead, they'd just turned out the lights and gone upstairs to bed. Bailey still remembered the looks of distaste the two policemen had given her mother when one of them said the man had been dead for nearly twenty-four hours before they were called.

Bailey also remembered the way her mother had shrugged. She'd made sure her husband was well insured, so his demise didn't interrupt her life much. In fact, it seemed that Bailey was the only person on earth who missed him.

But now, today, Bailey knew that she no longer wanted to be the child who had been taught by her father that she was like him, that she was a person who let others control her—and that that's what she *should* do. Had her father told her those things because he felt as alone as she had? Had he needed an ally in his no-resistance campaign to make him feel that it was the right way to go?

Bailey tried to clear her thoughts. She'd grown up receiving the only love in her life from her father, but to receive that love, she'd had to constantly take what was handed to her. Whenever she tried to stand up to her mother, she'd glanced at her father, and when she saw his look, which seemed to say that he wouldn't love her anymore if she became a shrew like her mother, Bailey had backed down.

A mere three years after her father died, Bailey had run away with James Manville, a man even more controlling than her mother.

So, she thought, what did she do now? It was all well and good to figure out the past, but what did she *do* with this knowledge? She could continue as she was, and disappear into Matthew Longacre, just as she'd become the shadow of her father and Jimmie. Or should she do something radical—kick Matt out of her house and say that she wanted to figure out her own life before she entwined herself with another man? Did she then see if she could make it in the world all by herself?

Not quite. Bailey already knew what was out there in the big, bad world. And she wasn't so full of this rebellious feeling that she was going to throw away a good man in the hope that another one would appear later, when she was ready. Also, she knew that she wasn't one of those women who wanted to spend her life without a man. There was a lot of bad about them, but they sure knew how to make you laugh! No, she needed a man in her life, that much she was sure of.

But then, wasn't it her *need* of Jimmie that had made her put up with a lot from him?

Put up with, she thought. What was that old saying? *Whatever you put up with, that's what you'll get.* She had "put up with" his affairs and . . . the chocolate, she thought, and again her nails bit into her already sore palms. In truth, hearing that Jimmie had sent her the chocolate when she was dieting, not his grateful clients, made her more angry than the affairs.

And the man from Heinz! At that memory, her nails dug into her palms so hard that she winced.

All right, she asked herself, what do I want to do with the rest of my life? Do I want to keep it as it is, or do I want to make some changes? Do I want to bury myself in this man, Matthew Longacre, or do I want to try to find out what *I* can do? Not what I can accomplish while living as the shadow of a man, but on my own?

Changes won out easily. So what changes do I want to make? she asked herself. I want to prove to myself that I can *do* something, was her answer. She didn't want to be eighty years old and have to tell her grandkids that although she'd grown up in a time when women were running for president, she'd opted to stay home and fry cheese and onions for a bunch of men she couldn't really say she liked very much.

So what do I have going for me? she asked herself, then gave a little smile. She'd told Arleen that she'd been involved in Jimmie's businesses. She'd said that to keep Arleen from thinking she was "a ghost," as that nasty little Bandy had claimed. But the truth was, that Bailey *had* learned some things from Jimmie.

So, first of all, she had some knowledge of business. Second, she knew a few women who needed to do something with their lives as much as she did.

All right, she thought. Enough whining. No more poor little Bailey. She knew what she had to do; she just had to figure out how. If Jimmie were in a situation like this—not that he would ever be in something that he couldn't control totally—what would he do?

"Guerilla warfare," she could hear Jimmie say. "Underground. Do it, then tell them what you've done. When it's a done deal, they can't give you 'advice.' And make no mistake about it, Frecks, advice is about control—and control is power."

"Make a battle plan," Bailey said out loud. "And figure out who my soldiers are."

Smiling, she went into the house. She had to prepare dinner for Matt.

Thirteen

It was Patsy who gave Bailey the idea.

It was two days after she'd seen Arleen in the restaurant in Welborn, and Bailey had been going crazy trying to figure out what she wanted to do with her life.

Absently, she had cooked meals for Matt, and when he showed her his latest house plan, she barely looked at it. "A penny . . . ," Matt said, but Bailey didn't respond. Her mind was fully occupied with the questions of what and how and who.

Finally, it was what Patsy said that made the bells in her head start ringing. It was Patsy's turn to have them over to her house, and Bailey had shown up with a carload of food. She'd reached the point that she couldn't bear one more of Patsy's tasteless dips-and-chips.

"My problem with food," Patsy said, "is that I don't know what to serve before or after."

Bailey's mind was elsewhere. She'd been reading all that she could find about marketing what the industry called "specialty items," and it seemed that every avenue of the market was filled. There were gourmet jams everywhere, plus every conceivable sauce, mixed spice, and pickle; and as far as Bailey could tell, every country on Earth had a couple of lines of their products out. All she could see to do was repeat what others had already done. But what she really needed was a hole that could be filled.

"Before?" Bailey asked absently.

"You know, before the meal. What do you serve before the meal?"

"Hors d'oeuvres," Bailey said, not understanding what Patsy meant.

"I know that," Patsy said in disgust. "I know what the name of the food is, but I don't know what to serve."

"You can—" Bailey began, but Patsy cut her off.

"I know that I can make little puff pastry shells and fill them with some divine lobster concoction," Patsy said, her voice heavy with sarcasm. "I'm not stupid. I watch those TV cooks just like everyone else does, but I don't *want* to do that. Nobody seems to understand that there are people out here who really and truly hate to cook. We just want to get in and out of the kitchen as fast as possible. But we're all supposed to pretend to want to be Martha Stewart."

Bailey was having such a difficult time understanding what Patsy meant that she was coming out of her reverie to listen. "Pretend to be Martha Stewart?" Bailey asked. "What do you mean?"

"All those cooks on TV tell us that it's easy to make fabulous meals. All we have to do is add a little of this and a little of that, and bam! we have a great meal.

What they don't tell us is that we have to, first of all, think of what we're going to end up with, then we have to go to the grocery and buy all that stuff, then we have to create it. I don't have a brain that works like that. And I don't have the *time* to do all that! I buy a chicken, throw it in the oven, boil some vegetables and pour a canned sauce over them, and I can add water to some instant mashed potatoes, and eventually I can come up with a passable meal. When company comes, I want to do more, but I don't know what to do for befores and afters. You know, hors d'oeuvres and dessert other than ice cream."

Bailey stood there blinking at her. " 'Befores and afters,' " she said softly, and her mind seemed to go round and round. Pickled mushrooms on a platter. Chopped olives served on rounds of toasted bread. A packaged pound cake with brandied cherries poured over it.

"Befores and afters," she said again, then she smiled. Then she smiled more broadly. Then she threw her arms around Patsy and hugged her.

"What's going on?" Scott called from across the yard. "Can anyone get in on this?"

"Girl stuff," Patsy yelled in his direction, then she lowered her voice. "You wanta tell me what's in your head?"

"Top secret," Bailey said. "You have just given me the idea for my new business. Are you in or out?"

"In," Patsy said instantly.

"Then don't say a word to anyone, especially to anyone male," Bailey said quickly as she saw Matt approaching.

Ten minutes later, Janice said quietly to Bailey, "What are you up to?"

"I'm going to start a business, and I'm going to do it in secrecy. I'm not letting any man know what I'm doing for fear that he'll somehow, some way, talk me out of it. Are you in, or do you want to search your husband's tax records back *ten* years?"

For a moment Bailey thought she'd gone too far and that Janice just might throw her drink in her face. But when Janice spoke, her voice was so low that Bailey could barely hear her.

"I found a bank account," Janice said, her eyes on her husband, who was laughing at something Rick had said. "He doesn't know that I found it, and he doesn't know that I know what it's for—or should I say, *who* it's for? But I've diverted the interest, and I'm going to start diverting the principal. By the time he finds out about it, I'll have enough to leave."

Bailey caught her breath. She knew that she didn't like Janice's husband, and she'd often thought how she wouldn't like her mother-in-law supervising her children, as was the case in Janice's life, but Bailey had never seen anything that made her think that Janice wanted out. "I can't guarantee we'll make a profit," Bailey said. "We might lose our shirts."

"His shirt," Janice said. "We might lose *his* shirt." She then turned and walked away, but Bailey thought that Janice's shoulders were straighter and her head a bit higher.

By the next day, Bailey had figured out that the first order of business was to try to get Janice and Patsy to work with each other. First, she tried being sensible. "We can't open a business together if two of the partners don't speak to each other," she said after they'd ordered lunch. Both women looked at her with faces of stone. It was obvious that they had no intention of budging on this issue.

Bailey thought about playing therapist and asking what the root of their not talking was, then trying to fix it. But that thought lasted about thirty seconds. She didn't have time to start *two* careers.

That night Bailey served Matt grilled shrimp and steamed vegetables for dinner. It was a quick meal; she hadn't had time to cook something more elaborate. "When Patsy is going somewhere, and she wants Janice to go with her, how does she ask her?"

"Letters," Matt said as he bit into a shrimp.

"Letters?" Bailey asked, sounding as though she'd never heard of one.

"They don't speak, but they write to each other. Of course they don't address the letters to each other, but Patsy uses green stationery and Janice uses blue, so everyone knows who the letter is to. In fact, the whole thing started because of—"

Bailey held up her hand to stop him. "Don't tell me why they don't speak. I just need to know how to get them to communicate with one another now."

"Oh?" Matt said. "Speaking of which, what were you three discussing so seriously yesterday?"

"Food," Bailey said quickly.

"Patsy was talking about food," he said flatly, then watched as Bailey turned her face away so he wouldn't see how red it got.

"Yes, we were," she said, her back to him.

"I see."

Bailey turned back to him. "Letters are too slow. Do you think they'd do e-mail? How about a fax machine?"

Matt was looking at her hard. "What are you up to?"

It was on the tip of her tongue to tell him that it wasn't any of his business, but instead she smiled. "We're planning a surprise birthday party for Rick," she said. "And Patsy wants me to make a truly fabulous dinner for him. I think she's planning to invite about a hundred people." For a moment she stood there blinking at him, her breath held. Would he swallow this? And when exactly was Rick's birthday?

Matt grunted as he picked up another shrimp. "You'd better get a wiggle on then, because his birthday is in just three weeks. Let me know if I can do anything to help."

Bailey didn't say anything but went outside to cool off. She'd never been good at lying, and she was terrible at doing things in secret. "What you're thinking is written all over your face," Jimmie had said to her more than once. But now, she smiled. She had just told a whopper of a lie, the sky hadn't fallen on top of her and, what's more, it seemed that Matt had believed her. She looked up at the mulberry tree and grinned. She had just taken her first step on the road to becoming a devious, underhanded sneak—and by golly, it felt good!

Although Bailey got past Matt without too many problems, she almost destroyed their fledgling company before it began when she offended Janice. It was their first private meeting, held in Patsy's sewing room. "No man will bother us in here," Patsy said. "Not after what I did to Rick."

"Okay," Bailey said, "I'll bite. What did you do to your husband?"

"Embroidered pink bunnies on all his underwear. He didn't know it until he was in the station changing his clothes, and a couple of the guys saw him. I think they ribbed him pretty hard."

"Was he angry?" Bailey asked.

"Oh, yeah, but I cried and told him that I'd made a mistake because I had too many interruptions while I was sewing. I couldn't concentrate. Then I showed him the new pattern I had accidently put on one of his expensive new shirts." Patsy held up a man's denim shirt. Across the pocket was embroidered a mother duck with four little ducklings behind her. Patsy put the shirt down. "No matter what they hear coming from this room, and no matter how much time we spend in here, neither my sons nor my husband will bother us."

Bailey looked at Patsy in admiration. Her methods were cruel to the point of inhumanity, but they worked.

But it was Bailey who caused the problem. They were trying to come up with a name for their company.

"It needs to be a 'thing,'" Patsy said. "It has to be something concrete so we can make a logo of it."

"Mother Duck isn't a good name," Janice said, her eyes on Bailey as though they were the only two people in the room.

"I was thinking of Rainbow Preserves, something like that," Patsy said stiffly.

Bailey wanted to groan. How were they going to do anything *together* when these two didn't speak? And now they were sniping at each other like first-graders. She wanted to relieve the tension that was growing in the room. "Why don't we name it The Golden Six? With that name, we'd sell everything we made right here in Calburn," she said, smiling.

To Bailey's consternation, the women looked at her with expressions of intense dislike. Patsy's lip was curled upward, and Janice's eyes were cold and hard.

"What did I say?" Bailey whispered.

"Why don't you just call it The Thirtieth of August and be done with it?" Janice snapped as she got up and left the room.

The venom in Janice's voice left Bailey breathless. But worse was what Janice had said. Jimmie's birthday was August 30. Had the women somehow found out who Bailey was?

No, Bailey thought, that couldn't possibly be it. Surely the date was a coincidence. But what had made Janice so angry? She looked at Patsy, who had her head down and was studiously looking at the notebook on her lap. "What did I say?"

When Patsy looked up at Bailey, her eyes were as cold as Janice's had been. "I understand that you're an outsider, but those six boys mean a lot to the people of this town, so I'd advise you not to make fun of them. And I'd especially advise you not to make any remarks against them to Matt."

"To Matt?" Bailey asked. "Why?"

Patsy looked at her as though she were daft. "Matt and Rick's father was one of the Golden Six."

For a moment all Bailey could do was blink at Patsy as she tried to remember what she'd said about those boys to Matt. He'd never so much as hinted that he was connected to them. "And what about Janice?" Bailey asked, and her tone didn't allow for Patsy to play games about pretending not to know who Janice was.

"Father," Patsy mumbled, bending her head again. "One of them."

An hour later, Bailey got into her car and put her head down on the steering wheel. The meeting had been a bust. This morning she'd awakened full of enthusiasm. She was going to start a fabulous business with two women who had become her friends and she was going to do it all in secret—secret, that is, from the men they were living with.

But now she felt as though her legs had been cut off. Her two "partners" refused to speak to each other, and their "business" meeting had turned into one of those girl things in which everyone walks away in silent anger.

"Women can never play the game," Jimmie used to say, as usual making no attempt to hide his male chauvinism. "You women get your feelings hurt, then you back out."

Bailey leaned back against the seat and closed her eyes. Part of her wanted to give up right now. Part of her said she should go to the nearest lingerie store and buy something sexy, then parade around in it in front of Matt. She had an idea that he was the kind of man who would propose marriage the morning after. Have a couple of kids, she thought. Make peanut butter and jelly sandwiches. Drive the kids to soccer practice and ballet lessons.

But even as she was thinking this, she put the key in the ignition and turned it. Okay, so the term *outsider* had hurt. Yes, she was an outsider. She was also obviously enough of an insider that her smart remarks about the town's history could hurt people.

At home she had three loaves of bread rising. She should go back, punch them down, and put them back in the proofing oven for the second rise. But she didn't. Instead she turned onto the highway, drove to Ridgeway, and parked in front of the library.

When Bailey handed her request slip to the girl behind the periodicals desk, the girl didn't blink. She's not from Calburn, Bailey thought, or she would have commented on the date. Minutes later, Bailey had the microfilm on the machine, and she was looking at the *Ridgeway Gazette* for August 31, 1968. She had to find out what Janice meant by her angry reference to that date.

"Tragedy in Calburn," the headline read.

What followed was the story of the murder-suicide of Frank McCallum and his young wife, Vonda. "Of the Golden Six, Frank was the talker," the article said.

He was the one with the voice, the one who could talk anyone into anything, and for years it seemed that everything he touched was indeed "golden." He left Calburn right after he graduated from high school, but he returned a few years later, a widower with a young son to raise alone. With his talent for talking and selling, he easily got a job at the local used car dealership. Within a year, he was made manager, and a year after that, he was selling more cars than any other dealer in the state.

But then Frank's luck seemed to change. Some said it happened when he used his voice to seduce a high school girl named Vonda Oleksy. The people at the Calburn Baptist Church were angry about what Frank had done, and many of them said that the Golden Six got away with too much. So Frank McCallum married Vonda, a girl half his age.

Not long after the marriage, Frank went to work drunk. No one knows exactly what happened or how it happened, but a car was left in gear, and, somehow, it slammed into Frank, pinning him against a concrete wall. For weeks afterward, he was in the hospital, and when he got out, he was a shell of the man he once was. He lost the use of his left arm, but, worse, he seemed to have lost his luck. Within a year of the accident, Frank was fired from his job at the car dealership. Broke, jobless, an alcoholic, Frank took his young wife and moved back into his childhood home, a mountain cabin without plumbing or electricity. We can only imagine the despair that he must have felt at the way his life had turned out.

But who of us can forget the glorious deeds of the Golden Six? Years ago, back in 1953, six boys had been sent away from their beloved hometown to attend another high school. They'd had to endure cruelty such as only the survivors of high school can understand. They were bullied, harassed, ridiculed. Yet did these boys retaliate in kind? No. Instead, when there was danger and there was need for heroism, the Calburn boys were there. No one in this half of the state hasn't heard of how the Golden Six saved the entire school when it was under threat.

But that was then and this is now. Somehow, Frank McCallum went from the top to the bottom. He fell from being a hero to living a life of desperate poverty and drunkenness, and finally, he fell to murder and suicide. We don't know the exact circumstances that drove him to these deeds; we only know the facts.

On the thirtieth of August, 1968, Frank McCallum shot his young wife, then turned the gun on himself. The coroner ruled it a murder-suicide.

The funeral will be held at Davis Funeral Home in Calburn on the second of September and, I am sure, the names of the pallbearers are familiar to us all.

Below was a list of names: Rodney Yates, Thaddeus Overlander, Frederick Burgess, and Harper Kirkland. And, at the last, was the name Kyle Longacre. Matt's father.

Bailey turned the wheel of the microfilm machine to the second of September. There was nothing in the headline of the front page on that day, but on page 6 it said, "All of Calburn in Mourning."

"Three days ago the bodies of Frank McCallum and his young wife were found in a pool of blood, both of them with their faces blown off."

With a grimace, Bailey skipped the next two sentences. Whereas the first article had been written in a sad, elegiac tone, this one seemed to be inspired by a love of lurid detail. She checked the bylines; yes, the articles were written by two different people. She read on.

But what no one knew three days ago was that other tragedies happened in Calburn on that fateful night. Gus Venters, a prominent and much-loved citizen of Calburn, hanged himself. His grieving widow told the sheriff that she had no idea why her beloved husband wanted to die. She said he had everything to live for. He had a farm and a business and two beautiful stepchildren who loved him very much. "I don't understand it," Mrs. Venters told this reporter.

Bailey grimaced when she read that. There was no mention that his wife was having an adulterous affair and had ordered her husband to get out.

She continued reading.

Also on the night of Frank McCallum's death, one of the Golden Six left town and hasn't been seen since. It was revealed at McCallum's funeral that Mrs. Kyle Longacre had managed to keep her husband's disappearance a secret for three days. But when Kyle Longacre did not attend his friend's funeral, wasn't there to be a pallbearer, the town knew that something was wrong. A man like Kyle Longacre would not have missed his longtime friend's funeral unless something was badly amiss.

This reporter was told by an anonymous, but reliable, source that Mrs. Longacre is the daughter of the socially prominent Winfield family of Philadelphia. However, there has been no contact with her elite family since Mrs. Longacre quit college just months before she was to graduate to marry the charismatic Kyle Longacre. The same source told this reporter, "I guess they didn't think that a son of Stanley Longacre was good enough for their family." Longtime residents of Calburn will remember that Kyle Longacre's father was the wealthiest man in several counties before he lost everything in 1958, and drove his car off a cliff, with his wife of thirty years in the car beside him. Their grave marker reads "Together in death as well as in life."

Due to the financial reverses, Kyle was forced to leave his prestigious northern university before he graduated. He returned to his hometown of Calburn and began to make a living as a traveling salesman. Soon after he returned home, the young society lady he'd met at school defied her family, married Kyle, and lived in Calburn with her husband, whose work kept him away for much of their married life.

But that great romance seems to have ended just three days ago. This reporter was told that Kyle Longacre wrote a note to his wife—the contents of which she would not reveal—then left town. He leaves behind his wife and two young children, Matthew, aged five, and Richard, three. When questioned, Mrs. Longacre said that she planned to take her children and go home to her family in Philadelphia.

Bailey leaned back in her chair. Matt's mother hadn't gone home, or if she had, she'd returned to Calburn. What happened? Bailey wondered. Had Matt's mother appeared on her family's doorstep, her two young boys with her, and been refused entrance?

That poor woman, Bailey thought. Her family had disowned her for marrying the man she loved; then they'd kept to their word even when she'd been abandoned.

And poor Matt, Bailey thought. All his life he'd been
fighting to regain what should have been his.

Bailey rummaged in her bag for a notebook and a
pen. At the top of a page she wrote: "30 August 1968,"
then she began to make a list.

Gus Venters hanged himself
Frank and his wife—murder-suicide
Matt's father left town forever
Jimmie's birthday—1959

Bailey put down her pen. But *was* that the date of
Jimmie's birthday?

Jimmie hated clairvoyants and anything to do with
fortune-telling. Bailey had lived with him for years
before she understood that it wasn't that he didn't
believe in them; it was that he feared what they might
see. At a dinner party a woman, minor aristocracy, had
happened to be an amateur astrologer. She'd asked Bailey when Jimmie's birthday was. But when Bailey said it
was August 30, the woman had said, "I don't think so.
He's not a Virgo. No, James Manville is anything but a
Virgo. Can you get me the *true* time and place of his
birth?" she'd asked. "I'll do a chart for him."

Bailey hadn't told Jimmie what the woman had
said, and she certainly hadn't asked him where and
when he was born—she knew she'd receive no truthful
answer. And, worse, he'd wheedle it out of her who had
asked such a question. Then, Bailey knew, she'd never
see the astrologer again, and she rather liked the
woman. "Don't mention your . . . hobby to anyone
here," Bailey said quietly, and the woman had nodded
in understanding.

Now Bailey remembered looking up once to see Jimmie staring at her intensely, as though he was trying to read his wife's interest in the old woman, who was wearing enough fake diamonds to fell a smaller person. That night, Jimmie had asked her what she'd found so interesting about the woman, and Bailey had chattered inanely about finding her so very interesting because she'd traveled all over the world. Jimmie had looked at his wife with one eyebrow raised, and she knew he'd known she was lying. But she stood her ground and didn't tell him the truth. That was the last time she ever saw the countess.

What Bailey remembered most strongly about the astrologer was that she had said she'd stake her life on a bet that James Manville had not been born on the thirtieth of August.

Now Bailey looked at her watch. It was after three, and if she was going to get home to make Matt's dinner, she'd better leave. But as she reached for the wheel to rewind the film, she saw a note at the bottom of the article: "See reprint of original story starting on page B2."

There was no way on earth that she could resist turning the film to the second page of the second section of the newspaper.

The truth was, until today the whole idea of a group of high school boys who were called the Golden Six had seemed like a joke, some local event that had happened long ago and far away. She hadn't even been interested enough to read the book Violet had given her. Until today, she didn't think she knew anyone who had a connection to the young men. Now she'd learned that Janice's father was one of them, and so was Matt's. Why did Matt's father abandon his wife and two children? Was

Kyle Longacre so devastated over the murder-suicide of his childhood friend that he could no longer bear his hometown?

Bailey read the story of what had happened in 1953, the event that had given the boys the name of the Golden Six, and by the time she finished, she had to admit that what those boys did had been pretty heroic.

The first part of the article recounted the story Violet had told her, about the fire at the high school and the students being bused to Wells Creek.

But the reporter hadn't just reported. She'd spent some time researching, and she'd interviewed several people, so she was able to present not just the facts but a story. She told how the parents of Calburn had so driven the school board crazy about which schools they wanted their children bused to that in the end, all the students' names had been put into a hat and drawn out. It was because of this random assignment that all girls were sent to one school while another received only two girls. And it was because of the drawing that six boys who had grown up in the same town but not really known each other came to be together.

The reporter told a little about each boy, and although she tactfully never said that the boys came from different social classes, it was definitely implied. She said that the boys were from such different back- grounds that they never would have become friends if they hadn't been isolated together.

There was Thaddeus Overlander, a studious boy with born-again Christian parents. "Taddy" had never been allowed to attend so much as a basketball game at Cal- burn, much less participate in a social life. Frederick Burgess, called "Burgess" by all, was an athlete, a great hulk of a boy, who found studies "difficult." Harper Kirkland lived alone with his mother, the last of the family that had founded Calburn and, according to the reporter, had once owned it all. But Harper's grand-father had sold the land off bit by bit, then frittered away the money until all the Kirkland family owned now was the small Calburn newspaper.

Frank McCallum and Rodney Yates were cousins, raised in the mountains of Virginia in a hardscrabble existence. They were attending high school in Calburn because they were staying with one of Rodney's seven brothers, a young man who'd quit school when he was in the sixth grade. Rodney and Frank had wanted to do better for themselves, though, so they were determined to finish school.

The reporter described Frank as a persuasive speaker who had a part-time job selling ads for the newspaper.

"And one has only to look at Rodney Yates to see what his talent is," the article said. At that Bailey turned through the film to see if there were any photos, with no luck. She went back to the article. "Rodney is an extremely handsome young man," the reporter wrote, "and it's rare to see him without several young ladies nearby.

"And then there's Kyle."

When she read that, Bailey drew in her breath. What was Matt's father like? What was the true nature of a man who could walk out on his wife—a wife who had given up her heritage and her family for him—and his small children?

"Kyle is the golden boy," the reporter wrote. "Every-one in Virginia and probably several other states knows of Stanley Longacre and his incredible success. They've seen the mansion where Kyle lives, the mansion his father built. But then a great many people in Virginia live in houses built by Stanley Longacre. It seems fitting that a man who has produced so much should produce a son like Kyle: handsome, athletic, a straight-A student, on the debating team, the yearbook staff, elected class president by his fellow students every year since the fourth grade."

"But he abandoned his wife and children!" Bailey muttered in disgust, then began to read again.

On that autumn day in 1953 someone, a man with an "ominous voice," had called the school and said he'd planted a bomb somewhere and that "they would never get out alive." Less than a minute later, black smoke began filling the corridors of the school. In the ensuing chaos, it had been the six boys from Calburn who made sure that every student got out safely.

When the reporter arrived, all the students were outside, the fire department and the police were there, and several of the students were crying. She wrote that at first she'd assumed that fear was causing the tears, but a couple of girls said, "We've been so mean to them," so the reporter began to ask questions. She was told that the students of Wells Creek had not wanted the extra students from Calburn, so they'd made them unwelcome. "Dead rats in their lockers," she wrote. "Hazing, name calling, ostracizing at every opportunity. It must have been horrible for the students from Calburn, but, in the end, they stepped above their treatment and risked their lives to save others."

Bailey read the account of what happened that day. Taddy told reporters that after they were told to evacuate the school, he'd glanced out the window of his classroom and seen smoke coming out of the gym. He saw a couple of the football players banging on the door, so he thought maybe they were trapped inside. Since the door to his classroom was blocked with students scrambling over each other to get out, Taddy climbed out a window, went down the fire escape, and opened the door for the football players to get out. Some of them were being treated for smoke inhalation, but thanks to Taddy, none had been seriously hurt.

Rodney said he heard screams from the girls' locker room, so he ran that way. The outside door to the locker room was bolted. He couldn't get it open, so he went around to the windows. The locker room was in the basement, and the windows were also locked, but shop class was nearby, so Rodney ran in, grabbed a crowbar, and wrenched open the windows. The girls climbed up on the benches and slid out through the windows to safety.

Here the reporter recorded her interview with Rodney verbatim. "Isn't it true that some of the girls were naked?" she asked Rodney.

"Yes, ma'am, they were."

"And you gave them your own clothing to cover themselves, is that right?"

"I gave them my jacket, my shirt, T-shirt, and my trousers."

"And that's why you're now wearing only boxer shorts, and your shoes and socks?"

"Yes, ma'am, that's why."

Bailey couldn't help smiling at the interview. She could imagine the beautiful young man standing there wearing little because he'd given his clothing to cover some frightened girls.

The article went on. "But it was Kyle Longacre who was the superhero. There was a gas mask, a souvenir of WWI, in a glass cabinet. Kyle broke the glass, grabbed the mask, put it on, then leaped onto a desk and climbed up into the attic of the old building. He told this reporter that when he saw the smoke coming out of the ceiling, he knew that whoever had planted the bomb had probably put it in the attic. He said that he didn't think about what he was doing, he just pulled the stairs down and went up them.

"And you got the bomb?" the reporter asked.

"Yes," Kyle replied, and the reporter said that he seemed reluctant to talk about what he'd done.

The reporter went on to say that while Kyle was being interviewed, a fireman said that what Kyle had done was the stupidest thing he'd ever heard of in his life, and he didn't know if the kid should be given a medal or locked away for his own good. Then a woman came over, shook Kyle's hand, and said that he'd saved her daughter's life. The woman went on to say that she lived in a house built by Kyle's father in the Golden Sixty development, so called because the land had once been sixty acres of broccoli that had gone to seed and covered the field with yellow flowers.

The reporter concluded the article by saying, "I don't know about the Golden Sixty, but these boys are sure the Golden Six."

"And that," the newspaper editor had added at the end of the article, "is how they got their names."

Fourteen

Bailey pushed the food about on her plate. Again, she hadn't had time to cook anything special for dinner, so she'd stopped at Boston Market and picked up a couple of pot pies, hoping that Matt would think she'd made them. But Matt was eating in silence and seemed to be deep in thought about something—as Bailey was.

Her mind was full of what she'd read that afternoon. Those six wonderful boys! They were just high school boys who'd been made to feel miserable by the other kids, yet when there was danger, they'd risked their lives to save the other students. What kind of kids cared that much?

She could imagine what bookish, unsocial Taddy must have been like. She had no doubt that the football players of the school had tormented him mercilessly. Yet the boy had climbed out a window, shimmied down a drain-pipe, and rescued them all.

And Kyle had grabbed a gas mask and gone directly toward the bomb. What if it had gone off? He'd had time to get out, so why didn't he run for his life? What interest did he have in a school where the other kids hazed and ridiculed him?

How could a young man like that later leave his wife and children?

"Why didn't you tell me your father was one of the Golden Six?" Bailey asked quietly, but she didn't look up at Matt. When he was silent, she raised her head and saw that he had eaten little and now was moving bits of chicken about on his plate.

"It didn't seem important," he said after a while, then put down his fork and leaned back in his chair. "I could have picked these pies up for you," he said, letting her know that he knew she hadn't cooked them.

"I was busy," she said, "and I didn't have time—" She cut herself off, realizing that he'd changed the subject. "Why didn't you tell me?"

"Since when have you been interested in the Golden Six?"

His tone was hostile, and she knew that he was trying to put her off, but Bailey didn't back down. "If I'm going to live in this town, I think I should know more than I do. Today I offended Janice. I made a crack about the Golden Six, and she was furious with me. Patsy told me that your father and Janice's were part of them. I guess I thought it had all happened so long ago that it had no connection to today. But it does." Looking at him, she said softly, "Do you know what made your father leave?"

Matt didn't answer, but got up and left the room.

Bailey gave a great sigh. Today seemed to be her day for offending people. She got up, cleared the table, and put the dishes in the dishwasher. When she was finished, she turned around, and Matt was standing there, a shoe box in his hand.

"Want to see some pictures?" he asked.

"Yes," she said, smiling in relief that he wasn't angry as she followed him into the living room.

He sat down on the couch, then motioned her to sit beside him. They had developed unwritten rules between them that said she took the couch while he took the big easy chair. But tonight they sat side by side, and Matt put the shoe box on the coffee table.

"I don't have much about him," Matt said as he lifted the lid. The box was old and worn; it was for a pair of children's shoes, size eight. "My mother threw these photos away about a year after my father walked out on us. It was only by chance that I saw them and fished them out of the garbage."

Matt didn't say so, but she had a feeling that he'd never shown the contents of this box to anyone. His hand shook a bit as he lifted the lid. "I was crazy about my father. He was hardly ever at home, but when he was, he was the center of everything. He was . . ." Matt hesitated. "He was . . . don't laugh at me, but he was glorious. He could do anything. He read a lot, mostly nonfiction, while he was on the road, so he knew a lot about how the world worked. I was only five, but maybe because, for most of the time, I was 'the man of the house,' so to speak, I was an old kid, and I had a lot of questions. My father never brushed me off as I saw other fathers do."

Matt reached into the box and pulled out a photo. It was one of those wallet-size heavily posed photos that fill high school yearbooks.

Bailey took the picture and looked into the eyes of a younger, slighter Matt. "I can see you in him. He's a good-looking man."

"Was. He's dead now."

Bailey wanted to ask questions, but she felt that if she was quiet, Matt would be more likely to tell her about himself. He handed her another photo. It was of six boys standing in front of a car with the round fenders of the 1950s.

"They're——" he began.

"I can guess who they are, but let me see if I can guess who is who," Bailey said, holding the photo closer to the bulb in the floor lamp. "This one in the letter sweater is your father, of course."

"Right," Matt said, smiling.

"And this one has to be Rodney . . . Roddy. Heavens! But he was beautiful."

"Yeah. Right after high school he went out to Hollywood for a couple of years, but he couldn't act. Or maybe he had too much competition. Whatever, he came back here."

"Like Frank did," Bailey said.

"Did you finally read that book on your bedside table? The one Violet gave you?"

"How——" She put up her hand. "No, don't tell me how you know what's in my bedroom and who gave me what. But, no, I haven't read that book yet. I spent the afternoon in the Ridgeway library, reading the newspaper accounts."

"Ah."

"What's that mean?"

"It means that you haven't heard all the story, not if you've only read what was in the newspapers." He nodded toward the photo in her hand. "So, go on, tell me who is who in that picture."

"Frank must be the skinny one on the end. Is that a cigarette in his hand?"

"Unfiltered. But are you sure he isn't Taddy?"

"No, Taddy is the tall one on the other end, the one who looks scared."

"You're not bad at this, are you?"

"And Burgess is the big one squatting down in front." She lifted the photo higher and looked hard at the young man standing beside Kyle. Harper Kirkland was short, thin, and as cute as a cherub on the Sistine Chapel ceiling. He reminded her of someone, but she couldn't think who. "What happened to them?"

Matt took the photo from her and put it on the table beside the other one. Inside the box were folded pieces of paper; he kept each photo in its own little envelope to prevent scratching.

"Burgess ran his father's lumber business for years, went bankrupt, and died when the plane he was piloting crashed. I think it was 1982 or 1983. Rodney married a couple of times and had a lot of kids. Taddy taught science at Calburn High until it closed, then died of a heart attack two years later. He never married. Frank and my father, you know about."

"What about Harper?"

Matt hesitated before answering. "He was one of America's first victims of AIDS."

"I see," she said, then bent forward and looked at the photo again. "Sal Mineo. Remember him? That's who he looks like." She looked back at the photo. "If those kids at Welborn had known *that* about him, his life probably wouldn't have been worth much."

Matt handed her another photo. This one was of a smiling, laughing young couple. He was wearing a school letter sweater, and she had on a big circle skirt and a tight sweater with a fuzzy little collar. They looked like actors in a stage presentation of *Grease*.

"Your parents?"

"Yes," Matt said softly. "That was them in the days before my grandfather went bankrupt, before he drove his car over a cliff and took my grandmother with him."

The bitterness in Matt's voice made Bailey shiver. "They look so much in love," she said, holding the photo. "Look at her eyes! She's looking at him as though she'd—" She broke off.

"As though she'd follow him anywhere?" Matt asked, his voice sarcastic. "She did follow him. But years later he left town and never came back. He left the woman who loved him more than life with two young children to support, and much too proud to ask her parents for help."

"How did your family survive?"

Matt leaned back against the sofa, and for a moment he didn't speak. "I remember a childhood of work," he said softly. "That's all there seemed to be. My mother ran the local grocery store for a tightfisted old bastard, and she left us in the care of a slovenly old woman who watched soaps on TV and ignored my brother and me."

Matt took a breath to calm himself. "I did my best to see that my little brother was fed and kept safe. I was a big kid, so I started mowing lawns for money when I was nine. On the day my father walked out on us, I was transformed from a child into a man. He took his high school medals, wrote a note to his wife, then left."

When Matt looked at Bailey, his eyes were black with anger. "You know what the note said?" He didn't wait for her answer. " 'Forgive me.' That's all he wrote. Just two words."

"But you didn't forgive him, did you?"

"No. When a man makes a bargain, he stands by it."

"As you did with Cassandra?"

"Right. Until her actions let me out, I stayed. I'd made the vows, and I meant them."

"Your mother never contacted her parents?"

"No. Too much pride." He smiled. "And don't look at me like that. I know that I inherited her pride. Patsy's told me often enough. But my mom wouldn't take money from her parents, and she never took any money from me. I worked all through school, every minute I could, and I saved every penny of it. My mother said she wanted me to go to college. She said that school was the only way that I wouldn't end up like her, and saying that was the closest she ever came to complaining."

"I wish I could have met her," Bailey said. "But if *I* had been in the same situation, I would have complained, and I would have gone to my father on my knees and begged him for help."

Matt looked at her with raised eyebrows. "Oh? Now why don't I think that's true? Why do I have the impression that maybe, possibly, you have more pride than my mother and me put together?"

Bailey looked away. He saw too much. "Did your mother see you graduate from college?"

"No. She died the year Rick was a senior in high

school, and six months later he married Patsy. Rick said he wasn't like me, that he didn't have my drive, and he couldn't bear to live alone. He said Patsy would give him someone to live for. He was smarter than I was. He knew what was good for him, and he went after it. He's been very happy with Pat and the kids."

"But not you. You haven't been happy."

"No, not me. I've always felt that something was missing from my life, that there was a big empty place inside me."

"Did you ever find out where your father went, or why?"

"A few years ago, I received a package. A woman who owned a boardinghouse in Baltimore sent it, and she wrote that her boarder said that if he died, she was to mail me the package."

"Let me guess. It was from your father."

"Yes. All his high school medals, the ones he'd taken with him, were inside. There was no note, nothing but the medals. At the time I was too involved in my own life to do anything more than mutter, 'The bastard,' and toss the whole box into the top of the closet. But later, during the divorce, when everything was being separated, I found the box and dropped it into my suitcase."

"A suitcase that you'd packed for going home to Calburn."

"Yes. I think it was in my mind that I needed to figure out where to go from here, and Calburn, home, was where I needed to figure it out."

"And have you found out anything so far?" Bailey asked softly.

"The truth is that I'd like to know what happened to

my father. I grew up hating him and knowing I would never have done what he did, but I'm older now, and I've realized that people don't live by their brains alone."

"Right," Bailey said. "People live by their emotions. Their emotions can drive them to do all manner of extraordinary things."

"Speaking from experience?" Matt asked, his eyes twinkling, obviously trying to lighten the mood. "What do you say that we go see a movie? How about if we do something normal for a change?"

"That sounds nice," Bailey said as she watched Matt put the photos back into the box. But as he lifted the folded papers to straighten them, one fell to the floor, and Bailey reached down to pick it up. He hadn't shown her all the photos in the box, and she wondered why. Did he have secrets, just as she did?

The photo she picked up was of two teenagers, a boy and a girl, both of them pudgy and sullen-looking. They were wearing ill-fitting clothes, and the boy had a complexion that even in the out-of-focus black-and-white photo looked splotchy. "Friends of your dad's?" Bailey asked, unable to keep the smile out of her voice. She couldn't imagine the well-groomed class president, Kyle Longacre, being friends with these two.

"No, they're—" Matt began, but cut off when Bailey wouldn't release the photo.

Slowly, with a face as white as the woodwork behind her, she moved the photo closer to the light. "Who are these two?" she said, her voice a husky whisper.

"I don't know," Matt said. "That was in the batch of photos I found in the garbage. Do *you* know who they are?"

"No," Bailey said, then stronger, "no, of course not.

How would I know someone in *your* photos?" But the way Matt was looking at her made her know that he didn't believe her. Bailey gave a laugh that she hoped sounded carefree and unconcerned. "They just reminded me of a couple of truly dreadful people I used to know," she said. "It gave me chills for a moment."

"Want to tell me about them?" Matt asked softly.

"They aren't interesting," she said quickly, then stood up. "You know, I'm going to pass on that movie, if it's all right with you. I think I'm a bit tired, and I'd like to go to bed and read for a while. Well, good night," she said before he could reply, then she nearly ran to the privacy of her bedroom, where she shut the door and leaned against it.

The teenagers in the photo were Atlanta and Ray, and they were standing in front of the house that Jimmie had left her, the house that she was in now.

Fifteen

❧

Once she was in her bedroom, Bailey picked up her address book and turned to Phillip's numbers. Maybe she should call him and tell him what she'd just seen. Maybe it was significant that she'd seen a photo of Jimmie's brother and sister in front of the house that Jimmie had left her.

But Bailey put the address book down. She'd always known that this house belonged to Jimmie, hadn't she? And if he grew up here, so did his brother and sister. And it wouldn't be unusual for a person in a small town to have photos of other people in that town, would it?

As she opened her chest of drawers and got out her nightgown, she told herself that it would be best if she just stayed out of whatever had happened so long ago. She'd seen the way Janice had reacted today, and she'd seen the way Matt's hand quivered when he showed her photos of his father. It would make everyone feel worse if she started asking questions about the past. "Who are these fat, sulky teenagers, and what is a photo of them doing in with pictures of the Golden Six?" was not something she could ask. If she could make Janice furious with one remark, imagine what she'd do if she asked a hundred questions.

She put her address book back into the bedside table drawer and headed for the shower. All in all, it would be better if she concentrated on the business she was trying to start with Patsy and Janice.

Feeling better with the decision made, she turned on the shower water, then saw headlights reflect off the trees outside her bathroom window. It looked as though Matt had decided to go to the movie by himself.

Without thinking about what she was doing, Bailey turned off the shower water, put on her big terry cloth robe, and left her bedroom. The house had that empty feeling that it did when Matt wasn't there to fill it up. "Matt?" she called, but there was no answer.

Her heart beating in her throat, she walked softly down the short corridor to his bedroom. The door was slightly open. "Matt?" she called again, then put her hand on the door. If he shows up, I'll tell him that I was . . . She thought, but she couldn't come up for a reason for her snooping, not to herself, much less to tell him.

On his bed, which she saw was neatly made, was the shoe box full of photos. Bailey didn't think; she just sat down on the side of the bed, turned on the lamp, and removed the lid.

There were three photos that Matt hadn't shown her. One was of a very young Matt and his brother Rick, wearing pajamas, standing in front of a Christmas tree, surrounded by opened presents. Sitting on the floor, looking at his eldest son with eyes full of love, was his father.

The picture made Bailey, knowing what happened later, want to cry.

The second photo was of an older Matt sitting on his father's lap behind the wheel of a car. When Bailey looked on the back, the picture was dated July 1968. In less than two months, this man would walk out on his family forever.

Shaking her head, Bailey put down the picture and picked up the one of the two teenagers. She held the photo up to the light and looked at it for a long time. There was no doubt that they were Atlanta and Ray. And it was no doubt that the house in the background was the one Jimmie had left her.

Find out the truth about what happened, will you, Frecks? Jimmie had asked. But the truth about what? About Atlanta and Ray? Were they somehow connected to the Golden Six? Is that why their picture was mixed in with photos of Matt's family? Matt said he didn't know who they were or why their pictures were there, so maybe it was just a coincidence, or an accident. Maybe Matt's mother had thrown out lots of pictures, but Matt had saved only the ones of his father. Maybe this photo had been stuck to the back of one of the good ones with a bit of ketchup.

Bailey turned the photo over. There was no sign of ketchup or any other stain, but there was a faint date penciled on the back. She turned the picture this way and that and all she could make out was 196—. The last number of the year, she couldn't read.

Slowly, she put the photos back just as she'd found them, then stood up and smoothed the bed. She didn't want Matt to know that she'd been snooping.

She went back to her own bedroom and took a shower, and as the water cascaded down on her, she decided again that it was best not to ask any more questions. What had happened was over long ago, and it was better to let it stay dead.

Sixteen

❧

After two more days with Janice and Patsy, Bailey admitted defeat. It was clear to her that the three of them had the knowledge to run the company once it was started, but getting it started was out of their league. For one thing, they couldn't even agree on a name. And where were they going to get the money, if they did get themselves organized?

Bailey made herself a cup of tea, took a pen and a sketch pad outside, and tried to come up with some ideas for a name and logo for the company, but she was stymied. After an hour, she went back inside to get more tea, and on impulse, she picked up the cordless phone and her address book, took them outside, and punched in a number.

As the phone rang, she held her breath. What would her reception be?

Carol Waterman answered on the first ring. All Bailey had to do was give her name, and words came flooding from Carol's mouth. "I thought maybe you were Phillip calling. He's never home now, and the children and I haven't seen him in a month. He wants to quit working for 'them,' and he's told them twice that he's quitting, but their response has been to give him more money— so much money that Phillip agrees to stay a while longer. Phillip won't tell me what those two are up to, but from the look on his face, it's not good."

While Bailey was listening, she was doodling on the sketch pad. In front of her was the mulberry tree, and she idly outlined the undulating branches of the old giant. For the life of her, she couldn't work up any sympathy for Carol. What had the two of them expected when Phillip took a job with lowlifes like Atlanta and Ray? That receiving billions would turn Atlanta and Ray into nice people?

"So what you're saying is that you have time on your hands and access to lots of money."

Carol hesitated. "I guess I am," she said tentatively. "What do you have in mind?"

"I was wondering if maybe you'd be interested in joining in a business that I and a couple of friends are starting."

"What kind of business?" Carol asked cautiously.

"It's—" Bailey looked at the sketch on her pad. "Before and After is what we're working on now. It's a branch of . . . of the Mulberry Tree Preserving Company."

"I won't have to cook anything, will I?"

"No, that's my job."

"I see," Carol said, and her voice was cold. "So what else do you want from me, besides to give you and your friends money?"

Bailey knew too well what Carol was feeling. When she was first married to Jimmie, a lot of people had offered her a lot of things, but she soon found out that all they wanted was his money. "How about publicity?" Bailey said off the top of her head. "Advertising. Think you'd be any good in that area?" Heaven knew that she and Janice and Patsy weren't!

Carol was silent so long that Bailey thought she was going to hang up. "Before I married Phillip, I was training to be an actress."

Bailey wanted to say, What good is that to us? but she didn't. She couldn't afford to offend Carol, a person with access to money. "Maybe you could . . . You could . . . be the lead actress in our commercial."

"Great! What's the plot of it?"

"We're still working on it, and of course we'll need your input."

"You haven't written a word, have you?"

Bailey laughed, and when she did, the tension left her body. "Not even one. I can cook; Patsy can run a factory; and Janice is a money manager. But the three of us are stuck about what to do to let people know that we have a bunch of jams and jellies to sell. You think you could help us?"

"Maybe," Carol said slowly. "If I can find time between hair and nail appointments. You know how *that* is."

"All too well," Bailey said, trying to keep the excitement out of her voice. She'd called Carol hoping to get money, but talent as an actress was even better. "Maybe you could—"

"Get the next plane out of here and meet with you and your new friends and do something with my brain besides decide whether to wear the navy or the black?"

Bailey laughed. "Do you know where I live now?"

"I have no idea, but I have a pencil right here in my hand."

Bailey gave Carol the address, hung up the phone, and managed to sit still for half a minute; then she jumped up and started dancing. "Yes!" she said as she grabbed a branch of the mulberry tree and kissed it. "You old sweetheart," she said, as she grabbed her sketchbook and went inside and upstairs to Matt's fax machine. Now all she had to do was persuade Janice and Patsy that this was the right name for their company.

Bailey photocopied her sketch and sent her idea to both Janice and Patsy. To Patsy, she said she wanted her to sew a label like her sketch. Janice faxed back that everyone would think they sold only mulberry products. Then Patsy faxed that most Americans have no idea what a mulberry is.

"This could go on forever," Bailey muttered. Jimmie always said that he hated any decision that everyone agreed with.

"Good!" she faxed back to them. "If they don't know what a mulberry tastes like, they won't have any preconceptions. If either of you have any better ideas, I'd like to hear them."

For an hour there was silence from the fax machine, then Bailey received two notes, both of which said, "Okay by me." Since the wording was identical, she knew that, somehow, the two women had communicated with each other and come to an agreement.

"Thanks, Jimmie," Bailey said as she smiled at the faxes. Now she needed to go to the kitchen and start making some prototypes for the Before and After part of their brand-new company.

Bailey was experimenting with a strawberry-cherry mixture in which she used no alcohol. How could she make the sauce taste as good as though it was flavored with kirsch without using the liqueur? She'd found out that selling food flavored with alcohol involved obtaining a liquor license, something that none of the women was ready to take on. Janice said, "Let's save that as a goal for 2005," and the others had agreed.

Maybe if she extracted the juice, boiled it down, and added a little almond flavoring, she would create the flavor she wanted. With that thought, she went into the pantry to look for her *chinois,* the conical strainer set in a frame. It took nearly ten minutes before she saw the *chinois* on the top shelf of the pantry.

"Matt!" she muttered. He'd put the dishes away last night, and for some odd reason, he'd obviously thought that the strainer should be put on the highest shelf, a shelf that was at least three feet above Bailey's head.

There was a ladder in the barn, and she knew that she should go get it, or even get a chair, but it all seemed so time-consuming, and the fruit was bubbling. Bailey stepped onto the lowest shelf and held her breath to see if it would hold her weight; then she remembered that she was no longer heavy enough to break shelves.

Holding on to the shelves above, she stepped up until she could reach the strainer. But as she grabbed it, she saw something sticking out of the boards at the back of the shelf. This room was the only one that hadn't been remodeled. Bailey had refused to allow Matt and his beer-drinking friends to touch its perfection. It had been cleaned, and that was all.

Curious, Bailey put the *chinois* on a lower shelf, then stepped higher to reach the tiny piece of paper sticking out from the boards. Hanging on with one arm, she slowly pulled on it, and out came a rectangle of white. Bailey knew instantly that she was looking at the back of a photograph.

Slowly, she turned the photo over, and what she saw made her draw in her breath. In the foreground of the picture were two people. One was a giant of a man, blond, with eyes that didn't look too intelligent. But he had a smile on his face that was so sweet Bailey almost smiled back at him. He had his arm playfully around the neck of a boy who looked to be about fourteen or fifteen.

The boy had a horribly deformed cleft palate.

Slowly, Bailey got down from the shelves and walked closer to the window to look at the photo in the light. The boy in the photo was Jimmie. She'd recognize the set of those shoulders anywhere, and the eyes were the same. And she was sure that the blond giant was the man who'd once lived in her house, the man who had hanged himself in her barn.

She looked at the photo in the sunlight. In the background were three other people, a woman and two men. The face of the woman was clearly visible. She was small and thin, and not particularly attractive; her face was long and pinched-looking. Since she was openly sneering at the back of the big man and Jimmie, her disapproval plain to see, Bailey was sure she had to be the adulterous wife.

The men in the background had their faces turned to

profile and were a bit out of focus, so Bailey couldn't identify them.

Who would know who these people are? she wondered. Matt? No, he was too young when this photo was taken. It didn't have a date on it, but she guessed by the clothes that it was late 1960s or early 1970s.

"Violet," she said aloud, then she went back into the kitchen, turned off the pot of simmering fruit, put a dish towel on the glass shelf in the refrigerator, and set the hot pot on top of it. As she ran toward the front door, she grabbed her car keys, and fifteen minutes later she was at Violet's house.

Violet was sitting on her front porch, her head back, snoozing.

Bailey didn't bother with any preliminaries. "Who are these people?" she asked as she thrust the photo at Violet.

Violet awoke instantly, unstartled, as she looked up at Bailey. "And nice to see you too," she said as she took the photo. "Go get my glasses. They're in there somewhere," she added as she nodded toward the door.

It took Bailey ten minutes to find Violet's reading glasses, and another five to wash them. By the time she got back outside, Violet was asleep again, the photo on her lap. "So tell me," Bailey said loudly, holding out the reading glasses.

Slowly, Violet put on her half glasses and looked at the photo, while Bailey took a seat across from her. "I don't know who the two in front are. They're—"

"I know who they are. I want to know about the people in the back."

Violet raised her eyebrows at Bailey. "Know who they are, do you? You've been doing some research. Is the kid in the front, the one with the lip, the guy you were lookin' for?"

"Never mind that. Who are the people in the back?"

"What do I get out of it?"

Bailey narrowed her eyes at Violet.

Violet laughed. "Okay, let me look. I don't know who the woman is, but that one is Roddy, and the one way in the back is, I think, Kyle."

"The Golden Six," Bailey said under her breath. "So he *was* involved with them."

Violet stared at Bailey hard, then lifted the photo and looked at it again. "The big guy must be the man my friend told me about, the guy who hanged himself in your barn. Isn't that big ol' tree in the back the one that's at your house?"

"Yes," Bailey said absently. "That's my mulberry tree."

"If you want to know about this kid in the picture, why don't you ask him?"

"He's dead," Bailey said before she thought, then looked up at Violet with wide eyes.

"You better be careful there, or you're gonna start givin' away information instead of pullin' it out of ever'body else." Violet laughed when Bailey looked away, hiding her face. "What I meant is, why don't you ask *him?*" She pointed at the photo.

"Who?"

"Rodney."

"He's alive?"

"Honey, 'sixty-eight may seem like a long time ago to you, but it wasn't. Roddy is still alive, married to a girl less than half his age, and he's still poppin' out kids. Janice didn't tell you that she has half a dozen half brothers and sisters?"

"It seems that people in Calburn tend to leave out the more interesting parts of their history," Bailey said softly.

"Unlike you, who are so open and honest and tell everyone everything about yourself," Violet said.

Bailey got up, took the photo from Violet, and started to leave.

"What is it you gals are plannin' to do that you're so all-fired secretive about?"

Bailey drew in her breath. Did everybody in Calburn know *everything?*

"Don't look at me like that. I think your secret's safe around town, it's just that I hear more than other people do. I have a lot of friends around here."

For a moment Bailey looked at Violet speculatively. As far as she could piece together from what little she'd been told, in her younger days, Violet had been the local prostitute. And now she was the local drug dealer—or at least marijuana dealer. Bailey had had enough encounters with people of Violet's generation to know that most old hippies didn't consider marijuana a drug. "You wouldn't know anything about making a film, would you?"

Violet gave a little smile. "Before I came here, I lived in L.A., and I was a production secretary for sixteen years."

"Does that mean you typed, or you were on the set?"

"Let's just say that a lot of the time the director was too drunk or too busy with his love life to do his job, so I took over. What kind of film you plannin' to do? Porno?"

"With you as our star," Bailey shot back at her.

Violet laughed. "In my younger days . . . Okay, I'll stop the smart cracks. What do you need?"

"A TV commercial. Something simple. We have an idea about what we want to sell, but we don't know how to sell it."

"So tell me what's in your head. I've done enough script rewriting that I think I could do a one-minute script on my own."

"Think you can get along with Janice and Patsy and not start a war?"

"Maybe. How badly do you need a script written?"

Bailey wasn't going to say that they were desperate to find people who knew something about anything. She shrugged as though she could take Violet's help or leave it. "Do you know how to draw a map?"

Violet took her time in answering. "A map that shows you how to get to Roddy's house up in the mountains?"

"Yes," Bailey said.

"You won't like it up there. And you've got 'money' written all over you. He'll try to get it. And you're too pretty to be around him."

"I'll take my chances. So how much do you charge for your help?"

"I got weeds in my garden that are taller than the plants."

Bailey tightened her lips. "Vegetables, but no hemp plants. I draw the line at illegal substances."

Violet laughed as she heaved her bulk out of the chair. "Come on. You can make us some lemonade so we'll be cool while we talk about whatever it is that you're tryin' to sell. And you can tell me how Matt is."

Bailey's head came up. "You and Matt didn't— You haven't—"

"Not him or his daddy," Violet said as she walked past Bailey and into the house. "But I sure did *want* to!"

Seventeen

As *Bailey drove up* the gravel road toward Rodney's house, she was still feeling guilty about Matt. She wasn't a good liar, and she wasn't a good actress. Last night she'd been jittery and nervous about what she was planning to do today, and she knew that she was keeping many secrets from Matt. It wasn't that she *had* to tell him what she was doing, but he didn't deserve all the lies and evasions she was giving him.

At dinner last night she'd tried to be carefree and happy, and to make light conversation. But the truth was, she was pumping Matt hard for information. She wanted him to tell her all he knew about Rodney Yates, and about the man's situation now.

"Why ever didn't you tell me that one of the Golden Six was still alive?" she asked as she dumped mashed potatoes on Matt's plate. "It was such a shock when Janice mentioned her father. I was so embarrassed that I didn't know he was still alive."

"That's enough," Matt said softly.

"Oh, sorry," she said when she glanced down at the eight-inch-high pile of potatoes on his plate. She turned back to the stove.

"Janice didn't mention her father to you or anyone else," Matt said with conviction.

Bailey had to close her eyes for a moment to recover. Caught in a lie! She dumped green beans and almonds into a bowl. Brazen it out, she thought. "Okay, so I stopped by Violet's today, and she told me that Rodney was alive."

"From what I was told, you drove through Calburn doing sixty, and you spent all afternoon at Violet's."

Bailey knew that if she answered that, it would be angrily, and if she got angry, she'd reveal more than she wanted to. She sat down at the table, picked up her fork and looked at him. "I now live in this town, so I'd like to know its history. I offended Janice once, and I don't want to do it again. Could *you* please tell me about her father?"

Matt kept his head down for a few moments before he looked at her again. "You want to tell me the *truth* about why you're asking so many questions of everyone in town?"

Bailey made no reply to that; there was nothing she could say.

"All right," Matt said when he saw that she wasn't going to answer. "You win. Janice despises her father, has nothing to do with him. He's an old lech, an alcoholic. He's had money, but he drank it all. Janice's mother and Patsy's were identical twins, daughters of the town's doctor. Patsy's mother married a dentist, and Patsy has had a nice house and nice clothes all her life. But Janice's mother fell for the beautiful Rodney and married him. Rodney spent all the money her father left her, ran around on her, and made her short life miserable."

Bailey could hear the anger in his voice. "And Scott?" she asked softly.

Matt leaned back in his chair and pushed his half-full plate away. "Sure you want to hear all the dirty little secrets about Calburn?"

Bailey did and she didn't, but she couldn't stop herself from nodding yes.

"Janice was determined not to do what her mother did, so the minute she graduated from high school, she moved to Chicago and got a job in an exclusive men's clothing store, a place where she could meet rich men. During the two years she was there, she was engaged twice but she broke it off both times. They weren't what Janice was looking for. But then one day Scott Nesbitt walked into the store. He was the youngest son of the richest man in a little town about twenty miles from here. He was young, handsome, charming, and, most important, malleable. Scott never had a chance. Janice went after him, married him within six months, then persuaded him that he never should have left Virginia. The truth was that Janice wanted to return to Calburn and throw her newfound wealth in people's faces."

Matt took a breath and looked around the room for a while. "Janice made Scott what he is today. She worked twenty hours a day, and she took a lazy, spoiled young man and made him into . . . well, made him into the person you know." Matt glared across the table at her. "Is that what you wanted to hear?"

She was taken aback by his hostility. "Yes. I mean, no. I just thought that—"

Matt didn't let her finish her sentence as he got up and left the table. "I've got some work to do," he muttered as he climbed the attic stairs, but he paused halfway up. "Oh, by the way, my brother's birthday was six months ago."

Bailey put her head in her hands. She wasn't doing very well at "no involvement."

Now, in the car, she glanced down at the map that Violet had drawn for her and saw that, if she was following it correctly, she should reach Rodney's house soon. But there were no street signs on the dirt roads that led up into the mountains, and twice she'd made wrong turns and had to turn back. She'd had to drive her four-wheel-drive across a shallow stream and around a fallen log. Her driving lessons hadn't prepared her for this kind of terrain.

By the time she reached the cabin she felt as though she'd been on a safari. She parked under a tree and looked up the hill at it. "Don't let it shock you," Violet had said. "It's dirt poor, and Rodney makes it that way."

Bailey drank from her bottle of water as she stared at the cabin. It was difficult to believe that the same planet could hold this place and those houses of Jimmie's. The whole structure was about to fall down, with one side of the porch already collapsed. One corner of the roof had a hole in it.

In front of the cabin was dirt, trampled hard by many feet. A few scrawny chickens wandered about, then, as Bailey watched, a couple of dirty children ran out from under the porch and chased each other across the hard-packed ground.

A third child, older and a boy, scrambled out from under the porch, then halted when he saw Bailey's car. She wondered why they hadn't heard her drive up, but when she turned off the engine, she heard shouting coming from inside the house.

"Maybe now's not the right time," she said aloud. "Maybe I should go back and ask Matt—"

She didn't say or think anything else because, suddenly, a man appeared on the porch with a shotgun—and he was aiming it at her.

"You want to get the hell off my property?" the man shouted.

"Yes, I do," Bailey yelled out the window, then grabbed her keys from where she'd tossed them onto the passenger seat. "I'm going now," she called as she put the key into the ignition—then dropped them on the floor.

There weren't any curse words vile enough to express her annoyance as she ducked under the dashboard to search for the fallen keys.

But she didn't find them before the door to her car was thrown open.

"You try to serve me any papers, and I'll blow your head off," came the voice outside the open car door.

Bailey came up so fast she banged her head on the dashboard. "I have no papers for you," she said frantically. "I came to ask some questions."

Feeling like something out of a gangster film, she held both hands straight up in the air, to the roof of the car. Standing outside the car was a man with a heavily lined face; he looked to be a hundred years old, but his movements were that of a younger man, and he was holding the shotgun aimed directly at her head.

"Questions about what?" he said suspiciously.

"The—" What could she say that she was *sure* wouldn't offend him? "About the Golden Six," she said quickly, then closed her eyes tight in preparation for being shot.

When nothing happened, she opened one eye. He was grinning at her!

"Well, now, so you've come to meet me and ask me about the good times."

"I came to meet—" She was going to say that she'd come to meet the beautiful Rodney Yates, but from the way the man was looking at her, and from what he'd said . . . But this ugly old man couldn't possibly be . . .

He was watching her, and he'd lowered the shotgun only about an inch.

"You," Bailey said. "Yes, I came to meet you. You're Rodney, aren't you? You look . . . a . . . Well, you look just like all your pictures." Bailey was sure that a lie of that magnitude was going to get her shot, but instead the man grinned more broadly, reached out, put his arm around her shoulder, and pulled her out of the car. Bailey almost gagged. His breath was foul, and the hand on her shoulder had half-inch-long fingernails with what looked to be years of dirt under them.

She wanted to get back into her car and get away from this awful place and this dirty man as fast as she could.

"You're sure pretty," he said, and his hand began to run up and down Bailey's arm as he pulled her closer. "Hey! Wait a minute. You aren't here to do to us what that other one did, are you?"

Bailey had to piece that together. "Oh, you mean Congresswoman Spangler."

"Congress, ha!" Rodney said, then spit a glob on the ground about an inch from Bailey's foot.

"No, I'm not," she answered.

He grinned again, exposing teeth that hadn't been brushed in years. "Then you come on in, and I'll show you about that old hag, and I'll tell you what she did."

They were at the foot of the stairs up to the porch of the cabin now, and the house was dirtier than any place she'd ever seen in her life. How could people live like this? she wondered.

Rodney held her tighter as they went up the stairs, and Bailey could feel her body getting stiffer by the moment. "Here, now, watch that step. It's a little bit broken, and I've been meanin' to fix it, but I been real busy lately."

Bailey looked down to see a rotten board that had probably been there since the 1930s, and just managed to step over it. When she nearly lost her balance, Rodney took the opportunity to run his fingertips across the side of her breast. Bailey thought maybe she was going to be sick.

The inside of the cabin was worse than the outside. They stepped into a room furnished with dirty, broken old chairs and a couch with half of its legs missing, making it about four inches higher on one side than the other. "Have a seat," Rodney said, and there was a leer in his voice. He was motioning to the high end of the couch. If she sat on that end, she'd slide down to the low end, probably where he planned to sit.

"I'll, uh . . ." She looked around. There was a small wooden chair to one side. "I better take this one," she said as she moved it opposite the couch. "Bad back. I need the support."

"You know what the cure for a bad back is, don't you?" Rodney said, putting his face near hers, and she had to work to keep from moving away from his foul breath. "You need more exercise. You know what I mean? More of the ol' . . ." He made a circle with the finger and thumb on one hand and stuck his index finger of the other hand through the circle.

You owe me, James Manville, Bailey thought as she gave Rodney a weak smile that she hoped wouldn't show her revulsion.

Rodney bent over her and ran his hand down her arm. When it started to stray toward her breast, she twisted her shoulder.

Smiling, Rodney stood up. "What you need is a little drink."

"No, thank you. I just—"

"You're refusin' my hospitality?" he said, all humor gone from his face.

"No, I just—"

"Well, good then, we'll have a little drink, then you and me can spend the rest of the day . . . talkin'." He wiggled his eyebrows at the last word as though he knew she wanted to spend the day doing something else with him.

Bailey was sure she was going to be ill, and if the man weren't still holding a shotgun, she'd have left.

The next moment she nearly fell out of the chair when Rodney bellowed, "Woman! Get out here. Can't you see we got company?"

There were two doors out of the room they were in, one open and one closed. Through the open door, Bailey could see a dirty, rumpled bed. The closed door opened a bit, and the pale face of a girl who looked about thirteen or fourteen peeped through.

"Out!" Rodney shouted, and the girl stepped into the room.

Bailey was shocked to see that she was heavily pregnant. She didn't look old enough to be out of elementary school, much less having a baby.

Bailey looked up to see Rodney watching her, and there was pride on his face. "Mine," he said smugly. "I'm good at makin' babies. You got any?"

Bailey could hardly take her eyes off the girl, who was looking down at the floor and awaiting orders.

"You got any?" Rodney said louder.

"Any? Oh. You mean babies. No, I don't have any children."

"Well, maybe I can help you," Rodney said. "Maybe you and me—"

The door behind the pregnant girl slammed open, and out stepped a beautiful girl of about fifteen. She had on a worn-out dress, but it was clean, and her blonde hair was clean and tidy.

"She don't want any of your kids, and if you touch her, the cops'll be out here again," she said as she handed Rodney a can of beer.

"Nobody asked you," Rodney snapped. "And where's her drink?"

"She don't want a can of warm beer at ten o'clock in the mornin'. Do you, miss?"

Bailey gave both of them a weak smile. "I really just wanted to ask a few questions."

"About the Golden Six?" the girl asked, and there was so much derision in her voice that Bailey was taken aback. "About the glory days when he wasn't a bum and worthless?"

"Get out of here!" Rodney shouted. "Leave me and my visitor alone."

The girl didn't so much as blink at the order, or at the

volume at which it was delivered. "You leave her alone, you hear me?" She turned to Bailey. "He touches you, and you call out, you hear?"

Bailey could do nothing but silently nod.

"So go ahead and ask him your questions. He knows all about those six boys, and he'll talk all day if you'll sit and listen. His life stopped on the day Frank McCallum died."

With that she put her arm tenderly around the pregnant girl's shoulders, led her from the room, and closed the door behind them.

"Don't pay her no mind," Rodney said as soon as the door closed. "You'd think a daughter'd have more respect for her father than that girl does for me. The other one, the young one, she's my wife." He looked at Bailey. "Now you just ask me all you want." He gave her a threatening look. "Unless you're writin' another book that's bad about us."

"No, I promise I'm not writing a book of any kind. I . . ." She couldn't think of a lie quick enough to explain why she wanted to know about him. And, truthfully, at this moment she couldn't remember why she was there.

"That other one, that Spangler woman, she was eaten up with jealousy, and jealousy is a real strong emotion. I never felt it myself 'cause I never had reason to be jealous of any man, if you know what I mean. I had more than my share, so I didn't need to want what somebody else had."

He looked at Bailey as though he expected her to tell him that he was still a fine-looking man.

"Did you know a boy who had a harelip?" she blurted out.

"A couple. You wanta see a picture of that T. L. Spangler?"

No, not really, Bailey wanted to say, but she just gave him a tiny smile.

Rodney put down his shotgun—at last—and went to an old cabinet in one corner. The upper half of the cabinet had doors that were about to come off their hinges, but the bottom doors had a big padlock on them. Rodney reached into his pocket and pulled out a chain with a key ring and a dozen keys on the end of it. He inserted a key into the lock, then turned back to Bailey. "Can't be too careful around here with so damned many kids around."

Again, all Bailey could do was smile in reply.

She could see that the inside of the cupboard was clean and in perfect repair. Lying on a shelf were two leather-bound photo albums, and Bailey knew enough about quality goods to know that these albums had cost a lot. A wave of anger shot through her. His children lived in filth, but he had beer and leather-bound photo albums.

As though he were handling a priceless object, Rodney withdrew the top album, then carefully opened it about two-thirds the way through. "Missed it by one page," he said as he walked toward her. "Usually, I find whatever I want on the first try, but you're makin' my heart thump so hard I can't think straight."

Why oh why hadn't she brought Matt with her? she wondered. Or Violet? Or a .45?

She took the album he held out so reverently and looked at the photo he was pointing at with his dirty fingernail.

"There she is. That's your T. L. Spangler when she was in school with us. Ain't she about the ugliest thing you ever saw?"

Bailey looked at the girl in the photo and had to admit that she was what was sometimes called "unfortunate." She had frizzy hair that stood out around her head, thick glasses, crooked, protruding teeth, no discernible chin, and a bad case of acne.

"Now look at this one," Rodney said as he flipped the page.

There was a cover torn from a *Time* magazine. On it were the faces of three women and the headline "Tomorrow's Future." Bailey had to read the fine print to see that the woman in the foreground was Senator Spangler. Her hair had been straightened, she didn't wear glasses, her teeth had been fixed, she now had a chin, and her skin had cleared up.

"Good surgeon," Bailey said in admiration. "Wonder who did the work?"

Rodney was looking at her as though she were stupid and missing the point entirely. He flipped the page back. "That girl was mad about Kyle. She wanted him. She did everything on earth to get his attention when we were in school, and when he wouldn't touch her, she swore she'd get him back. That's why she wrote that book."

"I see," Bailey said. She handed the album back to him. "So, uh, Mr. Yates, you don't remember a boy with a harelip?"

Rodney closed the album and carefully put it back in its place inside the cabinet. "How old was he in 1968?"

"Nine," Bailey said.

"No, I don't remember any kid like that. Sure he was from Calburn?"

"Yes. I—" She had been about to say that she had a photo of him in front of the mulberry tree at her farm, but something was keeping her from telling him that, and certainly from saying that she had a copy of the photo in her car. "You know, I think I better be going."

"You can't go yet," Rodney said, advancing on her. "I got three albums full of pictures. You and me, we could sit down with them together and look at every picture."

Bailey got up. "Maybe another time," she said as she headed for the door. *Maybe when I have an armed escort with me.*

Rodney put himself between her and the door. "You can't go yet. It's too soon," he said in what Bailey was sure he meant to be a sexy voice.

She put her hand on the door latch and pulled. In the next two seconds, she was out the door, down the steps, and heading toward her car. Just let me get out of here, please, she prayed.

"Wait a minute!" Rodney called from the porch.

Bailey stopped walking, but she didn't turn around.

"I forgot. Lucas McCallum had a harelip, but he was fourteen that summer. Big kid, hulking."

Slowly, Bailey turned around to look at him.

Rodney made a motion with his shoulders that Bailey had seen Jimmie do a thousand times. "He was an ugly kid. I mean, *real* ugly. Upper lip split open all the way up into his nose. You could see the gums above his teeth. And his ears stuck straight out. *That* the boy you're lookin' for?"

"McCallum?" Bailey said.

"Yeah. Frank's kid. You heard of Frank, ain't you?"

"Yes," Bailey said softly. "One of the Golden Six, the one involved in the murder-suicide."

"Yeah, that's Frank. Luke was Frank's kid, and he left town after Frank died. Never heard from him again—

not that anybody cared. He had a real chip on his shoulder. Would fight anybody. Real angry kid."

Bailey knew without a doubt that Lucas McCallum and James Manville were one and the same. In spite of what her brain said she should do, she found that her feet were moving back toward the house.

"That's right," Rodney said, "you come on back here, and I'll tell you all about Frank. He was a wonderful man."

"Lucas," Bailey said as she reached the stairs. "Tell me about Lucas."

"Yeah, sure, whatever," Rodney said as he opened his arm wide for her to step inside the circle. "You come on back in here, and I'll tell you whatever you wanta know."

This time Bailey had to sit on the high end of the couch, and as she hung on, she kept visualizing the movie *Titanic* and the people holding on to the railing as the ship went down. In their case, the sea was awaiting them; for her it was Rodney's hands. She wasn't sure which was worse.

She had to listen to Rodney tell the whole glorious story about how the six divine boys had saved a whole school. Bailey hung on to the couch arm, trying not to slide down the seat onto Rodney's lap, and tried her best to get him on the subject of Lucas.

It was probably only about forty-five minutes that she had to wait, but it seemed like hours. "What about Lucas?" she asked for the twentieth time.

Rodney frowned, annoyed that she'd interrupted him again. "He wasn't much, and he wasn't there when all the real stuff, the important stuff, happened. It was later that Frank went off and came back with that . . . that—" Rodney waved his hand in dismissal.

"What about Luke's mother?"

"Never met her. Never wanted to. If she had a face like that boy's, she probably drugged Frank to get him to go to bed with her, then lied that it was his kid. Frank was always a generous guy. Give you anything he had. He probably took that kid on just to be nice. Frank was like that."

"Saint Frank," Bailey mumbled, and Rodney looked at her sharply.

"How come you're askin' me so many questions about this kid? You know him? He still alive?"

"I don't think so," Bailey said, and didn't like the way Rodney was looking at her.

"That boy was uglier than Spangler, and even meaner. Are you writin' a book for him?"

"No," Bailey said, "of course not." The way he was looking at her now was beginning to make her nervous in a different way.

Rodney looked at her for a long moment, as though trying to figure out whether or not to believe her. "So how come you want to know about that ugly kid and not us heroes?"

"I, uh . . . I . . ."

His gaze was getting sharper by the second. She had to come up with something.

She took a deep breath. "I want to open a canning business, and I was told that the man who owned the farm I have used to can things, and I wanted to know about him. We, I mean, *I* looked on the Internet, but there wasn't anything on there about who used to own the farm."

He was frowning at her in such a way that the hairs on her neck were standing up. As unobtrusively as she could, she got off the couch and started slowly backing toward the front door. "That's all there is to it. I was just curious about the farm I bought and wanted to know more about it. You see, there's this big mulberry tree on it, and—"

Rodney's eyes opened wide. "Mulberry tree?" he said quietly. "Lord have mercy! Are you that widow woman that's livin' on Gus's old place?"

Instantly, Bailey felt relief. "Yes! That's me. I heard his name was Guthrie, but you're probably right, and it was Gus. Poor man. Did you know that he hanged himself?"

One minute Rodney was sitting on the end of the couch and Bailey was a foot away from the door, and the next he had her by the neck and was trying to strangle her. "Gus Venters was an evil man! Evil, I tell you, and he deserved to die! He deserved it!"

He pushed her against a window, and Bailey was holding on to the sides so her head wouldn't go through the glass, while at the same time trying to get Rodney's hands from around her throat.

Suddenly the window opened outward and Bailey fell backward—into the arms of a young man. He staggered backward a few steps with a muffled "Umph!" When Bailey recovered herself enough to open her eyes, she looked up into the blue eyes of a man she'd seen in several photographs: Rodney Yates. Time travel? she thought. I've fallen through a window into the 1950s?

But the next second the young man dropped her to her feet, grabbed her hand, and started running. "You have the keys?" he yelled over his shoulder.

It took her a second to know what he meant, then she saw her Toyota at the foot of the hill, and behind her she could hear Rodney's angry shouting. Just as they reached the car, she heard the sound of a shotgun blast, then the roar of a car engine.

"Let's *go*, lady!" the young man shouted as he vaulted into the driver's seat. "Where the hell are the keys?"

Bailey was still dazed from all that had happened in the last minutes. What had changed lecherous old Rodney into a murderer? Her neck hurt so much she didn't think she could swallow. "On the floor," she managed to whisper.

He moved to the passenger side, stuck his head under the dashboard, and within seconds held up the keys. Turning toward the sound of a car engine, Bailey saw a huge black truck with giant wheels coming toward them. She didn't think about what she did; she just reacted. She grabbed the keys from the young man's hand, leaped into the driver's seat, and jammed the key into the ignition.

During the search for the keys, Rodney had driven his black truck down the hill and was now about to block the only way Bailey knew how to get down the mountain. When she saw the truck coming toward her, she knew there was only one way to go: directly toward it. If she took the time to turn around and try to find another way to get down the mountain, he'd be on top of her in a flash. Instead, she put the car in drive and floored it.

"No!" the young man shouted. "Go *down* the mountain. Over there! That way! Get out of here! When he's this mad, he'll kill and ask questions later."

Bailey glanced at the narrow path between the trees where the young man was pointing, but she'd have to stop, then turn to reach it. Rodney could easily hit her from the rear. She kept going straight at the truck, gain-ing speed with every second. One of them had to move, or they were going to smash head-on.

"Turn! Turn! Turn!" the boy shouted over and over.

But Bailey didn't turn. Rodney did. At the last second, he jerked the wheel of his truck to the right and missed hitting her by inches.

"You're insane, you know that?" the young man shouted at her.

Bailey slowed the car and threw it in reverse while it was still rolling. "No. I've just spent a lot of my life with a man who knew how to play hardball." She glanced at him. "You buckled up?"

The young man grabbed the seat belt and buckled himself in.

"We're going down now," Bailey said as she looked ahead and saw that Rodney was still turning around. She knew that he would come back for her, and this time, even if it cost him his life, he wouldn't turn away. "You can use the element of surprise only once," Jimmie had told her. "After that, you need to use brains and skill."

"Okay," she said aloud. "It's time for brains."

"Who are you talking to?"

Bailey hit a bump that made both their heads hit the ceiling. "Somebody I used to know. What's your name?"

"Alex," he said. "And where did you learn to drive?"

"I think it was Bermuda." So far, she'd been going down a meadow, but there was a fence ahead of them, and a boulder in her path. She veered so sharply that they turned on two wheels. "No," she said. "It was in South Africa. Johannesburg." There was an old road to her left, and again she turned sharply. "No, that wasn't it. We were in—" In front of her was a stream with some fairly big rocks in it. If one of them hit the bottom of the car, it could tear out the whole underside, then they'd be stranded.

Bailey turned right, then left, in midstream and missed the two big rocks. When she got to the other side, she said, "Actually, I think it was—"

"Tell me later," Alex said, holding on to the dashboard with both hands and casting sideways looks at her.

"Do you by any chance know the way down to the highway?"

"I thought you knew—" Alex began, but stopped. "Okay, slow down. There's an old road along here somewhere, but it hasn't been used in years. It's probably covered with logs. Besides, I think you lost my dad a long way back there."

"Your dad?" Bailey said, looking in her rearview mirror.

"Yeah, he—" Alex's eyes widened as he glimpsed his father's truck through the trees. "He knows which way you're headed, so he'll cut you off. He's going to ambush us."

Suddenly, Bailey stopped the car, then backed up.

"What are you doing now?" Alex yelled.

"I'm going back the way I came. If he's down there, then I'm going another way."

"But you can't. You made it across that stream once by sheer dumb luck. You can't do it again."

When she had the car straight and aimed down the hillside, she looked at him. "In or out?"

Alex took a deep breath. "In," he said as he braced himself.

In the next second, Bailey floored the accelerator and hit the stream at full speed. And for the second time, she managed to twist the car around the rocks.

When they were on the other side, Alex said, "I need a drink."

"You're too young to drink," Bailey snapped.

"I'm too young to die, but that isn't going to keep me alive."

Bailey jerked the wheel sharply and turned onto the road that she'd come up the mountain on. For a moment she almost relaxed, but then Rodney and his big black truck came roaring out from the trees, and Bailey went down the trail at fifty miles an hour.

"What the hell did you do to him?" Alex yelled.

"I don't know," she yelled back. "I mentioned Gus and Luke and the mulberry tree, and he went insane."

She swerved around a rock and nearly sent Alex through the windshield. "He's getting closer," she said as she looked in her rearview mirror.

"Half a mile. If you can stay in front of him for half a mile, you've got it. He can't drive on the highway. Too many DWIs, among other things. He steps out of these mountains and the sheriff will lock him up forever."

"Is there a shorter way out of here?"

When Alex said nothing, she glanced at him.

"Where?" she yelled.

"It's an old logging road. Impassable. You can't go that way!"

"Where?" she shouted again.

Alex lifted his hand and pointed, and she could see an opening through the trees just ahead of them. "Hold on," she shouted, then turned the car in a spray of gravel and headed down the old road.

Alex looked out the back. "He won't follow us this way. He knows he can't make it. He knows—Holy shit! He's right behind us."

"Watch your language!" Bailey said as she ran over a four-inch log and sent their heads banging into the ceiling.

"We're gonna die any second, and you're telling me not to cuss?"

"The Lord is my shepherd," Bailey said. "I shall not want. He maketh me to lie down in—"

Alex turned to look at what she was seeing. There was a bridge that had been whole the last time he saw it, but now half of it was in the river. The deep, fast-moving river. "—in green pastures. He leadeth me beside the still waters. Yea though I—"

"—walk through the valley of the shadow of death—"

The next sound was their screams in unison as the car went flying off the bridge and sailing over the river.

When the car hit the other side, they landed hard, and for a moment they were both too dazed to comprehend that they had made it, and they were alive.

Alex recovered first. He looked out the back window and saw his father on the other side of the river, getting out of his truck—with his shotgun.

Alex looked at Bailey, and Bailey looked at Alex.

"—I will fear no evil—" they said together, then Bailey pushed on the accelerator, but the car had stopped. She turned the key, but it wouldn't start. Alex leaned across her and looked at the gauges.

"Lady, you're out of gas."

Before Bailey could reply, Alex had grabbed her hand and was pulling her across the seat. Hunched down, they ran around the front of the Toyota, and stayed there until they heard two blasts of Rodney's shotgun.

"Now! While he reloads," Alex yelled, then they started running.

They didn't stop until they reached the highway.

"We're safe now," Alex said, "so you can slow down. By the way, what's your name?"

"Bailey James," she said, and put out her hand to shake his.

As they stood there beside the highway, eighteen-wheelers whizzing along behind them, they smiled at each other. Then they started to laugh.

"I have never been so scared in my whole life," Alex said.

"Me neither."

"You! But you were great. Cool and calm. You must drive like that for a living."

"I'm a housewife," she said, and that sent them into new peals of laughter. "I've probably driven a total of a hundred and fifty miles in my life."

"Then that explains it," Alex said. "Anybody with any experience would have known she couldn't have done something like that."

They walked along the highway, laughing together for about a mile, before Mr. Shelby happened along and gave them a ride to Bailey's house.

Eighteen

❦

When Matt got home that night, Bailey was asleep in a chair in the living room. She had on her nightgown and bathrobe, her hair still damp from a shower, and he thought she looked about twelve years old. Lately, things between them hadn't been going the way he wanted them to. It seemed that no matter what he tried, she pulled back from him.

She was involved in something secret with Janice and Patsy, and honestly, he didn't blame her. Scott and Rick had laughed about how they'd distracted their wives from their "silly little ideas" about opening a business.

"My wife is *mine*!" Scott had said. "I'm not having Calburn say that I can't support my family."

And half a dozen mistresses, Matt had wanted to say, but didn't.

Rick had been milder, but just as adamant. "Patsy

seems to have forgotten how tired she was when she had to get up every morning and go to work."

"And when she went to work every day, you got stuck with half the housework," Matt said, feeling no compulsion to hold back from telling his younger brother what he thought.

"That has nothing to do with it," Rick said. "I just think it's better if Patsy stays home with the boys."

Matt had had to stand by and watch the men stop their wives from opening their business, and because of the unwritten male code, he couldn't tell Bailey what was going on. But she knew. And, worse, when Matt asked for her help with his design business, he knew she thought he was doing the same thing as Scott and Rick.

Matt knew that he was losing ground with Bailey, but he didn't know how to show her that she could trust him, that he wouldn't betray any of her secrets—or undermine whatever she wanted to do with her life.

He walked quietly across the room and touched her hair. He wanted to make a pass at her, wanted to make love to her, but with the way she was feeling lately, he was sure she'd turn him down. And he didn't think his pride could stand that.

Quietly, he bent and picked her up in his arms. "Ssssh," he said when she started to waken. "It's just me."

She snuggled against his chest and went back to sleep, but when he tucked her into bed, she awoke enough to catch his arm. "I did something today," she said.

"Oh, and what was that?" He sat down on the edge of the bed and smoothed her hair back from her head.

"I met Rodney Yates."

He paused in smoothing her hair. "You should have

told me you wanted to meet him, and I would have gone with you."

She gave a big yawn. "Mmm. Sorry. I should have. He's kind of crazy."

"Very much so. Go to sleep now, and you can tell me everything in the morning."

When he got to the door, she said, "Matt?"

"Yes?"

"I brought one of Rodney's children home with me. Just for a while. Is that okay?"

"It's your house," he said, but when she started to say something else, he smiled. "Sure, it's okay. I think it's time someone did something about those kids anyway. Maybe we can find them foster homes. Together. It'll be something we can do together."

"Yes," she said softly, her eyes closing. "Together. The three of us."

The idea of him and Bailey and a child made Matt smile, and as he closed her bedroom door, he thought that maybe everything was going to work out all right after all.

The next morning, Matt awoke to a nightmare. It was as though he'd been transported back to Patsy's house. The bathroom was a pigsty. Every towel in the cabinet was wet and had been slung across every surface. The tub was rimmed with greasy gray scum. There was hair in the sink, and the mirror was speckled with what looked like shaving cream.

When he left the bathroom, he nearly tripped over a box in the hallway. Suspicious, he investigated and found out that all his storage boxes, at least fifty of them, had been removed from the spare bedroom and put into his attic office. He couldn't get to his computer, or his drafting table.

Downstairs again, he flung open the door to the extra bedroom and saw that all his things had been cleared out so completely that all that was left was the bed and . . . well, all the furniture that Bailey had put in there originally.

Calm down, he told himself. She told you that she'd brought home one of Rodney's kids, and you can't expect a kid that's been brought up like he was to keep a bathroom tidy. Poor child has probably never seen an indoor toilet.

But still, it hurt to see all his possessions removed and put elsewhere, as though he was no longer living there.

In the kitchen, Matt went to the jar that Bailey kept filled with her homemade granola, and found that it was empty. He looked in the oven. There was no scrumptious omelet waiting for him. In fact, when he looked in the refrigerator, there were no eggs. And no milk.

Bailey walked into the kitchen, and she looked better than he'd ever seen her. There was a light in her eyes that he'd never seen before.

"Good morning!" she said brightly. "You got in late last night."

"Yeah, I—"

"I put it in the wash," she shouted over her shoulder, cutting Matt off from what he'd been about to say. She looked back at Matt. "Oh, sorry. Alex was looking for his shirt, but I told him . . . But then, you heard what I told him. Are you okay? Do you need something?"

Matt gave her a helpless, little-boy-lost smile that had made a few women weak-kneed. "Breakfast?"

"Oh, yeah, sure, but you're going to have to fix it

yourself. Alex and I have to leave. We have to . . . uh . . . do something."

"Oh," Matt said, keeping the smile plastered on his face. "But I couldn't find the cereal."

Bailey opened a cabinet and pulled down a box of Cheerios.

"From a box?" Matt said, shock in his voice.

"Sorry, but Alex ate all the granola I made. Have some eggs."

"There aren't any." He was having to work hard to keep smiling.

"Oh, that's right. I made Alex and me an omelet last night."

"There were a dozen eggs in there yesterday."

Bailey shrugged. "Were there? I guess so, but Alex and I were very hungry last night, so I guess we ate all of them."

"How can a kid eat an entire dozen—" Matt began, but stopped when Alexander Yates entered the room. Matt had been expecting a child of nine or ten, but in walked a fully grown young man—and he had a look in his eye that said he knew exactly what Matt was thinking . . . and feeling.

Matt wanted to remain cool, but he didn't. "What are you doing here?" he snapped.

"I'm her partner in crime," Alex said, then he and Bailey laughed together. In fact, Bailey laughed so hard that she had to sit down.

"Did you see—" she said.

"When you ran straight at him, I thought it was my last minute alive," Alex said, laughing just as hard, collapsing in the seat beside Bailey. "And I didn't even realize that I knew that Psalm."

"You were perfect on every word."

They looked at each other and said in unison, "And I will fear no evil."

"When that window opened, I thought I'd fallen—Oh, Alex." Bailey clutched his arm; she was crying with laughter.

When Alex looked up to see Matt scowling at him, he gave a little shrug, as though to say, What can I say? The ladies love me.

Bailey wiped her eyes, and got up to go to her bedroom to get a tissue.

Matt was close behind her. "Do you know who that kid is?"

Bailey was having a hard time sobering from the laughter. "He's one of Rodney Yates's children. I told you about him last night. By the way, it was very nice of you to carry me into—"

"He is *not* a child; he's a *man*. You brought a strange *man*—not a child, a man—into this house, a man you don't know anything about—and you let him spend the night here. You're even *feeding* him. Don't you realize he could be dangerous?"

Bailey blinked up at Matt. "My goodness, but you're right. But then I didn't know you, and I let you sleep here, didn't I? And I feed you and, gee, I think you're a bit more dangerous-looking than he is. No danger of tripling *his* rent, is there? Now if you'll excuse me, I have some things I need to do." With that, she closed her bedroom door in his face.

Matt kicked a dirty towel that was lying in the middle of the hallway.

Nineteen

The next month flew by, and during that time, Bailey was so busy that the Golden Six never crossed her mind. And the truth was that she was fed up with them. Alex asked her repeatedly what she'd said to his father to send him into a rage like that, but what Bailey told him made no sense.

"He only gets like that when his latest wife says she's divorcing him," Alex said thoughtfully. "So I wonder what it was about what you said that sent him off."

Bailey looked across the breakfast table at Matt, but Matt wasn't speaking to either of them. And Bailey had to admit that Matt's jealousy of Alex felt good.

It turned out that Alex was living in Calburn with one of Rodney's sisters and had only been at the cabin for a few days while he visited his half siblings. Bailey wasn't sure how it happened that Alex moved in with her and Matt, but he did. Later, when she was told that Rodney's sister was taking care of six grandchildren, and they all lived in a two-bedroom, one-bath house, she didn't blame Alex for taking advantage of the situation. But it was all right because Bailey enjoyed his company.

"He's a nice kid," Bailey told Matt. "He works after school in Wells Creek, and he saves all his money to give to his family. If it weren't for Alex, they'd have nothing."

Matt had muttered a reply.

Even though Alex had a job and made good grades in school, he still found time to rehearse for the school play. His teacher told Bailey in an adoring voice, "Alex is a natural at acting. All he has to do is read through a scene once, and he's memorized it. He doesn't need much rehearsal. He could just show up the night of the play and be perfect."

Matt had gone with Bailey to see Alex act.

Afterward, she and Matt were in his pickup on the way home. "Alex is a very good actor," she said. "All through the play I was thinking that I might call a man I used to know and see if he could get him a screen test in Hollywood."

"What a great idea!" Matt said enthusiastically. "How about calling him tonight? You could arrange a screen test for the kid tomorrow. I'll pay for his flight to Hollywood."

Bailey laughed.

"No, really. I'll charter a jet for him," Matt said, making Bailey laugh harder.

Carol had flown in the day after Bailey called her, and she was eager to work. Oddly, she and Violet hit it off well, and Carol moved into Violet's house. Two days later there were eight trucks outside the house: carpenters, plumbers, electricians, painters, landscapers, appliance delivery, furniture, and a cleaning crew. Three days after that, Carol's daughters, aged eight and twelve, flew down with their nanny for the weekend, but they didn't return home on Monday. Instead, they stayed with their mother, and Carol enrolled them in the local school.

And as though she knew that only work would keep her sane, Carol wrote a one-minute TV commercial to promote the Mulberry Tree Preserving Company, then used Phillip's money to buy time during a collegiate football game that would be shown in three states. After she had the ad scheduled, she went into a frenzy of production design that had Patsy's sewing machine running twenty hours a day. And Carol recruited nearly every person Bailey had introduced her to in Calburn to have some part in the commercial.

At the beginning of the second week, Arleen showed up on Bailey's doorstep with twenty-eight suitcases.

"How did you find me?" Bailey gasped.

"You can hide from the world, but everyone in this town knows where you are. Don't give me that look. They don't know *who,* just where. So, dear, where's your guest room?"

"I have three bedrooms, and two men are living with me, so—"

"Oh, my, you *have* changed," Arleen drawled.

Bailey had six pots of jam on the stove and four crates of strawberries that needed to be capped, so she didn't have time to exchange bon mots with Arleen. "You'll have to stay in a hotel."

"Can't, dear. I'm broke. Flat."

Bailey started to tell her that that was no problem of hers, but then she had an idea. It was a long shot, but she thought Janice and Arleen might like each other. Janice was always trying to overcome her background, so Arleen might impress her. Years ago, Janice had pushed her husband to buy the Longacre place, the enormous house that Matt's grandfather had built to show the town how rich he was. "The house that bankrupted my grandfather," Matt had said. Scott had bought the run-down house for next to nothing and remodeled it. "A never-ending process," Janice had said.

"Let me make a call," Bailey said, and ten minutes later, a wide-eyed Janice had appeared in her Mercedes and taken Arleen away with her, along with as much of her luggage as they could get into the car.

After Arleen arrived, and Carol immediately cast her in her commercial, there was no possibility of keeping what the women were doing a secret. But by that time they were so deeply involved in starting the business, they didn't have time to listen to anything a man said to dissuade them.

Besides, there was strength in numbers, and there were six of them.

The women spent several evenings together calculating how much money they could raise. Patsy held a huge garage sale, and Arleen sold two Paris ball gowns to a Richmond shop. Each woman did what she could to contribute to the communal bank account; then, with nervous hearts, they prepared to make an offer on a factory in Ridgeway. But before the offer had been written up, the realtor gave them the astonishing news that the owner had dropped the price by a third. Bailey was sure that this new price had something to do with a meeting that Violet had with the owner, but she knew better than to ask for details.

Janice was up to her neck in setting up the books, getting licenses, and researching codes for running a canning factory.

"For a woman of aristocracy, Arleen sure knows how to deal with money," Janice said in admiration. "She's better than a calculator for adding and subtracting in her head. And brother! can she bargain. I've never seen anything like it. She got the decorator to put up silk curtains in my dining room for half what I was told that cotton curtains were going to cost. And I don't know where she got those rugs, but—" Janice put up her hands in amazement. "And what she says to my mother-in-law has to be heard to be believed. I thought the old hag would run and tell Scott that her ladyship would have to go, but the old bat eats it up. The nastier Arleen treats her, the harder my mother-in-law tries to please her."

Patsy was having a wonderful time hiring all the women who had worked for her years before, women she'd had to lay off because the canning factory was closing. And she loved that she now had an excuse to give her husband and sons most of the housework to do. "Like the old days," she said dreamily. "When I had a job."

At one of their tasting meetings at Bailey's house, they talked of designing a brochure to send out to small groceries and wholesalers, but here they were stumped. Not one of the six women was an artist or knew anything about computer design or Web sites.

"You know who you should get?" Alex asked one morning at breakfast. "Carla."

Bailey had to think where she'd heard that name before.

"Opal's daughter," Matt said.

"You mean the girl with the multicolored hair and the various body piercings?"

"See?" Alex said. "Right there, you can see that she's an artist."

"Actually . . ." Bailey said.

Matt looked at her. "You get Carla involved in this, and her mother will find out, and Opal's the biggest gossip in Calburn."

"It's okay," Bailey said. "The only people we wanted to keep it a secret from were you three men."

She'd meant to make Matt laugh, but instead she saw red rise on his neck. "I'm not your enemy," he said, then got up and left the table.

The next day at school, Alex asked Carla to come home with him, to Bailey's house, and Bailey was amused to see that Alex couldn't quit looking at her. Bailey had been afraid that Carla was going to be as sulky as she had been in her mother's salon, but she wasn't. She was enthusiastic and had some good ideas— and she seemed to know everything about how to create a Web site. In no time she had put together a good-looking brochure, then recruited Alex and Patsy's twin sons to address envelopes.

"How does she do it?" Bailey said to Matt. Carla had three gorgeous young men obeying her, but as far as Bailey could tell, she wasn't interested in any of them.

"Same way you do," Matt said as he left the room to go upstairs to the attic. He'd cleared the boxes out and was now spending most of his time up there. But then, since the house was filled with people working on the Mulberry Tree Preserving Company, there wasn't much room for him downstairs.

For some reason, they began to receive orders even before the brochures were mailed.

"Did you notice that all these orders are from men?" Patsy asked. "*Directly* from the men. Am I just old-fashioned, or don't most company presidents have secretaries?"

"Violet," Carol said as she licked an envelope. "She called in a few favors."

Bailey started to ask a question, but when Patsy and Janice gave her a hard stare, she closed her mouth. "Okay, so which do you like better, the cherry or the blueberry?"

Three days before the commercial was to air on TV, the phone rang at 3:00 A.M., waking Bailey.

It was Phillip, and he was in a noisy bar; she could hardly hear him.

"Bailey, I don't have much time," he said. "I just paid fifty bucks to some guy to use his cell phone so no one can trace the call back to me. I've got to warn you— except that I don't know exactly what I'm warning you about. Atlanta and Ray are scared of something. They're liquidating everything, putting it into cash, and moving the money out of the country. You'll probably see something about it on the news."

"Phillip," Bailey said, "I don't mean to be negative, but what does this have to do with me? It's their money, and they can do anything they want with it."

"Bailey, are you *sure* James didn't get your mother's permission to marry?"

"He couldn't have. He didn't even meet my mother until *after* we were married. You know that we eloped."

"Yes, of course. But are you *sure?*"

"Why are you asking me this?"

"Because Atlanta and Ray have been asking me questions about you—a *lot* of questions. I said that when you were told I was taking a job with them, you walked out, and I don't know where you went."

"Phillip, none of this makes any sense, except that Atlanta and Ray are crazy and always have been. My marriage to Jimmie wasn't legal, plus his will left me nothing, and Atlanta and Ray are his only living relatives."

"Are they?"

"What? I can't hear you."

He didn't say anything for a while, but the noise lessened, so she thought he must have moved to a quieter spot. "*Are* they his relatives?"

"Of course they are! Jimmie hated them. Why else would he put up with them unless they were his relatives? No one would put up with *friends* as repulsive as Atlanta and Ray."

"I don't know anything for sure, but I wonder if maybe they knew something about him that he didn't want others knowing. You know how secretive he was about his past. What if they knew something horrible? Something James had done? And, Bailey, I've been thinking about a lot of things. James wasn't the kind of man to overlook details. It's hard for me to believe that he didn't know you were just seventeen when he married you. And if he knew that, he would have obtained your mother's permission."

"But he didn't know, and he didn't get any permission. He would have told me."

"But *you* didn't tell *him*. Maybe he was waiting for you to confess to him. But you didn't, did you?"

"No, I didn't. If I had, we could have married legally.

But it's okay, Phillip, stop worrying about me. I'm okay. *Very* okay."

"Bailey, listen——" There was a beep in the phone. "Oh, no, the battery is dying. Listen, Bailey—what if, somewhere, there is a permission slip from your mother? What if you and James *were* legally married? What if Atlanta and Ray aren't blood relatives of his? That would mean all those billions are yours, not theirs. And what if the person who knows that you were legally married has come forward with that information? Maybe that's what's stirred Atlanta and Ray up now."

"But Jimmie's will——"

"The will states that the money goes to his brother and sister. If a court were shown that they weren't his relatives . . . Bailey, have you seen anything since you've been there that would link Atlanta and Ray with James?"

Bailey didn't want to tell him about seeing the photo in Matt's shoe box. She didn't want to get involved. It was better to put Atlanta and Ray and even Jimmie behind her.

"You've heard something, haven't you?" Phillip said. "What is it?"

She sighed. Even over the phone she couldn't get away with a lie. "Nothing. I just saw a photo of some kids, and I think they might have been Atlanta and Ray."

"Oh, God!" Phillip said. "Bailey, you don't know how important this is. You *must* find out anything you can about them. If I could prove that they aren't blood relatives of James, I might be able to stop this madness. And if you know anyone who would know if you were married or not——"

"I don't want all that money!" Bailey said, and her voice came out as a shriek. She could feel the flashbulbs, hear the reporters asking her how she felt about anything and everything.

"This isn't just about *you*!" Phillip shouted into the phone. "Those two are shutting down and selling off all of James's businesses. Thousands, maybe millions, of people will be affected by this. Can you find out anything at all?" There was another beep on the phone. "Promise me that you'll find out what you can. Swear to me. It's very, very important."

"All right," Bailey said reluctantly. "I'll—" She stopped; the phone had gone dead in her hands. "I'll do what I can," she said, then grimaced.

She put down the receiver, then looked up at a soft tap on her door. "Yes?" It was Matt.

"Everything okay?" he asked. "I heard the phone."

"Yeah," she said, but Phillip had upset her. Lately she'd come close to forgetting that she'd ever been James Manville's fat wife. It had been days since "what Jimmie said" and "what Jimmie did" had run through her mind. She'd been very worried about Arleen or Carol making a slip, but they were used to keeping secrets. One afternoon Carol had said, "Do you think I want them to know that my husband works for billionaires?" The way she said it made Bailey laugh. She made "billionaire" sound as though it were a contagious disease.

"No," Bailey said to Matt, but she didn't look at him. "Just an old friend. Celebrating. It's his birthday."

When Matt didn't move, she knew that he knew she was lying.

"Yeah," he said coldly. "Or maybe it was a wrong number." He didn't give Bailey a chance to say any more before he closed her door, and she heard him turn and go up the stairs to the attic. He wasn't going back to bed but upstairs to work.

Bailey tried to go back to sleep, but Phillip's call had upset her too much. Why hadn't he asked about Carol? she wondered. Or his daughters? Surely he knew that his entire family was in Virginia with Bailey. Or did he?

An hour later Bailey got up, dressed, and went to the kitchen. By the time Alex got up, she'd made a six-inch-tall stack of crepes, with four different sauces. Matt came to the table, but he didn't eat or say much.

Even when Alex said, "Good thing you've lost your appetite, old man. Men your age put on weight real easy," Matt didn't respond.

"What's wrong with him?" Alex asked when Matt left the house to go to work.

"Just . . . adult things," she said, sounding as though Alex were five.

"Ah, sex," he said, smiling at her. "You're right. I have a father like mine, and I have no idea about sex."

"It isn't sex," Bailey said with heavy sarcasm. "Not between Matthew Longacre and me. I can assure you of *that*."

"Yeah?" Alex said, rolling up another crepe and filling it with ricotta cheese and orange-infused sauce. "What's the matter? Old Matt can't? Because that's the only reason, if he isn't."

"Whatever are you talking about?"

"Lust, Miss B. Old-fashioned lust. The kind that causes wars. That man is so hot for you that he's about to come apart."

"You're crazy, and you're going to be late. Stop eating and go!"

"If you don't believe me, you should go up to him and put your hand down—"

"Out! Get out of here! And do try not to become like your father."

He grabbed his books and ran toward the front door as she heard the school bus stop in front of the house. "I'm too beautiful to ever end up like him," Alex called, then grinned when Bailey laughed.

Twenty

❧

The commercial was a great success. Everyone gathered at Bailey's house to watch it, and she had to admit that the men, once they realized the women were going to open a business no matter what they did, had given in graciously.

"I've been so excited about all this that Rick and I've had the best sex of our lives," Patsy confided to Bailey. "He wants me to open *two* businesses. What about you and Matt?"

"Three," Bailey said quickly, then smiled when Patsy giggled.

Bailey had set up food outside, but they were so nervous that none of the women could eat anything while they waited for the commercial to come on. For a moment Bailey stood back and watched everyone. Mother Theresa once said that what hurt people more than poverty or illness was feeling that they weren't needed. And now, looking at the people gathered under her mulberry tree, she was sure that Mother Theresa was right. All the women there today, herself included, had changed in the last weeks, and it was because they felt that they now had a purpose in life.

The biggest change had been in Arleen. In all the years that she'd hung around Jimmie, Bailey had never been able to stand her. She was a parasite. But Arleen had turned out to be a great asset to them, and in the last weeks she'd put on weight as she'd tasted and retasted Bailey's recipes. She nixed half the designs that Carla proposed, saying that they looked as though they were intended for "trailer trash." "Careful," Bailey had said, "your origins are showing." In the end, it was thanks to Arleen that they ended up with a simple label that conveyed that the product was classy and elegant, but also affordable.

Carol had been a good influence on Violet; the older woman had dropped twenty pounds, and Bailey hadn't seen her with a joint in her hands for days.

"It's time," Carol said, and everyone halted for a split second before they all ran toward Bailey's back door. Alex and Patsy's twin sons became jammed in the doorway—with Carla in the middle.

"Stop that!" Patsy said as she swatted her nearest son with a rolled-up catalog.

Laughing, the boys moved back and let Carla go ahead of them.

Bailey sat on the couch beside Matt, and they all held their breaths as the football game took a commercial break. Without a thought, Bailey took Matt's hand in hers and held it.

In the commercial, a woman and her two children (Carol, her youngest daughter, and Carla) were sitting in their family room watching TV. The room was a mess, and all three of them were wearing sloppy, everyday clothes. Suddenly, the husband (Alex wearing a mustache) burst into the room, saying that his boss and his wife had come home with him and were expecting dinner. "I'm sorry, Hon," Alex said, "but I told him what a great cook you are."

Carol said that she had made a pot roast for dinner. "But what do I serve before and after?" she wailed.

The camera went to Carla, who said, "I know, Mom. How about using those preserves you bought at the grocery?"

The next scene was played in double time, with Carla in the kitchen, dressing her mother (her pulling panty hose on was hilarious), while Carol opened jars from the Mulberry Tree Preserving Company and made a beautiful plate of hors d'oeuvres. The youngest daughter took a frozen pound cake from the freezer and poured a jar of marinated cherries on top of it.

The camera slowed down to show a beautifully coiffed and dressed Carol (three hours with Opal, under Arleen's direction) serving hors d'oeuvres to her husband's boss and his wife (Mr. Shelby and Arleen, who was wearing Chanel). The last scene was the two couples sitting at the dining table, finishing the cake. The boss turned to Alex and said, "You get the promotion and the raise."

When the commercial was over, Patsy grabbed the remote, turned the set off, and looked at everyone. "Well?" she said.

Rick started the applause, then everyone joined in. Matt got the bottles of champagne out of the refrigerator and filled glasses. "To the Mulberry Tree Preserving Company," he said, and everyone drank.

Laughing, they went outside to the food, dissecting every aspect of the commercial. But Bailey hung back and found Matt alone in the kitchen.

"Did you like it?" she asked. "Really like it?"

"Yes," he said softly. "It was great. It got your point across, and it was funny. You couldn't ask for more."

"What would you change?"

"Nothing," he said. "I wouldn't change anything."

They were alone in the house. "Matt, I'm sorry about lately. It seems that—"

Bending, he kissed her on the nose. "It's okay. You don't owe me anything." He went back into the living room and picked up the remote, Bailey right behind him. "You mind if I catch the news?"

"You mean the football scores, don't you?"

Matt smiled. "You're beginning to know me too well."

"Maybe not well enough," she said, and looked him hard in the eyes.

Matt's smile grew warmer. "How about another glass of that wine, and maybe we could—"

"Snuggle down and watch an old movie?" she asked.

"Certainly snuggle down," he said, smiling back at her.

"Two glasses of champagne coming up," Bailey said, then disappeared into the kitchen.

When Bailey returned, the news was on, and when she heard the name "Manville," she halted, standing behind the couch, a glass of champagne in each hand.

A woman on the news was crying. "They've closed the plant," she was saying. "And I have three kids to support and no job."

The newscaster looked back at the camera and said,

"This is just one of many plants and factories that Atlanta and Ray Manville have shut down in the last few weeks."

When Bailey gasped, Matt turned to glance at her, but her eyes were on the TV.

"The Manvilles have put Wall Street in a turmoil as they dump stocks, sell everything that once made up the empire of multibillionaire James Manville, and turn it into cash."

On the screen was Ray, surrounded by reporters and furious people who'd lost their jobs. He was flanked by three bodyguards and four lawyers as they pushed their way through the crowd. Ray stopped in front of one microphone. "My little brother knew how to run all these businesses, but my sister and I don't. We're just simple country people, so we're selling up and getting out," Ray said, then started pushing again.

"But what about all the people you're putting out of work?" the reporter asked.

"They'd be out of work when we went bankrupt, wouldn't they?" Ray snapped at the man.

As Ray got into a waiting limo, the camera went back to the reporter. "It's been estimated that Atlanta and Ray Manville have so far collected one-point-four billion—that's *billion*—dollars in cash. And where are they putting their dollars? Not in an American bank. Since the accidental drowning of James Manville's former attorney, Phillip Waterman, yesterday—"

That's when Bailey dropped the glasses of champagne on the floor, and when she stood there in frozen silence, her eyes wide and staring, Matt came around the couch and led her to sit down. He was listening to the TV, but he was watching Bailey.

"—the business liquidations have doubled," the reporter continued. "No one knows the reasons behind these sales—and especially not the reason for the speed. Back to you, Nancy."

In the newsroom, behind the heads of the two anchor-people, was a photo of the late James Manville and his wife, and the reporter was speculating on where his widow was now. "Could she have prevented this, Chuck?" the woman was saying. "If his wife of sixteen years had stayed and fought, would this be happening now?"

Suddenly everything in Bailey's mind started spinning, and the walls seemed to be closing in on her. She slumped forward and would have hit the floor if Matt hadn't caught her. He picked her up in his arms and carried her down the hall to her bedroom.

"Is she okay?" he heard Carol ask from behind him.

"Fine," Matt said, trying to keep his voice calm. "She dropped the glasses and cut her hand, and she's a little faint. We'll be out in a minute."

"I'll clean it up, and if you need anything, let us know," Carol called through the door.

Matt put Bailey on the bed, then went to the bathroom to get a cloth soaked in cold water. Sitting down by her on the bed, he put the cool cloth on her forehead.

Instantly Bailey tried to sit up, but Matt pushed her back down. "Get hold of yourself. Calm down. Don't let them see that you're upset, or they'll ask questions."

"I . . . I don't know what you mean. I—"

Matt wiped her face with the cold cloth. "James Manville is your Jimmie, isn't he? I recognized you in the photo. Your face is thinner now, and your nose is different, but it was you."

When she hesitated, Matt said, "Don't even *think* of lying to me! There were so many odd things about you, like how you don't know how to do simple things, like order from a catalog, yet you've been all over the world. And you— Anyway, I knew you'd either been isolated in some rich prison or— Truthfully, I couldn't come up with an answer to explain what you were like. All I've known is that you have one really big secret."

"And now what do you plan to do about it?" she asked suspiciously.

"Hit you up for a loan," he said.

"I don't— Oh, I see. That was a joke."

"A bad one. Is the Phillip who drowned the same man who paid for cleaning and clearing this place?"

As that memory flooded back to her, Bailey put the back of her hand to her mouth. "Phillip. He's Carol's husband. The girls' father. Oh, Matt, she doesn't know. She's been angry at him because he's been working such long hours, so I don't think he knows she's here. Knew," Bailey said, and tears came to her eyes.

"Stop it!" Matt said, his hands on her shoulders. "You can't do this. Who was the call from, the one in the middle of the night?"

"It was Phillip," Bailey said, choking back tears. "He was warning me about . . . I can't think. He was warning me about something, but I can't remember what."

"Since you've been here, you've been asking a lot of questions of everyone. Why?"

"Jimmie asked me—I mean, he left me a note with his will. He wanted me to find out what happened."

"Happened about what?"

"I don't know. It's just—" She broke off as she opened her bedside table drawer and removed her address book. Stuck between the pages was the note that Phillip had given her.

Matt took the note and read it. "What does this mean? He wants you to find out the truth about what?"

"I don't know," Bailey half shouted. "I don't know," she said again, then lay back on the pillows. "What am I going to tell Carol? I don't know how, but Phillip's death is my fault. Maybe if I had found out the truth, and maybe if I'd listened to Phillip, maybe—"

"Your only fault has been in not confiding in me," Matt said. "Now, listen, here's what I want you to do. I want us both to go back out there and pretend that you haven't heard devastating news. I'll tell Violet to keep Carol away from all media until you and I can talk to her. And I'll think of something to get rid of all of them as soon as possible. Then you and I are going to sit down and have a talk. Agreed?"

Part of Bailey said she wanted to stand on her own two feet, but another part wanted to put her head on Matt's big shoulder and let him take over. The cowardly part won out.

"Thanks," Matt said when he saw her face relax. Taking her hands, he pulled her off the bed, smoothed back her hair, and looked down at her. "Not bad," he said. "You look like you've just had a tumble."

"No such luck," Bailey said, sniffing.

"Now she tells me," Matt said with such sincerity that Bailey came close to smiling. He took her hand. "Now, come on, chin up, we'll get rid of them soon."

Matt did as he said. They went outside, and everyone looked at them in speculation. Matt went straight to Violet and whispered something to her, but no one noticed because they were all staring at Bailey. When she couldn't meet their eyes, they smiled, as though they knew what she and Matt had been doing in her bedroom. All it took to make all of them leave was for Matt to yawn and say, "Whew, it's been a long day."

Everyone except Alex said they needed to leave. Patsy said something to Rick, Rick said something to his two sons, then they whispered something to Alex. Alex said, "But I hate video games." That's when Carla walked over to him and struck him in the ribs with her elbow. "Hey! Why'd you— Oh, yeah, I think I'll leave too," he said, then he winked at Bailey.

Thirty minutes later, Bailey and Matt were alone in the house. He made her a strong cup of tea and set her down on the sofa. "Now talk," he said.

It didn't take long for Bailey to tell Matt every fact she knew. That her billionaire husband had died suddenly and left his fat widow with nothing had been on the news across the globe. Matt had seen the note, and all Bailey had been able to find out in her time in Calburn was that Jimmie had, maybe, been Frank McCallum's son.

"Then who the hell are Atlanta and Ray?" Matt asked.

Bailey's eyes widened. "How would I know? For all that this town is Gossip Heaven, there are big secrets everywhere. If Jimmie is one of Frank's kids, then I guess Atlanta and Ray are Frank's other kids." She put her hands over her face. "This has all happened too fast. When I saw them in your photo, I—"

Matt pulled her hands down. "My photo? What are you talking about?"

"You have a photo of Atlanta and Ray in your shoe box," she said.

"Those two ugly teenagers?" Matt asked, narrowing his eyes at her. "And you flat-out lied to me that you didn't know who they were."

"I—" she began, but he waved his hand.

"I'll get my box." He left the room and came back moments later with the shoe box, then held up the photo. "I've never paid much attention to this picture and I've thought many times that I should throw it away, but I didn't." He put the box of photos down on the coffee table. "I want you to tell me every word that Phillip said to you when he called."

Bailey had to admit that her mind had been so full of starting the business that she hadn't listened very carefully to Phillip, so it was hard to remember the details. And what she did remember had to be explained, so Matt could understand.

After a while he got up to get Bailey another cup of tea. When he returned, he said, "Maybe Manville had your mother sign a permission slip but never told you he'd done it."

"That's what Phillip said, but that doesn't make sense. I told Jimmie that I would be nineteen on my next birthday. There would have been no reason for him to think that he needed to get permission from my mother. I told him—"

Suddenly, Bailey's eyes widened. "Oh, my God."

"What is it?"

"I . . . I don't believe this."

"What?!"

"When I met Jimmie, he gave me an award. I was in the—" For a moment, Bailey was too stunned to speak. "I was in the under-eighteen division."

Matt leaned back against the couch. "I want you to tell me every word about the day you met him. Everything."

Twenty-one

❧

"*I'd like to know* who in the hell said I'd do this," James Manville said, sneering at the little man with the badge on his chest. Jimmie was tall and big, and he was wearing black leather racing gear. His lion's mane of hair and his thick mustache added to the size of him.

"It was, uh, part of your contract, sir," said the little man. "The fair guaranteed your car a place in the—"

"All right," Jimmie snapped. "What is it I'm supposed to judge? Flower arranging?" He looked over the head of the little man to his two employees, and they chuckled quietly at their boss's joke.

The little man didn't know Jimmie was making a joke. "No," he said as he consulted his clipboard. "It's preserving. Jams and jellies." He looked up at Jimmie. "I apologize, sir. To ask someone of your stature to judge something as lowly as this is unthinkable, and of course I will see that whoever did this is fired. He—"

"Where?"

"You mean who?"

"No!" Jimmie snapped. "I mean what I say. Where is the preserving exhibit?"

"It's, uh, this way, sir," he said, trying to keep up with Jimmie and his entourage.

"Lillian, he liked you!" Sue Ellen said.

"No, he didn't," Lillian Bailey answered, clutching the four blue ribbons she'd won. "He was just being polite."

"Are you kidding? How many judges kiss the cheeks of the winners?"

"Why would he—" Lillian began, but she couldn't continue, because the fourth time that James Manville had kissed her cheek, he'd whispered, "Meet me by the Ferris wheel at three," and Lillian had nodded.

"I have to go," Lillian said, then ran toward the main arena, where she knew her mother and sister would be. Dolores was planning to sing today, right after the first car race. The race *he* was in, Lillian thought, and a thrill shot through her.

Her mother and sister had been assigned a small area at the back of the arena. It was open at the front, canvas on three sides. A piece of plywood was set across sawhorses at the back, and Dolores sat in front of a mirror, applying mascara. She had on her smallest cowgirl outfit, the one with all the fringe.

"There you are," Freida Bailey said when she saw her second daughter. "Don't just stand there, make yourself useful. See what you can do with your sister's hair."

Lillian picked up the hairbrush and began to stroke her sister's hair.

"Would you mind!" Dolores snapped. "I'm going to get mascara all over myself if you keep jerking me around like that."

"Sorry," Lillian said, then drew in her breath. How was she going to tell them that James Manville—*the* James Manville—had asked her to meet him? Would they grab her and squeal in delight, as Dolores and their mother did when Dolores won a singing contest? "I won," Lillian said.

Freida was looking in the big trunk that they carried from show to show. "I can't find your little pistol," she said.

"It's in there somewhere," Dolores said. "Keep looking."

"I won," Lillian said louder, then caught the brush in her sister's hair. Dolores yelped in pain.

"Really, Lillian!" Freida said. "It's wonderful that you won another blue ribbon, but then your jams always win, don't they? Couldn't you make yourself useful and help? Your sister is going onstage in ten minutes, and it's rumored that James Manville is going to be in the audience. He's not married, and he's rich."

At that statement Freida and her eldest daughter looked at each other and laughed.

And suddenly, Lillian couldn't stand being there. "Oh, no!" she said. "I forgot. I have to——" For the life of her, she couldn't think of a quick lie. Instead, she just turned and ran out of the arena, and when she heard her mother call, she kept on running. She had hours before she was to meet "him," and she wanted time alone to savor the anticipation.

"*I can't believe this,*" Matt said. "You were seven-teen years old, and Manville was how old?"

"Twenty-six," Bailey said.

"And I guess you did meet him at the Ferris wheel?"

"Oh, yes," Bailey said, and closed her eyes in memory. When she blocked out all that had happened since then and thought only of that one wonderful day, it was the sweetest memory of her life. "Yes, I met him, and I had a glorious day. Jimmie was like a kid. It was as though he'd never been a child. We went on rides, and he took me to see his race car. At that time he was known as much for his daredevil racing as for the money he'd made. They opened the speedway just for him, and he took me for a couple of laps around the track. He even let me steer."

"He let you know that he *liked* you," Matt said softly.

"Yes," Bailey said. "He made me laugh, and he did like me, old-fashioned *liked* me. He liked what I said and did. He liked the look of me, and considering that I was fat and had a nose the size of—"

Matt put a fingertip over her lips. "Manville saw what you really are. He saw inside you, and he approved."

"Yes," Bailey said. "Sometimes I've thought that approval may be the strongest aphrodisiac in the world."

"It is when you've had little of it in your life," Matt said softly. He was holding her hand and caressing it.

"Right," she said. "But it wasn't one-sided. I also felt something needy inside him. If I'd been older, I would have been cynical. I would've thought he was a dirty old man out for the virginity of a young girl. But I'd been hit on by an older man before, and it felt creepy. Jimmie made me feel wonderful. And in spite of our age difference, I didn't feel we were different." Bailey looked away for a moment. "Maybe it was because when I met him I was an old woman, or at least that's the way I saw myself, and he was a man who seemed to have missed out on being a child."

"How long did you spend with him that day?" Matt asked.

"Hours. All afternoon and into the evening."

"Didn't your mother worry about her seventeen-year-old daughter being out alone for all that time?"

"I don't think so," Bailey said. "But then, she and Dolores were busy."

"But surely someone would have told her that her daughter and the infamous James Manville were on the rides together."

"We didn't know anyone at that fair. It was in Illinois, and we lived in Kentucky."

"Hmmm," Matt said. "Go on. What happened next?"

"That's all. Jimmie and I were going up the side of the roller coaster when he said, 'You wouldn't want to marry me, would you?' and I screamed, 'Yeeeesssss,' all the way down."

Bailey got off the couch and walked to stand by the fireplace. The memories were making her sad. Where had she and Jimmie gone wrong? When had the bad started?

"At the bottom of the roller coaster, he took my hand and started pulling me. 'Where's your mother?' he asked.

"And that's when I panicked. I stopped in my tracks, because I knew that if we asked my mother's permission to marry, it wouldn't happen. He'd probably be turned off by one of them. Or maybe one of them would steal him away, since both of them were beautiful. At best, I knew they'd take months to plan a wedding, and I couldn't see Jimmie standing still for all the buttering up that would go on. In an instant I could see everything. And, before you ask, no, I wasn't tempted to lose my one and only chance with a man like James Manville by telling him I was just seventeen years old. And as he often did, Jimmie understood my hesitation completely."

Bailey took a deep breath. " 'Are you sure?' Jimmie asked. 'Yes, I'm sure,' I told him. 'No hesitation?' he asked me. 'None.' 'I'll take care of you,' he said. 'I know you will,' I answered, then I put my hand in his and followed him to his car.

"Three hours later, we were married. And I didn't see my mother and sister again for three months. By then they'd had time to adjust to the idea of my being married to James Manville."

Matt gave her a one-sided smile. "Welcomed you home with open arms, did they?"

"Open wallets is more like it."

"I'm not a lawyer, but to be legal, I think Manville would have had to get your mother's consent *before* the marriage. Was there time? Could he have done so? Was there any hint from any of them that they knew that you were to marry Manville *before* the ceremony?"

Bailey tried to remember every detail of that first visit. "Jimmie said I had to make it up with my family, so we went back to Kentucky to see them. Maybe some women would have been triumphant, but I was embarrassed. I felt I'd done something wrong by eloping. And I so very much wanted approval from them."

"Think back," Matt said. "Try to remember everything that was said that day."

Bailey closed her eyes and tried to concentrate. "I remember that there were a lot of new things in the house, a few pieces of furniture, and a dishwasher had been installed. And some repairs had been made to the house. I think I remember that the roof looked new. I never spoke of it but I knew they'd accepted money from Jimmie, but then he was generous like that."

"And how did your mother and sister act toward you?"

Bailey swallowed. Some hurts never healed. "They were cool and distant, like strangers. I wanted my mother and Dolores to fall on me with great hugs and tell me they were so happy for me. But instead they—"

Bailey turned away for a moment, then looked back at him. "I don't like all this dragging up of the past. It's ugly, and it *hurts*."

"Remember that woman on TV crying because she had lost her job and she had three children to support?" Matt said softly. "I imagine she and a lot of other people are in pain now."

Bailey closed her eyes again. "It was as though they didn't remember me, as though I'd never been part of their lives; I was a stranger to them. Instead of giving me a Coke, like she and my sister were having, my mother had bought a china tea service. She poured me a cup of tea and asked if I wanted one lump or two. I'd never drunk a cup of hot tea in my life, and I'd never even heard of lump sugar. It was all so strange."

"Did either of them say anything at all?"

"Not much. I just remember chitchat. Rainy weather, that sort of thing. Jimmie just sat there, leaning back on a chair, amused some of the time, and sometimes so bored he nearly fell asleep. I so wanted it all to be *fun*. I wanted my mother to drag out my baby pictures and tell Jimmie all about me when I was a child. Instead, at one point, my mother called me Mrs. Manville. 'Thanks to *you*,' my sister said nastily, then my mother gave her a look to shut her up. I was so jealous of that look. It was so like family. It was—"

"Back up," Matt said. "What did your sister mean, 'Thanks to you'?"

Bailey shrugged. "I don't know. Just some family thing, I guess. I wasn't a part of it."

"Tell me again what your mother said."

"She said, 'More tea, Mrs. Manville?' Then my sister said, 'Thanks to *you*.' "

"Did your sister say that to you or to your mother?"

"I thought she was talking to me, but I was looking at Jimmie, and—" Bailey opened her eyes wide. "Do you think my sister was saying that I was Mrs. Manville thanks to my mother?"

"Maybe. Think of the timing. When could Manville have obtained your mother's permission?"

"He couldn't have. We went straight from the roller coaster to a waiting preacher. There was no time to—" She looked at Matt.

"Waiting," he said. "A *waiting* preacher. He knew you were underage because you had won in the under-eighteen division. He must have made up his mind to marry you when he gave you the blue ribbons. By the time you met him at the Ferris wheel, he'd already arranged everything, or else she would have come after you. I can't imagine that a small-town fair wasn't abuzz with gossip about a celebrity spending the afternoon with a teenager. Some busybody would have made it her duty to find your mother and tell her."

"He preplanned the wedding," Bailey whispered.

"Was he the type of man to have made the decision, then been so sure you'd agree that he went ahead with the arrangements?"

"Oh, yes. That's exactly what Jimmie *always* did. It was a philosophy of his. He said that most people were indecisive fools, and that even if you worked for years to get them to see reason—meaning, to see his point of view—they could go backward in a second. So he'd have contracts ready before he went into meetings. The second they agreed, he'd present the documents."

"I think maybe he saw you, wanted you, and knew you were under eighteen, so he began doing what he had to to get you."

"Then you think he *did* get my mother's permission?"

"Yes. And, what's more, I think Atlanta and Ray may have recently been told that that piece of paper exists, and they know that if it shows up, they'll lose everything. That's why they're liquidating as fast as they can, to get as much money out of the country as they can."

"But where is the paper?" Bailey asked. "Where's the permission slip? It didn't show up when the accountants went through Jimmie's papers."

"There's someone who knows."

"Who?"

"Your sister. My guess is that she either has it or knows where it is."

Bailey gave a little smile. "That's a good thought. Why don't I just call her and ask? I'm sure she'd love to tell me. I talked to her just—let's see—it was a mere three years ago. She was screaming at me that I'd ruined her life. She said it was *my* fault that her first husband had divorced her. I never knew if Jimmie was the one who arranged for her husband to get a job offer in the Middle East or not, and the truth is that I didn't want to know. But Dolores was sure that he had. The fact that Jimmie set up annuities for her and her daughter, bought them a huge house in a gated community in Florida, and kept supporting her through husbands number two and three meant nothing to her. In her mind, *I* had made her life miserable."

Bailey took a deep breath to calm herself.

"Okay, so maybe *you* can't ask her, but there must be someone who can, someone who could get information out of her."

"I don't know who," Bailey said.

"Okay, let's put our minds to this."

But try as they might, they could come up with no solution.

After a while, Matt stood up and looked at his watch. As though she could read his mind, Bailey knew what he was thinking. They had put it off long enough: they had to tell Carol that her husband was dead.

Twenty-two

❧

Matt wouldn't allow Bailey to go to Violet's house by herself. Instead, he drove her there, then told her that he'd wait as long as she needed. When Violet saw the two of them standing at the door, she gathered Carol's two daughters and ushered them out to the backyard. Matt gave Bailey's shoulder a reassuring squeeze, then left her alone with Carol.

It was two hours before Bailey walked out of the house into Violet's backyard, where Matt was playing with the girls and Violet was sitting on a chair and watching them.

"How is she?" Matt asked.

"As well as can be expected. Carol said she left Phillip and didn't even tell him where she was going. She wanted to shock him enough that he'd quit working for Atlanta and Ray. But the money they were offering was something that Phillip wouldn't turn down."

Bailey looked up at Matt. "You know something, I think Phillip was lying to his wife. I think there was some other reason why he didn't leave Atlanta and Ray. Jimmie once told me that Phillip had a lot stashed away, and he never struck me as greedy. Phillip told me that what he liked about working for Jimmie was that he was never bored."

"What now?" Matt asked, glancing up at the house.

Bailey looked at Carol's daughters on the swing set. Violet was pushing them, and they were yelling that they wanted to go higher and higher. For all that the oldest was twelve, in Calburn, she was still a little girl.

"Carol has to tell her children that their father is dead. She has to—"

When Bailey started to cry, Matt pulled her into his arms, then waved at Violet to let her know that they were leaving. They didn't say anything on the ride home.

At home, Matt treated Bailey as though she were an invalid, putting her on the couch, wrapping a quilt around her, then scrambling her some eggs that were heavy on the butter.

"You've had a hard time of it," he said softly as he sat down beside her and smoothed back her hair.

"You know," she said, putting her empty plate down on the coffee table, "I lost my husband, and because of the money, I wasn't allowed to mourn him. Did you hear what they said about me on the news today? That what Atlanta and Ray are doing might be *my* fault. Yet after Jimmie died, they talked about how I was a 'master controller.' I saw shows where therapists talked about 'women who manipulate.' And now—"

Matt was smiling at her.

"What's so damned funny?"

"You," he said. "When I first saw you, you looked like you were scared of everything in life. You looked like you were afraid to step foot out of the house, but look at you now. You're ready to fight the world."

"Maybe—" she began, then said, "You have something on your chin."

Matt wiped at his chin. "Did I get it?"

"No. Come here, let me," she said; then, when Matt leaned toward her, she grabbed his shirt collar and pulled his lips to hers.

There was something about being so close to death that made her want to live. Today Carol had cried and said all the things that Bailey had thought after Jimmie's death, that she'd never hold him again, never laugh with him.

Bailey had wanted to say, But at least you have friends who will mourn with you. Bailey hadn't had that luxury after Jimmie's death. Instead, she'd been labeled by the world as such a horrible person that her husband had disinherited her.

Matt kissed Bailey back, but he pulled away quickly, then looked into her eyes. "I'm not an easy make," he said softly. "I play for keeps."

She stared right back at him. "I'm not going anywhere."

With that, Matt smiled, then swooped her up in his arms and carried her into the bedroom, where he put her on the bed. When he made a motion as though he meant to leave the room, Bailey grabbed his arm. "Where—" she said.

"To get some protection," he said, his eyes hot.

Bailey didn't let go of his arm. She didn't say anything, but she looked up at him, her eyes asking him not
to leave.

"Are you sure?" Matt said, and his voice was husky.

"Yes," she whispered.

He smiled at her in such a way that she thought
maybe there were tears in his eyes.

Then, the next moment he was on her. Weeks of
pent-up desire made them tear at each other. Clothes
went flying about the room. It was a happy, joyous time,
with both of them wanting to block out the last horrible
hours.

Bailey wanted to forget the many weeks of loneliness.
The joy of feeling a human body against her own was
what she needed.

"Beautiful," she said when she saw him nude, her lips
on his skin.

"Sure?" he asked. "I thought maybe the water trick
had turned you off."

All Bailey could do was laugh, a low, throaty laugh,
as her lips and hands ran over his skin, felt the muscle of
him, felt his hips between her thighs, and the weight of
him— Oh, heavens, but the deliciousness of a heavy
man on top of her!

"I love you, you know that, don't you?" Matt said
into her ear, just before he sucked her lobe into his
mouth.

All Bailey could do was nod, because when he entered
her, all thoughts fled. She was a primal being, and she
was at the very basis of what life was all about.

Matt slammed into her until Bailey's head hit the
headboard; then, somehow, she was hanging over the
bed, her head hanging down toward the floor. To brace

herself, she put her hands on the wall, and Matt kept going.

When he came, Bailey screamed, and her body went so limp that if Matt hadn't caught her, she would have hit the hardwood floor headfirst.

With one arm, he pulled her up onto the bed and tucked her under him, then they lay there in a pool of sweat for a moment.

After a while Bailey felt his body stiffen, and she knew that he had something serious to say to her. "You know, don't you, that you could be . . ." He trailed off.

"With child?" she said and Matt nodded, smiling at her use of the old-fashioned phrase.

She raised herself on one arm to look down at him. Twenty-four hours after she'd met Jimmie, she'd been married to him, but she'd come to know Matt well before she went to bed with him. She knew what a kind, sweet man he was. She knew that his pride was his downfall, and there were times when she could see that little boy who'd so hungered after all the things he'd missed in life.

"No," she said. "I couldn't be."

"Oh," he said, and his face fell. "I see. You're using something."

She stroked his dark hair away from his sweaty forehead. "I happen to know that the only way to conceive is through oral sex."

"Yeah?" Matt said, eyes twinkling. "Is that right?"

"Yes. My best friend in high school told me that. She said that as long as a man and woman don't put their mouths on each other's 'things,' the girl can never get pregnant."

"I see," Matt said. "Then we'd better not try that."

"Certainly not when we're this dirty," Bailey said.

"You're right," Matt said, then he smacked his forehead. "You know what I forgot to do? The plumber—you remember him?"

"How could I forget? He's the one who gave me the onion-flower cutter."

Matt laughed. "He told me that I was to check if that big bathtub in your bathroom works. And I never did."

"That's horrible of you!" Bailey said. "Really dreadful. What kind of friend are you?"

"The worst," he said as he ran his mouth along her bare shoulder. "How can I make it up to him?"

"Try the tub out now?" Bailey suggested.

"Mmmm," Matt said, as he kissed her neck. "But you better stay with me and make sure I do it right."

"On one condition," she said.

"And what is that?"

"No oral sex. Absolutely anything on this earth except oral sex."

"Scout's honor," he said, then he picked her up and carried her into the bathroom.

"Matt," she said, "were you ever a Boy Scout?"

Matt just laughed.

Twenty-three

❦

When Bailey sauntered into the kitchen the next morning, Alex was there, and he had the table filled with food. She stared, unable to comprehend what she was seeing. There were cinnamon rolls hot out of the oven, pancakes, hard-boiled eggs, and little sausages.

"I thought you and the old man might be needing some refreshment this morning," Alex said in a way that made Bailey blush and turn away to look at the tea-kettle. "Have a good time last night?"

"Watch your mouth, and what time did you get in last night?" Matt said from the doorway.

"Ten," Alex said.

"It was two A.M.," Matt said. "If you're going to live under this roof, young man, you're going to follow some rules."

"I've already got one father," Alex said, glaring at Matt.

Bailey stepped between the two of them. "Both of you are five years old. Where were you last night, Alex?"

"With Carol," he said; then, when both Matt and Bailey looked at him in astonishment, he shrugged. "Older women like me. They confide in me. Give me an old lady, and she wants to bare her soul to me. And, occasionally, bare other things. Not that Carol . . . Poor lady."

"How is she?" Bailey asked.

"Okay. But she was pretty angry at her husband. She regrets that they didn't make up before he died."

Matt took a seat at the table, and Bailey went to pour hot water into her teacup, but then, as she stood at the window looking out at the mulberry tree, what Alex had said hit her. He'd meant to be flippant, but . . .

She turned to look at Matt, and he was watching her, waiting for the same thought to hit her. For a moment she and Matt stared at each other, wide-eyed.

"Did I miss something?" Alex said.

"I think we may have a job for you," Matt said softly.

"An acting job."

"Doing what?" Alex asked suspiciously.

"We need someone to get a woman of—" Matt looked at Bailey. "How old is your sister?"

"Forty-one."

"She's that much older than you are?"

When Bailey nodded, Matt turned back to Alex. "We need someone to meet a forty-one-year-old woman and find out about a piece of paper, if it exists, and if it does, where it is."

Alex looked from one to the other. "I'm going to need more information than that," he said.

Matt looked at Bailey in a silent question: Was it all

right to tell Alex about Jimmie? After a moment's hesitation, she nodded, and Matt began telling Alex all that he needed to know. He had, of course, seen Bailey on TV on the arm of her flamboyant husband.

It was when they got to the part about Dolores, Bailey's sister, that Matt turned to her. "If your sister is forty-one now, that means that when you were seventeen, she was already twenty-six."

"Yes," Bailey said, not seeing his point.

Matt and Alex exchanged one of those male looks that said that women had inferior minds.

"So?" Bailey said.

"And didn't you tell me that she was beautiful?"

"Yes," Bailey said. "She looked like a beauty queen. In fact, she won several pageants."

Matt smiled. "So let me see if I have this straight. Dolores was twenty-six, beautiful, and unmarried."

Alex looked at Bailey. "And you were seventeen, fat, and had a nose big enough to shelter a flock of geese from the rain."

"Is there a point to this?" Bailey said, narrowing her eyes at both of them.

Matt and Alex smiled at each other, then Alex nodded toward Matt, as though to say, You take the honors.

"But in spite of the differences between the two of you, you bagged the man half of the women in America wanted. Right?" Matt said.

"I never looked at it that way," Bailey said, "but I guess you're right. I did."

"And all your sister has done to you in retaliation is withhold knowledge that could gain you billions?" Matt said, wonder in his voice.

"I can't believe she didn't kill you," Alex said cheerfully as he bit into his third cinnamon bun. "Slowly. Real, real slowly."

"My goodness," Bailey said, thinking about what they'd said. "I really *did* live out the Cinderella story, wicked sister and all."

Matt and Alex laughed, then Matt turned to Alex. "Well? Think you can find out about that paper?"

"Sure," Alex said. "It's a done deal. But I'll need a motorcycle and a full set of leathers. Chicks like motor-cycles, and they like leathers. Can you afford that, old man?"

Bailey turned away to look out the kitchen window as Alex and Matt bickered in the background, and smiled. Home, she thought. She was home.

Twenty-four

❧

Bailey couldn't attend Phillip's funeral for fear of being recognized, but Violet and Arleen went. Bailey and Matt cuddled up together on the couch and watched CNN at every possible moment. There was little coverage of the funeral, though, except to say that James Manville's widow did not "come out of hiding and attend the funeral of a man who had been her friend for more than half her life," as one reporter put it.

"Yet another strike against me," Bailey said. "No matter what I do, it's wrong."

Matt didn't say anything. He agreed with her, but he knew that showing his anger wouldn't help the situation.

Atlanta and Ray did attend the funeral, and there was a shot of Atlanta weeping into a handkerchief. "I can't believe this happened," she told reporters. "He was our friend as well as our attorney."

The coverage was played against a background video of scenes from James Manville's life.

"It's hard for me to believe that Manville and those two were related," Matt said. "The three of them don't look anything alike. And not any of them look like Frank McCallum. Are you *sure* that all of them are blood relatives?"

"That's what Phillip asked me, too," Bailey said, her eyes on the TV. After a moment she felt Matt looking at her. When she turned toward him, he was staring at her, and he looked as though he was angry. "What?!" she asked.

"Phillip said that he didn't think Manville and those two were related? He said this when? During his last call to you? The one that I asked you to repeat *word for word? That* call?"

Bailey gave a weak smile. "Uh, yeah. Did I forget to mention that he said he wondered if Atlanta and Ray were Jimmie's siblings?"

"Yes, you did," Matt said softly. "What else did you 'forget' to tell me?"

Bailey took a deep breath. "Did I mention that I found a photo of Jimmie with the man who hanged himself in the barn?"

"One, two, three, four . . ." Matt began, narrowing his eyes at Bailey. "That photo better be in my hands by the time I reach ten."

"Or what?" she said defiantly.

"Or no more oral sex," he answered.

Bailey was off the couch and back with the photo before he reached eight. But she didn't hand the picture to Matt. "Look, before you see this, I have to tell you something. By the time I met Jimmie—actually, by the time the world met Jimmie—he'd had some surgical work done on his face. I think maybe he'd had quite a bit of work done."

"What kind of—" Matt began, but then he stopped and held out his hand for the photo.

Slowly, Bailey handed it to him.

"I see," Matt said, after looking at the photo for a long while. "And you're sure this kid is the man you were married to?"

"Oh, yes. When you live with a man that long and know him that intimately—" She broke off because Matt was looking at her in a way that let her know that he didn't want to hear about her "intimacy" with another man.

"Where did you get this picture?" he asked.

"I was looking for my *chinois,* you know, that conical strainer that you put on the top shelf in the pantry? You'd put it up so high that I had to climb on the shelves to get it, and I saw the corner of this photo sticking out between the boards."

"The only room in this house that hasn't been taken apart and put back together is that pantry," he said thoughtfully. "Wait here while I get my crowbar."

"Oh, no, you don't," Bailey said. "That room is also the only one in this house that was nice from the beginning, and you're *not* going to destroy it."

"Did it occur to you that Phillip Waterman's death probably wasn't accidental? That he found out something that cost him his life? And since he was warning you days before he died that those two goons were trying to find out where *you* are, maybe you're next on the list to have an 'accident.' "

"No," Bailey said, swallowing. "I can't say that I did

think of that. You'll put my pantry back together?"

"That'll be easier than trying to put your *body* back together," he said as he walked toward the door.

"I'll take everything out of it," she called over her shoulder as she started running for the pantry.

"Nothing," Matt said, looking at the bare walls. He had removed every shelf and every board nailed onto the studs, but there was nothing inside except years of dirt, dead insects, and dehydrated rodents.

Bailey tried not to weep as she looked at the naked, ugly walls of her once-beautiful pantry. The boards were stacked on the ground outside the kitchen door.

Matt leaned against the doorjamb. "Let's look at this logically. First of all, there could be nothing else here. That one photo being stuck in between the boards could have been a fluke. On the other hand, if a person felt the need to hide one thing, then he probably needed to hide more, so there's probably a motherlode somewhere. And if there is such a treasure trove, it's either here in the floor or in the barn. So where do we look next?"

Bailey didn't even look down at the wonderful old floor, its wide boards worn with years of use. "Barn," she said. "I feel in my heart, right down to my toes, that if there is anything hidden, it's in the barn. After all, the man did . . . well, hang himself there, so I'm sure that whatever he wanted to hide, he would have hidden it in the barn."

"Right," Matt said, "pantry floor it is."

"I hate men," Bailey muttered as Matt put his crowbar under the first board.

"What did you say?" Matt asked as he pulled the first board up.

"I said that I— What is that?" she asked as she peered over his shoulder. In the hole that the board had revealed was the corner of a metal box.

"You aren't curious, are you? Actually, I think maybe we should wait on this," Matt said, moving back from the hole. "In fact, I think I'd like something to eat."

"Get it yourself," Bailey snapped, then grabbed the crowbar from him and pried up the second board. When she'd removed four boards and the box was exposed fully, she looked up to see Matt lounging against the doorjamb, a smirk on his face.

With her nose in the air, Bailey pulled the box out of the hole and carried it past him to take outside. "If you ever again want to eat anything I've cooked or share my bed, you'll wipe that look off your face."

Matt's face changed to serious so suddenly that Bailey laughed. "Here, you take the dirty thing outside while I get us something to drink. And if you open that box before I get there . . ."

She let him imagine his punishment.

A few minutes later, she joined him outside. Matt had wiped the dirt off the outside of the box and was sitting on a chair, looking up at the mulberry tree and patiently waiting for her to show up.

"You do the honors," Matt said as he took the glass of lemonade from her.

It was an old metal box, with the outside printed, "Earnest's Crackers. Good for the digestion."

Bailey took a deep breath before she pulled the lid off the box. What would she find inside?

What she saw was heart-stoppingly familiar. There were four blue ribbons on top, all of them for preserving. Lifting the ribbons, Bailey looked at them, then sat down on a chair and held them, running her fingertips over the slick surfaces. She'd never seen these particular ribbons before, but they opened memories.

"What is it?" Matt asked, watching her.

"I just never put two and two together before now, that's all. I was told that the man who hanged himself had put up jams and pickles and that he'd sold them in town. By the time I saw his photo with Jimmie, though, so much had happened that I'd forgotten about his canning. But in the photo, I saw that he and Jimmie were friends."

Matt was frowning in concentration, trying to understand her point.

Bailey looked up at him. "The first time I saw Jimmie, I had just won a blue ribbon for my raspberry jam." She looked down at the ribbons she held. "A ribbon almost identical to this one."

"You think there was a connection?"

"I think maybe what I did, putting the fruit in the jars, entering a contest and winning, was something that strongly reminded Jimmie of someone else he knew . . . and probably loved."

Matt leaned toward the table, looked into the box, and withdrew a stack of edge-worn index cards fastened with a rotting rubber band. The band fell away the moment he touched it. "Hmmm," he said loudly, then began to read the headings on the cards. "Ginger Jelly. Wild Blueberry Marmalade. Caramel Apple Butter."

"Give me those," Bailey snapped, then snatched them

out of his hands. "Don't you know that a canner's recipes are secret?" she said as she looked down. "Oh, my goodness. Two teaspoonsful of lemon juice. Of course! Why didn't I think of that?"

"If they're secret, then maybe we should respect the dead and burn them?"

Bailey opened her mouth to say something; then she smiled. "Sure. Who needs more Brandy Peach Conserve in the world?" She held out the cards toward him. "*You* burn them."

"I hate women," he said, smiling, as he removed the envelope from the bottom of the box.

Matt and Bailey looked at each other, and a feeling—*this is it*—passed between them. Matt held out the envelope toward Bailey, but she shook her head, so he moved the two chairs close together, and with their shoulders touching, they opened the envelope.

In it were two photographs. The first one was a copy of the same photo that Matt had found. Atlanta and Ray were teenagers, standing in front of the mulberry tree where Matt and Bailey were now sitting, and looking into the camera with sullen hostility. On the back of the photo was penciled, "Eva and Ralph Turnbull, 1966."

The next photo was a studio portrait of the man who had hanged himself and an older woman, who didn't look very happy. She wasn't pretty, and the turn-down of her mouth added to her overall picture of misery. But the man looked sublimely happy. His light colored eyes—the photo was black and white—had a faraway look to them anyway, but in this picture, they looked rapturous.

Both the man and the woman had on suits, both of them with flowers in their lapels.

"Wedding," Bailey said. "This is a wedding photo, and she did *not* want to be married to him."

Matt turned the picture over. On the back, written in what looked to be a child's block lettering, was, "Hilda Turnbull and Gus Venters. Married May 12, 1966."

"It looks like the two kids weren't his," Bailey said.

"Or three kids. How does Manville fit into this?"

"You don't think that this woman was once married to Frank McCallum, do you? Didn't I read that Frank left Calburn right after graduation, but returned a few years later with a young son?"

"Yeah," Matt said.

"What if Frank went away, married this woman Hilda Turnbull, had three kids right away, then divorced her? But what if she said she didn't want the youngest child, the one with the cleft lip?"

"So Frank returned here to Calburn with his youngest son; then, years later, this Hilda showed up with the other two kids?" Matt looked at her with admiration. "Not bad sleuthing. For a girl," he added.

When Bailey threw a pillow at him, he caught it, then pulled her into his arms and began kissing her.

"Who would know?" Bailey said, her mouth on Matt's ear.

"Know what?" His lips were running down her neck.

"Who would know more about these people? We can't very well go back to Rodney. He went crazy when I mentioned Gus's name."

"Mmmm," Matt said, his lips moving farther down her throat. "We could ask Violet when she gets back from the funeral," he said.

"Right. Her, uh, connections to all the men in this town."

"No," Matt said. "We can ask her what Burgess told her." He had unbuttoned four buttons on her blouse.

Bailey pulled away to look at him. "Burgess? The football hero? Were he and Violet lovers?"

"I assume so, since she was married to him."

Bailey stiffened in his arms. "Violet was *married* to one of the Golden Six? And no one told me about this?"

At her tone, Matt moved away with a sigh. He knew that there was going to be no more lovemaking until this was hashed out. He ran his hand over his eyes. "That's why she came to Calburn. Burgess went to California on business back in the sixties, and he returned home with a wife. I was just a kid then, but I still remember hearing how she shocked people."

"While she was married?!" Bailey asked, wide-eyed.

"No," he said in disgust. "Not that way. It was the clothes she wore and the way she acted."

"Oh, I see. Miniskirts and go-go boots."

Matt smiled. "My mother once told me that Violet had shocked everyone because she didn't wear a hat or gloves."

"That *is* shocking," Bailey said, smiling. "Was your mother also shocked by her?"

"I think my mother rather liked Violet, although she never said one way or the other, but when I was a kid I saw the movie *Bonnie and Clyde* on TV, and when my mother saw I was watching it, she said, 'That's what Violet was wearing the first time I saw her.'"

"Right," Bailey said. "One of those movies that sweeps

the country with its fashions. So Violet came from California, wore the latest of the latest, and was married to one of the Golden Six."

"Right. Burgess had bought the house that Violet lives in now years before, and they lived there until the lumberyard went bankrupt and Burgess was killed in a plane crash." Matt grimaced. "A lot of people said he went down on purpose. I heard that he was never the same man after Frank's death."

"That's what people said about Jimmie," Bailey said under her breath, then her head came up. " 'Murders called suicide,' " she said.

"What does that mean?"

"Arleen—"

"You mean the woman you foisted on Janice? The woman who whenever I've asked you where you met her, you've run into another room rather than answer me? *That* Arleen?"

Bailey waved her hand in dismissal. "You want to pick a fight or listen?" She didn't wait for his answer. "Arleen said that one night years ago Jimmie said something about 'murders called suicides.' "

"What exactly did she say?" Matt asked.

Bailey put her hand to her temples. "She said that Jimmie said that all his money couldn't right some wrong that had happened when he was a kid. Arleen said that he said something about 'murders called suicides.' "

Matt looked at her for a moment. "So how many suicides do we have now?" He held up his fingers to count them off. "Frank McCallum. Gus Venters. And Frederick Burgess."

"You think one of them was a murder?"

"Yeah," Matt said, "and I think that one of the murders has to do with James Manville and those two creeps who are selling everything off and converting it to cash."

Bailey took a deep breath. "And you don't think Phillip Waterman's death was accidental, and you think that my life may be in danger."

"Yes," Matt said softly.

Twenty-five

❧

It was three days later that Alex returned. During those three days, Matt neglected his designing job to search the Internet for information about Hilda Turnbull, Gus Venters, Lucas McCallum, Eva and Ralph Turnbull. He could find nothing.

Bailey was trying to give her attention to the Mulberry Tree Preserving Company, but she was having a difficult time of it. Violet and Arleen were still with Carol and her children. Violet had called Janice once to tell her that they were sorting out Phillip's possessions, and that Carol was taking it all pretty hard. "We'll be back when we can," Violet had said, then hung up.

At dinner Matt told Bailey that he'd been unable to find anything about anyone, either on the Internet or in the town records. "It's as though they never existed."

"Been erased, more likely," Bailey said as she served

Matt swordfish with a sweet-and-sour sauce. "I'm sure Jimmie did it. I know his biographers looked long and hard to find out what they could about his early years but they couldn't find anything."

"But he couldn't have erased everything everywhere," Matt said in exasperation.

Bailey just gave him a raised-eyebrow look, as though to say, Think not?

With each day that passed, Matt was becoming more nervous, but he was trying to hide his worry from Bailey. What if she were recognized? What if Arleen or Carol made a slip and said something about Lillian Manville? Alex knew who Bailey was, and he was with Bailey's sister. What if Alex told Bailey's sister where Bailey was? What if Alex was as lowlife as his father, and the two of them plotted against Bailey?

By the time Alex returned, Matt thought his head might burst from the worry.

Matt was in bed beside Bailey, but unable to sleep. He'd had yet another frustrating day of finding out nothing. When he heard the low rumble of the motorcycle, he glanced at Bailey to see that she was sleeping soundly, then slipped out of bed and went outside.

Alex had turned off the bike and was removing his helmet.

"Where the hell have you been?" Matt snapped.

"And it's good to see you, too," Alex said blandly.

Matt calmed himself. "Sorry. Did you find her? We heard *nothing* from you all this time." He couldn't prevent himself from this reprimand.

As Alex glanced toward the dark house, Matt could see from the porch light's dim glow that the boy was exhausted, and the anger left Matt.

"She asleep?" Alex asked.

"Yeah," Matt answered. "You look beat. Want something to eat?"

"I could eat the tires off the bike," he said, "but I need to talk to you in private. I think you and I need to decide what to tell her."

Matt knew that the 'her' was Bailey. He nodded. "I'll get you some food and meet you in the barn. There's a shower in the office if you need one."

Alex just grunted in reply, then turned and started walking toward the barn.

Twenty minutes later, Alex was seated on a hay bale, his hair wet from the shower, wearing the clean clothes that Matt had brought him, and ready to talk.

"I crashed it," Alex said, his mouth full.

"Crashed what?"

"The bike. I didn't want to waste time, so I asked a few questions in the stores around where she lives, found out that she lives alone, then ran my motorcycle through the front window of her house. When she said she'd call an ambulance for me, I made an attempt to leave, as though I was afraid of being found by the police. She loved it; invited me to stay so she could personally nurse me back to health."

Matt just sat there blinking at the young man in wonder. Words like *audacious, fearless,* and . . . *stupid* came to mind. He refilled Alex's glass of iced tea. "If you wrecked the bike, how—" He nodded toward the barn door. Outside was the motorcycle that Alex had ridden up on.

"New one. She bought it for me."

Matt's eyes widened. "Where'd she get the money? I figured that when Manville died, her income would be cut off."

"I don't know where it comes from," Alex said, "but she's got lots of cash. I couldn't find out about her money in the little time I had with her, but I know that it's not from a legitimate source. Lord! but that is one angry woman! She said that she has to keep her money in a dozen different accounts so nobody will know how much she has. And she whines constantly about having to live in a 'dump' like the one she has, when she can afford better. But 'they' won't let her show her wealth." Alex shook his head for a moment. "She has a six-bedroom mansion set on four acres that look like something out of a magazine. Her swimming pool could be used in the Olympics."

"Did you find out anything about Bailey and the marriage?"

"Yeah, Manville got her mother's permission." When Matt opened his mouth to speak, Alex held up his hand. "But Dolores doesn't know where the paper is. When she told me that, she laughed and said, 'But *they* don't know that I don't know,' then giggled like a kid."

Matt waited while Alex took a long drink of tea, then returned to the food. "I want to know every detail," Matt said.

Alex put his plate of food down on the floor, then lifted his shirt and turned around. On his back were deep scratches, the kind of scratches left by a woman in the throes of passion.

Matt gave a low whistle.

Alex picked up the plate again. "No wonder she's lost three husbands," he said. "I never saw a woman so full of hate." He glanced toward the door of the barn. "And every bit of that hate is directed toward Bailey . . . Lillian. Dolores truly and deeply hates her sister. She believes that Lillian—I mean Bailey—took Manville away from her. But Dolores never even met the man until after he'd married her sister. Does that make any sense to you?"

"Yeah, sort of. Go on."

"Dolores says she wasn't there when it happened—the signing, I mean—or she would have stopped her mother. Dolores was onstage, singing. She says she was singing for Manville, but he was—"

"Go on," Matt said impatiently. "Tell me about the paper." He was afraid that Bailey would wake up, find him gone, and start looking for him. He could already tell that he didn't want Bailey to hear what Alex had to say.

"Dolores said that on that day in hell—that's what she calls it—three men in suits showed up with a type-written piece of paper and—get this—one of them was a notary public. Dolores said her mother didn't have time to think, and that the 'poor woman' hardly knew what she was doing. Dolores said the notary asked to see her mother's driver's license, then one of the men 'ordered' her to sign the paper 'if she knew what was good for her.' The notary put his seal beside the signature, then all three of the men left with the paper."

"Her mother wasn't given a copy?"

"No. Dolores said her mother was so bedazzled—that's her word—by it all that she didn't even tell Dolores until late that night."

"Didn't Dolores wonder where her teenage sister was?"

"Apparently not," Alex said, looking into the picnic basket that Matt had loaded with refrigerator containers full of food.

"Nice family," Matt said. "Go on. What else?"

"That's it. Dolores said that the only time the paper was ever mentioned again was at their mother's funeral. She said she got Manville alone and asked him what had happened to the permission slip. Dolores said she'd only meant it as a joke, but she said Manville got real angry. She didn't understand why until it dawned on her that Lillian probably didn't know about the paper. She figured Manville didn't want his wife to know that he'd been so sure of getting her that before he even asked her to marry him, he'd had all the paperwork done. Dolores said she figures that she's the only person who ever beat James Manville at anything. She said to him, 'So, where'd you put the paper, *Jimmie?*' Dolores said that, as far as she knew, until that moment, Lillian was the only person in the world who'd ever called him by the nickname. Dolores said Manville sneered at her, but it made her feel great. She said he told her, 'I gave the paper to the person I trust most in the world.' Dolores was gloating; she said she thought this meant he didn't trust Lillian, and to Dolores, the fact that Manville left Bailey no money was proof of his distrust."

Alex took another bite. "I've sure missed Bailey's cooking! Anyway, at the funeral, Dolores told Manville that she'd just seen the cutest little Mercedes convertible. It was white with a red interior. So the next week some guy shows up and hands her a set of keys to a white Mercedes convertible. With red leather interior, of course. And, after that, Dolores received a yearly six-figure allowance from Manville, and if she wanted anything extra, like a country club membership, Manville gave her that, too."

"But it wasn't enough," Matt said softly.

"Not by a long shot. And now Dolores says that she's tapped into the heart of all that should have been hers." Alex swallowed, then said, "For the life of me, I can't figure out how she thinks Manville was hers if she'd never met him."

"If you're asking me to explain women, I haven't lived long enough." When Alex yawned, Matt said, "Come on, kid, you need to get to bed, and tomorrow, early, I'm sending you to stay at Patsy's house. The less Bailey hears about the details of this, the better."

Twenty-six

❧

Violet called Janice again to let her know when she and Arleen would be arriving home. Janice told Bailey, so Matt and Bailey met the plane.

Arleen seemed to think it was normal to have some-one waiting to meet her and deal with her luggage, but Violet was suspicious from the first moment. She arranged it so she sat in the backseat of the Toyota with Bailey.

"What do you want so much that you came all the way to the airport to get us?" Violet asked softly. In the front seat, Arleen was talking nonstop to Matt about the funeral and who had been there. "Mrs. Manville," Violet added.

"Who else knows?" Bailey asked quickly.

"Just us, but it won't be long before they find you."

"They," of course, were Atlanta and Ray.

"They grilled Carol pretty hard, but she told them nothin'. At one point Carol nearly got hysterical. She thinks those two had Phillip murdered."

Bailey drew in her breath. "Does Carol know why?"

Violet looked at Bailey for a long moment. "No, but you do, don't you?"

Bailey hesitated while Violet waited in silence. The older woman looked much better than she had when Bailey first met her. She was dressing better, and the weight loss made her stand up straighter and move more easily. "There is a possibility that all Jimmie's billions belong to me and not to them," Bailey said at last.

At that Violet leaned back against the seat and shook her head. "In that case, honey, you could hide in one of those caves in Afghanistan, and they'd still find you."

"And meanwhile, Atlanta and Ray are putting people out of work and—"

"Oh Lord! a do-gooder. You better get out of Calburn before—"

Bailey didn't want to hear advice about where she should hide and how she should start running and never stop. It was only a matter of time until Atlanta and Ray found out where she was, but until they did, she was going to do what she could to find out all she could. "Why didn't you tell me you were married to one of the Golden Six?"

"What on God's green earth that has to do with those two money-grubbin' murderers is—" Violet cut off as she looked at Bailey's face, then gave a little smile. "I see. You and that gorgeous man of yours are onto somethin', aren't you?" When Bailey didn't answer, Violet smiled broader. "So what's he like in bed? And don't bother tellin' me you don't know. You two were givin' each other looks hot enough to set the runway on fire."

Bailey narrowed her eyes at Violet. "I am *not* going to satisfy any of your sexual fantasies. I just want to know anything your former husband ever told you about Frank McCallum's son."

"Frank's son?" Violet said, puzzled. "I didn't even know that Frank had a son. He— Wait a minute. Didn't I hear that he had a retarded kid that stayed up in the mountains? Never came down. Nobody ever saw the kid."

For a moment Bailey looked out the window, and her stomach turned. Jimmie. A man as gregarious and as social as Jimmie hidden away in a cabin in the mountains. How many years? Was the isolation imposed on him or voluntary?

Violet was watching Bailey intently. "Harelip," she said softly. "Was the kid retarded or just deformed?"

There was a lump the size of an orange in Bailey's throat, and she couldn't speak. The few words Violet had just said explained so many things about Jimmie. He couldn't bear to be alone even for seconds. He craved being accepted by society. The first day she'd met him, he'd ridden the rides as though he'd never been on them before—and maybe he hadn't.

Violet patted Bailey's hand as they pulled into her driveway. "Drop Arleen off, then come back. I'll tell you what I know."

It was two hours later that Bailey and Matt drove into Violet's driveway. They'd stopped by the grocery and loaded the back of the car with bags of easy-to-prepare food to leave for Violet, plus a leg of lamb and wine so Bailey could cook the three of them dinner. "You take Violet outside and talk to her about Carol while I cook," Bailey told Matt. "Then the three of us will talk about the Golden Six."

"What's bothering you?" he asked. "You've been too quiet ever since we picked them up at the airport."

Bailey almost said that there was nothing wrong, but she didn't. Instead she told him that Luke McCallum was said to be retarded, and that he'd lived in seclusion in the mountains.

"We're not talking the Middle Ages," Matt said. "The kid's mouth could have been fixed. It *was* fixed."

"So why wasn't it repaired when he was a child?" Bailey asked. "That photo of Jimmie was when he was a teenager. Even if there was no money for the surgery, there are welfare agencies. Surely, with a case like that one a doctor could have been found who would have done the work for free. Jimmie—" She stopped and took a breath. "Jimmie used to give a lot of money to doctors to perform free surgeries on malformed children."

Matt gave Bailey a soft kiss. "Eventually we'll find out everything, and we'll start by finding out what Violet knows."

But after Bailey had served them the lamb and a cold cucumber soup, as they sat outside and ate, she and Matt found out that Burgess had told his wife little.

"When I met Burgess in California," Violet said, "I had only recently escaped from a hardscrabble life in Louisiana. My mother had six kids, all with different fathers, and—" She waved her hand. "That doesn't matter now. I was young and pretty, and I thought that if I could just make it to Hollywood, I'd instantly become a movie star."

Violet smiled at her naïveté. "You can imagine how that worked out. Four months after I got to California, I was doin' the same thing my mother had done to earn a livin'. But even though I was doin' rather well at it, I'd seen where a life like that led. I'd seen that I wasn't always gonna be young and pretty, and I knew that someday I was gonna look like this."

She motioned down toward her own body, but neither Matt or Bailey smiled at her self-deprecating joke.

"Anyway, one day my car broke down on some back road, and this big, slow-movin' man from Virginia stopped to help me. I knew right then that I was at a crossroads of my life, and I decided to take the opportunity. I put on my best helpless-little-girl act, made up lots of stories about my past and my present, and a few days later Burgess and I were married, and we came back here to Calburn to live."

Violet glanced toward her garden as though to see if Carol really had cut down all her marijuana plants, but they were indeed gone.

Bailey got up to get dessert, a mango-infused crème brûlée, and when she returned with two bowlfuls, one for Matt and one for Violet, she said, "Go on with your story. Did you like it here in Calburn?"

Violet laughed. "It was all right. Borin', but okay. I made an attempt at bein' a housewife, and I did okay. Burgess was easy to please. Except when he told some long-winded story, he didn't talk much, so I got lonely sometimes. He was a nice man, though."

"What did he say about the Golden Six?" Matt asked.

"Not a word. In fact we'd been back here for months before I heard of them. Somebody at the grocery mentioned them and said that my husband had been one of them. I didn't think anything about it except as a joke, so that night, I was sort of teasin' him, sayin' I'd heard he was a 'Golden Boy.' He shocked me because he got angry. Burgess *never* got angry. Never! But he did that night."

"And that made you curious," Bailey said.

"Nope. Curiosity ain't one of my faults. I'd seen too many people with too many nasty little secrets in my life, so I wasn't interested. If he didn't want to talk about the Golden Six, I didn't either."

Violet finished the last of her dessert. "Good dinner. Carol has me eatin' six kinds of green things at each meal. I'm beginnin' to hate that color! And her idea of dessert is sugar-free Jell-O."

"What happened on the thirtieth of August, 1968?" Matt asked softly.

"Ah," Violet said. "That's when everything changed. That summer all six of 'em were here. My husband went from bein' home every night to bein' gone every night— and all day. All that summer they were callin' me from the lumberyard and askin' me when Burgess was comin' to work. They needed decisions to be made, but they couldn't find him."

"Why were they all here in Calburn?" Bailey asked.

"Different reasons. That little fruit, Harper, said he'd come back to see his mother because she was dyin', but he didn't spend much time with her. Burgess told me Harper was a big-deal producer out in Hollywood and that he was givin' up a lot to stay with his sick mother. I couldn't stand the little creep, and I was sure he was lyin', so I called somebody I knew in L.A. and asked some questions. It was just as I thought: Harper Kirkland was a nobody. He'd worked on a few sets as best boy—you know, he bangs the clapper"—Violet gestured as though clapping the board that shows the scene and the take number in a movie—"but the creep caused so many fights that he was always fired. He earned a living turnin' tricks."

"Fights?" Matt asked. "What kind of fights? Fistfights?"

"Yeah. Whatever. He did bitchy stuff like tell one person one thing, then another somethin' else. He loved to stir up trouble."

"And my father was home all that summer," Matt said. "He'd broken a bone in his ankle and couldn't drive."

"Yeah," Violet answered, looking at Matt. "I only met your dad a couple of times, but he was a real nice guy."

"So nice he abandoned his family."

"So all the six were here, and Frank . . ." Bailey said, encouraging Violet to go on.

"Yeah," Violet said. "On the thirtieth of August Frank shot his young, pregnant wife, then himself."

"And Gus Venters hanged himself in a barn," Matt said.

"And I wonder if Jimmie saw it all," Bailey said softly.

"My husband changed after that night," Violet said. "After that night he became depressed, deeply depressed, and he stayed that way until his plane went down and ended his misery."

For a moment the three of them sat in silence, then Violet spoke and broke the spell. "After my husband died," she said, "I found some scrapbooks he'd kept when he was a kid. You wanna see them?"

"Yes!" Bailey said before Matt could answer, and fifteen minutes later they had the table cleared and the dishes in the dishwasher Carol had had installed. Bailey had to admit that Carol had done an excellent job of remodeling the old kitchen. She'd had the worn linoleum removed and the wide pine floorboards refinished. She'd had a cabinet by the sink removed so the dishwasher could be installed, but none of the other cabinets had been replaced. They'd been cleaned, and the worn-out old hinges replaced, but Carol had wisely not even repainted them. The sink, the old stove, and even the retro refrigerator had been cleaned and repaired but not replaced. In the end, the kitchen looked as it probably had when it was installed back in the 1930s. And Bailey had to admit that the effect was marvelous.

"Here they are," Violet said as she put three scrapbooks on the coffee table in the living room, then sat down on a newly upholstered chair. In this room too Carol had done nothing but return it to its original state, and again it looked great, perfect for the style of the house.

For an hour, as it grew dark outside, the three for them drank coffee and liqueurs and went through the scrapbooks. Violet said, "I haven't seen these in years," as each person picked up a scrapbook.

There was nothing remarkable in the scrapbooks, just the usual high school clippings and photographs, but when Bailey thought about what had happened to the laughing kids in the pictures, the books were rather sad. For the most part, the pictures were from when Burgess was in school in Calburn, not in Wells Creek.

At one point, Matt pointed to a photo and asked Violet, "Is this Bobbie?" and she'd said yes in a way that made Bailey ask who Bobbie was.

"Burgess's older brother," Violet said quickly.

"Died when he was a kid," Matt said just as quickly, then he looked back at the scrapbook on his lap. And the way he said it made Bailey know she was going to get no more out of him, just as she'd not been able to get more out of him about what Alex had found out from Dolores. All Matt would tell her was that Dolores had said that, yes, Jimmie had had her mother sign the paper, and he'd given the paper to "the person he trusted most in the world." Other than that, Bailey could get nothing out of Matt, not whether Alex had liked Dolores or not, whether they were going to continue to have contact with each other, nothing. The only thing that Matt would discuss with her was the fact that she had been legally married to James Manville, and now all they had to do was prove it.

"And figure out how to run a billion-dollar empire," Bailey had mumbled, but Matt had just smiled at her.

"What are these?" Bailey asked as she opened a big envelope that had been at the back of one scrapbook. Inside was a thick stack of carefully cut-out newspaper clippings.

Matt looked at Violet. "She hasn't read the book," he said.

Bailey narrowed her eyes at him. "I've been a little bit busy trying to figure out a way to support myself and spending hours in the kitchen trying to fill your growing belly."

"And doing a damned fine job of both!" Matt said with enthusiasm.

Violet chuckled and nodded toward the envelope full of clippings. "After the paper named the boys from Calburn the Golden Six, Harper jumped on the bandwagon and wrote a bunch of articles about the boys that glorified them. The articles were half truth and half— What?" Violet looked at Matt for help.

"Comic book," he said, staring down at the book on his lap, his eyes wide.

Bailey doubted if Violet noticed it, but she could see that Matt had seen something that interested him a great deal.

Abruptly, Matt gave a great yawn and looked at his watch. "You mind if we borrow these and read them later?"

Bailey could see from the way Violet grinned that she probably thought Matt had suddenly had a sex attack. "Sure," Violet said. "Take your time. Those things have been stored in a closet for years, so it's not like I need 'em."

Fifteen minutes later Bailey and Matt were in her car and heading home, the scrapbooks on her lap. She asked the question she was dying to ask: "So what did you see?"

"Burgess's social security number. It was on a copy of an application for his first job."

"So?" Bailey asked.

"I can feed it into the computer and see what comes up."

"But what good will that do? The man's dead."

"I don't know what to expect," Matt said, "but it's a lead. If that ex-husband of yours did erase the past, surely he missed something somewhere. Maybe he didn't erase all there was to know about Frederick Burgess."

As soon as they got home, Matt ran upstairs to his computer, and Bailey checked her phone for messages. There was seventeen, all from Janice and Patsy about the business. By the time she got off the phone to the two of them, it was too late to read the scrapbooks. Besides, Matt had already showered and was waiting for her in bed.

She took a shower and slipped into his arms, and quite a while later, as she was drifting off to sleep, she murmured, "Find anything?"

"I put his social security number into a search service. They'll get back to me with what they have within twenty-four hours. Probably nothing," he said. "There was nothing on the Turnbull name."

"Mmmm," was all Bailey said before she fell asleep.

The next thing Bailey heard was a distant shout, then Matt threw open the bedroom door.

"Look at this," he shouted, shoving a piece of paper in front of her face.

Bailey was too sleep-dazed to focus. "What is it?"

"This is—" Matt had to take a few breaths to calm himself. "The search came through on Burgess's social security number, and it gives addresses for 1986, 1992, and 1997."

Bailey pushed herself up in bed. "That doesn't make sense. The man died in—"

"Nineteen-eighty-two. But his plane was so burned that they found nothing, not even teeth."

Bailey grimaced. "It's a little early in the morning—" she began, then her eyes widened as she looked up at Matt. "Are you thinking that Burgess could still be alive?"

Matt held out the paper to her, and she looked at it.

"I'm confused. These are addresses for a man named Kyle Meredith."

"It's him," Matt said.

"What makes you think that? I know Kyle was your father's name, but—"

"Burgess Meredith, the film star, remember?"

"Yes," Bailey said slowly as she looked down at the

paper again. "The last address is Meadow Acres Rest Home in Sarasota, Florida. Oh, heavens! There's a telephone number."

"Yes," he said, "and I've already called, but they don't answer calls until nine A.M."

"Okay," Bailey said, catching Matt's excitement. "We'll just have to wait until nine. What time is it now?"

Matt didn't have to look at his watch. "It's seven-twenty-two."

"Okay," Bailey said, "we'll just be calm and wait. I'll make crepes. They take forever."

She made four batches of them, burning one batch because her eyes never left the clock. Matt sat at the dining table with a newspaper in front of his face, but from the way he kept glancing at the phone, Bailey didn't think he was doing much reading.

When the clock clicked onto nine, Matt grabbed the phone and pushed the redial button. The call was answered on the first ring. Matt had to clear his throat to be able to speak. "Is a Mr. Kyle Meredith still living at your rest home?"

"Yes, he is," the receptionist said. "Who's calling, please?"

But Matt didn't answer. Instead, he hung up the phone and looked at her. "He's there."

She took a breath. "You make the plane reservations while I pack, and call Patsy and ask if Alex can stay with them."

"Right," he said, then they nearly fell over each other as they started running.

As she and Matt took their seats on the plane, he handed her the book by T. L. Spangler. "I think it's time for you to read this," he said.

Bailey opened to the title page and read that the author had written the book to fulfill her requirements to obtain a Ph.D. in psychology.

It didn't take Bailey long to see that Ms. Spangler believed that the boys planted the bomb in the school themselves, and that they had planned the whole rescue mission. Spangler shared her theory right away, then went into what interested her the most: the psychology of the boys.

Bailey began to read.

The class system in any society is interesting, but in small-town America, it is more so. What happens when the class system is removed? When the rich woman and the poor man are marooned on an island, what happens? If the woman has a skill, such as sewing, she may, perhaps, be able to keep her status. But what if the woman has no skill and the man marooned with her is a carpenter? What becomes of their status then?

The loss of a class system is what happened in 1953, in Wells Creek, Virginia. Six boys, who had grown up in nearby Calburn, Virginia, were well established as to who and what they were by the time they reached their teens.

Kyle Longacre was from the richest family in Calburn. To display his wealth, Kyle's father had built a mansion on a hill that looked down on the small town. As a result of his father's money, in school in Calburn, Kyle was the prince. People in the hallways parted when he walked by; everyone wanted to know him, be with him.

Frederick Burgess was the captain of the football team, the boy who led his team to victory—on the rare times when the team was victorious, that is.

Harper Kirkland was from old money, with his family able to trace their ancestors back to the first settlers in Virginia. It didn't matter in Calburn that Harper's grandfather had wasted what money the family had left on the horses, or that he'd sold the family's run-down plantation to buy his mistress a town house. And it didn't matter that the only thing the family still owned was a tiny local newspaper. In Calburn, the Kirkland name was treated with reverence because people knew what it meant.

On the other hand, in Calburn, Frank McCallum, Rodney Yates, and Thaddeus Overlander walked through the halls unnoticed. Sure, Frank was known to be able to "talk anybody into anything," and people could see that Rodney was beautiful, and the teachers all knew that Thaddeus was smart, but these traits were overlooked in Calburn because of the boys' parental origins. Frank and Rodney were cousins and had grown up in poverty. Nice girls in Calburn didn't look at Rodney because he was a "hillbilly," and Frank was shunned for the same reason. And Thaddeus, well, "Taddy" had parents who were of a religious sect that never allowed their son to participate in any social function. Taddy was the quintessential "nerd."

When the six boys were sent to spend their senior year at a school outside Calburn, their pasts were both erased and magnified.

No one in Wells Creek knew about Harper Kirkland's family being the oldest in that part of Virginia. He got no perks for being who he was. In Wells Creek, there were kids who had parents much richer than Kyle's contractor father. And Wells Creek had several boys who were better football players than Burgess.

By the move to another high school, these three boys were demoted.

But the other three boys were promoted. In the first week in the new school, in speech class, Frank was assigned to give a "persuasive speech." In Calburn, had he given such a speech, the response would have been tepid, after all, the other kids knew "who" he was. But in Wells Creek, Frank, probably for the first time in his life, was judged not on "who" but on "what." He gave a speech that was so persuasive that he was given a standing ovation.

Rodney, as handsome as any matinee idol, was ignored in Calburn because of his origins, but in Wells Creek, the girls giggled and fluttered their lashes when he passed them.

Thaddeus, largely ignored in Calburn, was adored by the math department in Wells Creek because of his ability to do long, complicated calculations in his head, and the school body, unaware of his social standing, began to call him "the Whiz."

Perhaps it was the shock of finding himself on

the bottom for the first time in his life, or perhaps he just needed to prove himself, but whatever the reason, within the first weeks of entering Wells Creek, Kyle Longacre began to make his way upward in the new school. Perhaps he wanted to prove that he didn't need his father's money to be "the prince" of the school and that he could attain such an accolade on his own. Even though he knew only a few people at the school, Kyle Longacre ran for president of the class. He joined the yearbook staff and the debating team.

Burgess, perhaps wanting to be the star of the team as he had been in his hometown, began to arrive early and stay late for football practice, and it was said that because of his extreme effort, his game improved dramatically.

Harper joined the newspaper staff, and at the end of the first month, when the boy who had been the editor of the paper for three years fell down the stairs and broke both legs, Harper took over.

By Christmas, all six of the boys had made themselves known in Wells Creek. Three of them were on their way to establishing themselves in as high a position as they had been in Calburn. And the other three were beginning to enjoy a status such as they'd never before had.

Perhaps it was the success of these "outsiders" that made the Wells Creek students so angry, for they too had their class system. Frank McCallum was taking the place of a student who had been known for his excellent speeches since he was in the sixth grade. That boy's father was the richest in Wells Creek.

The handsomest boy in Wells Creek High School began to hate Rodney Yates when the girls whispered among themselves that "Roddy" was a great deal better looking than he was.

Jealousy. One of the most powerful emotions there is began to rear its ugly head in the small town of Wells Creek. And to combat that jealousy, the students of Wells Creek tried to get the status back in line. They decided to investigate these intruders and use what secrets they could find to return the social structure to what it had been.

In small towns, everyone knows everything about everyone else, but, by unwritten law, it is often decided not to tell all. For example, sometimes everyone in a town will know that a child's father is in prison, but the town will choose not to state this fact out loud in an attempt to protect the child.

And while Wells Creek had its own code of protection, it had no such code of ethics to protect the outsiders from Calburn. Some industrious students went to Calburn, got the locals talking, and found out the "secrets" of the six boys from Calburn. They then told these secrets around Wells Creek High School.

It was told at Wells Creek how Frank and Rodney had been raised in unimaginable poverty, and the name "hillbilly" was once again attached to them. In Calburn, it was an open secret that Kyle Longacre hated his overbearing father, who loved to flaunt his wealth. In Calburn people put up with Stanley Longacre's bragging and generally obnoxious personality because they wanted to buy the houses he built. But when stories of Kyle's father were told in Wells Creek, the students began to laugh at Kyle behind his back. The possibility of his becoming class president was abandoned.

And although no one knew for sure, it was believed that Thaddeus Overlander wore long sleeves year-round to hide the bruises that his fundamentalist father gave him. Whispers went round the school about the odd religious services that Taddy attended.

Harper was said to be "in love" with Kyle—and this was in 1953, when no attempt to understand such a love was made.

And then there was Frederick Burgess, a murderer at four years old. Everyone in Calburn knew the story of Burgess, as he was called, and his older brother, Bobbie. Bobbie Burgess was one of those rare children who possessed scholastic aptitude and athletic ability in equal abundance. He was the head of the debating team and captain of the football team, and on Sunday afternoons, he tutored underprivileged children in reading. On the twelfth of July, 1940, when he was sixteen years old, Bobbie was washing the family car while his four-year-old brother Frederick played inside. A neighbor, also outside, saw what happened. The child, playing that he was his big brother and driving, moved the gearshift. The car, parked on an incline, rolled backward, trapping Bobbie's foot, then running over him and killing him instantly.

Frederick did not inherit the intelligence or the

athletic ability that his deceased brother had had, and it was said in Calburn that his parents despised their younger son for what he'd done, for what he'd taken from them. In fact, one person in Calburn said that Burgess's father had often expressed the wish that his second child had never been born.

Bailey looked up from the book. "I don't think I can read any more," she said as she closed the book. "High school is difficult enough, but what those kids had to go through was horrible."

"But if the torture ended when they graduated, why did all the rest of the bad stuff happen to them?"

"I don't know," Bailey said. "Maybe it was their destiny. Are you sure you have the address?"

"Yes," Matt said distractedly.

"What are you reading?" She put her head on his shoulder.

"Nothing. I was just thinking how everything leads back to the Golden Six. No matter what we want to know, it always leads back to those six boys."

"Your father," Bailey said softly.

"It happened before he was my father. Anyway, I was thinking that the more we find out about them, the more likely we are to find out who Manville trusted."

"And if that person is still alive," Bailey said.

"Yes. If," Matt answered.

Twenty-seven

❧

"*He's never had* a visitor before," the nurse said to Bailey and Matt a few minutes after they entered the rest home. "Well, a couple of friends from work have visited him, but no family."

"Where did he work?" Matt asked.

"High school football coach," the nurse said, looking at them in speculation, as though to ask why they didn't know that. "If he's your uncle—" she began, looking at Matt.

"Family feud," Matt said. "You know how those things are."

"Sure," she said as she stopped in front of a door. "All right, now here are the rules. He's a very sick man, so if you upset him, out you go. Understand?"

Both Bailey and Matt nodded as they stepped past the woman to enter the room, and right away Bailey wanted to leave. The man on the bed looked as though he barely weighed a hundred pounds, and tubes were coming out of him everywhere. His left arm was strapped down, and a drip was slowly entering his veins. An oxygen tube was across his face. Machines all around him measured his breathing and his heart rate.

"Matt, I—" Bailey began, her hand on his arm.

But Matt stepped forward to the man's bedside. "Mr. Burgess," Matt said firmly, "we'd like to ask you about the night Frank McCallum died."

In the next second all hell broke loose as the man opened his eyes and alarm bells started screaming. In an instant the door opened, and a doctor and two nurses ran into the room, pushing Bailey and Matt aside.

Bailey stood back, clutching Matt's hands in hers as they watched the doctor examine the patient and the nurses switch off the machine alarms. After a moment Bailey heard a voice say, "I'm all right. Get off of me!" and she breathed a sigh of relief. "I was having a bad dream," the voice said. The doctor and two nurses were blocking their view, but Bailey knew it was Burgess speaking.

"Would all of you get the hell out of here and let me talk to my guests?" the voice said.

The doctor turned around and gave Bailey and Matt a hard look. He hadn't been fooled by his patient's lie. "You upset him again like that, and I'll personally escort you out of here," he said, then the three of them left the room.

Bailey walked to his bedside. The man in bed was emaciated, wasted by whatever was eating his life away, but his eyes were bright and alive. And she could see past his wrinkled face to the young man she'd seen so many pictures of.

"I think we'd better leave," she said. "We've—"

"What?" he said. "Already almost killed me?" Burgess said, then coughed.

Bailey got a glass of water with a straw in it off the table and held it while the man drank.

During this, Matt had been standing at the foot of the bed, his hands white-knuckled as he gripped the rails.

"You're Kyle's boy, aren't you?" Burgess said. "You look like him, only fatter."

"He eats a lot," Bailey said, smiling.

Burgess turned to her. "And who are you?"

Before Bailey could speak, Matt said, "Lucas McCallum's widow."

"Oh, Lord," Bailey said, then sat down on a chair beside the bed. She was sure that this news would certainly kill the man. The machines made some beeps, but no alarms went off.

"Manville," Burgess said after a moment. "James Manville. I saw him once. I was in Oregon buying lumber, and someone said that James Manville had just come into town and was going white-water rafting. Like everyone else, I wanted to see him, so I was in the crowd that watched him get in the boat. Just before they took off, he waved at us, and I thought my heart would stop, because I was looking into Luke McCallum's eyes."

"Did he see you?" Bailey asked.

"Oh, yeah. He saw me, and when he did, the arrogant look of James Manville left his face, and he was that scared little boy again. But I put my finger to my lips and shook my head to let him know that I'd never tell, and Luke smiled back at me. I always liked Luke."

"I want to know *everything* about him," Bailey said.

But Burgess smiled. "Sorry. Can't help you there. All I know is that Frank left town right after graduation, stayed away for a few years, and when he came back, he had a kid with him. I once asked Kyle why we never saw the kid, and Kyle said that he was deformed, so Frank kept him hidden away up in the mountains so people wouldn't make fun of him. It wasn't any of my business, so I never asked any questions about him. I never even saw the kid until he was a teenager. He used to sneak down out of the mountains and visit . . ." Burgess paused for a moment. "A farm. There was a nice little farm on—"

"Owl Creek Road," Bailey said. "The old Hanley place."

"Yes! That's it. Have you seen it?"

"Yes," Bailey said softly. "It's beautiful. There's an old mulberry tree in the back that—" She stopped; the man's machines had begun to beep wildly. "I'm sorry, I've upset you. I think we should go."

"No, please don't leave," Burgess said. "It's lonely here, and I'd like to talk. I go days without saying a word. I used to be known as a pretty good storyteller."

Bailey looked at Matt, and he smiled.

Burgess was silent for a moment as he looked from one to the other of them. "Maybe you'd like to hear about the Golden Six and what really happened."

"Yes," Matt said. "We'd like to hear anything you can tell us."

For a moment Burgess closed his eyes. "Dying has made me want to tell the truth." He opened his eyes and looked at Bailey. "It was all caused by that bitch, T. L. Spangler. You know that?"

"I read most of the book," Bailey said softly. "All that I could stand to read of it, that is."

Burgess shook his head. "No, not that part. Not what was written in that book. She tried to justify the horror she'd caused, but she knew what she'd done. I hear she's in Washington now," Burgess said, then smiled. "Politics. Backbiting and underhanded tricks. That's where she belongs." He paused a moment to calm himself. "It all started with a bet, a bet that Roddy lost, a bet that changed the lives of a whole lot of people. If you've read the book, then you know all about that social class crap she harped on, but some of it was true. We were kings in Calburn and nobodies in Wells Creek.

"But what that ugly woman didn't write in her book was that *she* was behind all the hatred that happened in Wells Creek. You see, Roddy— Is he still alive?"

"Yes," Bailey said. "He's alive. And he's mean and he's crazy, but he's still marrying little girls and producing babies."

Burgess smiled. "Then he hasn't changed at all. He always was mean and crazy, but back then he was also beautiful, and few people outside Calburn could see past that beauty. Your father could," he said, looking at Matt, who'd taken a seat beside Bailey. "Kyle couldn't stand Roddy, just plain detested him, and contrary to what's been written, it had nothing to do with Roddy's 'parental origins' or his 'social status.' Roddy was born mean, and he never changed."

"And my father disliked him," Matt said thoughtfully. "But I thought the Golden Six were—"

"One for all and all for one?" Burgess said, then tried to laugh, but when the machines started beeping again, he calmed himself and held up the arm that was filled with needles. "I'd take them out, but they'll just put them back in," he said with a sigh. "Now where was I?"

"A bet," Bailey said. "You said it all started with a bet."

"Yes. I remember that day clearly. We were in Wells Creek High School, standing by the lockers. It was Kyle, Roddy, Frank, and me. Roddy was trying to impress Kyle. Talk about an impossible task! But Roddy was even more full of himself back then, so he bragged to Kyle that he could get any girl in the world. For some reason, instead of ignoring him as he usually did, Kyle turned around and glared at Roddy. Then Kyle gave this little smile that I'll never forget. 'Her!' Kyle said. 'Get *her*.' It was Theresa Spangler. Have you seen a picture of her?"

"I have," Bailey said, then looked at Matt. "Have you?"

Puzzled, Matt said, "Sure, she was on the cover of *Time*."

"No," Bailey said, "not a recent picture. Have you seen what she looked like in high school? Back then, she was—"

"A dog," Burgess said. "A real bowzer." He closed his eyes for a moment as he remembered that day. "Roddy went to her and gave her his best sexy looks, his oiliest, most lustful come-on lines, but Spangler wasn't affected by him. She told Roddy to drop dead, that she wanted nothing to do with him.

"You should have seen his face." Burgess chuckled. "Roddy thought all the girls at Wells Creek were mad for him, but here was this dog telling him to get lost. By then a crowd of girls had gathered, and they were whispering among themselves. Roddy's pride was hurt, so he said, 'Who'd want an ugly old hag like you anyway?' and started to walk away. But Spangler—" Burgess had to take a breath before he could go on.

"Loudly, down the length of the hallway, Spangler said, 'You might have beauty, and I might be ugly, but I have brains and you don't. I can get my face fixed, but you can't get a brain. Someday I'll be in the White House, while you'll be in a shack dreaming of the days when you were beautiful.' "

"Yeow!" Matt said. "She was certainly right on the money, wasn't she? Smart girl."

"A good memory, anyway," Bailey said. "But she stole the whole thing from Winston Churchill."

Both men looked at her as though to ask what she was talking about. "A woman Winston Churchill disliked was sitting beside him at dinner, and she said, 'You, sir, are drunk,' and Churchill said, 'And you, madam, are ugly, but I shall be sober in the morning.' "

Both men were still looking at Bailey in question, silently asking what her story had to do with anything. "Roddy could have pointed out the woman's plagiarism," Bailey said, but the men kept staring at her. "Right. I forgot. You're boys. You probably think Roddy should have punched her in the nose. Oh, well, what *did* he say?"

"Nothing," Burgess answered. "Roddy was beautiful, not smart, so he said nothing, and everyone in school laughed at him.

"But what none of us from Calburn knew was that no one made fun of Theresa Spangler, because she was dangerous. All the kids in Wells Creek had learned in primary school to stay away from her. If they didn't, their lunches 'disappeared.' Or they found chewing gum in their hair. Or there were 'accidents' on the playground.'"

"A dirty fighter," Matt said.

"The dirtiest," Burgess said. "She never did anything in the open. The kids all knew who had hurt them, but the teachers never did. They felt sorry for Spangler because she was so ugly, so if a kid said Spangler did it, it would usually be the innocent kid who got punished.

"In high school, the snotty little leader of the cheer-leading team once made a rude remark about the ugli-ness of Theresa Spangler, and the other girls laughed. The next day someone put green dye in the shampoo of all the girls on the team. After that, everyone in Wells Creek High School treated Theresa with the utmost respect."

"I'm sure her methods were bad, but at least she fought back," Bailey said. She had too frequently been called "ugly" herself, and she'd fantasized often about revenge.

"I know what you're thinking," Burgess said. "She was right to get revenge, and maybe she was. But that girl played too dirty, and she didn't forgive. After those cheerleaders laughed at her, Spangler didn't stop at dye-ing their hair green. They led lives in hell for that whole year. The next year, three of them moved to other schools, and the other three . . . well, let's just say that they desperately needed therapy."

"So you boys had inadvertently chosen the most for-midable person in school to pick on?" Matt said.

"Yes. And she took her rage out on *all* of us. She set herself a goal to undeclare us the heroes that the bomb scare had made us. On the next Monday, Kyle opened his notebook, and inside was some jock's homework. Four of them were waiting for Kyle after school. They beat him so badly he spent two days in the hospital."

Burgess shook his head. "All six of us were accused of awful things that year, but we were innocent. An obscene note from Roddy was found in some football player's girlfriend's locker, and only by luck did he escape a beating. Part of Frank's shirt was found outside the girls' locker room, and he was accused of being a Peeping Tom. Taddy was accused of cheating on a test. And Harper was locked inside Kyle's locker by four boys who said he was spying on them. They did it on a Friday afternoon, and we didn't find him until Saturday night. We had to break into the school to get him."

"And you?" Bailey asked. "What did they do to you?"

" 'Murderer' written on my locker. And it was written inside my books and on anything that had my name on it."

For a moment the three of them were silent.

"*Was* it all a setup?" Bailey asked quietly. "The bombing, I mean. Did you all plan it, or were you really heroes?"

"Yes and no," Burgess said. "In a way we planned it because we fantasized about doing it for days beforehand, but I don't think any of us really thought about planting a bomb in the school."

"Except Harper," Matt said softly.

"Exactly. How'd you guess?"

"I think maybe my dad told my mother the truth because one time there was a news piece on TV about a bomb going off somewhere, and my mother said, 'Better check Harper's whereabouts.' She didn't mean for me to hear her, but I did. At the time I was so young that I thought she meant a harp, a musical instrument, but what she'd said was so puzzling that I remembered it.

Years later, I heard the name Harper, and I put two and
two together."

"So how did it happen?" Bailey asked.

"It started out as loneliness, just as Spangler said. We
were strangers in a school that didn't want us, and we
desperately wanted to find our places."

"Spangler said that Frank and Rodney and Thaddeus
were better off in Wells Creek than they had been in
Calburn," Bailey said. "She said Frank had impressed the
whole school with his persuasive speech."

Burgess snorted so loud that one machine began to
beep, and he had to take a couple of breaths to calm
himself and quieten the machine. "You know why
Frank had such a good voice? He'd been chain-smoking
since he was eleven, and his lungs were charbroiled.
Spangler wrote that book to impress her teachers. We
were *all* misfits. The only thing that woman got right
was that since we were the only boys from Calburn, it
threw us together. And she was right when she said
that in Calburn we'd never been friends. Nerds like
Taddy don't rub elbows with shining stars like Kyle
Longacre."

Bailey glanced at Matt and saw that his mouth was in
a hard line. Obviously, he didn't consider his father a
"shining star."

"The first weeks were awful," Burgess said. "We were
alone and lonely and we missed our school, where we
knew the rules. Every afternoon we had to wait forty-
five minutes to an hour for the bus to pick us up to take
us back to Calburn. And, like kids then did, we stayed
apart from the girls. The first time the bomb was mentioned, as usual, we were complaining about how much
we hated Wells Creek High School."

❧❧❧

"*What would you do* if someone bombed this place?" Harper asked the other boys as they stood in the little kids' playground and waited for the bus to arrive.

"Run," Roddy said, and they all laughed.

"I'd get the hell out of here, and hope that they all blew up," Frank said.

"No!" Harper said fiercely. "That's not the way to become heroes."

"Heroes? Who wants to be a hero?" Roddy asked.

"Look, we have to stay in this school for a whole year, and it can be heaven or hell," Harper said. "Which do you want?"

Frank started to walk away from the idiotic turn the conversation had taken, but Kyle's words held him back.

"I'm listening," Kyle said. "What do you have in mind to do?"

"Nothing," Harper said. "I don't plan to *do* anything. It's just that I want to be a writer, and I like to play, What if? It's my favorite game."

"You mean besides trying on ladies' hose?" Burgess said.

Harper looked Burgess up and down. "Want to try a pair?"

Kyle interrupted them. "Okay, I'll bite. What would make us heroes?"

"It was just something I was thinking about for a story, that's all. I was thinking what I'd do if the bomber struck here."

"Push the lot of them into an elevator shaft then throw a stick of dynamite after them?" Taddy said, and everyone looked at him, surprised at the violence in his voice.

"Just the opposite," Harper said. "I'd rescue them. I'd be the calm one while they were running around in terror. I'd direct them toward the exits, and I'd take over while the teachers and students were going crazy. Then later I'd be modest when I was talking to reporters." At this he demonstrated, with his head down, then looking up shyly. "Shucks, ma'am, 'tweren't nothin'."

They were all laughing at Harper, and Kyle said, "Nice idea. We'll lead them out the exits and make a stand for Calburn."

"And what if the doors of the classrooms are locked?" Taddy asked.

"And who would rescue the naked girls in the gym?" Rodney asked.

"What about the little kids downstairs?" Burgess asked. "I'd like to get them out."

"And me," Frank said. "I'd help with the little kids, too." Then when they all looked at him, he shrugged. "I like kids. Better than adults, anyway."

"What about you, Taddy? Who would you like to save?" Kyle asked, and Taddy grinned.

"I'd save the football players. They'd be . . ." He thought for a moment. "They'd be locked inside the gym, and smoke would be pouring into the room. They'd be coughing and sure they were going to die, then I'd . . . I'd break open a window and lower a rope down the side of the wall and help them climb up."

His story was so vivid that the others laughed, but Harper was serious. "What do you break the window with, and where do you get the rope? And if they get out of the place one at a time, do the others die of smoke inhalation?"

For a while they were all silent, glancing down the road, waiting for the bus, and the discussion seemed to be over, but Harper wouldn't let it die. He turned to Kyle. "What would *you* do?"

"Catch the bastard that did it," Kyle said instantly, as though he'd been thinking about it. "I'd put on my cape and fly into the smoke and catch the criminal."

"But what if the bad guy was long gone?" Harper asked.

"I'd walk toward the bomb and take it out even if I had to throw my body over it."

When Kyle saw the others staring at him, he gave a half smile and said, "So sue me, I want to be a hero. I'd like to be the opposite of my old man."

"And that's how it started," Burgess said. "It was just a story we made up to entertain ourselves during the long wait for the bus."

"But then it really happened," Bailey said.

"Yes. Harper planted the bomb in the school, and between you and me, I think he'd done it before. Several bombs had gone off around the area during that summer, and I think Harper planted them all. In Wells Creek, there were actually a half dozen of them placed around the school, but during the confusion Harper managed to sneak around and remove most of them before the cops found them. They weren't real anyway, just smoke.

"Anyway, by the time they went off, our fantasy had been talked about so much among us that we knew exactly what our jobs were. And Harper had done his homework; everything we needed for the rescue was right where it needed to be. And when the reporters came, even our speeches of humility had been rehearsed.

"But what hadn't been rehearsed was Kyle's wrath.

"That night Kyle went to each house, got us out of bed, and had us sneak away to have a little 'meeting' with Harper. Kyle was furious, and he threatened Harper that if he ever did anything like that again, we'd cut him out of our group. We'd shun him and leave him on his own."

"But you came out of the bombing as the Golden Six," Matt said.

"Yeah, that was something we hadn't planned." Burgess paused a moment. "For a while it was great. We were heroes in Wells Creek, and we ruled Calburn. Everyone everywhere loved us."

"Until Roddy insulted Theresa Spangler," Matt said.

"Right," Burgess said, then smiled. "By that time we'd pretty much forgiven Harper since everything had worked out so well. In fact, we were doing better than we ever had in our lives thanks to him. Then after Spangler was insulted, horrible things began to happen to us, but Harper saved us."

"He wrote the articles," Matt said. "But Bailey hasn't read them." Quickly, he added, "That's not a criticism, dearest."

"I didn't realize you two were married," Burgess said.

"We're not," Bailey said.

"She only started sleeping with me—" Matt began.

"Would you mind?!" she said to Matt, and both men laughed. "So tell me about the articles."

"Harper's family owned the Calburn newspaper, and his mother stayed home and had Harper wait on her hand and foot, while her deceased brother's oldest son ran the newspaper. Sort of. Harper's mother was a tyrant, and she tried to rule anyone who got within twenty miles of her.

"Right after Roddy made Spangler angry, she started telling people that she believed we'd planted the bomb ourselves. She said that heroes didn't just appear in one day, that there had to be something leading up to them. But it's my experience in life that people want heroes, so for the most part the other kids ignored her. So she went to Calburn and pretended she was writing an article about the Golden Six and asked a lot of questions."

"Just as she did many years later for her book."

"Exactly," Burgess said. "She got people to confide in her, then spread what she had learned around, and the students began to hate us.

"Because we weren't from Wells Creek, we didn't know where the evil gossip was coming from. It was Roddy who found out. Some girl told him while they were in the backseat of a car.

"And when Harper heard, he got angry. He said that no cross-eyed, buck-toothed, frizzy-haired Medusa was going to win over him.

"What Harper did was to tell his mother that if he was going to be a writer, he needed to start young, so he needed to have his work published in *their* newspaper *now*.

"His mother allowed Harper to have anything except freedom, so she agreed, and Harper wrote his first story. But when Harper's cousin, the editor of the paper, read the first column, he refused to publish it. 'I can't publish this,' he told his aunt. 'Have you read this thing? It says that Kyle Longacre is a cross between Galahad and Buddha, a "champion of the underdog," he calls him. I've known Kyle all his life, and he never championed anything except a football. He's a nice kid, but he's no saint. And your son has portrayed that Thaddeus Overlander as a great mathematician who's secretly working with the government to save the world from destruction. And Burgess is—'

" 'I think the article shows great imagination,' Mrs. Kirkland said.

" 'This isn't imagination, it's libel. And, besides that, it's all a great whopping lie.'

" 'My son wrote it, so you will publish it, or you will no longer have a job,' she said, and that was that.

"And that's when everything *really* began. Harper took all the bad stories that Spangler had used against us and twisted them around so they became good traits. He portrayed Frank as a man with the voice of the angels, and said Frank had worked his way up past unimaginable poverty, all with his voice. As a result, Frank was asked by a local radio station to announce the football scores.

"Kyle was said to be a young man of noble character, a throwback to ages past, so he was given any job in school that called for someone trustworthy.

"Roddy was made out to be irresistible to women, and it got so that he couldn't open his locker without love notes falling out.

"Taddy was said to be brilliant, and as a result, he was given special attention from the teachers, which made his grades soar.

"For himself, Harper hinted that he'd written books under a famous pen name, so he was constantly being stopped in the halls and asked if he was so and so."

Burgess paused for a moment, and Bailey gave him another drink of water. "As for me, everyone in the county knew what had happened when I was four, but instead of hiding it, Harper wrote an essay about me that had anyone who read it crying. He portrayed me as living under the burden of great tragedy, from which I was suffering every moment. More papers sold the day that essay came out than any day before, and after that, 'murderer' was never again written on anything I owned."

When he'd finished this story, Bailey could see that Burgess was worn out. His skin was beginning to turn gray. She gestured silently to Matt that they should leave. He nodded, but still, the big question hadn't been answered.

Matt took a breath. "James Manville had a very important piece of paper, and he said he gave it to 'the person he trusted most in the world.' "

Burgess smiled. "That would be Frank's mother, Martha. She raised Luke."

Bailey's heart fell as she visualized the paper being thrown out with an old woman's effects. "Oh, thank you," she said, looking at Matt and trying not to let her disappointment show. "I think we've taken enough of your time. We'd better go now."

"Yes, I am tired," Burgess said, "but a good tired. I feel lighter now."

Bailey gathered her things and prepared to leave, but she couldn't resist one last question. "Why did you marry Violet, then leave her?"

"A lot of reasons. I had some friends in California, and one of them lived out in the country. He said, 'Burg, how long has it been since you were laid?' Next thing I knew, he was calling some prostitute he said was the best he'd ever had. It sounded good to me until he started talking about watching, and that's when I left. I was two miles away when I saw this girl stopped by the side of the road. Her beat-up old car had broken down, and I instantly knew who she was. I knew that when she got to where she was going, it wasn't going to be pleasant for her, so I felt a bit guilty, and I stopped to fix her car.

"The whole time I was working, she was putting on an act about being young and innocent, and how she sang in the church choir back home.

"But even though I knew she was lying with every breath, I liked her. And, what's more, I knew that she wanted my life. Not me, exactly, but my life. And that was odd, because not many pretty girls want to marry a lumber salesman and move to some nowhere town."

For a moment Burgess paused and smiled. "Besides, I liked the idea of taking a prostitute back to Calburn. It appealed to me to imagine introducing her to my old man as his daughter-in-law. And if Violet and I had kids—" Burgess gave a little smile. "Let's just say that I was planning to tell my old man some interesting things on his deathbed."

"Did you love her?" Bailey asked.

"Exactly as much as she loved me. And I don't mean that in a bad way. Violet and I liked each other; we were well matched."

"But you faked your death and walked away."

"No, I didn't plan it. The plane crashed and I walked away without a scratch, and as I looked at that wreck, I thought that maybe if I left my life, left that town and those people behind, I could be someone else."

"Did it work?" Bailey asked.

"No."

"Because of what happened on the thirtieth of August, 1968?" Matt asked, and that's when the alarms started screaming again, and this time the doctor pushed them out of the room before they could even say good-bye.

"I guess that's that," Bailey said once they were in the lobby. "I know! Since Frank grew up in a mountain cabin, maybe they used the permission slip to paper the walls, and it's still there."

Matt laughed, then shook his head as though to say that he didn't know what to try next.

"Excuse me," came a voice from behind them. "Mr. Meredith wants you to have this." The nurse was holding out an address book.

Bailey took the old, worn-out book and looked questioningly at the nurse.

She lifted her hands. "Don't ask me. He just said to give you that."

"Thank you," Bailey said as she walked through the door Matt was holding open for her.

Once they were outside, she opened the address book and flipped through a few pages. They were all addresses in Florida and looked like mostly business acquaintances.

"Try the letter *M*," Matt said. "For McCallum."

Bailey ran her fingers down the letters, then slipped her nail under *M*. There, at the top of the page, was the name Martha McCallum, and a telephone number.

Matt had his cell phone out before Bailey could get her breath. She stood in silence, breath held, as Matt asked the person who answered about Martha McCallum.

"She is?" Matt said. "She's alive? Lucid? Thank you very much," he said, then hung up.

"Where?" Bailey asked.

"A rest home outside Atlanta."

When Bailey started turning around and looking at the buildings around them instead of walking toward their rental car, Matt said, "What are you doing?"

"Looking for the nearest travel agent."

He grinned. "We have like minds. Remind me that when this is over I'm to tell you that I love you."

Bailey didn't pause as she started for the car, but her heart was pounding in her ears. "Okay, I'll remind you."

Twenty-eight

❧

Matt's cell phone rang at three A.M. He and Bailey were in a hotel in Sarasota, and booked on an early-morning flight to Atlanta. They couldn't get seats together, and they'd had to pay a lot to book a flight just hours before it left, but they were going.

When the phone rang so early, Matt was sure it was bad news, and when he flipped the cover open and saw that it was his brother calling, he knew it was very bad. Quietly he got out of bed and took the phone into the bathroom. "What's happened?" he said into the receiver as he shut the door. He had to resist an urge to say, Who has something bad happened to?

"Alex has been arrested," Rick said. His voice was calm, but Matt knew his brother was very upset.

"What for?" Matt asked. "Speeding? DUI? Why the hell did you allow a kid that young out so late? You know he's—"

"Murder," Rick said. "Alex has been arrested for murder."

Matt sat down on the side of the tub. "Tell me," he whispered, as he imagined Alex in a barroom fight over a girl.

"Have you ever heard of a woman named Dolores Carruthers?" Rick asked.

Matt was sure his heart was going to stop. "Yes," he managed to get out.

"She was murdered yesterday, and the police say Alex's prints are all over her house. And she had skin under her nails, and Matt, the boy has deep scratches on his back. If the DNA matches—" Rick took a breath. "What the hell was he doing with her anyway? She's forty-one, and Alex is seventeen."

Matt ran his hand over his face. This was all his fault. If Alex was convicted—

"Are you there?" Rick said.

"Yeah, I'm here."

"Who is this woman?"

"Bailey's sister," Matt said.

Rick didn't say anything for a while. "This is bad, isn't it? And you're involved in it, aren't you?"

"Up to my neck."

"Is Bailey James Manville's widow?" Rick asked softly.

"Yes."

"Oh, God, Matt, the police are looking for her too. I told them we'd never met the woman. They showed us a picture of her, and I—"

When he broke off, Matt said, "You what?"

"Now I understand. Patsy saw the photo, too, but she didn't say anything. She let *me* tell the police that 'we' had never seen the woman before. But after the police left, after they took Alex away, Patsy said, 'I have to go see Janice.' You know she's not said Janice's name in umpteen years, and all I thought was, Good, maybe this mess will make them stop that stupid feud of theirs. But—"

"She saw that Lillian Manville was Bailey."

"Yeah, I think so," Rick said. "Where are you two?"

"In Sarasota. We—"

"Florida?!" Rick said. "But that's where the woman who was murdered lives. Do you mean to say that you and Bailey were in the same state when she was killed? Does Bailey have a reason to kill her sister?"

"There was a lot of hatred and billions involved. Think that's reason enough?"

Rick's voice lowered. "Do you think you and Bailey could be called co-conspirators in this murder?"

Matt took a deep breath. "Yes, I think that's not only probable, that's likely."

"Matt . . ." Rick said, and he sounded as he did when he was a child asking his big brother to protect him, to shield him.

"All right," Matt said, "just stay calm. Say as little as possible. Bailey and I are flying out of here this morning. There's someone we need to see, and she might have some answers about why these murders have happened."

"Murders?" Rick said, his voice rising. "Plural? As in more than one?"

"I'll explain everything later. Listen, I'm going to shut this phone off, so you can give the number to the police, and you can honestly say that I didn't tell you where we're going or who we're going to see. Remember that: you know *nothing*."

"Okay," Rick said, sounding six years old again. "But why did James Manville's widow come here to Calburn? What—"

"Gotta go," Matt said, then pushed the button to end the call. He moved the switch on the side of the phone to disable it.

For a moment he stayed in the bathroom and tried to calm himself. Murder was not in his realm of expertise. Part of him wanted to panic, but he knew he couldn't. He had to keep a clear mind so he could think about what must be done. Should they return to Calburn? Since he and Bailey had sent Alex, who was underage, to Dolores, it was probable that he and Bailey would be charged as accessories to murder.

Matt took a few minutes, then left the bathroom. Bailey was sitting up in bed, waiting for him.

"What's happened?" she asked, her eyes serious.

Matt debated whether or not to tell her, but she was a grown woman, and she deserved to be told the truth. "Your sister has been murdered, and Alex has been charged and taken into custody. The police are looking for you, for both of us, so if we want to get out of here, we'd better do it *now*."

Bailey sat there blinking at him.

"How much cash do you have?" he asked.

"I don't know. A hundred, maybe. Why?"

He could see that she was working hard to hold herself together. "Because we're going to drive to Atlanta, and we've got to pay cash for gas. We can't use credit cards because they can be traced."

Bailey looked up at him, her face calm, but her hands were clutching the bedcover hard. "Shouldn't we go back to Calburn to be with Alex? Why should we go to Atlanta? What could some ancient woman—if she's not senile—tell us that could help Alex?"

"I don't know," Matt said honestly, "but if Manville trusted this woman enough to leave the paper about your marriage with her, then maybe he trusted her with other information. You have any other ideas of how to help?"

"No," she said slowly. "No, but Alex must be so frightened. And my sister—"

Matt grabbed Bailey's arms and pulled her up out of the bed. "You can cry later. You can have a nervous breakdown later if you want—in fact, we'll both have one—but now you have to get dressed, get packed, and get going."

Twenty minutes later they were in the rental car, but Matt didn't start the engine. "I want to check on something," he said, then got out. There was an ATM machine on the side of the bank next door to the hotel, and he stuck his card in and punched some buttons.

Minutes later, he got back into the car and started the engine. "Frozen," he said. "My bank account has been frozen."

Bailey just nodded and buckled her seat belt.

Twenty-nine

Martha McCallum was eighty years old, much younger than Bailey and Matt had speculated. They'd been in the car for nine hours straight, arriving in the late afternoon, too late to visit the nursing home. They'd used all the cash they had for gas and food, so they couldn't afford a motel. Matt pulled the car down a dirt road, where they had a dinner of the last of the bread and cheese and shared a gallon of springwater. When the sun went down, they snuggled together in the tiny backseat and tried to go to sleep.

"Your foot," Bailey said.

"Right," Matt said as he moved his foot. "Maybe one of us should sleep in the front. Or one of us should do a Daniel Boone and sleep outside on the ground."

"Bugs or a gearshift," Bailey said. "I can't decide which."

He pulled her head down on his shoulder and smiled. He was glad she was able to make a joke, because from the way she'd cried for the first three hours of their trip, he thought she might never smile again.

At nine the next morning, they were in the lobby of the nursing home, waiting to see Martha McCallum. They'd both had sponge baths in the rest room of a nearby service station and done their best to look presentable.

The rest home they were in today was quite a bit different from the one Burgess had been in. His had been clean and comfortable, homey even, but this one was plush. As Bailey looked up at the huge, double, curving staircase, she said, "And here I thought the Yankees had burned Twelve Oaks."

"She'll see you now," the receptionist said; she was wearing a suit that Bailey knew had a designer label.

"Think Manville paid for this?" Matt whispered to Bailey.

"Excuse me," Bailey said loudly to the young woman. "Who owns this place?"

"It's owned by one of the late James Manville's corporations," she said, smiling as she stopped by a door.

As Bailey stepped past Matt, she raised her eyebrows as though to say, See?

Martha McCallum's suite was beautiful, and Bailey recognized the hand of an interior designer. It was done in French country, and all the antiques were real.

"Well, well," came a voice from a wooden-framed chair to their left. "So, Lillian, you finally found me."

Bailey turned to look at a small woman wearing a perfectly pressed silk shirtwaist dress, discreet gold earrings, and a strand of pearls. She also had on a small gold watch and a gold bracelet. It was a simple costume, but Bailey knew that everything the woman was wearing was of the finest quality and had cost the earth. The woman's face had few lines on it, and her long, blondish gray hair was softly pulled back to the nape of her neck and tied with a Hermes scarf. Bailey wondered if the same surgeon who had repaired Jimmie's mouth had done this woman's facelift.

"Yes," Bailey said, then took a seat on the couch when the woman gestured.

"And who is this lovely man?"

"Matthew Longacre," Bailey said, and the woman shook Matt's hand before he sat down.

It was Bailey who began to talk. "You seem to have the advantage on us, since you know me, but I've never heard of you. I don't mean to be rude, but we have a clock over our heads that is ticking, and when it goes off, it's going to explode, so we need to know all that you can tell us as fast as you can tell us."

"Yes, of course," Martha said. "I heard about your sister this morning. I'm sorry, dear, for her death, but she never was much of a sister to you, was she? Luke detested her." Martha waved her manicured hand. "Forgive me, but I've never been able to call him anything but Luke."

"What did Jimmie . . . my husband tell you?" Bailey asked.

"Everything," Martha said. "Absolutely everything. I don't mean about business—he never talked to me about that—but he told me everything about you, and about Eva and Ralph and how your sister extorted money out of him, and—"

"My sister? How—"

Martha looked at Matt. "You know, don't you? It

took me a while to piece it all together, but you sent that beautiful young man to Dolores to find out about the permission slip, didn't you? When I read that he was one of Roddy's children, I can tell you that my heart nearly stopped. Did he find out everything you needed to know from Dolores?"

"Yes, I think so," Matt said, studiously ignoring Bailey's hard stare. He knew she was just realizing that Alex had told him a lot more than Matt had told Bailey.

"You found out about the car Luke had to give Dolores, and the yearly income, and all the other things?" Martha asked.

"Yes, ma'am, I did," Matt said, still refusing to look at Bailey.

"And Lillian, dear, what did he tell you?"

"It seems that he told me very little," Bailey said, her mouth a hard line.

Martha smiled. "Men do try to protect us, don't they? By the way, I see you had your nose fixed, and you lost all that weight Luke kept on you."

"Yes," Bailey said, turning away from Matt. "And you? Jimmie's surgeon?"

Martha's smile grew broader. She had beautiful, expensive dental work. "Yes, the same man. He was used to keeping secrets."

"And where did Jimmie get the money for all the surgery he must have had?" Bailey asked.

Martha hesitated. "Some money had unexpectedly come into my possession . . . a box full of money, so I gave it to Luke and told him to use it any way he wanted to." She smiled. "He used it wisely. He got his mouth fixed, then used the rest to start making what would become billions." She smiled again, pride on her face.

"Do you have the signed permission for Lillian's marriage?" Matt asked after a moment.

"Yes." Martha looked at Bailey. "Luke was always terrified that you would leave him. Did you know that?"

"Yes," Bailey said softly, then her eyes filled with tears. "I killed him."

At that Matt looked at her sharply, but Bailey kept her eyes on Martha.

"No, you didn't," Martha said, and when Bailey started to speak, she raised her hand. "Before you tell me that I don't know the whole story, let me assure you that I do. Three nights before he died, Luke called me and told me that you'd asked him for a divorce."

Matt moved his hand across the couch and clasped Bailey's hand.

"But Luke wasn't despondent over it," Martha said. "He was elated."

"Elated?" Bailey said. "He *wanted* a divorce?"

"No. He was elated that you'd finally put your foot down. Luke used to tell me that you didn't love him enough to be jealous."

At that Bailey had to get up. She walked to the window and, for a moment, gazed at the beautiful grounds that surrounded the rest home; then she looked back at Martha. "Jealous? He thought I wasn't jealous of all those tall, skinny, beautiful women?"

"They meant nothing to him," Martha said softly.

"They meant a lot to *me!*" Bailey said, then calmed herself. "Was he going to give me a divorce?"

"No, of course not," Martha said, smiling. "He was going to court you. He said it was something he owed you. Do you know where he was going when his plane crashed?"

"No. Business. Jimmie was always visiting the places he owned." Her voice lowered. "Like this one."

Martha smiled. "Isn't it lovely? When Luke was a child, and he and I were alone in that horrible old cabin, we used to make up stories about what we'd buy if we had all the money in the world. Frank saw to it that we had TV, books, and magazines, so Luke and I knew what was available in the world, even if we couldn't have it."

"And what did you two wish for?" Matt asked.

"I just wanted normal things, like a house with an indoor toilet, but Luke wanted to own the world. 'And I'd give it all to you and my dad,' Luke said. He adored his father."

Bailey looked at Martha. "Where was Jimmie going the day he died?"

"You really didn't know? He didn't so much as hint?"

"No," Bailey said. "I was very depressed at the time. I was tired of everything, all the moving around, all the people who despised me, and all of Jimmie's women." She said the last with anger in her voice.

"But what was it that you wanted more than life itself?" Martha asked.

"I . . . I don't know," Bailey said, puzzled.

Martha looked at Matt. "What does she want?"

"Kids," he said. "She gets real gooey every time she looks at one."

Bailey looked at Matt in astonishment. "I do no such thing."

"What about those twins you saw at the grocery store?"

"Those were exceptionally cute babies," Bailey said defensively. "And I—"

Martha's words cut her off. "He's right. Children. Luke wasn't about to have his own child and risk it inheriting his lip, so he arranged a private adoption."

At that Bailey sat back down on the couch beside Matt. "Adoption?" she whispered.

"Yes. You know how Luke was. He arranged it all in just a few days, and he was flying to some state out West to pick up the child. He meant to surprise you."

"Put it in a box and wrap it up?" Matt said, sarcastically.

"Yes, that would be like Luke," Martha said, watching Bailey as she struggled with this news. "I told him he should treat you like an adult, and you two should go through the adoption together, but Luke said, 'Frecks is too sentimental. She'd want to adopt a whole orphanage full of misfits. But I'm too selfish to stand more than one of them taking her time away from me, so I'm going to get her a little blonde-haired, blue-eyed girl.' "

"That sounds just like him," Bailey said, blinking back tears. For months now she'd been carrying the burden that maybe Jimmie had been so despondent about her asking for a divorce that he had committed suicide.

"Feel better now?" Martha asked.

Bailey was too choked to answer, but she nodded vigorously. Yes, she felt better. She felt relieved of the heaviest burden she'd ever carried.

Martha motioned to Matt to hand Bailey a tissue from the box (elegantly covered in bird's-eye maple inlaid with walnut) on the table.

Bailey took the tissue and blew her nose. "Then it really was an accident."

"Oh, no," Martha said. "Eva and Ralph Turnbull killed Luke."

Bailey halted, the tissue halfway to her nose, and Martha looked from Bailey to Matt.

"Atlanta and Ray?" Matt asked.

"That's what they call themselves now, but they're still Eva and Ralph."

"Turnbull," Matt said. "Not Manville and not McCallum."

"Heavens no!" Martha said. "Those two murderers are no kin to me or my son—and they were never related to Luke."

It took Matt and Bailey a moment to digest what she was saying.

"Phillip said he didn't think Atlanta and Ray were related to Jimmie."

"Blackmail?" Matt asked.

"Yes. Blackmail. If Luke didn't claim them as kin and give them millions, they said they'd tell the world about his childhood in Calburn. And if people learned of Luke's early life, he might receive what he most dreaded." She looked to Bailey to supply the answer to that riddle.

"Pity," Bailey said. "Jimmie couldn't bear for anyone to feel sorry for him."

"Right."

"There's more to it than that, isn't there?" Matt said. "Bailey told me about a 'murder called suicide.' Was he referring to his father's death?"

For a moment, Martha turned and looked out the window, then she looked back at Bailey. "I don't know if I should tell the story or not. Part of me wants to let the secrets die with Luke. He worked so hard and paid so much to keep his childhood from the world." For a moment she was quiet as she blinked back tears. "When

I heard of Luke's death on TV—no one called and told me, because no one knew about me—I knew *they* had killed him. Luke made a lot of people angry."

"Yes," Bailey said. "I warned him about that. He sometimes cut people to the quick."

"But then Luke had been cut so many times that it was all he knew," Martha said. "Eva and Ralph found it easy to bribe someone who worked for Luke to tell them what he was doing. When they found out that Luke was about to adopt a child, they couldn't allow that, now could they?"

"An heir," Matt said.

"Right." She looked at Bailey. "Your sister found out at your mother's funeral that you didn't know Luke had obtained your mother's permission to marry. And Dolores knew that if you didn't know about the paper, then you thought you and Luke weren't really married. Shame on you!" Martha said. "How could you believe that someone like Luke would have overlooked something as important as that?"

"When I was married to Jimmie, I didn't think about legalities much," Bailey said in her own defense.

"So Atlanta and Ray and Dolores worked together?" Matt asked.

"No, I don't think Dolores was any match for those two, but Dolores had a big mouth. Sorry, dear, but all one had to do was get her to talking about her younger sister, and Dolores told anyone anything."

"She told Alex about the signed permission after knowing him only a day," Matt said.

"Yes, and it cost her her life," Martha said.

"Atlanta and Ray do it?" Matt asked.

"Oh, yes. Just as they killed Luke and his attorney,

they killed Lillian's sister. I've tried hard to protect Luke's past so that the world would never find out about it, so I kept quiet after Luke's death. It was harder after that lawyer died and left two little children behind. How is his wife doing?"

"Taking it hard," Bailey said.

"Yes. Luke told me that theirs was a good marriage."

"You keep saying he told you," Bailey said. "Did he call you?" There was a hint of jealousy in her voice. Yes, Jimmie had been to bed with many women, but Bailey had survived by knowing that Jimmie *talked* to no woman but his wife.

Smiling, Martha pointed toward a cabinet along the far wall. It was large and of waxed pine, and Bailey doubted if it had cost less than a hundred grand. She opened both doors and looked inside. Inside were shelves full of pretty boxes covered with peach silk. Each box had a brass label on it and a date, each box covering about six months.

"Go on," Martha said, "open them."

Bailey pulled out a box, removed the lid, and looked inside. In a neat row were letters, each one in an envelope of Jimmie's monogrammed, green stationery.

"A letter and a photograph," Martha said softly. "Every other week since July 1978, he sent me a letter and a photograph. And he also kept my bank account filled with money. And, by the way, dear, Luke was born in 1954, not 1959. He was so proud of his new face that he nipped a few years off his age."

Bailey opened one of the letters and read.

Frecks was mad at me when I got home last night, but I soon got her in a good mood again. She lost four pounds while I was away, so I got the chef to bake that chocolate mousse cake she loves so much. I know, I'm a devil, but I like her fat. She's all mine that way.

Bailey folded the letter and put it back into its envelope, but she couldn't help removing the enclosed photo and looking at it. It was a picture of her, sitting on a chair on the patio of their house in Antigua. Near her were a dozen people, all with drinks in their hands, all seeming to be laughing.

But Bailey was alone in the middle of the crowd, and her face showed her misery. No wonder they disliked me so much, she thought; then she looked across the room at Matt. I'm much happier now, she thought as she slipped the photo back into the envelope, replaced it in the box, put the box away, and resolutely closed the cabinet doors. That part of her life was over. James Manville had not killed himself because his wife had asked him for a divorce.

"How do we prove that Atlanta and Ray murdered Jimmie?" Bailey said.

"Actually, I have proof," Martha said, then smiled at Bailey's and Matt's identical looks of astonishment. "I've had months, and thanks to Luke, I've had unlimited funds, so while the rest of the world was crucifying you, dear, I hired investigators."

"To find out what?" Matt said sharply.

"Who was near that plane for forty-eight hours before Luke took off in it. And I had some men—actually, about a dozen of them—go up into the mountains, find the wreckage of Luke's plane, and bring every piece of it down."

"I thought the police did that. Jimmie's body—" Bailey began.

"The police searched the wreckage, but only superficially. They weren't looking for evidence of foul play because two young men at the little airport where Luke kept his plane said they'd begged Luke not to fly the plane. They said they'd told him that there was something wrong with it."

"No," Bailey said. "I could believe that Jimmie slammed a plane into a mountainside in one great flash of drama; he'd be in control then. But he'd *never* go up in a plane that was malfunctioning and let a piece of machinery have control over whether he lived or died."

"That's just what I thought," Martha said, smiling, her eyes twinkling. "I was sure Atlanta and Ray paid those two young men, so while everyone else in the world was looking at *you*, I was quietly having my own investigation conducted."

"And you found out that the plane had been sabotaged."

"Yes," Martha said. "It was quite simple, really. The fuel gauge had been tampered with, so Luke ran out of gas in midair."

For a moment they were quiet, then Matt said, "If you found a broken gauge, couldn't it have broken in the fall?"

"Yes," Martha said, "but we didn't find a gas gauge, broken or not."

"Then how —" Bailey began, then her eyes widened. "He had a black box on board."

"Yes," Martha said, smiling.

Bailey turned to Matt. "I forgot all about this. Jimmie and I were watching the news one night when a jet had gone down. The reporter kept talking about the black box that recorded the words of the pilots. I remember that Jimmie said, 'I ought to get one of those so I can'—" Bailey stopped talking.

"So he could tell you that he loved you before he went down," Martha said softly, and Bailey nodded. "Yes, that's what he wrote me that he'd told you. He had a system put in his plane, and he did it in secret, as he did so many things."

"And your men found the box," Matt said, "because they knew to look for it."

"Yes," Martha answered. "Jimmie spent his last moments trying to get the plane down safely, and while he was struggling, he was talking so the recorder would pick up his words. He told what was wrong with the plane, who he'd seen at the airport, and how to prove that Eva and Ralph—that's what he called them—had murdered him."

"But you didn't turn this information over to the police," Matt said.

"No," Martha said. "I didn't because Luke asked me to make his murder known only if his beloved Lillian was in danger. 'She'll find you,' he said just before he went down. 'And when she does, tell her that I love her.' Those were his last words."

For a moment, Bailey looked away. When she looked back at Martha, she said, "I want to hear the story. I want to know the truth. I want to know about a 'murder called suicide.'"

Thirty

❧

"I don't know when the bad started, whether it was with Vonda, the Turnbull woman, or when Frank lost the use of his arm," Martha said as she poured them tea from the silver pot. She'd picked up her phone and ordered a "breakfast tea," and ten minutes later a feast had appeared. It had been wheeled in on a table that could hardly hold it all. There were tiny sausages wrapped in flaky pastry, three kinds of eggs, broiled tomatoes, and enough scones and muffins to start a bakery.

Matt and Bailey spent about thirty seconds trying to be polite, before starvation won out and they nearly leapt on the food.

"The Turnbull woman owned my farm," Bailey said, her mouth full. "The canner's wife."

"Yes," Martha said, watching the two of them eat but

politely refraining from asking how long it had been since they'd had a meal. "Hilda was a secretive woman and rarely told anyone much, but word around town was that when she was quite young, she'd married a very rich, very old man. From what I heard, people figured she hoped he'd die right away so she could have his money."

"Wait a minute," Matt said. "You keep saying 'You heard.' Where were you?"

"And where was Jimmie?" Bailey asked.

Martha took a breath. "Luke and I stayed alone together up in the mountains. When Luke was little, Frank took him into town a few times, but people stared at the baby so much that Frank left him with me. He came to see us on weekends."

"Why didn't you have Jimmie's face repaired?" Bailey asked.

Martha took a while before she answered. "I'm afraid to tell you because you'll hate my son—and me."

Bailey shook her head. "Maybe I will, but I have so many other people to hate that you and Frank will be far down on my list."

Both Martha and Matt laughed.

"I've had many years to think about the reason all of it happened, but I think it boils down to love. I don't know how to explain, but"—Martha's eyes bored into Bailey's—"maybe I don't need to explain it to you. Luke loved really hard. If you were ever on the receiving end of Luke's love, you must know what I mean. Luke's love was what kept Frank and me going. Does that make sense?"

"Oh, yes," Bailey said. "It was a smothering love, but you couldn't leave it either."

"Right," Martha said. "And I was at fault too." For a moment she looked about the room. "May God forgive me for it, but what did I have if Luke got his mouth fixed and left me? I was a widow and poor. Frank was my only child, and I knew better than to think that if Luke was gone, Frank would visit me nearly as often. Luke and that cut in his upper lip made us a family."

Matt was watching Martha, seeing the way her hands wrung each other. She was obviously carrying a heavy burden over what she'd done to her grandson. "What about Hilda Turnbull?" he asked gently.

"She——" Martha said as she tried to get herself back under control. "I saw her once. She was short, scrawny, and had fierce-looking eyes."

When Martha seemed to lose her train of thought, Bailey said gently, "Did her old husband die?"

"Yes," Martha said, seeming to regain herself. "But not until Hilda was nearly forty years old and she had two half-grown kids."

"Eva and Ralph," Bailey said.

"Yes."

"Why hasn't anyone from Calburn recognized them? They're on TV often enough," Matt said. "Why hasn't anyone said, 'Hey! Those two are Hilda Turnbull's kids, and they have nothing to do with James Manville'?"

Martha smiled. "First of all, people in Calburn rarely saw them. Hilda kept them in one boarding school after another, then sent them to summer camps. They were dumpy, uninteresting kids, and no one paid much attention to them. Luke wrote me that a couple of buildings at the schools they attended burned down, and he was sure Ralph had done it, but no one ever suspected him because he was so——"

"Nothing," Bailey said. "He looked like nothing, but he always made my flesh crawl. He and Atlanta worked as a team. When they visited us, she'd knock something over to get our attention, then zip! some expensive little ornament would slide up Ray's sleeve. I didn't know if Jimmie saw it, and I wasn't going to tell him that his brother was a thief, but then Jimmie started buying reproduction Fabergé boxes. When I asked why he was buying those awful things, he said, 'They won't know the difference, so let them steal fakes,' and we both laughed."

"Go on about Hilda," Matt said.

"Sometimes Luke used to write me about . . . well, about what had happened—some of it, anyway—and he said he figured Hilda married Gus so she'd get his work for free. When Hilda's old husband died, he left her two farms—the one they'd been living on, which Gus told Luke was worn out and useless, but Hilda had also inherited the old Hanley place in Calburn, a farm that had been in his family for generations. His great-great grandmother, I believe it was, had been a Hanley.

"After the old man died, Gus didn't want to leave the town where he'd grown up, and since he'd been offered two other jobs, he told Hilda he was quitting."

"So she married him," Bailey said.

"Yes. She married him, but she refused to take his last name. He was twenty-eight, and she was thirty-nine. Gus would never have scored high on an IQ test, but he was a great cook, and he could make things grow. Luke used to say that Gus could put a steel spike in the ground, and it would grow into a tree. Like you," Martha said, smiling at Bailey. "Luke said you were as talented as Gus, but that you have the brains of a college professor."

"For once I agree with something Manville said," Matt said as he put his arm around Bailey's shoulders. She was blushing.

"We were told that Hilda Turnbull was having an affair with a married man," Bailey said. "Was it Frank?"

"Heavens, no! That was Roddy."

"I should have guessed," Bailey said under her breath. "He seems to be at the heart of anything bad that happens."

"Yes, Roddy played a big part in all this, mainly because he was after Hilda's money. It was rumored that she had many thousands of dollars hidden somewhere in her house. But in our family, it was Gus who was the problem. You see, Gus threatened to take Luke away from Frank. I don't mean he threatened Frank in words, but by 1968, Luke was fourteen, and he was starving for companionship."

"Always was," Bailey said. "Never got enough of it."

Martha shook her head. "I'm not a good storyteller. I need to backtrack some, back to 1966, back to when Frank got married. One night my son got drunk, and when he woke up, he was looking into the barrel of a shotgun, and he was horrified to see that he was naked and in bed with an equally naked high school girl. Later, he told me he didn't remember ever having seen the girl before. But her father—who was holding the shotgun—gave Frank the choice of marrying her or having his brains blown out, so Frank married her.

"Her name was Vonda Oleksy and, from the beginning, Frank couldn't stand her, and he knew she'd tricked him into marriage. All her silly little girlfriends couldn't wait to tell Frank that, since Vonda was thirteen years old, she'd been saying that when she grew up, she was going to marry one of the Golden Six. It didn't take Frank long to realize that he was some sort of prize to her, and once they were married, she had no interest in him. She was mean, lazy, and stupid, and he would have divorced her if she hadn't had four brothers and a father who were meaner and stupider than she was. They said that if Frank divorced Vonda, he'd find Luke or me dead."

Martha paused a moment. "The worst part of the marriage was that, because of her, Frank became an object of ridicule around Calburn. He was thirty, while Vonda was just seventeen, so everyone assumed that Frank was a dirty old man who lusted after the young virgin. And it didn't help that Vonda told everyone her version of how they'd come to be married. Overnight, Frank went from being a respected man in town to being laughed at by everyone.

"Also, Vonda spent money faster than Frank could earn it. All day he was at work, she was shopping. He'd come home to see half a dozen new boxes piled in the living room, no dinner on the table, and last night's dishes in the sink.

"After a whole summer of trying to live with her, Frank sent Vonda up to the cabin to live with Luke and me."

Martha stopped for a moment, and her mouth twisted into an ugly shape. "That girl *hated* Luke. Frank had warned me that Vonda could be cruel, but I was trying so hard to get along with her that it took a couple of weeks for me to see the look of despair in Luke's eyes. She used to sit outside near Luke when he was doing chores like chopping wood, and truthfully, I thought it was nice of her. But one day I hid in some bushes to listen to what she was saying to my grand-son."

Martha had to take a couple of breaths before she could go on. "She was telling Luke that his lip was from Satan, and it was proof that Luke was evil."

"Sick woman," Matt said.

"Yes," Martha said, watching Bailey, who was silent. "I told Frank I wouldn't have her there anymore, that he had to take her away. Since Frank loved Luke, he took his wife back to his house in town.

"Six weeks after he took her back, Frank showed up drunk at work, and that's when the car slammed into him and he lost the use of his left arm. But . . ." Martha looked away for a moment. "I saw Frank just a few hours before the accident, and he was cold sober, and he was happy. He wouldn't tell me what he was happy about, but he said, 'I've found a way to fix everything.' I didn't know what he meant, but I said, 'The only way you can fix anything is to get rid of that trashy girl you married,' and when I said that, Frank laughed harder than I'd seen him laugh in years.

"A few hours later, a car slammed into him and shat-tered his arm. Frank told the police he'd accidentally left the car in gear, but the police said he reeked of whiskey, so they wrote on their report that he was drunk. Later, when he was in the hospital, I told him I didn't believe he had been drinking. I said I thought Vonda's eldest brother had hit him with the car, and that Frank wouldn't tell the police for fear they'd hurt Luke or me.

"But Frank stuck to his story and I don't think he told anyone the truth."

Martha took a moment before she went on. "My son was fired from his job and given no workmen's comp because of the police report. After he was out of work, Frank found out that that horrible girl had either spent or given her relatives everything he'd saved over the years. He had no savings, and no income, and he had to sell his house in town to pay the debts she'd run up.

"By necessity, the two of them had to move into the mountain cabin with Luke and me. Frank swore to me that he'd keep his wife under control and that he'd take her away as soon as things got better. But things didn't get any better. Frank tried to repair car engines with his one arm, while his wife went to work in Calburn at a diner. Frank soon learned that he couldn't go into town because he'd hear snickers about how his young wife was on the menu."

Martha looked down at her hands for a moment. "Things did change. Frank made them change, but—" She looked at Bailey and Matt defiantly. "Frank was my son, and I loved him, and I know that what he did wasn't right. But I can understand why he did it. For years he'd been part of that blasted Golden Six—how I came to *hate* that term!—so he'd been treated like a hero. Then, suddenly, he became a joke to the same people who used to slap him on the back and be proud to be his friend. He had an unfaithful wife little more than half his age, and he'd lost the use of his arm and his job."

"Frank didn't feel like he was a man anymore," Matt said softly as Martha paused before she spoke again.

"The first time it happened, it was by accident. Gus Venters was a big, blond giant of a man, slow in speech and slow in his movements, and no one paid much attention to him. One day Frank was in town, and he saw Gus take some of his canned items into the store. I don't know what made him do it, but Frank made a derogatory remark about Gus, and the men around him laughed. It was the first time in over a year that Frank wasn't the butt of the jokes—or worse, the recipient of their pity.

"After that, it just escalated. I'd see Frank standing over a car engine and chuckling, and I knew he was making up more Gus stories. Eventually, those jokes became Frank's reason for going into town. 'Got any new Gus stories?' the men would ask him."

Martha closed her eyes a moment to give herself the strength to go on. "The problem was that Frank soon found out that to be funny, the jokes had to come close to reality, but since Gus rarely went into town, Frank knew too little about the man to make fun of him."

"Didn't you—" Bailey began.

Martha held up her hand. "Didn't I beg, plead, threaten, and shed tears to try to get Frank to stop? Oh, yes. I did. I said everything I could think of. And maybe if I'd kept my mouth shut, none of it would have happened. At first Frank practiced his jokes in front of Luke and me, but when I protested and Luke didn't laugh, Frank went into hiding. And when he started using Luke, he did it with such secrecy that I knew nothing about it.

"Frank told Luke he wanted him to hide and watch Gus, then Luke was to tell his dad everything. Luke didn't want to do it. Luke knew too well how it felt to be made fun of. But Frank got angry, which was something he rarely did with his son.

"In the end, Luke did it, but the spying backfired on Frank, because Luke came back with stories of how hard Gus worked, and how prosperous the farm was. Luke said the farm was like the Garden of Eden. This made

Frank angry again, and he shouted at Luke, 'Didn't you see any *bad?*' And Luke had shouted back, 'Yeah, that wife of his treats him like dirt, orders him around like he's a dog.' Luke had meant to defend Gus, but Frank just listened and smiled.

"The next day Frank went to town and had the people rolling with laughter over a parody of Gus being belittled by his militant wife."

"Awful," Bailey said. "Jimmie would have hated all of that."

"Yes, he did, and he told his dad he wouldn't spy anymore. But when Frank had no new Gus stories to tell, the people of Calburn began ignoring him again, so he and Vonda began to fight more.

"One night Luke had been kept awake all night by his dad and his stepmother screaming at each other, and Luke hated turmoil among his own family."

"Always did," Bailey said. "Jimmie didn't care if the world was angry at him, but if *I* was, he couldn't stand it."

"I think Luke felt a kinship with Gus from the beginning," Martha said. "To get away from the arguing, Luke went down the mountain and stretched out under a tree where he could see the Garden of Eden farm. When he awoke, Gus was sitting by him, offering him food. Years later, Luke told me that it was the best food he'd ever eaten in his life—which tells you everything about my cooking."

"And a friendship was born," Matt said.

"Yes," Martha said, "a friendship of kindred souls, a bonding between a couple of outcasts. But neither Frank nor I knew the friendship had started. Not long after that Frank got a job as a night watchman, so he was gone all night and slept all day. I was busy with household chores because I had to wash and iron Vonda's uniforms as well as Frank's, and I didn't have a washing machine. I was too busy to worry about where a big boy of fourteen was all day."

"He was with Gus?" Matt asked.

"Yes. Gus's wife was at work all day and fooling around with Roddy at night, so she had no idea Luke and her husband were together. I doubt if she ever saw Luke." Martha took a breath. "As always, everything bad started with Vonda.

"Frank was miserable at his job. It was all the way in Ridgeway, so he had no Golden Six background with them, and Gus stories didn't make them laugh. The other men at the job called Frank 'Slot Machine,' as in One-Armed Bandit, and from there it became 'Slots.' Frank couldn't quit, couldn't even fight back. He was in hell. His wife was staying out later each night; they spent hours every day fighting; and the more horrible it was at home, the more time Luke spent with Gus.

"But of course in a town like Calburn, you can't keep secrets forever. A few deliverymen had seen Luke with Gus, and they told what they saw. And with Vonda working in the diner, she heard.

"Then one Sunday afternoon, Frank stopped by the diner, and he was in the middle of a Gus story and making his old buddies laugh when Vonda, out of sheer spite, said, 'Gus is more of a father to your son than you are.' Everybody in the diner laughed even harder. At Frank. And that's when he knew that Gus Venters had won. Frank made people laugh at Gus, but in the end, Gus had taken away what Frank loved most in the world: his son.

"And that's when Frank's hatred began. All his anger at every rotten thing that had ever happened to him came out—and it was all directed at one man: Gus Venters."

"And all the anger came to a head on one night."

"The thirtieth of August, 1968," Matt said.

"Yes," Martha said. "The thirtieth of August, 1968.

"It started that afternoon when Vonda told Frank she was pregnant. I was away that day. A woman I knew was sick, so I'd gone to sit with her, but years later Luke told me every word of what was said. On that day, that woman told Luke something that not even I knew. My guess is that Frank told the boys in that"—Martha had to swallow against the lump in her throat—"that Golden Six, and one of them told Vonda."

❧❧

"*Whose is it?*" Frank yelled. He was drunk, as usual.

"It's a *man's*," Vonda shouted back at him. "Which is more than you'll ever be."

"I'll divorce you," Frank said. "And I'll tell the courts what you're really like. When I get through with you—"

Vonda laughed at him. "You take me to court? With what, old man? You have nothin'." At that, her head came up, and she saw Luke standing silently in the bedroom doorway. "You little sneak," she said. "You're always listenin', ain't you? Ain't it enough that you spend all day spyin' on that poor Gus? Poor ol' retard."

"He's smarter than you'll ever be," Luke shot back at her. "And richer."

"Are you talkin' down to *me?*" Vonda sneered at Luke,

then her eyes began to glitter. "Hey, Frank, why don't you tell this ugly kid the truth about his mother?"

"Shut up, Vonda, I'm warning you. You don't know what I can do to you."

"And what are you gonna do to me that ain't already been done?" she taunted. "Hey, kid, you chicken? Go ahead. Ask him about your mother."

"Shut up," Frank said, then went after her, but he staggered and fell, and his foot got caught between the wall and the coal stove.

Vonda looked at Luke, her upper lip curled in disgust as she looked at the boy's misshapen mouth. "Frank here met your mother in a bar in New Orleans. He was bein' nice to her because she had a lip just like yours. Oh, it'd been sewn together some, but it was like yours, and what's more, she was about ten minutes away from deliverin' a kid. You."

Luke looked down at his father on the floor, and as he realized what the woman was telling him, Luke's face went pale with shock.

"Luke—" Frank said softly, reaching out his hands, but he was still trapped and unable to move.

Luke stepped away from his father's seeking hands.

"Frank McCallum isn't your father any more than that Gus you're so crazy about is," Vonda said, smiling. "Or maybe ol' Gus *is* your father, who knows? And you know what happened to your mother? She didn't die right after you were born and have a pretty funeral, like Frank's told you all these years. She took one look at you, had a screamin' fit, and ran off. She couldn't bear to look at your ugly face."

Vonda's little dark eyes gleamed maliciously. "Frank felt sorry for you, so he brought you back here to this godforsaken hole and hid you away so nobody had to look at you." She looked down at Frank on the floor. "And after all that trouble you went to to take care of some old whore's deformed kid, he likes some dull-witted farmer better than he likes you."

❧ ❦

Bailey had her hand to her mouth as she imagined what a proud man like Jimmie must have felt, hearing something like that.

"Luke left the house after that, and he didn't come back for three days," Martha said. "But by then, it was all over. Gus Venters was dead. Hanged."

"In my barn," Bailey said softly.

"Oh, no. He was hanged from that mulberry tree in your backyard."

At that, Bailey clutched Matt's hand. Her beautiful, beautiful mulberry tree.

"You said 'was hanged,'" Matt said. "He didn't commit suicide?"

"No," Martha said. "*They* hanged him. That . . ." She struggled over the words. "The Golden Six. All six of them were in town that summer, and Frank went to them and told them—" Martha looked away for a moment, then back. Her voice was trembling when she spoke. "My son, Frank, got them together and told them that that sweet, lovely, *innocent* man, Gus Venters, had . . . that he had . . ." Martha had to pause for a moment. "Frank told them that Gus had raped Luke."

"May God forgive them," Bailey said.

"When I got home in the wee hours, Frank was a mess. He was curled up on the floor and crying hard.

And what was worse, he had a gun in his hand. He was planning to shoot himself.

"I couldn't understand what was wrong with him or what had happened. I kept asking if Luke was hurt or was he dead, but Frank would cry harder and say, 'It's worse. It's worse.' To my mind, if Luke was all right, it couldn't be too bad.

"I managed to get the gun away from him, but Frank had been drinking a lot, so I went to the kitchen to make coffee. The water bucket was empty, so I went outside to the well to fill it.

"A few minutes later I heard a shot, and I realized I'd stupidly left the gun on the kitchen counter. I dropped the bucket and ran, because I knew in my mother's heart that my only child had just been shot."

Martha took a breath. "My son was lying on the floor, dead, and standing over him was Vonda, the gun in her hand.

" 'They hanged poor ol' Gus Venters tonight,' she said. 'Strung him up from a tree. Roddy said they'd better make it look like suicide, so they moved him into the barn,' Vonda said to me, and I can still see the light in her eyes. She'd *enjoyed* killing my son.

"Vonda put the gun down on the table, stepped over my son's body like he was a sack of garbage, and picked up a metal box off the floor.

" 'While they was hangin' ol' Gus the second time, Roddy sneaked in the house and took this.' She opened the box, and I saw that it was full of money.

" 'Roddy's been sleepin' with that ol' hag, Hilda Turnbull, because he knew she had money hidden, and he wanted her to tell him where she kept it. It took a lot of pumpin' to get the information out of her, but he did it. And tonight Roddy got the box, only *he*'—she looked down at my dead son's body with a sneer—'he took the box away from Roddy, said he was gonna give the money back to ol' Hilda.'

"That girl looked up at me in triumph. 'But now I got the money, and I'm carryin' Roddy's baby, and he's waitin' for me outside. I just got the wrong Golden Six the first time around, that's all. But now, everything's gonna be just fine.'

"And that's when I picked up the gun and shot her right between the eyes."

Epilogue

✤

ONE YEAR LATER

Bailey looked through the heavy black veil covering her face at the people gathered at Martha's grave site. Matt wasn't with her, for there'd been no way to disguise his appearance. And if he were seen and identified, the journalists that stood on the periphery would find Bailey. As it was now, she stood among a dozen other women, all wearing concealing black veils, all of which had been made by Patsy. The press couldn't identify any of the women, and besides, they were looking for James Manville's widow, a woman a great deal heavier than any of the women who attended Martha McCallum's funeral.

As Bailey looked down at the closed coffin, tears of gratitude and love flowed down her cheeks. Martha had

sacrificed herself to preserve Bailey's anonymity. Martha
had sacrificed so Bailey could keep the happiness she'd
found. She had explained that she owed Luke for keeping him to herself for so many years, and the best way to
repay him was to give to the woman he loved.

So Martha had done everything. She oversaw the
lawyers and presented the evidence she held.

Martha hired private detectives, and they found a
woman who said she'd seen and talked with Dolores the
day after Alex had returned to Virginia. And half a
dozen girls in Calburn could testify as to exactly where
they'd seen Alex Yates and when. The charges against
him were dropped for lack of evidence.

Bailey had stayed up all night talking with Matt;
then she got on the telephone with Martha, and an
agreement was made. If Bailey stepped forward and
showed the court—and the world—that she had indeed
been legally married to James Manville, she would probably be awarded what was left of his billions. But if Bailey got the money, she'd lose her privacy.

"Do you mind?" Bailey had asked Matt tentatively.

"Mind losing billions?" Matt asked, eyes twinkling.
He smiled. "No. I don't want the money. I've seen what
money takes from a person. And, besides, I have everything I want right here."

She smiled at him, but she couldn't keep the tears out
of her eyes. She'd come to love him so very much.
Through everything, he'd helped her, and he'd stood by
her. Not once had he tried to hold her back from what
she'd needed to do.

Her hands had been in her lap, and once again she
twirled the engagement ring he'd given her the night
before.

"Could I have a big wedding?" she'd asked, and even to herself she sounded like a child.

"The biggest Calburn has ever seen. But—" Matt hesitated.

"But what?"

"If you don't let Patsy make your dress, our lives won't be worth living."

Laughing, Bailey had agreed readily.

It was the next day that they'd spent discussing the money and what to do about it. How did one manage billions but remain anonymous?

In the end, it was Arleen who helped them the most. For many years she'd supported herself by being, as she said, "a parasite." "But a good one, dear, a very, very *good* parasite." She went on to explain that she'd had to become a keen observer of people. "When your dinner depends on getting along with someone, you must quickly learn to like what they like and say what they want to hear."

To Bailey's astonishment, Arleen made a list of the people James had trusted the most. "If you want people to run your company, use these men," Arleen said as she handed the paper to Bailey.

"Not my company. Not *my* money," Bailey had whispered. "I don't want it."

It was Martha who agreed to inherit James Manville's fortune. She had a birth certificate showing that Frank was her son, and Frank's name was on Luke McCallum's birth certificate. With DNA testing and hair samples, it hadn't been difficult to show that Lucas McCallum and James Manville were the same person.

Martha had done it all, and she'd had to do it alone. Old, frail, and weak, she'd somehow gathered her strength to deal with lawyers and detectives and the press. No one who was near Bailey could help for fear of exposing Bailey, so Martha had had only the support of a woman she'd befriended in the nursing home, and a couple of nurses to monitor her health.

While the highly publicized trial of Atlanta and Ray was going on, Matt had flown around the United States to meet with the men on the list Arleen had given him. It had taken him all three months of the trial to pull it together, but by the time the guilty verdict came in, Matt had set up a board of trustees to oversee the industries that James Manville had once owned.

Through days and nights of work, Matt, Bailey, and the men on the list had set up a ten-year plan whereby the companies would eventually become autonomous. By the end of the ten years the companies would either have been sold and all the profits split among the employees, or would be run on a profit-sharing basis. The ultimate plan was that at the end of ten years, James Manville's empire would no longer exist.

By the time the trial was over, Martha had aged dramatically. It was as though she'd kept herself alive and healthy to accomplish this deed, and now that it was over, she wanted to rest—forever.

After Atlanta's and Ray's life imprisonment sentences were handed down, two nurses helped Martha sit down on the padded chair outside the courtroom. With shaking hands, Martha read a prepared statement about the future plans for James Manville's wealth.

In back of the reporters and outside the courthouse, people began cheering when they heard that they would still have their jobs. But the journalists were visibly disappointed. They'd wanted Martha to leave all the money to one person. The antics of heirs and heiresses made great copy.

"What about Lillian Manville?" someone shouted as soon as Martha had finished reading her statement.

Martha had smiled at the man. "She has been taken care of," Martha said, then before anyone could fire another question at her, she put her hand to her head and fell back against the chair as though in a faint. Immediately, the nurses hovered over her and a doctor came running from the wings. After a quick examination the doctor announced that Mrs. McCallum had had too much excitement and they had to leave.

"But what about Manville's widow?" someone shouted, but the doctor didn't turn around. He motioned for Martha to be put on a gurney and carried out of the courthouse.

For three days the news media swarmed outside the hospital where Martha McCallum lay in bed. The prognosis for her recovery had been good, but the doctors didn't take into consideration that Martha didn't want to recover. She had had enough of life, and she wanted to be with her son and Luke.

On the morning of the fourth day, Martha passed on, and the nurses said that there had been a smile on her face.

Bailey cried from the time Martha's death was announced until the time of the funeral. "I can't even go to the funeral," Bailey had said. "And there were all those years when we could have known each other, but James kept us apart."

"James," Arleen said softly, lifting her eyebrows at Matt. Now Bailey referred to her late husband as "James," not "Jimmie."

Matt put his arms around Bailey to comfort her, but he was smiling. At last, with the discovery of the truth, Bailey had been able to put James Manville behind her. She'd seen the good of him and the bad of him, and she was finally able to see him as a person. Her love for James Manville was no longer current. Now it was a memory.

"I think we can figure something out," Matt had whispered into her hair. Ten minutes later, he and Patsy had come up with the idea of dressing all the women involved in the Mulberry Tree Preserving Company in identical black veils and all of them attending Martha's funeral.

And now Bailey placed three white roses on Martha's coffin. One for Martha, one for Frank, and one for James, the boy who'd been "born" on that awful day in August.

Arleen put her hand on Bailey's arm. "Let's go home," she whispered through her veil.

"Yes," Bailey said. "Let's go home."

POCKET BOOKS
PROUDLY PRESENTS

WILD ORCHIDS

JUDE DEVERAUX

Now available in paperback
from Pocket Books

Turn the page for a preview of
Wild Orchids . . .

I can't say that I *liked* her very much, but she was the most interesting person I'd met in years. Best of all, I thought she could do the job and that she'd make no emotional demands on me. I needed some way to get back into writing, but since I hadn't found the road yet, I thought Jackie Maxwell and her devil story might send me in the right direction.

I'd read the gossip magazines and the Internet, so I knew people were saying that Pat had written my books. How she would have laughed to hear that! I'd also heard that my writing was linked to her and once she died, I couldn't do it anymore.

That was closer to the truth, because none of my books were fiction. They were fiction enough that my uncles and cousins couldn't sue me, but, basically, they were the truth. "Distorted truth" as Pat said. As she'd pointed out on that long ago, happy day, I'd had enough bad in my life to write many books. I'd written about every rotten thing that had ever been done to me.

But the truth that no one knew, not anyone at my publishing house or any friend, was that I'd written myself dry long before Pat died. The only book that was left in me was the one about Pat, and I was years and years and years away from being able to write that one.

In the six years since her death, I'd wandered around the country, moving the few belongings I still owned from one house to another. I'd settle into a community, look around and listen to see if anything sparked my appetite, and hope to find a reason to start writing again.

But nothing interested me. Now and then my publishing house would reissue some old book of mine, or put my few novellas into one book so it looked as though I was still publishing, but most people knew I wasn't. When I typed my name onto the Internet, I found three groups that were discussing my death. They listed "facts" that they believed were proof that I'd taken my own life the day my wife died.

The latest town I'd moved to was supposed to have great weather, but I hadn't seen it. It was also supposed to be "charming," but I didn't find it to be so. I'm not sure why I didn't move out the day after I moved in, except that I was tired. I was tired . . . not tired of living so much as tired of being brain-dead. I felt like those women who go through college, then get married and pop out three kids right away. They went from brain-overuse to not using their brains at all. I guess that's where I was. In six years I'd had a few brief affairs, but since I compared every woman to Pat, I'd found each one wanting.

About a year ago, I'd read something—I was a voracious, eclectic reader in those six years—about a witch that haunted some old house somewhere and it had sparked a tiny interest in me. I began to think about putting together a collection of true stories about ghosts or witches in America. Every state has those poorly written, locally printed books about regional ghosts, so I thought about collecting the books, doing masses of research, and publishing an anthology. A sort of *Ghosts of the U.S.* kind of thing.

Anyway, doing the research appealed to me. All I

needed was an assistant. But it turned out to be nearly impossible to find someone who was really useful.

Did I have a knack for finding losers? Was it something in me that attracted them? Several of the women seemed to be living in a romantic novel. They seemed to believe that I'd hired them because I wanted to marry them and share all my worldly goods with them. I got rid of those women fast.

Then I went through the ones who wanted everything spelled out for them. They wanted what they called a "job description." I gave in to one of them and spent an hour and a half of my life writing the thing. Two hours later, when I told her I wanted her to go to the grocery for me, she said, "That's not my job," and I fired her.

Some of them I fired and some of them quit. Truthfully, I think that all of them had an ideal in their minds of what it would be like to work for a best-selling author and I didn't live up to what they expected.

From my viewpoint, not one of them could follow an idea. They were like robots and would do what I told them to—as long as it didn't interfere with their "job description"—but they didn't take the initiative. And, too, many of them used their brains only for trying to seduce me to an altar. Free sex I would have taken, but it was "community property" that I saw in their eyes.

Just before I was to move yet again—to where I had no idea—I was having lunch with the president of the local university, and he said, "You ought to get an assistant like ol' Professor Hartshorn has. She's writing a book for him."

I wasn't much interested in what he was saying because I'd already scheduled the movers for next week, but I was being polite so I said, "What kind of book?"

He chuckled. "It's about Harriet Lane, with a great many passages about her violet eyes and her magnificent bosom."

I'd never heard of the woman, so he went on to tell me that she was President James Buchanan's niece. "I don't know where Hartshorn's assistant got her information, but I'd be willing to bet it's accurate. Miss Lane was an equal political partner to her uncle—who, by the way, was nicknamed 'Old Gurley.' If you know what I mean," he added, waggling his eyebrows.

Interesting, I thought. I needed an assistant who could think. "Is she writing the book *with* the professor?"

The president grimaced. "Hell, no. One time when I confronted him, he said there was already too damn much written about everybody, so he wasn't going to add to the pollution. But the trustees were on my case to fire him because he wasn't published, so Hartshorn started using his students to pretend he was writing." The president waved his hand, meaning he didn't want to explain that particular story. "Anyway, a couple of years ago, I received this hilarious chapter of a book about an obscure president's niece, and it had Professor Hartshorn's name on it as the author. Right away, I knew he hadn't written it so I gave it to my secretary—who knows everything that goes on in this town—and asked her who was capable of writing such a paper. She started telling me about a man who had a crush on a Victorian woman named Harriet Lane. Had pictures of her all over his office and always wore something violet because Miss Lane had violet eyes."

I was confused. "Hartshorn's assistant is a man?"

The president frowned at me. I knew that look. For a writer, you're not very smart, it said. I'd found out long ago that when you're a writer people expect you to understand everything about everything.

"No," he said, speaking slowly as though to an idiot, "that man was Hartshorn's assistant's father. He's dead. Her father is dead, not Hartshorn. Anyway, Hartshorn's young, female assistant sends me an extremely entertaining chapter every three months. They're too naughty to be published, but the Trustees and I love them. *The Misadventures of Miss Harriet Lane,* we call them."

While he was smiling in memory of Miss Lane's bosom, I was thinking. "If she's so dedicated to Professor Hartshorn she won't want another job."

"Hartshorn is an"—he lowered his voice—"what is colloquially known as an a-hole. I doubt if he's ever even told her thanks for saving his job. Although I did hear that he gave her a raise for decorating his office with a life-size mannequin of Miss Lane."

This was beginning to sound good. She was creative. And smart. Took the initiative. I needed those things. I didn't find out until after Pat died that I was a person who co-wrote. I need lots of feedback. I've never understood how other authors survived with the two or three words they got from their editors. You could spend a year writing a book and at the end all you'd get was, "It's good."

If I were honest with myself—and I tried not to be—I wanted a partner, someone I could bounce ideas off. I didn't want a fellow writer who was going to be competition, but I wanted . . . Pat. I wanted Pat.

But I had to take what I could get. "So how do I meet her?" I asked. "Through Hartshorn?"

The president snorted. "He'd lie. If he knew you wanted her, he'd drug her before he let you meet her."

"Then how—?"

"Let me think about it and see what I can come up with. A social setting might be best. I'm sure I know someone who knows her. For the next two weeks, accept all invitations." He looked at his watch. "Uh oh. I have a plane to catch."

He stood, I stood, we shook hands, then he left. It was only after he was gone that I remembered I hadn't asked what the assistant's name was. Later, I called Hartshorn's office and asked what his assistant's name was. "Which one?" the young woman on the phone asked. "He has five of them." I couldn't very well say, "The one who's writing the book for him," so I thanked her and hung up. I called the president's office but he'd left town.

"Two weeks," the president had said. I was to accept every invitation for the next two weeks. No one can imagine the number of invitations a celebrity in a small town receives in two weeks. I did a reading of *Bob the Builder* for a local nursery school—and was vociferously told that I had mispronounced Pilchard's name.

I had to give a speech at a ladies' luncheon, (chicken salad, *always* chicken salad) and had to listen to one shirt-waist-clad little old lady after another tell me that I used too many "dirty words" in my books.

I had to give a speech at a local tractor dealership, and ended up talking about the internal combustion engine—something I had to do to keep the attention of my audience.

I also accepted an invitation to a party at someone's house and that's when I finally met Professor Hartshorn's assistant.

At the party, I watched the people and tried to guess which one might be Hartshorn's assistant.

I noticed a group of girls who seemed to be friends. One of them was so beautiful she made me dizzy. Face, hair, body. Wherever she went in the room, eyes followed her—mine included. But after a while of watching, I began to detect a blankness in her eyes. The proverbial dumb blonde—or Titian red in this case. And her name was Autumn—which made me feel old. Her parents were no doubt former hippies—and my age.

There was a Jennifer who seemed to be angry about something and seemed to have set herself up as the boss of everyone. I knew it was her parents' house, but I'd be willing to bet that she bossed people wherever she was.

Heather and Ashley seemed normal enough, but Heather wasn't very pretty so, to compensate, she wore too much makeup.

The fifth girl was Jackie Maxwell and, instantly, I knew she was "the one." She was short, with a mass of softly curling, short dark hair, and she looked like a poster advertising "physically fit." Just looking at her made me stand up straighter and suck in my stomach.

She had a cute face and dark green eyes that seemed to see everything that was going on around her. A couple of times I had to look away so she wouldn't know I was watching her.

After a while, an odd thing happened. In the midst of the party, lovely little Autumn sat down on a chair smack in the middle of the room and began to cry. And cry right prettily, I might add. If Pat had been there she would have made a snide comment about how the girl managed to weep without squinching up her facial muscles.

But the girl going from laughing to tears in a second—and doing it in the middle of the room—wasn't what was odd. What was strange was that when this raving beauty began to cry, all eyes turned toward Jackie.

Even the woman who was blathering on at me about how she was writing a book "not like yours but deep, you know what I mean?" turned and looked at Jackie.

Did I miss something? I wondered. I watched with interest as Jackie went to this girl Autumn, squatted in front of her like some African native, and began to talk to her in the tone of a mother. Jackie had a voice that made me want to curl up with a blankie and have her soothe me. Turning to a man next to me, I started to say something, but he said, "Ssssh, Jackie's gonna tell a story."

Everyone in town—and eventually even the bartenders—tiptoed over to surround the big chair and listen to this girl tell a story.

Okay, I was jealous. No one had ever spontaneously listened to me like that. Only if there was a lot of advance publicity and I arrived in a limo did people listen to me with rapt attention.

So what story was she going to tell? I wondered. As all of us waited, she proceeded to cheer up this brainless little beauty queen with a story on how to write a Pulitzer Prize–winning novel.

Since my sales kept me out of the prize-winning circles, ("Money or prizes," my editor told me. "Not both.") I listened. And as she talked, I found myself wanting her to be even more critical than she was. What about the overuse of metaphors and similes? What about emotion? My editor called them "Connecticut books." Not too much emotion in them. Cool. Dignified. Cerebral.

We always want more, don't we? Prizewinners want sales; best-sellers want prizes.

When Jackie finished her story, I expected everyone to burst into applause. Instead, they acted as though they hadn't been listening. Odd, I thought.

She got up (even at her age my knees would have been killing me) looked straight at me, ignored my smile, then went over to the bar to get a drink. I followed her and nearly fell over my tongue trying to give her a compliment. Since the people who knew her hadn't said anything, I thought maybe they knew she hated praise.

Then I *really* messed up because I blurted out that I wanted her to work for me.

Brother! Did she laugh. When she told me that she'd work for me only if she had two heads, it took me a full minute to understand what she was saying. I didn't know exactly where the quote came from but I could guess.

Okay, so I can take a hint. I turned around and walked away.

I would have gone home then and probably forgotten about the whole thing (and would have had to work to not use the woman's "How to Write a Pulitzer Prize–Winning Novel" speech in a book—if I ever wrote again, that is) but Mrs. Lady of the House grabbed my arm and started pulling me from one room to another to introduce me to people. After several minutes of this, she told me that I needed to forgive Jackie, that sometimes she could be, well . . .

"Abrasive?" I asked.

Mrs. Lady looked at me hard. "My cousin worked for you for four and a half weeks and she called me every day to tell me what you put her through. Let's just say that Jackie doesn't have the franchise on abrasive behavior and leave it at that, shall we? Mr. Newcombe, if you're looking for an assistant, I think Jackie Maxwell just might be the *only* woman who could work for you."

When she turned away and left me standing there, if it hadn't been late at night I would have called the moving company and said, "Come and get me *now!*"

A few seconds later, I was trapped by a dreadful little woman who wanted me to personally publish her 481 church bulletins, many of which no one—meaning no congregation—had ever read. "Original source," she kept saying, as though she'd found George Washington's unpublished diaries.

I was rescued by Jackie. I meant to get her alone outside so I could apologize and maybe start over, but when I turned around, I saw she had been followed by an entourage of gawking girls. Within seconds I was bombarded with questions.

As the girls took me over, I could see Jackie inching away. I was beginning to adopt the philosophy of "if it was meant to be it will happen" when one of the girls dropped a bombshell on me. She said Jackie knew a true devil story.

Through my limited (mostly assistantless) research I knew that devil stories were rare. Ghost and witch stories were abundant, but devils . . . Rare.

After persuasion, Jackie told the story in a couple of sentences, but she told *all* of it in those two sentences. Someone once told me that if a person was a really good storyteller he could tell the story in one word and that word would be the title of the book. *Exorcist* is an example. Says it all.

Her story intrigued me so much that I thought maybe my ears would start flapping and pull me straight up. Wow! A woman loved a man the townspeople believed was the devil. Why did they believe that? And they killed *her*. Not him. Her. Why didn't they kill the man? Fear? Couldn't find him? He'd gone back to hell? What happened after she was murdered? Any prosecutions?

But before I could ask anything, Jackie dropped her glass—on purpose but I had no idea why—and all the girls turned into squawking hens and ran for the nearest bathroom.

I took a few moments to try to turn myself into their idea of a cool, calm, sophisticated best-selling author, then hightailed it after Jackie.

As soon as she came out of the bathroom some guy went up to her, said he had to leave and called her "Pumpkin." No one on earth looked less like a "Pumpkin" than that curvy little creature.

I didn't like him. He was too slick-looking for my taste. A used-car salesman trying to look like a stockbroker. And he was with a tall young man who looked like someone had turned the lights off inside his head. I'd be willing to bet six figures that those two were up to no good.

But then, maybe it was just that I really was beginning to want this young woman to work for me so I was getting possessive.

I again tried to get into a conversation with her and find out more about the devil story, but she seemed to be embarrassed because her friends had said that she should write a book. First of all, I didn't remember hearing that. It was probably when my ears were twitching and I was floating. Second, I wanted to say, "Honey, *everybody* wants to be a writer."

But as I chatted with her about her not wanting to be a writer, I found out she was getting married in three weeks (I guess to the salesman-broker). Then she more or less told me that she wouldn't work for me if I were the last man . . . Et cetera.

I went home.

Early the next morning I called the moving company and indefinitely postponed my move. I decided I really did need to figure out where I was going before I packed up.

By this time, I didn't have an assistant or a housekeeper, so I lived with dirty clothes and TV dinners—both of which made me think of my childhood. For weeks, I used every resource I had to try to find out about Jackie's story. I went on the Internet. I called Malaprop's in Asheville and had them send me a copy of every book they had on North Carolina legends. I called my publisher and she got me phone numbers of several North Carolina writers and I called them.

No one had heard of the devil story.

I called Mrs. Lady of the House (had to fish her invitation out of the garbage can where it was, of course, stuck to something wet and smelly) and asked her to please, pretty please, find out the name of the town in North Carolina where the story had happened, but not to tell Jackie or any of her friends I'd asked.

By the time I hung up I wanted to ask the woman to negotiate my next book contract—if/when, that is. She said she would get the name of the town, but only if I agreed to talk at one of her women's club lunches ("a reading would be nice and an autographing afterward"). In the end she set me up for three whole hours, and I was to get my publishing house to "donate" thirty-five hardcovers. All this for the name of a town in North Carolina. Of course I agreed.

She called back ten minutes later and said in her best silly-me voice, "Oh, Mr. Newcombe, you're not going to believe this but I don't have to ask anyone anything. I just remembered that I already know the name of the town where Jackie's story happened."

I waited. Pen ready. Breath held.

Silence.

I continued waiting.

"Is the twenty-seventh of this month good for you?" she asked.

I gritted my teeth and clutched the pen. "Yes," I said. "The twenty-seventh is fine."

"And could you possibly donate *forty* books?"

It was my turn to be silent, but I bent the tip of my pen and had to grab another one from the holder.

I guess she knew she'd pushed me to my limit because she said in a normal voice, no ooey-gooey gush, "Cole Creek. It's in the mountains and isolated." Her voice changed back to little-girl. "See you on the twenty-seventh at eleven-thirty A.M. sharp," she said, then hung up. I said the filthiest words I knew—some of them in Old English—before I hung up my end.

Three minutes later I had the number to the Cole Creek, North Carolina, public library and was calling them.

First, in order to impress the librarian, I gave my name. She was indeed properly impressed and gushed suitably.

With all the courtesy that I'd learned from Pat's family, I asked her about the devil story and the pressing.

The librarian said, "That's all a lie," and slammed down the phone.

For a moment I was too stunned to move. I just sat there holding the phone and blinking. Big deal writers don't have librarians or booksellers hang up on them. Never has happened; never will.

As I slowly put down the phone, my heart was beating fast. For the first time in years I felt excited about something. I'd hit a nerve in that woman. My editor once said that if I ran out of my own problems to write about, I should write about someone else's. At long last I seemed to have found a "someone else's problem" that interested me.

Five minutes later I called my publisher and asked a

favor. "Anything," she said. Anything to get another Ford Newcombe book is what she meant.

Next, I looked on the Internet, found a realtor who handled Cole Creek, called and asked to rent a house there for the summer.

"Have you ever *been* to Cole Creek?" the woman asked in a heavy Southern accent.

"No."

"There's nothing to do there. In fact, the place is little more than a ghost town."

"It has a library," I said.

The realtor snorted. "There're a few hundred books in a falling-down old house. Now if you want—"

"Do you have any rentals in Cole Creek or not?" I snapped.

She got cool. "There's a local agent there. Maybe you should call him."

Knowing small towns, I figured that by now everyone in Cole Creek was aware that Ford Newcombe had called the library, so the local realtor would be on the alert. I said the magic words: "Money is no object."

There was a hesitation. "You could always buy the old Belcher place. National Register. Two acres. Liveable. Barely liveable, anyway."

"How far is it from the center of Cole Creek?"

"Spit out the window and you'll hit the courthouse."

"How much?"

"Two fifty for the history. Nice moldings."

"If I sent you a certified check tomorrow how soon can it close?"

I could hear her heart beating across the wire. "Sometimes I almost *like* Yankees," she said. "Sugah, you send me a check tomorrow and I'll get that house for you in forty-eight hours even if I have to throw old Mr. Belcher out into the street, oxygen tank and all."

I was smiling. "I'll send the check and all the particulars," I said, then took down her name and address and hung up. I called my publisher. I was going to buy the house in her name so no one in Cole Creek would know it was me.

I knew I couldn't leave town until after the twenty-seventh of April when I had to pay the blackmail-reading, so I occupied myself by reading about North Carolina. The realtor called me back and said that old Mr. Belcher would give me the house furnished for another dollar.

That took me aback and I had to think about why he'd do that. "Doesn't want to move all his junk out, does he?"

"You got it," the realtor said. "My advice is not to take the offer. There's a hundred and fifty years of trash inside that house."

"Old newspapers? Crumbling books? Attic full of old trunks?"

She sighed dramatically. "You're one of those. Okay. You got a house full of trash. Tell you what, I'll pay the dollar. My gift."

"Thanks," I said.

The twenty-seventh was a Saturday, and I spent three hours answering the same questions at Mrs. Attila's ladies' luncheon (chicken salad) as I had everywhere else. My plan was to leave for Cole Creek early Monday morning. My furniture was to go into storage and I planned to take just a couple of suitcases of clothes, a couple of laptops, plus a gross of my favorite pens (I was terrified that Pilot would discontinue them). I'd already shipped my research books to the realtor to hold for me. And Pat's father's tools were on the floor of the backseat of my car.

At the luncheon Mrs. Hun told me that Jackie Maxwell was getting married the next day. Smiling—and trying to be gracious and amusing—I asked her to tell Jackie that I'd bought a house in Cole Creek, and was spending the summer there, where I'd be researching my next book, and if Jackie wanted the job, it was still open. I even said she could ride with me when I left on Monday morning.

Mrs. Free Books smiled in a way that let me know I'd missed my chance, but she agreed to relay my message to Jackie.

On Sunday afternoon I was shoving my socks into a duffel bag when there was a hard, fast knock on my door. The urgency of the sound made me hurry to answer it.

What I saw when I opened the door startled me into speechlessness.

Jackie Maxwell stood there in her wedding dress. She had on a veil over what looked to be an acre and half of long dark hair. The last time I'd seen her, her hair had been about ear length. Had it grown that fast? Some genetic thing? And the front of her dress was . . . well, she'd grown there, too.

"Is the research job in Cole Creek still open?" she asked in a tone that dared me to ask even one question.

I said yes, but it came out in a squeak.

When she moved, the dress caught on something on the porch. Angrily, she snatched at the skirt and I heard cloth tearing. The sound made her give an evil little smile.

Let me tell you that I *never* want to make a woman so angry that she smiles when she hears her own wedding dress rip. I'd rather—truthfully, I can't think of anything on earth I wouldn't rather do than be on the receiving end of anger like I saw in Ms. Maxwell's eyes.

Or was this after the ceremony and she was now Mrs. Somebody Else?

Since I wanted to live, I asked no questions.

"What time should I be here tomorrow?"

"Eight A.M. too early for you?"

She opened her mouth to answer but the dress caught again. This time she didn't jerk it. This time her face twisted into a frightening little smirk, and she very, very, very slowly pulled on that dress. The ripping sound went on for seconds.

I would have stepped back and shut the door but I was too scared.

"I'll be here," she said, then turned and walked down the sidewalk toward the street. There was no car waiting for her, and since I lived miles from any church, I don't know how she got to my house.

At the street sidewalk, she turned left and kept walking. Not a person or child was in sight. No one had come out to see the woman in the wedding dress walk by. I figured they were as scared as I was.

I watched her until she was out of sight, then I went inside and poured myself a double shot of bourbon.

All I can say is that I was real glad I wasn't the man on the receiving end of that anger.